Drawing from memory . . .

That night, Jeanette went to sleep reliving the party, always with Dr. Murer beside her or coming toward her or unwilling to leave her; sometimes they did not follow Mlle. Bernhardt into the house at all. Over the next few days, fantasy overlay memory more and more, though it never altered the departure points nor belied certain moments. If pressed by conscience, Jeanette might have admitted that making herself the object of romantic attention was half the pleasure of her daydreams. Nevertheless, she also believed in the magical air that had enveloped her and Dr. Murer on their walk through the back orchard, in the secret garden, on the terrace at twilight. And she responded to him—*him*, Dr. Edward Murer, so different from anyone else she knew . . .

"An engrossing story with complex, compelling characters. I'll never forget Jeanette, Edward, or Cousin Effie, and neither will other readers."

—Elizabeth ten Grotenhuis, professor emerita,
Department of History of Art & Architecture,
Boston University

"Keenum's deft handling of details makes *Where the Light Falls* a standout among painterly novels. As delectable and addictive as a Parisian pastry, the book is an art lover's delight."

—Lynn Cullen, author of *Reign of Madness*

Where the Light Falls

KATHERINE KEENUM

BERKLEY BOOKS, NEW YORK

THE BERKLEY PUBLISHING GROUP
Published by the Penguin Group
Penguin Group (USA) Inc.
375 Hudson Street, New York, New York 10014, USA

Penguin Group (Canada), 90 Eglinton Avenue East, Suite 700, Toronto, Ontario M4P 2Y3, Canada (a division of Pearson Penguin Canada Inc.) • Penguin Books Ltd., 80 Strand, London WC2R 0RL, England • Penguin Ireland, 25 St. Stephen's Green, Dublin 2, Ireland (a division of Penguin Books Ltd.) • Penguin Group (Australia), 707 Collins Street, Melbourne, Victoria 3008, Australia (a division of Pearson Australia Group Pty. Ltd.) • Penguin Books India Pvt. Ltd., 11 Community Centre, Panchsheel Park, New Delhi—110 017, India • Penguin Group (NZ), 67 Apollo Drive, Rosedale, Auckland 0632, New Zealand (a division of Pearson New Zealand Ltd.) • Penguin Books (South Africa), Rosebank Office Park, 181 Jan Smuts Avenue, Parktown North 2193, South Africa • Penguin China, B7 Jiaming Center, 27 East Third Ring Road North, Chaoyang District, Beijing 100020, China

Penguin Books Ltd., Registered Offices: 80 Strand, London WC2R 0RL, England

This is an original publication of The Berkley Publishing Group.

This is a work of fiction. Names, characters, places, and incidents either are the product of the author's imagination or are used fictitiously, and any resemblance to actual persons, living or dead, business establishments, events, or locales is entirely coincidental. The publisher does not have any control over and does not assume any responsibility for author or third-party websites or their content.

PUBLISHING HISTORY
Berkley trade paperback edition / February 2013

Library of Congress Cataloging-in-Publication Data

Keenum, Katherine.
Where the light falls / Katherine Keenum. — Berkley trade paperback ed.
p. cm.
ISBN 978-0-425-25778-4
1. Women artists—France—Paris—Fiction. 2. Americans—France—Paris—Fiction.
3. Paris (France)—History—1870–1940—Fiction. I. Title.
PS3611.E3453W47 2013
813'.6—dc23
2012039036

PRINTED IN THE UNITED STATES OF AMERICA

10 9 8 7 6 5 4 3 2 1

In loving memory of my mother, grandmother,
and great-grandmother, writers all

ACKNOWLEDGMENTS

Generous friends are the first to read portions of an unpublished novel or the manuscript in its entirety when a draft is completed. For their perceptive comments and unflagging support, I am deeply indebted to the late Mary Emery, Elizabeth ten Grotenhuis, Elizabeth Morgan, Sarah Novak, Elaine Fowler Palencia, Polly Shulman, Andrew Solomon, Susan Elizabeth Sweeney, and Christie Woodfin. A writer's maxim claims, "First thought, best thought." I would add, "First readers, best readers."

A finished manuscript is not enough, however; it must reach the professionals. Special thanks, therefore, to Polly, who introduced me to her agent, Irene Skolnick. Irene believed in the novel and sent it to Jackie Cantor at Berkley. Jackie then nurtured both the book and me with her skillful editing and patient, loving insights. Irene, Jackie, and their staffs made the process of bringing the work to publication a pleasure.

I also want to remember here three women whose inspiration has been constantly with me: Jeanette Sterling Smith Greve, whose escapade launched this story, went on to become a writer and an editor at *McCall's Magazine* early in the twentieth century. Her daughter, my grandmother, Dorothy Greve Jarnagin published two novels, wrote short stories, and talked wittily about grown-ups to children. *Her* daughter, my mother—journalist, puppeteer, and storyteller—taught me to write and to know that stories matter.

Finally, my deepest debt of gratitude is owed to my husband, John Keenum. He helped set the project in motion by his chance discovery that the family story about Jeanette's expulsion from Vassar was true.

He listened to me talk endlessly about my research, visited museums (and Paris!) with me, read early drafts, and reviewed the final edited manuscript. He told me to dedicate the novel to my three foremothers, not him; but he was along for every step of the way, and no one has ever been a better companion.

CHAPTER ONE

Vassar College, February 1878

S urely, there is nothing dishonorable about marriage!" protested Jeanette Palmer.

"About marriage, nothing. About elopement, everything." Hannah Lyman's thin, gray face conveyed the suffering of a long illness, the longer custom of wielding authority, and, at the moment, outraged disdain. "Miss Palmer, have you considered the possibility that, with your help, your friend has delivered herself into the hands of a cad who will ruin and abandon her?"

"Oh, Miss Lyman, not Beau, not—"

"A man who scorns society's approval in a matter as sacred as marriage is capable of anything. Moreover, no matter what has become of the fugitives, nothing mitigates the egregiousness of your own misconduct, which is the topic under discussion. Your actions will have a demoralizing effect on your fellow students, and the whole affair may damage this institution in the eyes of a larger public. Even to know of such a plan without reporting it would have been wicked, but to arrange meetings at the house of your aunt, to carry messages and deceive hall monitors, to impersonate Miss McLeod last evening in order to cover her flight—! Miss Palmer, there can be no place at Vassar College for so deceitful a girl as yourself. You are dismissed forthwith and will remain in your room until your departure."

"Dismissed? You mean expelled, for good?"

"Miss Palmer, whatever else you are, you are not stupid. You can have expected no less."

In fact, Jeanette had expected far less. An uproar was sure to follow the discovery that Abbie was gone, but she had naively believed that her own part in the plot would go unnoticed or at worst earn her demerits. She had not foreseen how great a calamity the elopement of a student would be to the Lady Principal of Vassar, who was proud that the college offered a full liberal arts curriculum to women but who insisted equally on ladylike behavior and moral purity.

"I shall wire your parents this morning to have you removed."

"Oh, please, Miss Lyman, don't say *expelled* in a telegram, please. The news will be all over Circleville before the messenger boy reaches the house. You don't know what a small town in Ohio is like."

"Your shame is of your own making, Miss Palmer, and you might as well get used to it. It will be with you for the rest of your life."

"But you don't have to humiliate my whole family, Miss Lyman! And I don't see how spreading scandal can enhance the reputation of Vassar College."

"How I conduct the business of this college is my affair, not yours," said Miss Lyman, leaning angrily against her knuckles on the desk. "To your room."

Nevertheless, she took Jeanette's point about scandal. FAMILY PRESENCE URGENTLY REQUIRED, she telegraphed, LETTER TO FOLLOW. Mail trains were swift and deliveries frequent. She could spell out the infamy of their daughter's behavior to the Palmers at length in the full confidentiality of a letter.

Jeanette left the office stunned. In the empty lobby outside the administrative offices, she shut her eyes tight and bit her fist. *There can be no place for you . . .* With a dragging footstep, she started up the front staircase of Main Hall's central block. Her hand slid ahead of her, caressing the wood grain of the polished banister—hers to touch now, but not for long.

The art gallery. In consternation, she remembered the canvas she had left on an easel in front of a painting she had been copying. She must retrieve that picture; it was hers, and she would not let them take it away from her. Nor could she bear the thought of leaving without ever seeing the other paintings again. She caught up her skirt and ran—up and up, past the living quarters and classrooms on the second floor, up to the third floor, with quick glances at every landing to make sure she was safe.

To her relief, the canvas was still there. From tall windows and skylights encircling a two-story dome, wintry daylight filled the gallery. In so much natural light, the college's collection of paintings could be seen to good advantage and so could thousands of water-colors, etchings, and engravings mounted in albums for the use of students and faculty. Scores of oil paintings hung one above the other, landscapes and genre scenes. Jeanette did not mind that most of them were small—oil sketches, preliminary studies for larger work that hung elsewhere, or finished paintings scaled to hang over a private owner's sideboard or mantelpiece. They allowed her to imagine places she had never seen; they told stories. Inside their gilt frames, they were richly colored; and in them for the first time, she had seen the magic of how an individual brushstroke could represent a petal on a flower in the foreground or the sail of a skiff in the distance. She had loved them wholeheartedly from the start.

She picked up her own canvas and held it out. Over a soft brown ground, she had chalked in outlines and blocked in swatches of cool green; she had just begun to work on the details of a sandy, gray church on the far side of a river. The original painting was called *The Shrine of Shakespeare*: Presumably the church was at Stratford; presumably the river was the Avon. Stratford-on-Avon was a place her mother had long dreamed of visiting, and this copy was to be a present for her. Jeanette fought back tears and wrapped the canvas loosely in a cover sheet so that it wouldn't stain her clothes. Holding it against her hip, she moved regretfully from one tier of pictures to the next, sure that the All-Seeing Eye, as the girls had dubbed Miss Lyman, would soon drive her out.

The bell for the next change of classes gave her a chance to dash to her room under the cover of a general crush in the halls. Instead, she yanked down an album of English watercolors, another of pen-and-ink drawings, and a third of etchings from their shelves. She banged them onto the farthest study table and sat with her back to the door. She flipped pages, keeping an ear out for approaching footsteps. The ruse worked. Someone came in but took no notice of her. After a while, whoever it was left. Jeanette, who had been sitting tensely, began to cry. *There can be no place for you here.*

The album lay open to pen-and-ink studies of rocks and trees by Ruskin. She wiped her eyes and blew her nose. She had copied similar drawings the first semester of freshman year when art students were introduced to techniques for drawing on paper. Why, oh why, hadn't she done more while she had the chance?

"You have had good training," Henry van Ingen, the chairman of the art department, had said when he first saw her work. "Where?"

"From a neighbor at home in Ohio. She studied in Cincinnati."

"At the McMicken School of Design? The same curriculum as in Munich, I hear." Van Ingen had chuckled, then shrugged in self-deprecation. "Well, well, we all do what we can in this New World. And you are lucky, Miss Palmer, you have picked up no bad habits—still, you have much to learn." He wagged a finger at her. "Work hard. For you, it will pay off."

Jeanette was one of the warmhearted, those who are encouraged by praise. Art class went from being her favorite elective to the center of her life at Vassar. She did work hard, as hard as Professor van Ingen demanded. When in her second year she had to choose between oils and watercolors for instruction, he had told her that if she took up oils, he would teach her himself.

"Learn watercolor on the side, of course—but not as a lady's accomplishment. The girls around you who are drawn to watercolor—*pissh*. They do not like mess, and they will not wait for oils to dry. They are impatient and dainty, two things talent cannot afford."

Naturally, she had followed his lead, but now, in disgrace, she looked with longing at an exquisite watercolor painting of sun through mist on the Salisbury plain. She should at least have spent more time with the albums.

Someone entered the gallery and walked rapidly toward her. She cringed. A hand touched her shoulder.

"Jeanette!" came a whisper, urgent and needlessly secretive. "What are you doing here? Everyone is looking for you. Don't you know you're supposed to be in your room?"

It was her best friend, Becky. Jeanette twisted around. "Of course, I know. *To your room!*" she whispered back, in an unmistakable imitation of Miss Lyman's voice.

"I knew I'd find you here if you weren't in the studio." said Becky, sympathetically. "Is it true?"

"About Abbie?"

"No, pea-brain, about you. They're saying . . ." Becky's voice trailed off apprehensively.

"Expelled," said Jeanette. "It's true. Kicked out. *Dismissed* is the word Miss Lyman used."

"Oh, Jeanette," said Becky, sinking into the chair beside her and leaning forward. "How awful. What are you going to do?"

"Paint."

Becky put an arm around her shoulder and tugged. "Good girl."

"What *am* I going to do, Becky? I don't even know what's going to happen to me next, tomorrow, much less after that. I can't bear the thought of going back to Circleville."

"Well, first things first," said Becky. "You might as well eat. If we get in the lunch line, they won't dare make a scene in front of everybody. But we have to hurry—the doors will close soon."

In the jostling lines outside the dining hall, they joined a few close friends, who crowded around Jeanette to hide her until the doors opened for everyone to march in together. Inside, her two remaining suitemates looked frightened when she approached the table assigned to their end of the dormitory hall. The duties of the resident hall teacher who had failed to prevent Abigail McLeod's elopement had already been transferred to a senior named Leticia. Startled at seeing Jeanette reappear, Leticia turned wildly toward the head table. With a frown, Miss Lyman signaled that Jeanette should be seated.

An embarrassed silence at their table was broken only by Leticia's strangled attempts to initiate conversation along approved lines. Jeanette ate slowly, with her eyes fixed on her plate, uncomfortably aware that all around the murmuring room diners were surreptitiously watching her. When a dull blancmange was set out for dessert, she bolted. Miss Lyman's eye bored into her back. The bell had not rung, but what did she care? She could not be dismissed again.

Her room might now be a prison, but Jeanette fled to it as a refuge. Her things were there, it gave her privacy—privacy all too full now that Abbie was gone. The suite contained three bedrooms and a common sitting room. A little wan daylight reached the sitting room from the outer bedrooms, but Jeanette and Abbie's room was on an interior wall adjoining the corridor. It was gloomy from lack of sunshine and, in spite of high ceilings, the air in it was stale. Jeanette seldom came here during the day, but now she leaned against the bedroom door frame and looked wistfully at the decorations they had all put out to give the sitting room personality. A satin shawl belonging to Abbie still swooped at an angle on a wall. Someone out in the hallway knocked.

"Who is it?" she asked, cautiously.

"Jeanette, it's Leticia. Please, open up. I'm supposed to make sure you are here and stay here."

Toady, thought Jeanette, angrily; go away. But she knew that her mother would expect her to be dignified even in disgrace. She opened the door with her head high and discomfited Leticia with a level, resentful stare.

"I won't abscond, if that's what you and Miss Lyman are worried about."

"It's not my fault," said Leticia, backing away.

Before the door was closed, Jeanette had forgotten her in a huge wave of undifferentiated misery. She cried and cried until she fell into a dull quiet on the borders of sleep.

No one else came, neither her suitemates nor her friends, until midafternoon, when word was sent up from the Lady Principal's office that Professor van Ingen wished to see her. For an instant, Jeanette's heart lifted at being remembered by her favorite teacher; but on the way, she felt it was far worse to see someone she respected than a wet noodle like Leticia. She had let him down.

"So, Miss Palmer, you are leaving under a very dark cloud."

She could not meet his eye. "Yes, sir."

"Do you have plans, may I ask?"

"No, sir."

"Then what are your dreams?" asked van Ingen, gently. A willingness to tease the girls made him popular; a deeper seriousness made him loved.

"Oh, Professor van Ingen," she said, looking up, "I want to be an artist, you know that. I want to paint."

"I am glad to hear it. You have talent, Miss Palmer—if not common sense. To assist your foolish friend to elope!" He raised his hands in a gesture of comic exasperation. "But talent is not enough. You need more training, much more training."

"I guess I'll have to try to get it in Cincinnati."

"Why Cincinnati? Why not New York or Philadelphia?"

"Because I'm from Ohio. It seems possible."

"You came to Poughkeepsie. That, too, seemed possible."

"But that was because my parents wanted me to come to Vassar. My mother is ambitious for women to be educated, and I don't have any brothers for Papa to send to Harvard. My coming here meant a lot to them."

"And to you?"

"Ye-ess," said Jeanette, hesitantly. "I wanted to get out of Circleville, and I do like to read. I like history and philosophy and science and things, really I do. I loved looking through Professor Mitchell's telescope."

"Ah, you earnest Americans," laughed van Ingen. "The artist in Europe, what he cares for also is music and drama and poetry and, of course, nature! Ah, well, now that you have fallen so low, you think your parents will agree to an *académie des beaux arts*, your McMicken in Cincinnati, for instance."

"They'll have to do something with me if they don't disown me altogether. My father calls the McMicken a trade school; maybe he'll think I need a trade."

"You are an artist; you will need your art," corrected van Ingen. "You might even make a living from it. A few women do. Look at Rosa Bonheur."

"I wish I could," said Jeanette, smiling with shy humor for the first time that day. "I've only seen engravings."

"There you are then! You must go places where you can see paintings, real paintings—big, public canvases and not just the little studies we have upstairs, admirable though they may be. Your papa is right: They are woodcarvers at McMicken, tools of industry. The technical instruction in drawing therefore is good. Design, too—decorative florals, scrolls, and the like. But for the fine arts, no.

"What languages do you have? English obviously. You could study in London; the Slade takes women students now, though perhaps not so readily foreigners—and the English are insular." Doubt came into van Ingen's voice. "Their styles are not international, not current." He was thinking out loud, and it lifted Jeanette's heart to be treated as a serious student. "For watercolor, yes, London. For sculpture, Rome—it would not hurt you, by the way, to take instruction in modeling clay. Clay will teach you much about form and volume. And, of course, you must visit Rome—such wealth of everything in Rome: sculpture, painting, mosaic, murals. But to be trained as a painter . . ."

Van Ingen tapped a pen against his teeth and regarded her meditatively. Even with pink coming back into her cheeks, this Miss Palmer was no great beauty; but she was pretty the way all the healthy young were pretty. Her curly brown hair was twisted into an unfussy knot to be out of the way, a good sign of a workmanlike attitude; the fashionable frizzy bangs they all seemed to wear these days showed a natural enough vanity. Intelligent hazel eyes, guileless American eyes. Eager. He wondered whether she had the necessary ruthlessness. "You would like Munich, I think. You are from Ohio. Do you speak German?"

"No, sir," said Jeanette, crestfallen. One more failure. "I did Latin and French in school."

"Well, then, it is obvious: It must be Paris. Munich is smaller; the competition is not so cutthroat. There is real camaraderie among the students in Munich, and good beer. But if you speak French, then by all means go to the top. Go to Paris."

Reality could reassert itself later. For the moment, Jeanette let flattered hope overwhelm incredulity, and she beamed. Van Ingen saw her pleasure, and his face took on a warning look.

"But one last sobering piece of advice, and this our good Lady Principal will approve. Learn discretion, Miss Palmer; you cannot afford mistakes. A whiff, and more than a whiff, of danger is exciting in a man, but a woman must be above reproach. It is the rich who commission portraits, and they usually know more about propriety than genius. If one more silly girl runs away with one more besotted youth, then Cupid laughs and the world changes not a jot. But when an artist throws away a career, then somewhere an angel weeps."

"And does the world change?"

Van Ingen waved a reproving finger. "Do not be bitter, Miss Palmer; you are too young. If the sky loses a star, perhaps no one will notice, but still the night is dimmer. We must try to shine. Here, I have written you a general letter of introduction. Perhaps it will be of some help."

Jeanette left elated. With the letter in hand, she almost pranced down the corridor, imagining herself in a triumphant return to Vassar, a world-famous artist, reclaimed by Alma Mater as a brilliant daughter, asked to address chapel, engaged to paint the president's portrait. The daydream vanished as soon as she met titillated glances from a knot of seniors whom she hardly knew. She hurried past. It was four o'clock, a hungry hour; she felt hollow and woebegone again.

"Hurry up, before we get chased out," said Becky, pulling her into the sitting room and closing the door after a quick scan of the hallway. "Irma's brought a spread."

"The box arrived from home today," said Irma, looking up from where she was laying out a big pound cake and an assortment of homemade cookies on the suite's big study table. Beside her, a third friend, Dottie, was busy boiling water for tea over an illicit spirit lamp.

Jeanette felt a deep rush of affection. She glanced through doors into empty bedrooms.

"Don't worry. Your dear suitemates are prudently staying away," said Becky. "They fear guilt by association."

"They may be right," warned Jeanette.

"Oh, we're not afraid," said Dottie. "*We* didn't carry notes or anything, the way they did."

"My mere presence contaminates. To hear the Lyman tell it, I'm an epicenter of moral degeneration. I'm not even sure I'm allowed out here; it's not my bedroom."

"We'll put a chair in the doorway," said Becky. "Sit. See? Now you're technically confined as ordered in your own little Bastille. Bread and water for the prisoner; or, better yet, let her eat cake. Fill up a plate, Irma, one of everything."

"Really, much as I love you for being here, isn't the whole suite off limits now?" asked Jeanette, settling onto the chair.

"Probably," said Becky, "but no official ban has been pronounced yet."

"They can't decide whether to try to pretend to the rest of us that nothing's happened," said Dottie, "or to hurl anathemas."

"Tell," said Irma, handing her a cup and plate, "tell, tell, tell. Talk with your mouth full if you have to. We want to know everything."

So Jeanette told; the other three listened; and then they all talked. They groaned, giggled, and commiserated. They tried to keep the noise down; but as they all suspected, Jeanette's suite was being closely watched. When she got wind of the party, Leticia chased everyone away.

After that, Jeanette was kept isolated. Since school policy prevented close friends from rooming together, the absence of her suitemates was no great loss. Still, it hurt to be shunned by them, and it was demoralizing to be so much alone. She took her meals in the infirmary. It was suggested that during morning classes, she should do calisthenics and run laps in a wide corridor designed for that purpose. She had her own books, but the art gallery, studio, and library were off limits. She was allowed to receive mail only from outside. Friends slipped a few clandestine notes under her door; she slipped rueful cartoons back under theirs when she was allowed to go out to the bathroom or meals.

Meanwhile, letters and telegrams were rapidly crisscrossing the country between Poughkeepsie and Circleville, Circleville and Manhattan. Miss Lyman to Judge and Mrs. Palmer. Judge Palmer to Miss Lyman. Mrs. Palmer to Jeanette. Judge Palmer to his sister Maude Hendrick in New York City. Mrs. Hendrick back to her brother. On the afternoon of the third day, Jeanette was handed a yellow Western Union Telegraph Company sheet. It read, ARRIVING TOMORROW MORNING STOP BE PACKED STOP EFFIE.

Oh, lord, thought Jeanette, Cousin Effie.

CHAPTER TWO

Cousin Effie

Iphigenia Palmer Pendergrast—Cousin Effie—was the perfect emissary from the Palmer clan to appease Miss Lyman. She bustled with efficiency when catching trains and the like but could never threaten anyone else's authority. For one thing, a decided overbite above a receding chin made her appear insignificant. For another, she had long since fallen into the habit of reflecting the attitudes of those around her. At thirty-seven, she was well into a respectable spinsterhood, lived in domestic subjection to her cousin Maude Palmer Hendrick, and accepted without complaint her role as general family dogsbody. She dressed in black in perpetual memory of a fiancé killed in 1862 at the battle of Antietam and largely forgotten by everyone else. On the morning she arrived to collect Jeanette, therefore, what Miss Lyman saw across her desk was a suitably distressed gentlewoman, whose oft-brushed but well-cut black cashmere coat and new kid gloves left no doubt as to her social standing and whose dismay at her cousin's transgression was a balm to feelings lacerated by three days of the McLeods' wrath and little sleep.

"I take it that you understand our position," said Miss Lyman, in a tone more gracious than she had used up till now.

"Of course, of course. I cannot tell you how abashed Jeanette's parents are. And to think, Gardiner McLeod's daughter! How the mighty have fallen." Effie clucked her tongue. "I trust the story of the elopement will be kept out of the papers?"

"That goes without saying. Though between you and me, I think the McLeods would do well to make a simple announcement of the marriage. The sooner the unfortunate circumstances are masked by the veils of propriety, the better for Miss McLeod—or Mrs. Calhoun, as I am thankful to say we may call her."

"Better for Vassar, too," agreed Effie, saying aloud what Miss Lyman would have preferred left unspoken.

"Just so. Well, Miss Pendergrast, unless you have further questions, I shall send for Miss Palmer and arrange for you to be taken to the train station."

"No need. I've hired a cab for the day," said Effie, becoming brisk and businesslike. "It's waiting around back at your stables. If you will have Jeanette's trunk brought down and give us luncheon, we should be able to make the two-forty back to the city; it's only a local, but there isn't an express until four."

Miss Lyman had not expected to be maneuvered into providing a meal for Miss Pendergrast; but if it expedited the removal of Miss Palmer, so be it. "I shall have the college kitchen send us something in my sitting room," she said, resigning herself to an uncomfortable party of three. She could hardly invite Miss Pendergrast to join the high table while Jeanette ate in the infirmary; she would not countenance Miss Palmer's return to the dining hall; and the instinct to control prevented her allowing the two women extended time together in private before they were out the college gates. She rang for her secretary and gave orders.

"Miss Palmer, your cousin has arrived to take you home," she said, a short time later when Jeanette entered.

"Yes, Miss Lyman."

Any inclination Effie might have had to scold her on behalf of the family melted away at sight of the child. To the inevitable pallor brought on by a lack of sunlight and fresh air in February, three days of being cooped up with her thoughts had added a pall to Jeanette's complexion; her eyes were shadowed by dark circles. Effie's weak mouth worked soundlessly.

Jeanette regarded her cautiously. "Hullo, Cousin Effie. It . . . it was good of you to come."

At even so slight an appeal, Effie's face was suffused by a flood of feeling. She rose, flung her arms around Jeanette, planted a kiss on either cheek, hugged her again, and stood back, shaking her head in disapproving regrets. It was the sort of confused emotional display that young Palmers, Hendricks, and Pendergrasts all over New York and Ohio dreaded in Cousin Effie.

"There now." Effie dabbed at her eyes with a handkerchief and brought herself to order. "And what do you think? Miss Lyman has asked us to luncheon. I call that most hospitable in the circumstances, don't you?"

Jeanette would have called it gruesome if she had dared. She smiled wanly. Miss Lyman did not smile back.

Somehow, Cousin Effie found the conversational resources to prattle meaninglessly through soup, a cutlet, a salad, and pie. Miss Lyman made aloof, polite replies or generalized observations of unimpeachable banality. And then, mercifully, it was time to go.

*   *   *

On the train, Jeanette and Cousin Effie found seats on the scenic, western side of the car. New Hamburg, Fishkill, Cold Spring, Garrison: Passengers getting on and off were a distraction. Cousin Effie too obviously watched and categorized them, whispering comments to Jeanette on their appearance or hazarding guesses about their errands. Shrinking into herself, Jeanette answered in monosyllables or tried to discourage the older woman by staring out the window at the handsome bluffs and fine expanse of the Hudson River. On other visits to New York City, the view from the train had delighted her. Today its beauty, depicted in paintings she would never see again, kept her tears close to the surface.

In the echoing bustle of Grand Central Station, the need to keep up with Cousin Effie drove everything else from Jeanette's mind. Effie became like some small animal on the alert, a squirrel or a rabbit, cutting through the crowd in a series of swift darts and zigzags. She engaged a porter, retrieved Jeanette's checked luggage, and tipped the man for delivering them to a hansom cab. Jeanette stumbled behind, banging a shawlstrap against her shins. By five, they were on their way to Twelfth Street, where Effie lived with Maude and Matthew Hendrick.

Outside the house, Effie deftly avoided mud and snow heaps at the curb while she paid the driver and directed him to deliver the luggage to the service entrance. Jeanette was attentive too late. She looked down to see dirty slush creep up into the hem of her dress; she was going to enter the house bedraggled as well as disgraced.

"Well, here we are," said Effie, superfluously, as she led the way up steep steps to the front door.

She rang the bell and pulled one of the double outer doors open to admit them into a vestibule. Almost simultaneously, inner doors were opened wide by Simms, the butler, who admitted them into a hallway that ran all the way to the back of the house. Its many-globed, gas chandeliers were inauspiciously dark. Only a few wall sconces gleamed feebly.

"Good evening, Miss Pendergrast, Miss Palmer," said Simms.

While Effie slipped easily out of her coat and handed it to him, Jeanette held the shawlstrap against her knees, hoping that he would not notice her wet skirt. Semidarkness was good for hiding dirt, at least, and the house was warm even if she was unwanted—warmer than anything at Vassar or in Circleville. Aunt Maude must burn coal at a furious rate.

"Miss, your hand luggage," said Simms.

"It's my portfolio," said Jeanette, holding back, but aware even as she spoke that her protective reluctance to let it go was ridiculous.

"I shall see that it is taken to your room," said Simms. "Miss Pendergrast, Mrs. Hendrick is in the upstairs parlor with Mrs. Vann."

Jeanette stiffened.

"We'll show ourselves up," said Effie. At the first landing, Jeanette paused briefly at a tall mirror to adjust her hat. How she wished her clothes were cleaner and better ironed! Ordinarily, any visit with her fashionable, married cousin Adeline, Mrs. Harold Vann, held a kind of glamour. Adeline had been and, after two children, remained a great beauty who dressed handsomely and was not above indulging in racy gossip. Her talk had always made Jeanette and the two younger Palmer girls, Sallie and Mattie, feel very grown-up or very small-town, depending on Adeline's mood. Jeanette did not relish coming under her scrutiny tonight, not as the topic of gossip herself.

"Well, Maude!" said Effie, brightly, as they entered the stuffy second-story parlor where Mrs. Hendrick spent most of her time in the colder months. "Here we are! And I hope you'll ring for a fresh pot of tea—we're both cold and famished, aren't we, Jeanette?"

Jeanette did not reply. Not only was it hopeless to treat this as a normal visit, but Cousin Effie was already fading into utter irrelevance, a shadow among the shadows on the edge of the room.

By contrast, the light of a well-placed oil lamp shone on Adeline, on her pearly complexion, on the complicated coils of her golden hair, on the small green hat over which she could swathe a scarf when she went outdoors. Her voluminous striped skirts spread theatrically over a green-and-salmon-striped love seat. They match, thought Jeanette with a peripheral part of her mind, and ever afterward thought of Adeline as a piece of handsome rosewood furniture with tautly pulled upholstery. But mainly she was forced to meet Aunt Maude's stern stare.

Mrs. Hendrick, with her bulk held rigidly by whalebone stays, sat imperiously in a high, wingbacked chair, facing the door. "So, Jeanette," she said, "you have humiliated your family and brought destruction down upon your own head."

"I—"

"Don't argue. You have." Mrs. Hendrick tugged hard at a bell pull as though that closed the case. "Your mother is on her way, as I assume she has written you."

"Yes, ma'am, she—"

"Then you understand it will be Sarah Palmer's duty, not mine, to make clear to you the anguish you have inflicted upon her and my brother. My duty is to Matthew Hendrick, and it requires me to protest your having dragged the house of Hendrick into scandal."

"Oh, be fair, Mother, how?" said Adeline.

"Did she not request that Beaufort Calhoun be included in the guest list for our Christmas soirée when she knew that the McLeods were invited and would bring Abigail?"

"Mother, there were three hundred people invited to that soirée, or you would never have included the McLeods in the first place. Beau Calhoun was a perfectly eligible young man, and if Abigail's own parents were present to chaperon, I hardly see—"

"Don't obscure the issue, Adeline. Whether or not it was under the McLeods' very noses that Jeanette aided the lovers, it was still under your father's roof."

"Honestly, Aunt Maude, I don't think they were planning anything yet when they met here," said Jeanette.

"They no doubt canoodled in the corners. That was the point of your invitation, wasn't it?"

"Well, at least to enable them to see each other."

"And you knew the McLeods disapproved."

"Yes, ma'am, that's why they had to seek out occasions—"

"Convicted by your own tongue, missy. Now, as you very well know, I have no use for bluestockings—Rachel McLeod included—and I can't think why anyone would waste a varsity education on a young woman in the first place. But since it was what your misguided mother and my equally misguided brother wanted for you, Jeanette, it was your filial duty to let yourself *be* educated and not to throw away the future provided for you—certainly not for the insipid daughter of two crackpot reformers. They tell me Rachel McLeod wants the vote for women."

"If she wins it for us, Mother, we'll all need to be educated," said Adeline.

Mrs. Hendrick snorted and returned to her main concern: "Jeanette, you have placed me in the position of having to drive over to those odious people's house to apologize, and I hope you are ashamed."

"Mother, do you think that's wise? We don't yet know what fiction the McLeods are trying to maintain."

"Gardiner McLeod will never keep his mouth shut on any topic, Adeline. Take it from me, the minute he heard they had run off, he sent after the guilty pair to retrieve Abigail before they could be married. He'll cane that young man from one end of New York to the other when he catches them."

"Oh, no, Maude," spoke up Effie, "the young people *are* married. Miss Lyman told me so."

"Then he'll seek to annul the marriage and cane the young man anyway."

"He'd better not," laughed Adeline. "A South Carolinian's sense of honor will end in pistols if he tries. But anyway, Mother, don't go. Mrs. McLeod will only think you are prying or gloating, which, of course, you will be."

"Nonsense. If I harbor the young lady who might have averted this tragedy and who may even now know where the runaways are . . ." Mrs. Hendrick paused inquisitively.

"I don't know, Aunt Maude, truly I don't."

"It had better be Europe or at least San Francisco," said Adeline. "They'll never be received in Charleston, much less New York."

Just then Simms entered, bringing in a portable table laden with a jug of hot water, more china, and plates of fish sandwiches and cakes. He set it down in front of Mrs. Hendrick.

"Jeanette, here, come sit by me," ordered Aunt Maude, patting a chair at right angles to her own. "No, no, Simms, no need for fresh tea leaves. Take the caddy away; you may go." She added water to the pot she and Adeline had already shared. Effie sighed.

Jeanette was grateful for any interruption and she was hungry, but a seat next to the Gorgon offered little hope of cake or sandwiches and no hope of escape.

"Well," said Mrs. Hendrick, "if you don't know where the fugitives are, what *do* you know?"

"That Abigail is happier, Aunt Maude."

"That what? Do my ears deceive me, missy?"

"Oh, Aunt Maude, Abbie was *so* unsuited to Vassar, and she and Beau are *so* much in love!"

"Don't gush, Jeanette; it's girlish. Besides, no girl in her right mind falls in love with a man named Beaufort Dabney Calhoun, even if he did go to Princeton."

"And even if his father once owned half the slaves in South Carolina," said Adeline. "The Calhouns are penniless now."

"Not penniless," said Jeanette, "they still own the land."

"Malarial swamp," said Mrs. Hendrick, "which they probably

still work with the same poor darkies. The McLeods were tireless abolitionists, Jeanette. It's no wonder they disapproved of him."

"Which is why Abbie and Beau had to elope," pleaded Jeanette. "It's not Beau's fault he was born to slave owners. Can't anyone see that the war is over?"

"Not in this household," thundered Mrs. Hendrick. "You are forgetting that your father and I lost a brother." Effie sighed again, more audibly. "And Effie lost her fiancé."

"I'm sorry."

Mrs. Hendrick snorted. "The young have ever been careless. To keep to the topic at hand: Do you mean to say that you defend what you did?"

Jeanette hesitated. If she had it to do over again, knowing the price, would she? "I will still defend what Abbie and Beau did," she said, slowly.

"Well, that's something," said Mrs. Hendrick. "If you are going to sacrifice yourself to a quixotic cause, you might as well believe in it." A lump rose in Jeanette's throat. "I suppose I had better know exactly what happened."

"Mother, you old fraud," laughed Adeline, settling back to listen, too. "We both want every delicious detail, Jeanette. It's why I came."

For the next hour, Jeanette tried to reconstruct events both before and after the elopement through a bewildering flow of questions and rebukes from Mrs. Hendrick, amused asides from Adeline, bickering between mother and daughter, and a stifled interjection now and again from Cousin Effie. "Matthew Hendrick will be arriving soon," said Aunt Maude at last. "He likes a pretty face. Effie, show Jeanette which room you have put her in. Have a wash and smarten yourself up a bit, Jeanette. Dinner is at eight, and the warning gong will ring at a quarter to. Will you stay, Adeline?"

"No, Mother, Harold will be getting home, too, and I want to peek in on the children before they are put to bed."

* * *

In the hallway, Effie and an exhausted Jeanette reached the staircase to the third floor just as Mr. Hendrick came up from the first.

"That you, Effie?" he asked, in the gloom. "Who's this you've got with you?"

"It's Jeanette, Matthew."

"Ah, yes! our miscreant!"

He spoke with such good humor that Jeanette reluctantly stepped forward. "Good evening, Uncle Matt."

Matthew Hendrick was a short, round man whose agile arms and legs were fitted into tight sleeves and trousers; his coattails seemed to flap of their own accord out of habit when he halted his energetic step. He rubbed his hands together. "Been stirring up the ladies, I hear, Jeanette!" He kissed her cheek.

Jeanette, grateful for his tone but at a loss for words, was rescued by Effie. "You must excuse us, Matthew, we're on our way up to change for dinner."

"You do that! Put on your prettiest dress, Jeanette," said Mr. Hendrick, patting her hand. "And pinch your cheeks for color—winter needs brightening up."

On the third floor, two bedrooms formerly belonging to Hendrick girls overlooked narrow gardens and faced the back windows of the next street over. Tonight, heavy draperies were drawn against the cold; but while each room had its own marble fireplace, they no longer served any purpose except to provide a mantelpiece on which vases and ornaments could be set. For heat, up-to-date steam radiators hissed and clanked. The air was already warm, though the profound cold of the furniture revealed that until a few hours ago, the spare rooms had been thriftily closed up.

"Would you prefer a bath and supper on a tray instead of coming down?" asked Effie. Her hands tugged nervously at her wrists.

"No, thank you," said Jeanette, who knew better than to appear difficult to Aunt Maude. "I've had enough of meals by myself."

"Oh, dear, yes, of course. Silly of me. Well, before I go, let me say just one thing." Effie gaped, and the chin of her open mouth virtually disappeared. "It was wrong of you to help Miss McLeod elope, Jeanette, but, but—it was very *romantic.*"

❦

CHAPTER THREE

Mrs. Palmer's Arrival

The next morning, Jeanette ate breakfast with Uncle Matthew and Cousin Effie (Mrs. Hendrick's breakfast was sent up on a bed tray). Back in her room, she wondered nervously how to spend the hours until her mother arrived. She wanted to block all thought of what was to come.

The bedroom was still, in many ways, a girl's room from twenty years earlier: simple wooden furniture, white-sprigged counterpane, thin linen liners at the windows where the pale-blue, winter draperies had been tied back to let in as much sunshine as possible. A pair of framed silhouettes from early in the century were the only decorations on walls papered in a silvery blue-and-white pattern. With all that white and a window facing northwest, the room was coolly and evenly lit; it would be a good place to work and might, for that matter, make a possible subject. She hoisted her shawlstrap onto the bed and spread out some sketches, looking for one she had made of her room at Vassar.

"May I see?" asked Cousin Effie, from the doorway. She peered inquisitively at a sketchbook that lay open to a page of pen-and-ink drawings of anatomical casts—hands, feet, arms, ears. They were drawn with a firm line and rounded by technically proficient cross-hatchings. "But these are good!" she exclaimed, when Jeanette moved aside.

"They're like finger exercises on the piano," said Jeanette. "Anyone can learn to draw shapes."

"No, they can't. Not like this."

Surprised but won over by Cousin Effie's matter-of-fact declaration, Jeanette explained what she was trying to do in some of the sketches and made excuses for others. On a page with a full head from a Greek classical statue, a little caricature filled an upper corner. In profile, it depicted a woman in a beribboned cap looking through a telescope, with her mouth dropped open.

"Why, that's Miss Lyman!"

"It was the germ for this." Jeanette wasn't sure it was wise to show Cousin Effie an irreverent cartoon, but she couldn't resist. Over a caption, *The famous Professor Maria Mitchell and Miss Hannah Lyman look at the stars*, two women stood back to back on a dwarf version of the Vassar Observatory, each peering through a handheld telescope. A stout one gazed rapturously up at the night sky, while her taller, thin companion stared indignantly down at a tiny, mooning pair over whom hovered a cloud of sparkles. Effie snickered at the schoolgirl joke. "Are there any other caricatures?" she asked.

Jeanette showed her Becky, Irma, Professor van Ingen, and the newest—the unfortunate Leticia in saucer-eyed terror. "And here's a study of Mother."

"Why, that's lovely—and it's Sarah to a T. My goodness, child, you ought to be a portraitist."

Jeanette seized her chance. "Let me draw *you*, Cousin Effie. Sit for me. Right now!"

"Oh, I don't know. I don't think . . ."

"This light is perfect, but I need a subject," said Jeanette. She steered her cousin to a seat on the bureau stool. "Now, tilt your head a little."

Jeanette worked quickly in pencil, but not too quickly. Bold relief would emphasize the defects of Effie's rabbity face. Instead, she blended feathery strokes to minimize Effie's overbite and emphasize her hooded eyes and wide brow. White chalk provided a few highlights.

"There."

"Oh, my. Well, I never. May I keep it? Please? If you give it to me, my dear, I shall treasure it forever."

"The chalk needs to be set."

Jeanette rummaged in her carpetbag; but before she could pull out a bottle of fixative, Effie's face had changed from naive pleasure to something more calculating. "You must limn Maude! Nothing will put her in a better mood than a portrait, especially if it's flattering." Effie jumped up, still holding the sketchbook. "Never mind about the chalk right now. Bring your pencil. She'll be in her parlor."

The second-floor sitting room was at the bright, southern end of the house. Sitting in her customary chair beside the double window, Mrs. Hendrick could keep an eye on whatever was happening on the street below while taking advantage of the sunlight for needlework. Her head, when they entered, was bent over an embroidery hoop. Continuing to stitch, she inclined a cheek slightly, which Effie obediently pecked.

"Maude," began Effie.

Mrs. Hendrick ignored her. Without looking up, she said accusingly, "Well, Jeanette, did you sleep the sleep of the innocent?"

"I slept well, Aunt Maude, thank you. In fact, I almost overslept."

"Sloth will not be tolerated in this house. Do you sew?"

"Not as well as Mother but—"

"Made what you have on, did she?"

"No, a dressmaker—"

"With three daughters to clothe, your mother should be a seamstress. Sit down," said Mrs. Hendrick, nodding to a chair on the opposite side of the table. "I am converting some worn-out sheets to a set of napkins and tray towels. Adeline prefers showier needlepoint and grand schemes, but I'm a merchant's daughter plain and simple and a merchant's wife." She looked up. "Sit down, I said. I'll start you with hemming to see how well you stitch."

Effie, who had been hovering with Jeanette's open sketchbook, slapped it onto the table at Mrs. Hendrick's side and hastily pulled her hand back. "First look at this, Maude."

Mrs. Hendrick squinted at the picture through her spectacles, then looked up at Jeanette. "Did you do that? When?"

"Just now, Aunt Maude."

"Upstairs," said Effie. "Isn't it beautiful? She can do yours, too. We could have the pair ready for Matthew and Sarah when they get here. Wouldn't it astonish them? And it would make Sarah proud of Jeanette instead of ashamed."

Jeanette blanched. "I'll hem," she said.

"Coward. How long will I have to hold still?" Aunt Maude's face was already freezing into an unnatural mask.

"It would only be a study, Aunt Maude," sighed Jeanette. "Perhaps you should go back to sewing. I'll sketch you occupied."

"That's right, Maude, look at this one of Sarah. Isn't it lifelike?"

Mrs. Hendrick's facial muscles relaxed as she glanced at the sketch of her sister-in-law sitting with a book. "Trust Sarah Palmer to find time to read. No wonder she doesn't sew. Well, I suppose drawing is the sort of ladylike accomplishment you young folk set great store by, even if some might call it the work of idle hands."

"I'll hem the next napkin for you, Maude," said Effie. Scooping up one of the several white linen rectangles already pressed under and basted around the edges, she began to take rapid, fine stitches.

Mrs. Hendrick snorted, but she made no other protest and went back self-consciously to her embroidery. She took no notice when Effie excused herself, saying that she must arrange the day's flowers and see that a fire was lit in the library.

The clock on the mantel ticked on.

The sketch of Mrs. Hendrick was less successful than the one of Effie, the shadings overworked, too strong. Jeanette frowned as she reluctantly handed the sketchbook to Aunt Maude. "I'd like to try again."

"It looks like me," said Mrs. Hendrick, mesmerized by a recognizable image of herself. After a few moments more, she began turning pages. "What are these?"

"Pieces of statuary."

"Who wants pictures of statues? Stick to drawing people."

"If only we could! But first you need to learn from ideal shapes; all the schools teach that way. And besides, nobody can afford to pay models for beginners."

"So I should be charging you?"

"I'll pay you with a better sketch if you like."

Mrs. Hendrick laughed. "Papa's granddaughter, I see—not too much the aesthete to drive a bargain. Another time."

The rest of the morning was spent in needlework. After lunch, Mrs. Hendrick installed herself and Jeanette downstairs in the library to be ready for Mrs. Palmer. Cousin Effie would be out for the afternoon. No one had thought twice about sending her to Poughkeepsie for Jeanette, but Mr. Hendrick would do the honors himself for his sister-in-law.

"Is there anything else I can do, Maude?" asked Cousin Effie, as she pulled on gloves. "I'm not sure I should leave."

"So you have said a hundred times, and for the hundredth time I repeat: I am quite capable of receiving Sarah Palmer in my own house by myself. If Sarah asks, we'll tell her the weekly meeting of the Children's Aid Society would falter without you. Run along.

"Here, read this to me." Mrs. Hendrick handed Jeanette *David Copperfield*, open to the chapter in which Steerforth's perfidious abandonment of Little Em'ly is revealed. Her heavy face maintained a placid absorption while she continued her morning's embroidery, only occasionally stealing a sly glance at her niece.

Jeanette took the point of the selection, but her increasing anxiety as they waited had nothing to do with Aunt Maude's estimation of her or her worries about Abigail's fate and everything to do with her mother's attitude. At last, the front doorbell rang, followed by indistinct voices in the entry hall.

"Aunt Maude, they're here!"

"Then what are you waiting for? Go greet your mother."

Jeanette ran. Because she had stayed East during the Christmas holidays, it had been nearly six months since she had last seen either one of her parents. Coming into the drawing room from the back of the house just as her mother entered from the front, she was struck hard by the fatigue in her mother's face. A corner of her mind noted also how dumpy her mother was, how provincially dressed; yet Sarah Palmer was formidable, too, in her dignified self-possession. When their eyes met, a questioning look crossed Mrs. Palmer's face, but her brow eased as if she were satisfied. At that signal, Jeanette ran forward, threw her arms around her mother, and broke into sobs. Mrs. Palmer clasped her briefly and rubbed her back, then pushed her away, holding her at arm's length.

"Oh, Mama!"

"Now, now," exclaimed Uncle Matthew, rubbing his hands energetically. "No tears in this house, no tears! Never allowed from my girls, you know. I like to see smiles on pretty faces."

"Don't cry, Jeanette," said Mrs. Palmer, quietly. "What's done is done, and we'll talk about it later. Right now, I must greet your aunt Maude."

So there it was. Appearances, even within the family, were what mattered. After hours of anxious waiting, to have her drama simply pushed aside hurt; but Jeanette resigned herself to the role of a child for the time being, to be seen and not heard.

When at last they were upstairs alone, Sarah Palmer lowered herself slowly onto her bedroom's one armchair and propped her elbows on the armrests. Leaning back wearily, she pressed her fingertips together in front of her chest and looked at Jeanette. "Well?"

Jeanette's unhappiness flooded up again, hotly. "Oh, Mama, I'm so sorry! I'm so sorry it's all turned out this way. Really I am!"

"I'm glad to hear it."

Mrs. Palmer's coolness was another slap, but not unexpected. Jeanette perched on the edge of the bed and tried to be equally cool. "What is it you want from me, Mama?"

"Genuine contrition and humility to begin with, Jeanette; and we need to understand each other if we are to plan sensibly for your future."

"I'm going to paint, that's all I know."

"Each of us has our favorite pastime."

"No, but art is much more than that for me, Mother! You always insist that women must think for themselves and do what they believe in, don't you?"

"That is hardly a practical answer, Jeanette."

"For me, it is. It means I have to go on with my training."

"What we'd like to do and what we can do are not always the same thing in this world." Mrs. Palmer sighed and put a hand to her forehead. "Don't protest, Jeanette. You are overwrought, and I'm tired. Go wash your face, and then I'll take a bath. I have five hundred miles of grime to get rid of."

The next morning at breakfast, Mr. Hendrick asked, "What's on the schedule, ladies, eh?"

"I have an excursion in mind!" announced Cousin Effie, making a quick gambit.

"I was thinking of a turn around Washington Square to stretch my legs," said Mrs. Palmer, mildly.

"We can go there, too," said Effie, "but first, Matthew, I want to show them the Tenth Street Studio Building. Jeanette is going to be an artist, you know, and—"

"Are you, my dear?"

"Yes, sir."

"She aspires to be one," said Mrs. Palmer.

"Well, in that case, she must see the Studio Building—a most interesting enterprise. Only artists for tenants," said Mr. Hendrick, "and very successful—they had to annex space next door a few years ago."

"And I happen to have made friends with a young man who has a studio in the annex!" said Effie.

"Young man? Made friends with?" growled Mr. Hendrick, facetiously. "You're a dark horse, Effie Pendergrast. Never a word till now, and you've been seeing a young man. I hope you have been well chaperoned."

"Go on, Matthew." Cousin Effie squirmed. "It was at the Children's Aid Society. Mr. Moyer teaches a mechanical drawing class there, but mostly he works in his studio. When I told him about Jeanette's drawing my picture, he said we should drop by."

"Perhaps another day with a more specific invitation—" began Mrs. Palmer.

"Oh, no need, Sarah. Nobody stands on ceremony these days," said Mr. Hendrick, cheerfully. "Take my advice: Run along and see what there is to see."

After that, Mrs. Palmer could hardly refuse; but when they set out, Jeanette was all too well aware that her mother was in no mood to be pleased. It helped that they had several blocks to walk. Whatever she thought of their ultimate errand, Sarah Palmer valued her reputation at home for moving in the larger world and observed the city with interest.

Down Fifth Avenue, Effie led the way briskly. On West Tenth Street, her step slowed as they approached No. 51. It was a large brick building, as wide as three of its neighbors put together and as high as four. Except for its unusually tall, wide windows, it might have suggested a warehouse or industrial workshops. Cousin Effie halted, clutching her handbag to her waist. "M-Mr. Moyer said to go in the front door," she almost whispered.

Mrs. Palmer waited with an ironic look of detachment. As the youngest and on probation, Jeanette hesitated; but then, not to be deprived of a look inside, she stepped up and held the door open.

Under the high ceiling of the main lobby, several women were mounting prints, watercolors, and drawings onto movable screens. Jeanette wanted very much to investigate, but almost at once Effie found Mr. Moyer's card on a directory board, and she had to follow her around to the annex.

The outer, double doors of Mr. Moyer's studio stood open and one of two inner doors had been left ajar. Effie peered around and knocked timorously.

"Who is it?"

"Mr. Moyer? It's Miss Iphigenia Pendergrast. From the Children's Aid Society. You said if . . . if ever I were—"

Jeanette's heart sank. Mrs. Palmer signaled a retreat with two tiptoeing fingers, but just then Mr. Moyer came to the door. A tall, loose-jointed young man in his twenties, with a quick, intelligent eye, he might have been an ambitious country law clerk if he had worn a coat instead of a painter's smock. He looked surprised to find three ladies at his door, but his face lit up in welcoming mirth for Effie. "Come in," he said, standing back. When Effie failed to initiate introductions, he held out a hand to Mrs. Palmer. "My name is Frank Moyer."

"Mrs. Joseph Palmer, Mr. Moyer; and this is my daughter, Jeanette. Please forgive this uninvited intrusion."

"Oh, not at all. Always open for business."

"Cousin Effie said we might see your studio," said Jeanette.

"By all means! Isn't it grand?" he said, waving his arm to encompass the room. "It really belongs to Payne Hedley, but it's all mine until June!"

It *was* grand, Jeanette thought, as big as the studio shared by all of Professor van Ingen's students at once and lit by broad windows that rose from shoulder height to the ceiling. Framed pictures crowded the paneled walls; unframed canvases on stretchers leaned against the wainscoting. The largest picture in the room was some seven feet high by nine feet wide, a panoramic landscape of jungly forest with a parrot and orchids in the foreground and mountains in the distance against a glimpse of luminous golden sky.

"Is this yours, Mr. Moyer?" asked Mrs. Palmer.

"Good lord, no, that's the *meister*'s. But thank you, ma'am, for thinking it might be. He's off in South America now, making studies for a companion piece, and it was my great good luck to be allowed to sublet."

"He's a follower of Mr. Church?" asked Jeanette, studying the handling of light on the distant mountains.

"Bull's-eye!" said Mr. Moyer, looking at her with more interest.

"And do you also paint landscapes?"

"Yes and no. In the afternoons, I fill in the backgrounds for Mr. Hedley's parlor-sized variations on jungle birds and flowers." He turned around a few of the canvases propped against the wall. They were all about eighteen by twenty-four inches, and all showed some tropical bird or other against a spray of lush blossom. "*Beaks and bouquets to pay the rent*, he calls them. Putting in twigs and sprigs earns me a share of the space."

"You mean he sells pictures that aren't all his own?" asked Effie, shocked.

"Everybody from Rembrandt on down has had workshop assistants!" said Jeanette, hoping that Mr. Moyer did not think he had been accused of shady practices.

"The genius does the interesting parts the patron pays for," explained Mr. Moyer, not in the least offended, "and we groveling journeymen work in his style to complete the background. But come take a look at this. Every stroke mine, I promise."

The picture on his easel showed a bare-legged young woman in a farm dress and apron, sitting on a split-rail fence as she gazed straight at the viewer.

"You are lucky in your model, Mr. Moyer. She has a lovely face," said Mrs. Palmer.

"Well, *I* think so," said Mr. Moyer. "She's my fiancée, and you'd never guess from my turning her into a frontier lass that she's just back from Europe. Wait! What am I thinking? Come with me; Susan may be in the gallery right now. There's a group of them hanging a show of works on paper to open in a few days."

"We saw them!" exclaimed Jeanette.

"Did you? Susan is deep into pastels these days; I hope some of hers are up already for admiration."

Back in the main lobby, he led them to a young woman who was hanging a pastel portrait of a little girl, matted and framed, on a line with several others.

"Susan, here are visitors I want you to meet," said Mr. Moyer. "Mrs. Palmer, may I present Miss Susan Whitmore, lately returned from Paris, France, soon to be the toast of New York City, New York. Susie, this is Mrs. Palmer and her daughter and my friend Miss Pendergrast from the Children's Aid Society."

Miss Whitmore was not quite as pretty as Mr. Moyer's portrait of her, but almost. Jeanette decided to be in love with the pair of them and not him alone. "We want everyone to come in and see that they can—and should—own original art," said Miss Whitmore, with a sweep of her arm to encompass the exhibition. "Would you like to look around?"

"Not now," said Mrs. Palmer. "I've put on enough meetings to know how much we'd be in the way at this stage."

"We'll come back when the show is open," said Jeanette, quickly. "And please, Miss Whitmore, may I stand off to one side and make a quick sketch of the scene to remember it by?"

"Do you draw? There's some scrap butcher's paper around here somewhere."

"I have a sketchbook," said Jeanette, pulling one out of her coat pocket. It was three inches by five, too small for most work but useful for jottings.

"Here! Just see what she can do," said Cousin Effie. She startled everyone by whisking Jeanette's picture of herself out of a handbag.

Jeanette's chagrin turned into excitement when Mr. Moyer held it for Miss Whitmore to see. "Do you have a teacher?" he asked.

"No. I've been told the best place to study is New York or better yet in Paris."

"Is Will Sartain taking on pupils, Susie?"

"It's worth asking. But if Paris is a possibility, then go," said Miss Whitmore to Jeanette. "I was at the Académie Julian. There's nothing like it here to prepare a woman for a career. It has the same curriculum as the École des Beaux-Arts."

"Oh, it was so inspiring, Aunt Maude!" exclaimed Jeanette, when they returned home for lunch and found Mrs. Hendrick in her upstairs sitting room.

"What did I say about gush, young miss?"

"Not to do it," said Jeanette, in no mood to be suppressed. She knelt down by Mrs. Hendrick's chair and crossed her arms on the armrest. "We went to some of the dealers' galleries, but first we met Cousin Effie's friend, Mr. Moyer, who introduced us to his fiancée, Miss Whitmore. She's an artist, too, and awfully good; I want to be as good as she is."

"And what about him?" asked Mrs. Palmer, in a tired voice. "If you are going to measure yourself, Jeanette, measure against the best."

"Him, too. He *is* good, Aunt Maude. It's scary to see how accomplished they are! Such competition! But Cousin Effie brought out my picture, and I showed Mr. Moyer and Miss Whitmore my letter from Professor van Ingen. They said maybe I should show samples of my work to a Mr. Sartain, and—"

"That was only politeness," put in Mrs. Palmer.

Jeanette clutched the armrests tightly. "Why should it be?" she asked, in a strained voice, without looking around at her mother. "And even if they were only being polite, it wouldn't hurt to try."

"It would hurt to be rejected, Jeanette. In any case, there's no point in wasting a busy man's time. You don't live in New York."

"If he agreed to teach me, Mama, that would be reason to stay."

"Let *us* see how good you are," commanded Mrs. Hendrick. "Bring down your best work, Jeanette. Put on a private exhibition just for the three of us here. Sarah, you must be curious about your daughter's progress."

"Maybe after lunch, Maude."

"No time like the present," said Mrs. Hendrick, who had had the advantage of morning coffee.

Jeanette knew her mother was hungry and the time unpropitious, but Aunt Maude was only too likely to lose interest by afternoon. And she wanted to show them her work, to show her mother why it mattered. Upstairs, she quickly gathered some samples and, with a flash of determination, snatched up her unfinished *Shrine of Shakespeare*. Mrs. Hendrick made a point of going through everything at a leisurely, admiring pace. She held up a page with a formal arrangement of hands drawn in pen and ink, taken from various plaster casts. "They almost look real, as though they could move."

"Hands are harder than cheeks or noses," said Jeanette. "They have so many subtle lines and angles. And they're expressive."

"Expensive, too," said Mrs. Hendrick. "A three-quarters portrait costs more than a head, and the price goes up with each hand you show. I know, because my father checked into it when he commissioned the portraits of him and your grandmother that hang in the library."

"Some day you must copy them for your father, Jeanette, and be sure to add in hands," said Mrs. Palmer.

Mrs. Hendrick ignored her. "This is pretty!" she said, picking up a watercolor with a maple painted in deep colors in the foreground and paler washes for distant hills.

"I did that on one of Professor van Ingen's sketching parties, and here's where I used the tree in an oil composition."

"The watercolor is livelier."

"I know," sighed Jeanette.

"But I'd rather have the oil on my wall. It's richer."

"That's why I want to master oils—people buy oil paintings. Look, this is a copy I was working on when—" Jeanette broke off.

"When you presented all of us with the problem of what to do with you next," said her aunt, darting a glance at Jeanette over her spectacles.

"Really, Maude, I think the problem of what to do with Jeanette is for her father and me to decide, not all of us," said Mrs. Palmer.

Not even me, too? thought Jeanette caustically, but she held her tongue. Mrs. Hendrick had gone back to looking at *The Shrine of Shakespeare*. "What did you learn doing this?"

"Well," said Jeanette, trying to keep her voice neutral, "you can see where I've chalked in the church building. The first task is just to get the outline and proportions right."

"That should be easy. It's all right there in front of you."

"Maybe it should be, but it isn't—not when you try freehand. So you use a grid—it's like enlarging a dress pattern. And next when you try to figure out the brushstrokes, you learn how the artist gets his effects, like this rendering of the texture of stone in the church. Also, here, let me stand it next to the autumn leaves: Do you see how, even though it's only half done, these sandy grays and bleached greens are going to induce a very different feeling from the brilliant reds and yellows? There's something restful and Old World about the original painting that I wanted to capture. It's called *The Shrine of Shakespeare*, Mama," she said. "I was going to give it to you."

"Then I wish you could have arranged to finish it."

"Why don't you finish it from memory?" asked Mrs. Hendrick.

"I—I wouldn't want to mess this up. Maybe a whole new canvas," said Jeanette, who was looking at her mother, not her aunt.

"This one has a certain value as it is," murmured Mrs. Palmer.

"As a reminder? That's what you mean, isn't it, Mama? Here, take it then, as is! Have it framed and hang it in the entrance hall by the front door. You can add a brass plate that says *Her Unfinished Career, by Jeanette Palmer*, and then nobody, nobody, nobody who comes into the house will ever be allowed to forget that your eldest daughter made herself unworthy and was cut off from her talent and training and everything she ever cared about. Only it isn't going to happen that way, Mama. You and Papa may try to stop me, but you won't be able to. You are not the only ones who have a say in what happens to me. I *am* going to paint. I'm going to find a way."

"Jeanette! I'm ashamed of such an outburst," said Mrs. Palmer.

In her corner, Effie twisted a handkerchief.

"Calm down this minute, young miss, and apologize," thundered Mrs. Hendrick. "Disrespect of elders will not be tolerated in this house, nor scenes. My girls were never allowed to make them."

Jeanette squeezed her eyes shut and hung her head while she collected herself. "I am sorry for the way I spoke. It was sarcastic and emotional," she said, adding under her breath, "but I am going to study art."

"Hmmph," said Mrs. Hendrick. "How much would you take for a copy like that—if it were finished, I mean?"

"Maude!" said Mrs. Palmer. "For the love of all that's holy, is this the time?"

"Might as well clear the air, Sarah. Suppose I were to let Jeanette earn her room and board by making a set of copies for me? Adeline is always saying we need to redecorate. Now suppose this Mr. Sartain—"

"But it isn't going to be Mr. Sartain or anybody else in New York, is it?" asked Effie, a little breathlessly. They all looked at her in surprise. "Didn't Professor van Ingen tell you to go to Paris?"

"Yes," said Jeanette, softly, with a catch in her throat. She stared at Cousin Effie questioningly.

"So much the better!" said Mrs. Hendrick, with a chuckle. "Adeline and Harold chase over to Paris every year or so to search out the latest and the best. Won't we impress them!"

"This is pie in the sky," said Mrs. Palmer. "Even if the money could be found—"

"My brother has made a big success in Ohio. Money is not the problem, is it, Sarah?"

"Not entirely, Maude. But setting that aside, and setting aside the question of whether Jeanette deserves the chance to go, she cannot just traipse off to Paris by herself."

"I won't," said Jeanette, whose eyes had never left Effie's. "You're coming with me, aren't you, Cousin Effie?"

"Oh, my," murmured Cousin Effie, "and I don't speak any French."

CHAPTER FOUR

An Attack in Cincinnati

Edward Murer customarily kept the Murer Brothers Pharmacy on Elm Street in Cincinnati open until eight o'clock at night. At six, when most other shops on the block closed up, he sent Hans, his clerk, home. There were few late customers; but, as Edward explained whenever his older brother Theodore urged him to shorten the retail store's hours, those few were likely to be emergency cases. They needed him, and he preferred to serve them in the ordinary way rather than be rousted out from his boardinghouse in an atmosphere of crisis. Besides, he could read as easily in the back room behind the counter as he could at home. At age thirty-seven, as he had ever since the end of the war, Edward relied on quiet orderliness to keep suffering and panic at bay.

One night in February, he was, as usual, slumped in the shabby easy chair he kept in the back room. It was faded to no color and gray at the seams with dust, horsehair stuffing showed through on the threadbare arms, and it sagged. But the bones in his lean body settled automatically among its familiar bumps and hollows. He would have said it was comfortable.

He was watching his right hand as it lay on a small side table where an oil lamp provided a pool of light just sufficient for reading. The latest copy of *La Revue des Deux Mondes* to come from Paris lay open on his lap. The journal was his primary link to the larger, Continental world he wistfully yearned for, but he could no more have said what was in this issue than predict whether his hand would move to unstopper a full bottle of laudanum that sat in the shadows beyond his fingertips. No, that was not true. He was pretty sure he would not succumb. It had been more than two years since he had given in to the apothecary's temptation.

From beyond the curtain of beads between him and the main shop came the muted hum of tiny gears winding up, followed by eight clear tones as a brass clock struck the closing hour. At its prompting, Edward withdrew his hand from the attenuated pool of yellow light and closed the magazine. He sighed. On the whole, he was glad of the victory but regretted the temporary solace of opium. He extinguished the oil lamp. After the dusky shadows of the back room, the yellow gaslight in the shop seemed artificially bright—

though not half so harsh and glaring as the new electrical lighting that was turning up in stores throughout Cincinnati and making Theodore, who had shares in Cincinnati Light and Power, a very rich man (it had been many years since Theodore, who ran the manufacturing wing of Murer Brothers, had actually worked in the drugstore).

As he closed up shop, Edward glanced outside. When the lamps were first lit near sunset, gaslight seemed briefly to extend the day; and on the more garish streets, like Vine, where store windows and beer halls blazed, it was part of the bright scene; but on the quieter side streets, the isolated pools of light were surrounded by darkness. In his present mood, Edward was irritated by their feebleness; they were like dots of campfires. He turned the *Open* sign in the door to *Closed*, pulled the shades, counted the till, entered the daily tally in the ledger, and locked up the cash in the safe. After exchanging his white pharmacist's smock for a black frock coat, he pulled on a smooth, warm overcoat with a fur collar, set a top hat on his head, and picked up his favorite ebony walking stick. Not a man specially given to extravagance or show, he nevertheless took advantage of prosperity to place comfort and a touch of elegance between himself and the memory of scratchy, thick army uniforms and the worse— far worse—lice-infested, thin rags that came later.

Twelve years separated Theodore and Edward in age—twelve years, which meant that when war was declared in 1861, Theodore, with a wife and five children, did not feel called upon to serve in the Union army despite his gratitude to the country that had welcomed the Murers and other German political refugees. When conscription became mandatory, Theodore took the legal recourse of hiring a substitute to go in his place. In contrast, at age twenty and unmarried, Edward had dropped out of medical school to enlist in the first month of the war. His mother wept, but his father was proud. Herr Dr. Murer had been a chemistry professor and liberal activist before the failure of the revolution in 1848 had driven him into exile and the humbler druggist's trade of his ancestors. When Edward came home at the end of the war, emaciated, coughing, and limping, Mutter was dead and Papa was a sad old man. An abashed Theodore had taken Edward into his own home. Papa made him a partner in the pharmacy as soon as Edward could return to work. A return to medical school was out of the question. At first, even after regaining strength and mental acuity, Edward could not face it. He had seen too many hacked limbs to stomach the surgery classes, he said; he had slipped in too much blood. He did not add that he had smelled too much vomit, piss, and shit in the mud of the battlefield ever to want to go back into a hospital ward. Eventually, he reenrolled in classes to master the use of botanicals and alkaloids; he found himself able to undertake the gentler alleviation of pain that came with dispensing drugs and sugar pills. Although he seldom smiled, he was observant and sympathetic. After his father's death, the neighborhood transferred their reverence for the old man to him. With his reserved demeanor, the flecks of gray in his dark hair and beard made it easy to imagine him older than he actually was. They called him Dr. Murer.

Out on the street, Edward lingered for a moment to let his eyes adjust to the uneven darkness. On a winter's night, nothing made the obscurity of the deeper doorways and alleys penetrable; but at eight o'clock, with a few other pedestrians out and the occasional carriage or streetcar passing, he gave no thought to danger as he made his way to a neighborhood tavern where every night he drank a glass of beer and ate whatever sausage or sauerbraten was chalked up on the bill of fare. In years past, he had varied the routine from time to time—going to other eating houses, dining at home with Theodore or friends, attending concerts—but not lately. Sunk in dull thoughts, he passed familiar sights unawares, but his nerves had lost none of the sixth sense he had developed too highly during the war. Almost before a rough arm had reached for his throat and another grabbed for his waist, he had wrenched away and struck out with his walking stick. His first blow caught his assailant on the shoulder hard enough to make him duck. In the brief scuffle that followed, Edward landed a second blow squarely on the man's head and then struck again, savagely, to knock him to the ground. He was prepared to beat him again and again.

"Lay off, mister. I ain't armed," whimpered the man, rising woozily to one knee and shielding his face with his arms. He mumbled something about being a veteran, a prisoner of war, bad times. "The whole damn country's forgotten, but lemme tell you, it's hard."

Edward jabbed the tip of his cane under the man's rough beard and forced him to raise his chin. Even in the gloom between streetlamps, he could see the flattened pockets under the fellow's eyes and guessed at the coarse skin; it was no doubt a face ravaged by drink. A bleakness in their eyes met.

"An-der-son-ville," declared Edward, fiercely, between clenched teeth.

The man pushed the cane away and crumpled back down to the ground, sitting with his head bowed between his knees. "Salisbury," he replied. "North Carolina. Hellhole."

"They all were," said Edward, beginning to shake.

He stood back; the hot flare of his anger drained away, leaving him empty. The wreck at his feet recovered quicker than he did and, without lifting his head, held out a beggar's palm. Edward stared blankly at it for a moment, then stepped farther away, still shaking. He turned his back and walked on.

He walked and he walked. He passed right by his usual tavern, recoiling from the smell of beer and cabbage and the babble issuing through the door as someone came out. At first, he was jumpy. He walked quickly, hitting the ground with a resounding tattoo of his cane. Over and over again, he relived the attack, sometimes angrily, sometimes made sick by an inexplicable sense of failure. Once or twice, he thought of going back but knew it was too late. Gradually, his step slowed. The wound in his leg began to ache. That pain he could ignore, and did; but to his horror, tears came suddenly to his eyes. Worse than the surprise of their hot, round wetness was the conviction that they were right and natural. The world, or his life anyway, called for them. Get hold of yourself, man, he thought. He could not stand on a city street and cry. He looked around to see where he was: He had walked out Liberty, almost to the railroad tracks. Ridiculous to have come so far. He must get inside somewhere. Not his drab boardinghouse room; he balked at that. He would go to Theodore's house, must go to Theodore's house; an instinct for safety drove him to his brother and his brother's wife, Sophie. He had walked so long and so late that the streetcars were no longer running. Just as well; he might not have trusted himself to get on board with other people. What if he cried? What if they asked questions; what if they stared.

It took him an hour of steady plodding, the last stretches up many flights of public steps that climbed steeply between bends in the road. By the time he reached Theodore's street high on Mount Auburn, all the houses were dark. If he had not been so exhausted, he would have been ashamed to trouble the family; but he could not afford the scruples of pride. In spite of his warm coat and the heat of exertion, he was shaking again. His teeth chattered.

He lifted the knocker and rapped three times, a hesitant, furtive summons. Useless, futile. He pounded harder, louder. He leaned his cheek against the door and beat it with his fist.

An upstairs window flew open. From above came Theodore's choleric voice: "What the devil—? Do you know the time? Who is it?"

"Theodore. It's me. *Ist Eduard. Bitte!*" he called. "Please," he whispered, into the darkness.

He awoke the next morning sluggish and disoriented. A pencil-thin streak of light blazed painfully white at the bottom of a window shade; it was not where it should be. An unfamiliar chest of drawers loomed in a corner. As he roused himself enough to remember being put to bed in his nephew Carl's room, he remembered the rest of last night, too, in a surge of misery. Coming to Theodore and Sophie might have been the only thing to do, but he abhorred the need, and the fuss and bother that followed. He couldn't bear to think now about what came next. His bad leg ached; so did his head and back. He rolled over onto his side, away from the hateful light, and fell asleep again. He bolted awake later to the realization that he must open the drugstore and half rose on one elbow. His head pounded. He knew that the pain was due partly to hunger (when had he last eaten? lunch yesterday?). What he didn't know, on second thought, as he hung over his arm, was whether food or the drugstore or anything else in the world mattered enough to force him out of bed. Maybe not, but a full bladder did.

Sophie, who had kept an ear out for any sound from his room, heard his footsteps stumble down the hall. When they stumbled back, she came upstairs with a tray. She found him standing in the middle of the bedroom, engulfed in a voluminous nightshirt borrowed from Theodore, looking around helplessly for his clothes.

"Get into bed," she ordered. Not for nothing had she spent a year nursing him back to health. She set the tray down on a bedside table and plumped his pillow against the headboard.

"The drugstore," he protested, feebly. He felt almost too sick to speak. "What time is it?"

"Nearly eleven o'clock. Don't worry, *liebken*, Theodore sent Carl over with his key to let Hans in. They'll run the store today."

Hans was the ablest pharmaceutical apprentice the Murers had ever taken on. Edward himself had overseen most of the boy's training and knew he was both methodical as a druggist and ambitious. Carl, moreover, a year out of high school, was already active in the family's larger business (unlike his older brother Christian, who had gone east to Yale University and showed no sign of returning). Carl could easily handle the ledger. Nevertheless, Edward shied away from the thought of the boys tampering with his supplies and his book-keeping unsupervised.

"They'll make a mess of it," he said, as he lay back in bed. Sophie picked up the tray, ready to place it on his lap. "But they'll have fun," he conceded, with a trace of the sweet smile that few other people ever saw.

The smile did not last. At the sight even of dry toast, his gorge rose. A pang of squeezing pain behind his left temple shot across his forehead and sent a sick wave down through his body. His hands went clammy; he panted. His face was chalky and drawn. Hastily, Sophie leaned him forward, propped a second pillow behind him for more support, and fetched a shawl to settle around his shoulders. Then she sat on the edge of the bed and poured him a cup of milky tea.

"Sophie, I can't—"

"Shhhh, dear. We've been through this before. Just a sip."

A sip of tea, a nibble of toast, wait. Another sip, another nibble, wait. Gradually, the headache subsided and his stomach settled. They had indeed been through this before, all too often, in that first year after the war when she brought him back to life, as he was inclined to say. For Sophie, too, it had been a year of healing. Despite her best efforts, she had lost both her daughters to a typhoid epidemic that swept the city during the fighting. It had done her a world of good to see her patient mend instead of die.

In all the hours they had unavoidably spent together, moreover, she had come to know Edward as the man he had become, not as the lost brother whom Theodore kept wanting to reappear. As he began to respond to the world beyond his bodily needs, he showed a sensitivity to small things that Theodore, best of husbands, never noticed. For his part, after the hideousness of the camps, it was balm for Edward simply to spend time with a woman whose voice was pleasant, who always smelled powdery and clean, who shared some of his interests and knew his sadness. There had come a mild day in late autumn when he approached her while she was hanging clothes in the backyard. She had looked up over her shoulder at him and smiled. Their eyes met tenderly, but then the moment passed. They both knew it, cherished it, and never once spoke of it.

Edward sat back with his eyes closed, patted Sophie's hand, and held it for a moment. "I ought to be stirring."

"Nonsense; rest. You were freezing last night when you got here. You may have taken a chill. You know in your condition that's dangerous."

"You're making an invalid of me."

"I am giving you a holiday, you donkey. But you—if you have your way, you will make yourself sick, and then I shall have you on my hands for weeks."

Once Edward resigned himself to being fussed over, lassitude set in. All day, he dozed fitfully. He would think he should get up, only to sleep some more: cottony sleep that brought him no refreshment. The oxtail soup Sophie brought him for lunch was excellent—a rich, brown, flavorful smoothness on the tongue—but he was too weary to care. As the day wore on, he grew duller and duller. Late in the afternoon, when Sophie got him up to move to the guest room, now fully heated, he padded down the hallway in sock feet, aware primarily that the wooden floor under the runner was cold and hard and that his bones ached. His eyes stung. He slept through Theodore's return that night.

On the second morning, he awoke ravenous. Hunger was a spur, but the main thing that got him going was habit—habit and the discipline instilled in him by his father, by Colonel Willich of the Ohio Ninth Infantry Regiment, and by years of running the store. A fresh towel and washcloth had been left for him on a chair, and his clothes were laid out: his own coat and trousers brushed, his boots polished, and fresh linen lent by Carl, who was closer to his size than the much stouter Theodore. What required more effort than bathing and dressing was going downstairs to breakfast. He was ashamed of having been ill.

Luckily, when he came into the breakfast room, his voluble fourteen-year-old namesake, Eddie, was rattling on to Theodore about an experiment in thermal dynamics that he was devising for school; he broke the stream of his talk only to rise and welcome his uncle with a brief "Good morning, sir," as unconcerned as if Edward were a familiar household fixture. Edward returned the greeting briefly and nodded to the others. Eddie plunged back into the technicalities of his project. Theodore, who understood both his brother's reserve and his son's lack of it, winked at Edward and for once let Eddie flow unchecked.

Breakfast had been set out on the sideboard, a very Southern breakfast of ham, biscuits, and redeye gravy (Hannah, the cook, was from Kentucky), along with the pickles and sausages Theodore loved and the novel canned grapefruit that was Sophie's current fad. Edward's appetite waned at the sight of so much food, but he took a thin slice of ham, a biscuit, and a few sections of grapefruit to please Sophie.

"There is coffee in the pot, or would you rather have tea?" Sophie asked, over Eddie's chatter.

"Coffee, please," said Edward. Hannah roasted the coffee at home and brewed it strong. It should banish the vestige of his headache.

In response to Sophie's bell, Hannah came to the dining room door. "How you want your eggs this morning, Mr. Edward, scrambled or fried?"

"Scrambled, please, Hannah." He would have to make an effort.

Carl pushed back the chair at the place set beside him. "Why don't you let Hans and me open up the store again, Uncle Edward? It's a rotten day outside."

It was. Gray with a sleety rain.

"I need to get my blood stirring."

"Well, I'll come with you and show you what we did."

"Hans can do that."

"You must come back here tonight," said Sophie.

"It will take me longer in the bad weather to come here than to go home."

"Yes, but the dinner here will be better."

"Infinitely better, but still a distance."

"Take the streetcar or a cab," said Theodore, who had caught his wife's glance. "I have business to talk over."

"Can't it wait?" asked Edward. His hands came to a standstill, and he stared at his plate.

Sophie and Theodore exchanged a look.

"Of course," said Theodore.

A little while later, when the men were all leaving for the street-car, Sophie quietly pressed Edward's arm. "Do pack a bag and come stay here a few days, *liebken*," she said. "Now that we've warmed up the guest room, we should make use of the heat."

But Edward did not return, not right away. He stubbornly told himself there would be nothing wrong with him if he took himself in hand. Needed or not, Carl had gone with him to the store, where Hans was waiting, stamping his feet in the cold at the door. The bad weather kept customers away, but the morning proved busy as Edward stepped in to help finish up some housecleaning the boys had initiated the day before, preparatory to taking a thorough inventory. He was not sorry for the extra help and even the company: Carl was affable with those few old customers who did come in, many of whom had watched him grow up, and his presence deflected appraising eyes from Edward's strained face. But after lunch, Edward sent Carl on to his real job at the company headquarters of Murer Brothers. By the afternoon mail, he sent Sophie a note of thanks for his

rescue and regrets for dinner that evening. At eight o'clock, with
some trepidation, he went through his routine of closing up shop.
The thought had crossed his mind more than once during the day
that he might go somewhere new for supper, but a change from the
tavern so convenient to his boardinghouse would make mockery of
his refusing Sophie's invitation on the grounds of wanting to keep
dry. His real reason for staying away was stubbornness: He knew it
and she knew it, but a certain loyalty required him to go through
the motions of pretending even to himself that he was simply being
practical.

At the tavern, the regulars argued politics as usual: old Forty-
Eighters like his father, socialists, radicals, and staunch Republicans.
If they ever turned from theory to current news, they were as likely
to be concerned about Kaiser Wilhelm and imperial Prussia as about
President Hayes and the mess in Washington. Edward, who seldom
joined in these ceaseless debates, did occasionally take on a game of
checkers. Not tonight. He made himself inconspicuous and left half
his pork chop, potato, and overcooked shell peas uneaten.

When he opened the door to his boardinghouse, the little bell
that rang at its every movement brought his landlady out from the
kitchen into the hall. She carried herself very straight and wiped her
hands on her apron.

"I didn't hear you come in last night, Dr. Murer."

"No, nor see me at breakfast, Mrs. Wiggins," said Edward, who
knew that although something more than prurient curiosity moved
her, she had a salacious mind. "I spent the night at my brother's."

"I don't inquire," said Mrs. Wiggins, loftily. "But I do have to
charge you for the breakfast, anyway, seeing as you didn't give me
no warning."

"Of course, Mrs. Wiggins," said Edward, wearily. Mrs. Wiggins's
system of charging for the rooms a month in advance and individual
meals at the end of each week caused endless wrangling with her
tenants.

Satisfied on the main point, she paused before returning to the kitchen and looked at him quizzically. "Nothing wrong I hope, sir?"

"Thank you, Mrs. Wiggins, nothing."

Edward's second-floor suite consisted of a bedroom, closet, and study, rented furnished. Over the years, he had added a few things of his own: a large cherry bureau and a glass-fronted bookcase from his mother's house, some prints on the wall, a good rug. They mitigated the secondhand, catch-as-catch-can racketiness of the place. He could, of course, have moved a long time ago, but inertia kept him there. He believed it suited him.

On top of the bookcase lay his most precious possession, a small, black leather-bound picture case. He deposited his cane in an umbrella stand, hung up his hat and overcoat, and walked pensively over to pick it up. "Why did I feel nothing, Marie?" he asked, cradling the case.

He opened the cover. A young woman—no, a girl just entering womanhood—stared out with a fixed solemn expression, her fair hair primly parted and combed flat against her head, her soft mouth held in a line. For the first time ever, Edward admitted to seeing it for what it was: a thin, metallic film of silver grays and black on a slightly shiny surface. It did not recall the prismatic wisps of Marie's blond hair escaping into the sunlight, nor the uneven pink flush of her skin, nor the full contours of her nose and cheek and lips. It had not for a long time. The light blue of her eyes emphasized by a darker rim to their irises was only a blank lightness in the photograph. Worse, he realized that the image of Marie in his mind was as static as the darkening tintype. Of her likings, of her mind and quickness, of her laughter, all that remained to him were odd flashes, now stylized fragments, a boy's memories—and he was no longer that boy. He snapped the case shut and laid it down again, clutching the edges of the shelf as he leaned over it in defeat.

After a few dazed, dry moments, he lifted the glass panel of the bottom shelf and from behind a row of books took out a small box.

From it, he withdrew a key to a locked lower compartment of the bureau, which he used as a sideboard. He crossed the room, bent down, turned the key, and pulled out a wineglass, a bottle of sherry, a near-empty vial, and a dropper. Half a bitter ounce of escape dripped into a glassful of musky sweetness to cover the taste.

He took the laudanum.

CHAPTER FIVE

"You Must Go"

In the army hospital where Edward had been sent after liberation from the Confederate prison camp at Andersonville, Georgia, opiates were administered freely as a kindness amid intolerable suffering. They not only killed pain and cured diarrhea but induced a euphoric sense of well-being in the starved, the dying, and the amputees. Edward had been given his share.

In the lost days immediately following his return to Cincinnati, Sophie had preferred to comfort him with warm food, cleanliness, and sunny quiet. When he had nightmares, she held him and rocked him as she had soothed her children, including the two who died. "He needs to learn he is safe," she said, "not to be blunted into a stupor."

Theodore agreed. As a pharmacist, he understood the benefits of laudanum (indeed, with a clear conscience he had profited handsomely from supplying it and other derivatives of opium to the Union army); but he also knew that patients grew dependent on it. He himself was judicious in prescribing it and frowned on the new, distilled, and highly addictive morphine. Edward knew everything Theodore knew and more. Once he was on his own again, therefore, his intermittent laudanum use had been furtive. He did not want his family or his customers to know how incomplete was his recovery.

On the first night he was home after the attack on Elm Street, he calculated the dose well. He woke up at his usual hour; and if his pupils were still slightly constricted and his manner dull at breakfast, Mrs. Wiggins would notice nothing. Liveliness was not required of her boarders, nor expected in the morning.

He dragged himself up and sat on the edge of the bed, his head in his hands, weighed down by an unfocused sense of dread. Memory of the night before crept back and, with it, certainty that the tintype of Marie would never again have power to move him. He had learned of her death when he came home from the war. She had been dead some fifteen years now; the past was gone. Early in his bereavement, whenever he saw a view that would have delighted her or passed a band concert in the park, the moment of recognizing a pleasure as hers had been sweet; the instant stab of loss that followed had been deep and real. Out of such moments, he had made a practice of addressing her mentally as if to share things with her. He let her voice rally him for his absurdities. When had the habit lapsed and faded? When was the last time he had thought of her at all? The realization that had felled him the night before remained true in the morning: His devotion to Marie was a sentimental self-delusion, which he had given up long ago without even noticing. For that matter, the real eighteen-year-old Marie was probably nothing like the girl he had repeatedly resurrected in memory. Obviously, she wouldn't be now, not if she had lived. But for all he knew, she had betrayed him while he was away. She hardly ever wrote, he told himself brutally, then felt ashamed. Why malign that sweet girl in his blue funk? Hating his room more than he hated moving, he went downstairs.

Mrs. Wiggins's tea was stronger than her coffee, a coarse black

China tea that stood up well to milk. He drank a large cup and ate toast. He had no appetite for her badly cooked eggs or dry chops, but the stimulant did him good.

Back in his room, he picked up the closed tintype case and bounced it in his hand. Smiling a little sardonically at the experiment, he pushed it open with his thumb. The image of the pretty girl was still a flat gray irrelevance. He was no longer shocked by its failure to move him, though some part of his mind grieved. He might as well throw it away. But he didn't. Some caution, or perhaps a flickering thread of light in the back of his mind, led him instead to bury it in the bottom of his handkerchief box.

At the drugstore, he kept his customary hours. It was a busy morning. A warm wind during the night had brought in the kind of balmy day that presaged spring, and with it all the patients who had been kept indoors yesterday by the sleet. The newer customers with simple needs or doctors' prescriptions to be filled were glad to see Hans, whose ruddy cheek and alert eye attracted them; the older ones, those who remembered the Ohio Ninth Infantry, *Die Neuner*, and those who needed a diagnosis, generally waited for Edward. He attended each one with forced concentration despite an incipient headache. Not even the newcomers, who were intimidated by the gaunt shadows under his cheekbones and his sunken eye, doubted the assurance with which he prescribed remedies and compounded dosages. Not even Hans.

That night he forced himself to attend a lecture on the *Reich-patentgesetz*, the new patent law in Germany. His head pounded. Saturday, he worked all day. Saturday night, he tried to lose himself in the raucous gaiety of a music hall but had to flee the noise and smoke. On Monday, his hand trembled in the morning, but he kept himself on the job. He was late to work on Tuesday; he took to walking instead of eating at midday. Hans began stepping forward to greet all customers. Edward's condition worsened. Finally, the mother of one of his slain comrades in the Ninth came in, a woman who had known the Murers back in Germany. She leaned past Hans at the counter to peer at Edward hunched over in his chair behind the bead curtain.

"Is it one of his headaches?" she asked, in an undertone.

"He's been like this for a week," whispered Hans.

"So. Go take a cab, tell the driver to wait, and fetch Mr. Murer."

"But—"

"Take the fare from the till if you are afraid Mr. Murer will not pay."

"It's not that, but—"

She waved away objections. "Tell Theodore Murer that Frau Lund is with his brother, and he must come. Now." She turned the placard in the window to read *Closed* and pulled down the shade.

Hans returned with Theodore, who had the cabdriver deliver himself and Edward to the house in Mount Auburn. This time, Edward did not resist when Carl was sent around to the boarding-house to pack a suitcase. Sophie installed him in the guest room. Hans and Carl took over the drugstore.

Although the symptoms of Edward's collapse were unnervingly like those of his postwar debilitation, a few weeks of poor eating and finally some laudanum were physically nothing compared to two years of near starvation. Theodore was inclined to give him more laudanum, at least for a few days, but Sophie was against it. "He is ashamed of his use," she said, "and it dampens his appetite. Let us try to bring him around without it." She started Edward at once on soups and custards, carried up on a bed tray. When he failed to pick up his spoon, she hand-fed him small swallows, a few at a time. When he closed his eyes, she held his hand gently until he was willing to try again. As soon as she could move him to solid food, she did, always in small servings. To please her, he forced himself to use a fork even while food still stuck in his throat. He had not been able to bring himself to ask Carl to find a newly opened bottle of lauda-num in his room; pride prevented his begging Theodore for more;

and he suffered through the days wondering at the body's insistence
on living. Meanwhile, the weather cooperated by turning warm and
dry. In the lengthening March afternoons, Sophie led him on walks
in the neighborhood; they made excursions by carriage to the sylvan
retreats of Burnet Woods, still leafless but picturesque and sunlit. He
rejoined the family table. In spite of an apathy born of self-loathing,
his physical health returned and with it a restlessness.

"It's time to sell out to Hans, Edward," said Theodore, one evening,
leading Edward into his study after supper. "Here." He held out a
glass with a small splash of brandy.

"Should I?" asked Edward, not reaching for it.

"Certainly! What do you take me for? You are no drunkard,
Edward, and you know it," said Theodore, stabbing the air at him
with a cigar, which he left unlit in deference to Edward's damaged
lung. "Besides, wine is—"

"—the foundation of civilization."

"You mock me, but it is true. Where is the cradle of civilization
if not the Mediterranean? And what grows there? The grape. The
ancient Hebrews, the Greeks, the Romans—they all drank wine.
What better to stimulate the flow of conviviality, the soul of human-
ity? And brandy—"

Edward cut him short. "In Turkey, the site of Troy, they grow
poppies."

Theodore placed the glass on a table at Edward's elbow, poured
a larger glassful for himself, and sat down. "Edward, opiates consume
the user. They isolate him; he does not eat. He gives no thought to
his fellow man."

"What you mean is, I'm all washed up."

"That is exactly what I do *not* mean!" said Theodore, pounding
the arm of his chair. He brought his temper under control. "No, but

I do say that you need a change; you grow stale. I would be the same if—"

"—if you had moldered on at the store."

Theodore waved aside the old quarrel impatiently. "After your recovery from the war, Edward, you took up many things. While Papa was alive, we played chamber music together, with Herr Schwartz, remember?"

"I was only the violist."

"*Ja*, but you were good. Or what about that fencing master? You went to his school on Vine Street?"

"Dancing master was more like it; you know that—you were the real fencer. Anyway, that was before the war, not after."

"So, so. Nevertheless, you did things. You got your medical training; you moved in the society of men. You came out to the laboratory and experimented. You invented new products. Your cure for chilblains allowed us to expand."

"Any pharmacist can compound salves and remedies, Theodore. We both know that, and we both know it was your business sense that made the real difference."

"Only half true! You are proud that your salves and remedies work, and so am I. Without a good product, a businessman has nothing to sell. And now to keep expanding, we need new products."

"Hire younger men."

"Edward, what I am saying is that when you take an interest, you contribute! Your mechanical suggestions for the production line paid off, too. You have a good mind; it needs to stretch again. The routine of serving individual customers—"

"—of caring for patients, Theodore. They are our neighbors—mine, anyway."

"Some ever since Germany, and your comrades in the war—I know," said Theodore, sympathetically, and yet with a touch of impatience. He started to light the cigar, remembered, and flung the match away. "Papa clung to Forty-Eight. For him everything always had to be measured by the revolution that failed. It was my big cause, too, but we lost. We came here. I put it behind me. What happened to you in your war was very terrible, but at least the Union was saved, enslaved men were set free. Don't you ever get tired of it, Edward, always this looking back?"

"Tired of it? I'm sick of it! Sick of myself. Sick of being watched and pitied, yes. Sick of gratitude; sick of what follows—impatience at having to be grateful. Oh, the devil! That bum was right; nobody remembers anymore but the old mothers. Yes, Theodore, I am sick to my soul; we have all seen that. Nostalgic, you think. Impotent is more like it." Edward, whose thin frame had become taut with anger, slumped back. He turned his face toward the fire. "In France, they call it ennui."

Theodore, who had been taken aback by the vehemence of Edward's outburst, was silent. In the soft semidarkness of the cluttered room, lit only by the fire and a small lamp, strong feeling ebbed away. If the two brothers had been strangers, they would have rubbed each other the wrong way. As it was, the attachment between them was strong.

"What I was going to suggest was travel," Theodore said. "Why don't you go somewhere?"

"Covington, maybe? Kansas?"

"I mean it; I am serious. New sights to make a new man. Not all of France is ennui, Edward—it is also gaiety and beauty and esprit. Or if not France, then Italy, England, maybe even Spain. Go back to Kiel if you want. You were eight when we left; you can only half remember it. Such lovely, gentle views in Holstein. Or go to Alsace— you remember the summers at Gran'marie's house? Go to Switzerland. Take the waters at Baden-Baden."

"You have something in mind." It was a measure of Edward's improved health that he could detect an unspoken purpose in Theodore's pleading and be almost amused by it.

Theodore shrugged like a man caught out; his eyes twinkled. "There is something I want you to do. I want you to accompany Carl to Europe."

"The Grand Tour! Stuff his Midwestern head with culture?" asked Edward, disbelieving.

"No—though that would not hurt. They are tabulae rasae, these American children of mine. That much Latin even they may know, though not a word of Greek. What do they know of music, of theater, of painting and art? The best Cincinnati has to offer," he answered himself ironically.

"I speak with a twang myself," said Edward. "I'm as much a hick as they are."

"That you are not! You grew up with Papa and Mutter. And you still read," said Theodore, pointing the cigar forcefully. He frowned as he caught the drift of his own thought. "Not that we have no reason to be proud in Cincinnati! It is a great city in a great country. The future lies on this side of the Atlantic, in the New World, you mark my words."

"Consider them marked."

"Where were we?"

"Back in the Old World. Perhaps at La Scala or the Prado."

"Or the Louvre. Painting. Painting requires what?—paint," said Theodore, resuming his mock lecturing style. "Pigments, dyestuffs, pharmaceuticals. Once upon a time, they were all the same thing. The family craft. Murers have pounded botanicals in mortars and ground minerals for generation upon generation. They still do, but on an ever larger scale. A chemist in England tries to make quinine and discovers mauveine. All Europe dyes itself purple, and in Baden the Murers take notice. These aniline dyes and synthetic drugs, Edward, they are leading to whole new industries."

"So Young Paul said. Repeatedly." The previous year, when their cousin Paul Murer's son had paid an extended visit to Cincinnati to learn American business methods under Theodore's tutelage, he had boasted endlessly about the new chemical plant his father was building in Freiburg-im-Breisgau.

"Is a return visit not in order? I want Carl to spend some time in Freiburg at Cousin Paul's new dye works and bring us up to date, maybe take a course at a *technische Hochschule*."

"*Hochschule?* Carl should go east to college, Theodore. If the future lies in America, send him to Yale or Harvard. You're a university man yourself, and he's a bright boy."

"Bright, but lazy. He gets by on easy comprehension and charm. Maybe if he sees what ambitious young men his age are doing abroad, his zeal will increase. Munich, Zürich, Freiburg. As for you, Edward, you are older and a cooler hand. I should be interested in what you have to say about what you see there, too.

"But first, we make it a vacation, eh? We all go. We shall start in Paris. My Sophie will buy the prettiest dresses at the fashion houses and promenade on the Champs-Élysées; we shall hear opera in the splendors of Garnier's Opera House; we shall go to the World's Fair and see what every nation on earth is bragging about in commerce and art. And then when we have taken our pleasure, you and Carl will set off on your inspections."

"I still don't understand, Theodore. Why me? Why not take him yourself?"

"Because I do not have the time."

"And I do."

"You could. Listen, Hans is too ambitious to remain a clerk forever. Take advantage: Make him the manager; we'll sell him a share in the store. Real wealth is moving out from downtown, but Over-the-Rhine will be crowded for a long time. Let the boy sweep with his new broom—put in an ice-cream soda fountain if he wants. They are all the rage."

"There isn't room."

"*Ach!* You see? You hold him back! And you! It's time to brush the cobwebs out of your brain, Edward. If you still want to be a pharmacist when you return, we can open a new branch of Murer Brothers here on the north side."

"But I won't want to."

"No, you won't."

They were silent again. After a while, Theodore mused, "As long as that man Bismarck is alive, I will not set foot in Germany. An empire for the Prussian Kaiser." He shook his head. "Forty-Eight was not your war, but it *was* mine. Maybe I have not forgotten, after all. But I am not so stubborn that I cut off my son from opportunities. You speak German and French; you can help Carl. And the two of you—you will enjoy each other. You are younger than I am. Old enough to temper his callow youth, but young enough to make him feel free away from his aged Papa."

You are younger than I am, thought Edward, studying his brother. Yet oddly enough, although he recognized in Theodore a stronger life force, more worldly success, and the greater capacity for spontaneous enthusiasm, inside Edward a tiny, persistent pride insisted that his own yearnings were turned toward finer things, that he felt more acutely and saw more clearly than Theodore. In all the years of his suffering, he had never seriously thought of suicide. Many times he longed not to wake to yet another day in the prison camp or to the barrenness of life after the war, but instinct rejected the violence of a gun to the head or the outrage of poison administered by his own hand. And somewhere something green lay dormant among his dry sticks.

"Are you sending me to look after Carl, or Carl to look after me?"

"Maybe a little of both, Edward; I am an economical man."

CHAPTER SIX

Arrival in Paris

At first, neither Mrs. Palmer nor Mrs. Hendrick gave any credence to the idea that Jeanette and Effie might go to Paris. Nevertheless, when Jeanette insisted that her father would at least allow her to consult with Mr. Sartain, Sarah Palmer had to agree. She went with her. Taking it for granted that Mrs. Palmer wanted her daughter to have further lessons, Mr. Sartain addressed most of his remarks to her. He professed admiration for Jeanette's samples, pointing out particular felicities; he regretted that his own class was full but named some other masters in New York who taught privately.

"A Miss Whitmore recommended the Académie Julian in Paris," put in Jeanette.

"Is that a possibility? It's an excellent school."

"It would take thought," said Mrs. Palmer, slowly.

Sensing a weakening in her mother's resistance, Jeanette went on. "When would a French school term begin?"

"In the fall, but a great advantage of Julian's is that you can join a class at any time."

On the way home, Sarah Palmer was thoughtful. She drew Jeanette's arm through hers and said, "Well, I admit I was proud to hear his praise. Now don't draw hasty conclusions, Jeanette!" she added, aware that Jeanette was exulting. "I must write your father."

So must I, thought Jeanette. So must I!

Then it was Aunt Maude's turn to take umbrage when she realized that her unpaid housekeeper had meant what she said. "Out of the question, Effie! Jeanette would have to be overseas for a year or two, and it would not be convenient to have you gone that long."

"But, Maude, you often point out that you can run the house perfectly well yourself," said Effie, "and, of course, you can. I mean, you *do*. And now with the children all grown up and gone, and Jeanette's education to be thought of—"

"My girls never had any such education. Besides, what, may I ask, would you expect to live on?"

"Well, you know Papa left me a small income—"

"Pin money and a dress allowance."

"Yes, but dear Polycarpus put me in his will, too, before he was killed, and Matthew has been investing my little nest egg all these years. I think there would be quite enough. I mean, I know it: Matthew has been giving me quarterly statements."

"Quite right," said Mr. Hendrick. "Our little Effie is a woman of independent means, Maude. She could indeed get by entirely on her own."

"In reduced circumstances, I have no doubt."

"Much reduced. Genteel poverty, you might say, but perfectly respectable. Paris, Effie? Paris, Jeanette? *Ooh là là!*"

It was the respectability, not the *ooh là là*, that reconciled Mrs. Palmer to the plan, despite her continued misgivings. To say that Jeanette would be accompanying an older relative to Europe was the sort of story that would arouse little more than conventional interest in Circleville, or perhaps even a touch of envy. More important, Judge Palmer came around and took over. A man given to bursts of enthusiasm followed by forecasts of ruin, and vice versa, he had been proud of his daughter's early successes at Vassar, wounded by her delinquency, and impressed by the encouragement she was given by Professor von Ingen and those in New York whom she consulted. Once into the planning stages, moreover, he became openhanded and sent Matthew Hendrick a sum to fold into Effie's capital. *Let our young women have visions and us old men dream dreams!* he proclaimed. As for

Aunt Maude, once she knew she was bested, she predicted a cold, stormy passage in April: "But you'd better go soon while hotel rooms and *pensions* are still available in Paris; there's a World's Fair on, you know." And so Judge Palmer ordered that tickets be purchased for an early crossing. *And damn the expense, safety first. Take a Cunarder.*

He also wrote Jeanette an earnest letter. *Every father wishes to give his children the best in life, and every man learns to his sorrow the need for second chances. I am blessed with the means to give you yours, Jeanette, but it comes with conditions. I had expected to pay for two more years at Vassar College. In the coming twelve months, after you reach Paris, I shall send you an allowance in four quarterly installments equal to the tuition and living expenses I would have paid in your junior year. If at the end of your first year you can convince me that another year of study is required and that you have deserved it, you shall have it. But two years is my limit. There are your sisters to consider, if nothing else, and I will not have you make yourself into a dilettante. Go with my love, and come home prepared to demonstrate that your calling is as true as your eloquent pleas have claimed.*

In the middle of April, Jeanette leaned against the rail of an English Channel ferry boat. Around her, every stretch of canvas, coil of rope, wooden plank, or metal surface was pearled with moisture. So was the ancient woolen overcoat Uncle Matthew had given her to ward off salt spray and steamer soot. Under an overcast sky, even sea water was drained of color. For twelve days, the Atlantic Ocean had offered an infinitely subtle range of bright blue, slate blue, jade green, purple; of fire and gold at sunset; of pewter and silver at dusk. Not so this last leg of the journey, notable largely for dingy whitecaps; but now the channel's choppiness was giving way to a slow heave and roll. Against the harsh grind of the boat's engine and buffeting wind, the shrill squeals of seagulls could be heard. A blur like a cloud bank along the horizon took on contours and gradually began to separate into undulating shades of green over a band of lighter tan. Jeanette stood eagerly on tiptoe and leaned out over the water. A white V in the chalk cliffs marked the entrance to Dieppe harbor.

She ran to the ladies' saloon to fetch Cousin Effie, who insisted on folding up her knitting properly and putting on her mackintosh. When at last the two of them returned to the rail, the bluffs of the Norman coast were clearly visible. As the ferry turned out of the open channel into the long harbor basin, the scent of the open sea was replaced by the more pungent smells of a seaport with an active fishing fleet. The French tricolors fluttered lightly on flagpoles along the quays and some of the buildings opposite—limestone town buildings, block after block of them, three, four, and five stories high, with gabled windows in their mansard roofs and tall painted shutters at the windows.

"Why, it's downright quaint," said Effie, "or really I should say elegant."

"Too beautiful for this!" To embrace her new life, Jeanette doffed Uncle Matthew's coat and flung it onto a bench alongside the wall of the cabin.

"I've been thinking. We might want to make a lap robe out of that," said Effie.

"Too late! If it makes some other shivering passenger happy, so much the better, but you won't catch me entering France in anything that hideous. Cousin Effie, we're in *France*!"

On the quay, they joined a cluster of passengers gathered around a cheerful Englishman holding up a sign: *Thomas Cook Travel Agency.* He directed them to the nearby train station, where they would have time for a bite of something to eat in the station buffet.

"And you're sure that our checked luggage . . ." said Effie.

"All part of the package, madam, part of the package. It will be waiting for you—"

"—when we've been through customs in Paris," said Effie with him, nodding her head. She had read and reread the company's instructions.

While they were talking, Jeanette tried to take in everything. It seemed impossible that she could simply walk across the stone paving and be in the streets of Dieppe, but there were no barriers, no fences, nothing to stop her. Other passengers from the ferry were walking off or entering the train station as if it were the most natural thing in the world.

"Oh, look at the coffee shop, Cousin Effie! I wish we had time. And the *bakery*. Come on, we do have time for that. Adeline's centimes!"

"We'll spend those in the station. No, wait, Jeanette! Come back! We're supposed to eat at the buffet!"

But Jeanette had dashed across the cobblestones toward a row of small ground-floor shops. A bell above the door of the patisserie jingled as she entered. In a glass display case were trays of pastries, glistening with apricot glazes or filled by swirls of piped cream, each with its white card marking the price in a Continental hand. They were like nothing Jeanette had ever seen in America. Behind the counter stood a woman, wearing a fichu. *"Bonjour, mademoiselle."*

"Bonjour, madame!"

The hard line of the woman's mouth softened slightly, but her very direct, superior look made Jeanette burn to appear as if she knew what she was doing. A tray marked *tartes d'amandes, 10 c,* caught her eye. They looked solid, rather like a macaroon; they might break in her handbag, but they wouldn't smear everything with pastry cream or jam. She asked for two.

As she stepped back out onto the street, her elbow was caught by Cousin Effie, who had been nervously watching the Thomas Cook party disappear through a door. "Never run off like that again, Jeanette, never, ever!" she scolded, as she hurried them across the cobblestones to catch up with their group.

Jeanette was impenitent. "We're not lost, and we won't miss the train."

Inside the station, some of their fellow passengers grumbled about station food, but not Jeanette and Effie. Their thrifty choice of an oyster stew *Dieppoise* was enriched with spring cream and served with crusty baguettes. The white linen napkins were generous, the flatware heavy; and the practiced flourish of their unsmiling waiter when he served them strong, black coffee from a long-handled pot so delighted them that they splurged and ordered apple compote to go with it.

Effie splurged again when she spotted a rack of English-language books at a stall in the main waiting room. "Just the thing for the train," she said, happily, procuring a cheap edition of *The Hunchback of Notre Dame.*

"You should read it in French."

"I can't."

"Not yet. Oh, I'll tell you what: I'll buy this and you can practice on it later."

Jeanette picked up the current issue of a glamorous-looking magazine called *La Vie Parisienne.* Adeline could have told her that it was too frivolous and sophisticated for a nice girl from Ohio, but Adeline was an ocean away.

The Thomas Cook agent secured second-class compartments for his charges. "Now, the train will be picking up additional passengers in Rouen, ladies," he said to Jeanette and Effie, as he handed them up into an empty one, "but first come, first served—you've nabbed the window seats."

Effie immediately took the one that would have her riding backward.

"Are you sure?" asked Jeanette.

"Yes, indeed. I'm going to read." Effie settled down with her Victor Hugo, adopting the absorbed concentration that discourages other travelers from choosing the adjacent seat.

Jeanette did not even pretend to look at her magazine but watched every movement on the platform. The elements of the scene were the same as those at an American depot—the parallel sets of iron rails, gravel, signal posts, black snouts and flared chimneys of locomotives—yet everything was different. Not only were the signs in French, but the cars were built differently; even the freight yard, as they slowly pulled past, had a look of its own—while beyond the tracks lay Dieppe. And then the town disappeared. The train plunged into the blackness of a long tunnel, and at the other end were no outlying buildings, no tree stumps, no raggedy scrum; they had passed abruptly and totally into the countryside.

Jeanette had never seen farmland so densely cultivated nor so tidily beautiful. First came walled gardens with feathery squares of new-sprouting carrots or radishes, then sheep and herds of small cattle wandering in among the trees of well-pruned orchards. Neither the English watercolors she had seen at Vassar nor the Barbizon landscapes for sale in New York had prepared her for the fairy-tale quality of Norman farmhouses and folds of hills, of crooked roads and red-twigged coppices on riverbanks. She tried to note down a few details in her pocket sketchbook; but even for single lines, her hand jiggled too much. She gave it up.

An hour later, the modern world began to intrude again in the form of large, smokestacked industrial mills on the riverbank as they approached Rouen. A ten-minute stop gave them a chance to stretch. They left magazine and book on their seats, and Effie brought down a carpetbag from the overhead rack to put on the seat beside hers. "I knew we should have kept Matthew's coat," she said.

When they returned, five more of the eight seats were taken, but book, magazine, and bag had been respected. "*Ah! par-donny mwa!*" exclaimed Effie, pretending surprise to find her carpetbag on the seat. She lifted it toward the luggage racks, which were now full, shrugged an apology that could have fooled no one, and put it back on the seat. She winked at Jeanette.

Jeanette shrank into the corner of her seat. Luckily for her peace of mind, the limits of Effie's French constrained her from trying to strike up conversation. She merely perused each of their new companions and returned to her book. Jeanette kept her head bent over and stared fixedly at a paragraph of gossip from the *beau monde* of the Jockey Club, which seemed to have nothing to do with racing. At a jerk when the train started again, she involuntarily looked out the window. Effie caught her movement. "Off again. Gay Paree, here we come!" she said, brightly. Jeanette made as repressive a noise of agreement as she dared. Once everyone was settled and the iron wheels were clacking rhythmically over rail joints again, she went back to watching steadily out the window.

Jeanette began to feel strangely trapped, unable to move without disturbing the man sitting next to her, ignorant of exactly where they were. An hour past Rouen, well aware that her mother did not approve of eating in public, she surreptitiously felt inside her handbag. The stiff tissue paper of her bakery packet rustled. No one seemed to notice. Fumbling, she broke off a pinch of fragrant tart and brought it to her mouth. It was rich, delicious. She stole another bite, and another, then slowly and carefully drew out the packet to offer Cousin Effie her tart. Effie fluttered her hands, no, then snatched the whole packet quickly and tucked it away. Jeanette leaned back in her seat, exasperated.

She began to feel a creeping fear. In New York, she had had to put all her energy into making this happen. In Dieppe, the astonishment of actually being in France had sent her spirits soaring. Now, as the train clacked on into the fading dusk, the enormity of attempting to shape a future in so strange a place overwhelmed her.

The railroad bed cut straight into a hill and, after passing under a fortified wall, continued in a deep cutting on the steep sides of which were pasted one giant advertising hoarding after another— *Biscuits Olibet; Domaine de St. Gabriel something, something*—just legible by ambient light from streetlamps high above. The train slowed

until, with a squealing whistle, it plunged into new darkness marked
only by a line of lantern dots. As it reemerged into the open air, the
other passengers began to pull down luggage and adjust their hats
and coats. Jeanette sat paralyzed. The tracks, having diverged into
many lines, ended under a vast zigzag of pitched roofs. Everywhere,
there were workmen, signal posts, and sheds. Locomotives were being switched on turntables; crowds of outward-bound passengers
milled on platforms; billows of smoke and steam rose. They had
arrived at the vast Gare Saint-Lazare.

On the platform, while the other passengers from their compartment
disappeared into the crowd pushing toward the station building,
Jeanette and Effie waited, as instructed, until their Thomas Cook
agent turned up and guided them down a few car lengths to where
an amassing throng of porters, baggage carts, and fellow passengers
from the ferry were herded together. "Next, it's the sheep pens,"
remarked one of the men. He shifted aside to acknowledge Jeanette
and Effie's inclusion in the group. At a signal, they all began to move,
lengthening out into what became a line for the customs enclosure.

"Now, ladies," said the agent, coming back to Jeanette and Effie,
"if you'll take my advice, you'll let me engage you a cab right now
ahead of time. It will cost a bit more, paying the driver to wait, but
you'll be set when you're through customs and find yourself standing
on the Rue d'Amsterdam with your life's belongings heaped around
you on the pavement. Agreed? Right you are, never made a wiser
decision in your life. Keep moving with the line, and I'll be back in
a tick."

He returned with a sheaf of cards with numbers, which he distributed to the passengers under his care. "Now there's a cab out
there with this number, see. Just give it to the driver and off you go.

"Not at all, miss, all part of the job," he said, when Effie tried to offer him a tip. "But the porter on the other side, he'll be expecting his fifteen centimes and deserves it, don't he, a man has to earn his living. But don't give more than twenty, whatever you do. No need to support highway robbery and raise expectations. Just show him your number, and he'll take you to the cab."

In the claims area, Frenchmen and incoming foreigners were sorted, questioned, stamped, and reunited with their trunks, then questioned, examined, and stamped again. Jeanette and Effie had nothing taxable to declare and roused no suspicions in the minds of the customs officials; the search of their luggage was perfunctory. The next thing they knew, they had been disgorged into Paris.

CHAPTER SEVEN

Getting Started

For their first week, Jeanette and Effie had reservations at the Pavillon des Dames, a hotel on the Left Bank recommended by Miss Whitmore. As soon as their porter found their four-wheeled fiacre, Effie handed him his tip and read off their address to the driver. Her accent was bad, but her delivery had the ring of authority. In dealing with city cabdrivers, she was back in her element.

Jeanette was not. The cab ride through a phantasmagoria of smooth, light-smeared boulevards and dark, cobbled side streets; arrival at an impossibly narrow hotel wedged in the middle of a block; its threadbare lobby and their spartan room—everything conspired to lower her spirits even more than the train station had.

At a restaurant across the street, where the receptionist sent them for supper, they did not know how to order. She went to bed in despair at having made such a mistake.

The next morning, she overslept. They were in Paris and could have found something to eat within a block's walk in any direction; but breakfast was included in the price of the room, and Cousin Effie would not hear of paying twice. She hurried them downstairs. In a basement room, where a number of tables were laid with white tablecloths, cutlery, and china, a few guests lingered over broken crumbs and last cups of coffee or tea. Effie returned their curious glances so frankly that the ladies looked away. Jeanette slunk into a chair at the one table still laid with rolls, butter, and marmalade; she almost apologized when a sulky waitress brought them pots of hot milk and coffee.

"Where shall we go first?" asked Effie, later, as she complacently buttered the flaking remains of a second croissant. "I suppose the bank, and then we'd better look for a place to live."

Jeanette shook her head. Her spirits had risen in response to caffeine. "First, the Louvre."

They went on foot. With the map in a guidebook given them by Uncle Matthew, they could find their way, whereas the omnibus system was confusing and a cab cost money. On the Pont des Arts, a wide, wooden-planked bridge opposite the Louvre, Jeanette could feel the pounding surge of the Seine beneath them. A damp wind caused most pedestrians to bow heads and hunch shoulders, but she let it blow against her face while she watched black-headed gulls bank and swoop among the barges and boats below. A couple of fishermen leaned over the iron rails ahead, poles extended; a loose dog trotted as confidently as if he owned Paris—as confidently as she hoped someday she would. And all the while, on the farther shore for whole city blocks stretched the limestone Palace of the Louvre.

They entered its precincts at the Place du Carrousel. Despite its festively promising name, it was a dull expanse of paving stone where

dingy flocks of pigeons halfheartedly rose and fell back with a flack-
ering of wings. The only spot of color seemed to be the red panta-
loons of some Zouaves in the distance, but to their left, overlooking
the courtyard, stood a monumental arch topped by a statue of a
splendid woman driving a chariot drawn by four horses. That was
better.

"There's been a fire in that part of the palace!" exclaimed Jeanette, looking past the arch to scorch marks, broken walls, and
empty windows.

"Of course," said Effie. "That's the Palace of the Tuileries. Don't
you remember? It was set on fire by the mob during the dreadful
Commune. Oh, dear me, first ours and then the Franco-Prussian
War. So many dead. Eighteen seventy-one." Effie clucked her tongue.

"In 1871, I was only eleven," said Jeanette. She turned her back
on the eyesore.

Inside the museum, Effie would have dutifully taken the galleries in the order prescribed by their guidebook, but not Jeanette.
"Look at all those people heading straight upstairs to the main picture galleries," she said, and set off, knowing that Effie would hurry
after her.

At the top of the main staircase, they came to the long, barrel-
vaulted Galerie d'Apollon. Effie, like most sightseers, wanted to bend
over glass cases containing enamels, vases, and precious stones, but
Jeanette would not stop until they had reached the Salon Carré,
which housed a selection of the museum's most famous paintings.
At its black-framed doors, she paused briefly to draw a self-conscious
breath before stepping into what she had been planning to be one
of the supreme moments of her life: She who was going to be an
artist was about to behold *Art* (at the back of her mind, a classically
draped allegorical figure flung forth a triumphant arm). Then a sob
really did catch at Jeanette's throat. At Vassar, painting had been
stacked upon painting; here it was masterpiece upon masterpiece.
Hung on somber walls of a plummy chocolate, guarded and kept at

a reverential distance by a barrier railing, the pictures climbed one on top of another toward a skylit ceiling, not thirty feet, but fifty feet high, the smaller canvases below, the larger ones above, each demanding the viewer's full devotion.

As Jeanette moved slowly through the room, the more she looked, the more she was overwhelmed. Many of the paintings were familiar from engravings, but black lines on white paper were as unlike the tactile beauty of pigment as printed notes were different from music. In the face of these miracles of composition and effect, of imagination, insight, and technical accomplishment, she wondered how she had ever had the temerity to think she could learn to do the same. Yet the gallery was crowded, not only by visitors, but by copyists, some of them obviously students and many of them women. Jeanette resolved to look only at the original paintings, yet she could not stop her eye from straying to the copies.

As she and Effie moved on to other, less crowded galleries, copyists became fewer in number and seemed more intent on study than on reproducing the most famous pictures. One darkly handsome man, well dressed and well equipped, was making an astonishing copy of a Rubens—not a copy, a recomposition. He painted with distinctive brushwork that reflected Rubens' curves, the glow of Rubens' flesh tones, and an exploratory, vigorous life of its own. It was something Jeanette would never have thought of doing, and it excited her. From a distance, she paused to watch. "I wonder who that was," she whispered to Effie when they were out of earshot.

As the days passed, they began to learn the omnibus routes and rode outside on upper decks when the weather was fine. They justified sightseeing as learning the lay of the land, but they also began to answer notices and look at rooms. When everything seemed either too expensive or too dismal, they drank a cup of chocolate in a tearoom and made a pilgrimage to the nearest point of interest. The

Vanns had advised them to look for housing only in the new neighborhoods around the Gare Saint-Lazare, where the plumbing was good. Tall north-facing windows showed that artists congregated there, it was true; but they both preferred the Left Bank, Jeanette for the ambiance, Effie for the lower prices. Toward the end of the week, just when it seemed they would have to pay hotel rates a while longer, they heard through Effie's willingness to talk to strangers at breakfast about a room in a *pension* around the corner on the Rue Jacob.

"It was cheap, yes, and had a flush toilet on the floor, but no heat and no bathroom," said the middle-aged lady who was detailing her own search for long-term lodgings. "No sitting room, no privacy. I can't think why the agent sent us there."

"For contrast, dear," said her companion. "He wanted us to take a more expensive suite—which we did."

"Well," said Effie to Jeanette, when the two ladies were gone, "it's close by."

They set out afraid that if the room was just what they wanted, it would already be taken. When they presented themselves to the concierge, he acted so uncomprehending that they doubted for a moment whether any room had ever been available at that address in the history of the *quartier*. Even pointing from themselves to a placard in his chamber window, *Chambre à louer*, did no good until they began to back away in defeat. Then he relented and turned them over to his wife, who led them up the stairs to the third floor, where she rapped on a door with a key before turning it in the lock. To their consternation, she led them through what seemed to be the foyer of someone else's apartment (behind a bead curtain was a sitting room) to reach a further staircase to the next floor. On the landing above, another rap at a door and the turn of a second key.

"*Bonjour, madame!*" barked the *portière*, as she opened the door for Jeanette and Effie.

A pregnant, sleepy-eyed woman in a housedress pushed herself up from a battered sofa. The *portière* curtly asked to be allowed to show the room. The occupant swept her arm around in a resigned gesture. At the back, a large bed was unmade; an open trunk at its foot was half filled; clothes—a man's as well as a woman's—were strewn around the room. The furniture didn't match; the figured wallpaper on uneven walls was water-stained and faded to the color of parchment. Besides being cold, the place smelled too much lived in.

Yet where two windows across the front of the building overlooked the street, the room was as light as a gray day allowed, and a geranium on the deep windowsill blossomed among healthy leaves. Another window on the side wall between the sofa and the bed gave out onto the roof next door, and with the corner of her eye, Jeanette was aware of light to her left. It came from a small window in an alcove tucked into a gable beside the stairwell. There on an easel was a canvas painted in loose brushstrokes, which depicted the woman on the sofa.

"Oh, your husband is an artist, *madame*," she said, in French.

A shy complacency warmed the wife's face. Yes, a student at the École des Beaux-Arts. That canvas was a mere *esquisse*, a sketch for a larger composition that had just been accepted for this year's Salon. He hoped to sell it and win some commissions. The room was convenient to the school, but, thank God, they were moving to a real apartment with a proper studio.

"I could work here," said Jeanette, softly.

"A kitten!" said Effie, coming into the room. "Oh, look, kittens!"

Jeanette burst out laughing. A gray-streaked kitten, which had fallen out of a basket under a table, was rolling on its tiny wire cage of a back, trying to grab and bite the scrap of tail sticking out through its fluff. Three more of the litter were absorbed in watching it from the basket. What was the word for kitten? *"Les petits chats,"* she said, in explanation.

"Ah, oui," said the renter, mournfully, as she looked down at them

with a hand placed on her own belly. They needed homes; she hated to drop them in the river.

The kitten on the floor gave up on its tail and twisted around upright with a jerk to bat a tiny white paw at one of its siblings. Effie bent forward eagerly. "Oh, tell her to leave one here!" she said, even though Jeanette had not translated the part about the river.

"*Pouvons-nous . . . peut-il . . . ?*"

While Jeanette struggled to frame the request, Effie turned a beaming face to the *portière*, who drew in a breath through constricted nostrils but shrugged as she exhaled. Why not? Cats kept the mice down—but it must go in and out the window, never down the stairs. *Madame* did not care for cats. *Madame* was Mme. Granet, the proprietress; but it seemed that Mme. LeConte, the *portière*, was the real power in the establishment, at least when it came to rentals. The present tenants would vacate on Friday morning, after which the room would be given a good cleaning to be ready for occupancy on Saturday, rent in advance and a deposit.

Back out on the street, Jeanette and Effie's jubilation turned to jitters. The room offered less comfort and less space than they had hoped for (what would the family say if any of them ever saw it?), and they realized that they had no idea how good or bad the food might be.

"All the same, it's a franc a day less than we had expected to pay, and that's thirty francs a month saved," said Jeanette. "Let's put a coin a day in a jar to make it real."

"That lovely ginger jar that Matthew gave me for the trip! What a good idea—ready cash against an emergency."

"Or a monthly treat, Cousin Effie! Rewards for living virtuously."

On Saturday, they were given two keys, one to the third-floor apartment with instructions always to knock, never to linger, and a separate key to their own room on the floor above. Mme. LeConte promised to send the carter up with their luggage when he arrived, but she left them to find their way alone this time. At the third-floor door, they took a deep breath and looked at each other. Effie took it upon herself to rap politely with her ear to the door. No response. Inside, they tiptoed to the shadowy staircase with a nervous eye on the beads, then scuttled. They whispered until the door to their own room was open. Then they breathed easier. The room was light. The too-much-lived-in look was gone, along with the odor of unwashed laundry, replaced by a welcome bareness and the smell of carbolic soap. From inside a covered basket beside a bottle of cream on the table came mewing.

"Kitty!" exclaimed Effie, joyfully. "Oh, the one with the white paws!" she said, lifting the kitten out and holding him up high in the air. "Boots, Boots I'll call you. Ouch!"

"Maybe you should call him Claws."

"No, no, Bootsie, mustn't scratch, mustn't. What you need is cream."

The kitten spat and bit until presented with the saucer of cream, whereupon he drank and consented to be petted. His sides began to vibrate in violent purring until, with equal violence, he fell sound asleep.

Jeanette propped herself on the edge of the deep windowsill where the geranium had sat. She pulled back a faded, checked muslin curtain to gaze greedily at the façades and roofs of the buildings opposite, the up-and-down clusters of chimneys and chimney pots. Soon every long crack in the stucco, every slipped roof slate, every sign on the shops below and window grille above was going to be familiar. She would know where all the nearby streets went. Out of the whirl of merging impressions and possibilities from their first few days, this room, this view came into focus as her first fixed point of reference. She had, after all, some small claim of belonging in Paris—a claim she must make good by succeeding. On Monday, they must find the Académie Julian.

CHAPTER EIGHT

One Step Back

On Monday morning, supplied with directions by Miss Whitmore, Jeanette and Effie walked across the river and up to the Rue Saint-Marc. In the middle of a block, two bushes in tubs flanked gates that stood open under a sign reading *Passage des Panoramas*. Jeanette paused to take a deep breath. "Now!" she said.

Inside, restaurants and small specialty shops crowded both sides of an arcade. Painted signs hung out at right angles overhead like banners; a tiled mosaic floor ran for two blocks. Above a second story of shops, the whole length was roofed with a peaked ceiling of glass. Jeanette and Effie walked slowly among the beautifully dressed shoppers, all of whom seemed to take for granted displays of jewelry, fancy stationery, and fashionable hats. Two blocks later, they emerged onto the busy Boulevard Montmartre. "But I know this is what Miss Whitmore said!" exclaimed Jeanette, in exasperation.

A grizzled *commissionaire*, with a numbered badge to certify he was licensed, stood at the entrance, waiting to pick up an errand. Effie nudged Jeanette.

"*L'Académie Julian?*" said the man, in response to Jeanette's question. "*Mais oui, mademoiselle.*" He led them back to the middle of the main arcade and along a transverse passage to a service staircase near a restaurant. Gesturing with his hands, he urged them to ascend. "*Montez-vous, montez-vous, mesdemoiselles. L'académie, c'est au-dessus.*" While Effie handed him a coin, Jeanette started up doubtfully.

Unlike the appealing shop fronts of the arcade, the staircase was dark and smelly from refuse in a back alley; and unlike the stairs at the Tenth Street Studio Building, it lacked the width to accommodate large canvases. Yet at the top was an office with a sign reading *Académie de la Peinture*. Jeanette glanced back at Effie with a gleam in her eye and knocked.

"*Entrez, entrez!*" came the voice of a young man.

He was laying aside a newspaper and bringing his feet down from the desk when they opened the door. The walls of the office, which was little more than a cubbyhole, were hung with drawings and paintings—nudes, caricatures, and portrait heads. The young man himself wore a paint-daubed smock.

Was this the Académie Julian? Jeanette asked, shyly but eagerly.

"*Oui, bien sûr, mademoiselle!*"

Jeanette explained her errand. She wanted to take lessons; perhaps she could observe a class. He listened with a mischievous air of amusement but put on a solemn expression to send her down the hall to the classroom where she would find M. Julian. He assured her there was no need to knock.

Afterward, she would remember how crowded and smoky the room was: heads, backs, shoulders, and the triangular tips of easels everywhere—men standing in back, blocking sight of others on low stools near the front; everyone working away with pencil or brush. Yet at the time, Jeanette hardly took in the students; for her eyes followed theirs to a round dais where, in a twisted heroic pose, stood—to her momentary astonishment and horror—a muscular, hairy, and completely naked man. Years before, she and her giggling girlfriends had spent one Circleville summer spying through the bushes on their skinny-dipping brothers and classmates; since then, she had seldom seen a man with so much as his undershirt showing. She heard a gasp behind her. Effie.

A large man, whose black hair and beard emphasized an anvil-shaped head, was perched on a stool near the door. Under a short jacket, his chest and arms seemed as muscular as those of the model.

"*Bonjour, mademoiselle,*" he said, in strangely accented French, as he turned to greet Jeanette. She was perhaps looking for him. His name was Rodolphe Julian.

"*Bonjour, M. Julian. Oui, s'il vous plaît.*" Jeanette squared her back against Effie.

M. Julian's quick, dark eyes took in everything: the nervous chaperon, the youth of the applicant, the American white cotton gloves clutching a portfolio.

"You wish to join a class, *mademoiselle,*" he said in French, addressing only Jeanette.

She collected herself. "A life class, *monsieur.*"

"May I suggest that one commence with studies of plaster casts? It is normal. Come this way."

"But I have already—"

M. Julian wagged an admonitory forefinger and winked. "Allow me to show you the class, *mademoiselle.* It will calm your esteemed aunt, and there you may show me your samples."

In a second studio, thirty or forty students, male and female, were drawing various objects: classical busts and statues, plaster-of-Paris body parts, torsos on stands like dressmakers' dummies. Many of the female students seemed to be Jeanette's age; some of the boys were younger. There were also older students, including a few ladies whose lace cuffs and enrapt glow of amateurish devotion could not have been better calculated to reassure Cousin Effie.

M. Julian cleared a space on a table to look at Jeanette's portfolio. Silently, he turned the pages of drawings and the two small oil studies she had included.

"*Bon, mademoiselle,*" he said, "my compliments. You draw with decision. You are indeed ready to move on to the live figure. For ladies, at this moment, I offer three ateliers.

"In the first, the model is fully dressed, often in costume from what I can boast to be the largest collection of antique and regional attire in any private teaching establishment in Paris. But, *mademoiselle*"—he held up his hand to forestall Jeanette's protest—"if you work there, you will be surrounded by artists from whom you can learn nothing. In the second, the model is partially draped with ample opportunity to study limbs and torso. That is the class for you. In the third, the model is completely nude as in the class for men, but—"

Jeanette was bracing herself to request the third when again M. Julian forestalled her.

"I reiterate, *mademoiselle*, for you the draped figure." He glanced quickly to Effie and back. "In a month or so, when your venerable companion is accustomed to your coming here, you may advance if you so desire. In the meantime, there is much to be learned about the fall of cloth as well as the articulation of limbs; you will need both in your career. You agree to my suggestion?"

"Oui, monsieur!"

With a bow, he swept them down the hall and, from the busy arcade below, out onto a side street, talking all the way. Jeanette understood little of what he said and Effie none, but he was so obviously in charge that she followed docilely.

They climbed stairs to another classroom crowded with easels and artists. Here the students were all women, and the seated model female. She was partially covered by a thin tissue of cloth across her lap. Again, Effie halted in the doorway, overcome by distress; but Jeanette found herself more curious than she wanted to admit. If dormitory life had exposed her to many half-clad girls, they had seldom been bare breasted. She would have felt freer to stare without M. Julian beside her.

A painter who had looked around when they entered set down her palette and made her way quickly around the edge of the room and into the hallway. M. Julian introduced her as the *massière* of the class, the student monitor who was in charge of collecting fees, paying the models, and attending to all such administrative duties. Also she would translate into French *comme il faut* anything that his Provençal accent had made incomprehensible. *Mademoiselle* would be studying drawing.

"*Ah, non, monsieur, pas le dessin—la peinture,*" said Jeanette. Not drawing—painting.

He wagged a finger. "*Le dessin,*" he repeated, and was gone.

"Oh, dear, shall we sort this out in English? American, are you?" said the *massière*, in a crisp British accent. She was in her late twenties, with light-brown hair pulled neatly back from a face of regular features and an enviably clear complexion. Her manner was that of the very capable only daughter of a widowed sea captain turned parson, which she was. "My name, in case you didn't catch it in M. Julian's murderous pronunciation, is Amy Richardson. Now what's all this about painting?"

"It's just that I've already moved on to working in oil at home. I didn't come to Paris to go back to drawing—and M. Julian did say that I drew with decision."

"Ah, yes, well, I'm sure you do; of course, you can always try another school—the Colarossi on the Rue de la Grande-Chaumière, for instance, takes women—and there are always private masters. But a word to the wise, Miss—*Paumeur* is Palmer, I take it? Right. A word to the wise, Miss Palmer: Julian's assessments are seldom wrong, however maddening they seem at the time. Were you working from the live figure in your previous studies?"

"No," admitted Jeanette.

"Well, it's quite different from still lifes and landscapes. I promise you, we all need to draw in life class before we try to paint the human body. Tell you what, why don't you come look at what some of the girls are doing and see where *you* think you fit."

The best of the painters could have been professional portraitists (some were); worse, the difference between the drawings of those who could make flesh look soft and those whose work still resembled plaster casts was all too evident. Between growing intimidation and embarrassment at disturbing a class in progress, it was all Jeanette could do not to bolt and find a place to cry. Her mother was right: Coming here was a pipe dream; she had been deluding herself.

"Take your time to think it over," said Miss Richardson, back outside in the hallway. "You know where to find me if you decide to join the class."

"I don't need time," said Jeanette. "I need to begin at the beginning or slit my throat."

"No blood on the premises, please! You won't be sorry, you know," Miss Richardson added, sympathetically. "If you have the talent, nothing short of treating it with the proper respect will do. And you will make progress here, I promise. You've no idea how much we learn from each other as well as the masters."

Before they left, Cousin Effie overcame her own dismay about models enough to ask about fees.

"Ah, the grim practicalities. Yes, well, there's a basic registration fee of one hundred francs, on top of which you pay thirty-five francs a week, or the better monthly rate of a hundred."

"Twenty dollars to register and twenty dollars a month, oh my." Effie clucked her tongue. "He's no gentleman, but he certainly knows his business."

"We knew there would be tuition," said Jeanette in an embarrassed undertone.

Miss Richardson's face twitched, but she said only, "You can also pay four hundred francs for a full six months, much the best deal if you know you're committed. Any questions, Miss Palmer?"

"When could I start?"

"This very afternoon if you came back with money and a sketchbook. If you do decide to join us, run down to the Quai d'Orfevres, number four, and tell the man you are starting at the Académie Julian. He'll outfit you at a very decent price. Nothing like the smell of a new sketchbook and all those lovely, clean, white pages."

Blank, beginner's pages, thought Jeanette.

CHAPTER NINE

First Interlude: Cincinnati

The prospect of a trip to Europe got Edward moving. He went to his tailor, who made him handsome new clothes that hung comfortably and lifted his morale. He began reading again, at least fitfully: history, technical papers on chemical processes given him by Theodore, Goethe. And he kept away from laudanum. His will-power was strengthened when he cut himself off from his secret supply—for as soon as he agreed to let Theodore sell the drugstore to Hans, he withdrew completely from the business. He kept only his little library of books from the back room, a few instruments, and their father's clock.

Packing up from Mrs. Wiggins's boardinghouse was harder, but not much. On the day he gave notice, he went over with Sophie to supervise some men from the Murer Brothers factory in loading his belongings onto a van. Before they took his mother's bureau, he furtively pocketed the almost-new bottle of laudanum he had stashed in it; later, in a moment of resolve, he threw it away. At Sophie's direction, everything was brought back to the guest room, which she had already partially emptied in a flurry of curtain-washing and cushion-beating.

"This is too much trouble for so short a time," said Edward. "Just store it all at the warehouse until we get back. Then I'll look for new rooms."

"You don't know when that will be," said Sophie, "and Mutter Murer's bureau deserves regular waxing in the meantime."

When everything was safely in place upstairs, she unwrapped one of his framed etchings, an evocative landscape of trees beside a river. "This is beautiful," she said.

"One of my little mutilations."

"Edward!"

"Cut out of a magazine. Five dollars an issue, from Paris. The latest one is in a box with my books."

"Five dollars an issue? I never suspected you of such extravagance!"

"Once a year, three hundred prints on heavy paper, some good, some not so good. I pore over an issue for months. There are always a dozen or more superb pieces and many more worth looking at again and again." As he was speaking, Edward pulled out more pictures from their wrapping paper, one by one. "At the end of the year, I sell the whole issue to a dealer I know to cut up for resale piecemeal. He frames my favorite picture for free and pays me three bucks fifty for the rest."

When Sophie told Theodore about it, he dismissed the exchange with a snort of impatience: "Edward! The mind of a shopkeeper. It's what holds him back. Why doesn't he just have his magazine bound and buy real pictures for his wall?"

As spring progressed, Sophie and Edward continued their afternoon walks and rides. He began taking walks by himself, too. At first for an excuse, he took the family dog on a leash; but Jenks was too used to roaming free through the neighborhood, and the battle of wills as he tugged or balked was bad for both their tempers. Edward gave up on the dog and instead went down the hill to buy a German newspaper and a daily hothouse rose for Sophie. "Edward, you shouldn't. You will spoil me," protested Sophie, after the third or fourth, but her face always lit up with pleasure. Sometimes, he substituted violets or a gardenia.

The future remained a void. He had nothing in mind for his return. Oddly enough, the store, which had been part of his life since he was a boy, had no hold on him. It seemed simply to vanish. He did not wake up thinking he had to go there; he didn't care whether Hans maintained his careful inventories; his hands did not miss the mortar and pestle or compounding knife. Something would have to replace them or his demons would rip at him again; but for the time being, he accepted Theodore's assumption that a year abroad would reveal as much to him as it did to Carl. Meanwhile, he thought no further ahead than the first weeks of touring with the family. They would go first to Paris to see the World's Fair. He bought a Baedeker and reread Balzac.

CHAPTER TEN

Bienvenue

A full six months? Oh, good show; you won't regret it," said Miss Richardson, when Jeanette and Effie arrived first thing Wednesday morning. She unlocked a small tin box to receive Jeanette's payment. "Here's a receipt; thank you very much. Do me a favor today or tomorrow and drop by the office. Show this to them and sign the registry for the Atelier Bouguereau et Robert-Fleury."

"William-Adolphe Bouguereau?" exclaimed Effie.

"Himself."

"But one of his pictures just sold in New York for ten thousand dollars! Oh, my, that should impress your parents, Jeanette. Studying with William-Adolphe Bouguereau."

"When you think about it, it's jolly good of him and the others to come around," said Miss Richardson. "I don't know what Julian pays them, but they can't do it for the money." She paused and looked at a knitting bag that Effie had brought with her. "Would you care to observe today, Miss Pendergrast?" Her politeness left no doubt that an exception was being made.

"Oh, I . . . would I be in the way?" asked Effie.

"Not at all. If you will just wait by the door, please, I'll set up Miss Palmer and get the model started. Then I can see about a chair for you."

Miss Richardson led Jeanette around the edge of the room, keeping her eye on the floor. "We'll have to find a place where there aren't any chalk marks—those are the spaces already taken. Here, this should do. I know it's a bit far back and at an angle, as you'll see, but you'll have a full view. Grab that easel against the wall, Miss Palmer.

"*Attention, mesdemoiselles. Je voudrais vous presenter une élève nouvelle*," she went on, in French, addressing the rest of the class. "Ladies, I would like to introduce a new student, Mlle. Jeanette Palmer from the United States, and her cousin, Mlle. Pendergrast, who will be sitting in this morning."

"*Et le bienvenue?*" someone called out, to a round of titters and expectant looks.

"*Cet après-midi,*" Miss Richardson called back, with a lift of her eyebrow and a meaning glance back in Effie's direction.

"I didn't catch that. What is this afternoon?" asked Jeanette, in a low tone.

"A customary little party at the newcomer's expense. You are going to commission Pauline, our concierge and maid-of-all-work, to provide the entire class with punch and cake at the end of the session. Don't worry, there's none of the horrid hazing the new boys endure at the Beaux-Arts—no duels with loaded brush, no stripping and painting you blue—but do be prepared for a certain level of juvenile jocularity."

Stools and easels scraped on the bare wooden floor as students shifted within the tight confines of space allotted to them. The model emerged from behind a screen. With her drapery thrown around her like a toga, she threaded her way to the front of the class, glancing neither to left nor right. She stepped up onto a wooden platform about two feet off the floor, sat down on a stool, and dropped a bundle beside her. When she let the drapery fall from her shoulder, an audible squeak sounded from near the door. Blood rushed to Jeanette's cheeks. Unsure which was more embarrassing— Cousin Effie, the public disrobing, or her own blushes—she forced herself to look directly at the model. Guided by a penciled sketch that lay on the floor, Miss Richardson was crouching to arrange the drapery to fold exactly as it had on Monday. When it was done, the model rolled her head a couple of times, shifted her shoulders up and down, and leaned forward gracefully into position with her back arched to show each disk of her spine. From the expression on her face, she seemed to be speaking to someone; she might be a sibyl or a beggar. Her black hair was caught up in filets, Grecian-style, but a few tendrils escaped over the nape of her neck. Even from Jeanette's angle off to the side, both breasts were visible.

Jeanette had to look away, unnerved by twinges in her own body. The page of her new sketchbook, propped up on its easel, provided a safe place for her eyes.

"It's awful, isn't it, that empty blankness?" whispered an English voice beside her. "Try to find the sternum and plumb a line down to the seat as the point of reference for everything else."

I know that much, thought Jeanette, irritably.

The speaker was a latecomer who had taken up position while Miss Richardson posed the model. She leaned sideways from her stool to be heard but immediately pulled back, as if afraid she had intruded; she turned a quick, shy smile toward Jeanette. Her smooth, brown hair was parted primly in the middle over a wide forehead. Her mouth was small, her chin pointed. She seemed gentle rather than condescending. Jeanette nodded. Even if it was not the blank page that disturbed her, a quick sketch to block in the main masses was just the thing to steady her nerves. An hour later the model was allowed her first break. She drew in a deep breath and let it out slowly while her shoulders dropped. Straightening up, she rubbed her right arm, bent and turned from the waist, stretched her limbs, wiggled her toes—all without shifting the carefully folded drapes. Without a word, she bent over to the sewing basket beside her and pulled out a small garment, which she began mending. Pauline, the maid, brought her a cup of coffee and a cigarette, which she accepted curtly as her due. Nobody else smoked.

"My name is Emily Dolson," said Jeanette's neighbor, as talk became general throughout the room. In an undertone, she added, "Would you like me to show you the ladies' toilet?"

"I'd be eternally grateful, and so would my cousin who is with me. Just a minute though, I've got to catch Miss Richardson. Miss Richardson, please! About the *bienvenue*—?"

"Shall I arrange it for you?" Miss Richardson looked Jeanette up and down with an appraising eye. "Right. We'll go for good-natured, not out to dazzle; on a budget yet not stingy; making do with last year's hat but never skimping on shoes. How's that?"

"About perfect!"

In the afternoon, while Miss Richardson set the model in a new pose, Jeanette looked around at the works in progress nearest her. Emily Dolson, she was interested to see, drew in delicate pencil with a very hard lead; already the shading was exquisite, though faint.

At four thirty, Pauline appeared, carrying a tray with a pitcher surrounded by an array of cups and mugs. The model unbent, rose, and, staring straight ahead, made her way to the screen through the cheerful crowd that was moving in the other direction. A few minutes later, Pauline returned with a second tray of brioches, *baba au rhum*, and pastry. When Jeanette settled up, she was glad Cousin Effie wasn't there (and glad she had cashed a rather large check at the same time she had withdrawn her tuition); but remembering what the Thomas Cook agent had advised about tipping the railway porter, she gave Pauline fifteen centimes, which, from the way Pauline bounced it in her fist, she deduced was satisfactory.

As Pauline began serving out the punch, a voice shouted, *"Le catéchisme!"* Jeanette was hustled up onto the model's dais and made to stand on the stool looking out over everybody else. If she had any illusions that a studio full of artists with the same ambitions as hers would be an uncomplicated sorority of reciprocal encouragement, she was now disabused. One woman in particular was clearly the center of a clique, which she held to one side.

"What is the first principle?" someone in the middle of the room demanded in French.

"Drawing keeps art honest," replied Jeanette, in English, and then read a motto posted over the door—*Le dessin est la probité d'art*—to a patter of laughter and applause. She had cleared the first hurdle.

The next questions were easy: They asked her name, her home town, her age. They asked her the name of her lover. "Nemo!" She had played this sort of game at Vassar. How many brothers did her lover have? "Legions." How much was he worth? "A sigh, *un soupir.*" The game was harder to play in French. She missed a question as the model stepped out from behind the screen, now dressed in street clothes, though her hair was still piled in classical ringlets and tied with a ribbon. Jeanette was chilled by an unreadable look that crossed her face. She felt a fool bobbing and swaying on the seat where the other woman had just employed professional skill to endure rigid bondage for hours.

"Madame!" called Jeanette. *"Merci . . . un gâteau . . . ?"*

Won't you join us? she wanted to ask, but a hush had fallen on the room. The model's face froze into anger. Looking away, she lifted a faded shawl over her head and, with a twitch of her skirt, cut her way through the crowd to the door and closed it behind her with a rap just short of a slam.

A voice from the clique drawled out, "And what was your latest *faux pas?*"

"She is proud, La Grecque," someone else explained to Jeanette.

"Second principle," called up a friendly American voice, "only the *massière* speaks to the model."

Awkwardness put an end to the game, and interest returned to the refreshments, as most of the class broke up into little conversational groups, largely by language.

"If you hadn't put your foot in your mouth, you might have had a triumph," said Miss Richardson, joining Jeanette and Emily. "But just as well not. This lot can be cruel to goats and turn viciously on lions. Better a safe mediocrity."

"I know I goofed, but what was so wrong? Are the models never included in celebrations?"

"Not by rights; they're not one of us, you see," said Miss Richardson. "Hired by the week. Of course, it depends on the personality. Some of them set out to ingratiate themselves with one and all, and I have to admit that the best are better at what they do than many of us are at depicting them. La Grecque keeps her distance. But even if she shoots daggers at you tomorrow, stare right back and draw for all you're worth. You'll be critiqued in the morning, and first impressions matter."

"By M. Julian?"

"Good lord, no. By M. Bouguereau."

CHAPTER ELEVEN

The Murers Abroad

The Murers traveled from Cincinnati to Philadelphia on settees and cushioned armchairs in one of the comfortable new railroad parlor cars. Years before, through the wooden slats of rattling, splintery cattle cars, Edward had watched blasted landscapes jolt by: trees hacked to stumps, houses burned, torn rags caught on fence posts, corpses tumbled down the railroad embankments—everything broken and trampled, ruined and dead. Now out of glass windows, he saw tilled valleys and wooded hillsides, prosperous small towns, or the high wilds of Pennsylvania. For years, Theodore had urged him to travel; he began to think he should have listened.

From Philadelphia, they embarked on the *Nordland* for Antwerp. Although Theodore refused to return to Germany, he never gave thought to booking passage on anything but a German ship.

To no one's surprise, Edward was a bad sailor and, in the grip of seasickness, too miserable to be ashamed. "Just get me to France," he said, with his eyes closed when Sophie hovered over the deck chair where he lay wrapped in blankets. "You can fatten me up there. If I live."

Later, as the ship passed England and crossed the North Sea, the weather grew uncharacteristically calm. The shallow waters off the coast of northern Belgium were yellow with suspended sand, endlessly sloshing forward and back; the waves were so gentle that Edward was able to stand at the rail for pleasure, not necessity. As they entered the wide estuary of the river Schelde, a lump rose in his throat. Land and river welcomed him home. He had not experienced such melting happiness in years. A memory of turning into a tree-lined driveway floated into his mind. Plane trees with curling plates of mottled bark. It was the driveway leading to his grandmother's house in Alsace, near Mulhouse. He had not thought of it in years; but yes, each time they made the turn, it was the same. Each time, overlapping discs of sunshine and light shade, a moment of expectation—he felt the same expectancy now, the same happiness. Always the moment when the carriage turned in at Gran'marie's lane . . . Tears came to his eyes and he laughed—partly to prevent weeping; partly at himself; partly, thank God, from mirth. He wiped his face as though it had been splashed with spray and leaned forward, resting his forearms on the rail.

"We sailed out this very river on an evening tide," he said.

"I thought maybe you were too young to remember," said Theodore, relaxed and genial, with an unlit cigar between his teeth.

"No. I remember. Lanterns were beginning to shine out low on the banks, but everything else was gray and gloomy. I remember the water hissing like this around the bow."

"Sandy water. Look at it."

"It was somber that night. Mutter was so sad."

"Was she? No—relieved." Theodore pointed his cigar at Edward and chuckled. "Up until the last minute, even after we were safely on board, she was sure that secret police would burst out from somewhere to arrest Papa and me. When the anchor was weighed in Antwerp, I think she let out a breath she had held since we left Kiel."

"But to leave home and country, everything she knew and everyone? Surely, Edward is right," said Sophie, comfortably, slipping her arm through Theodore's. "Poor mothers! Mine never stopped mourning a particular cherry tree that grew in an angle of her garden wall. Almost I think I would recognize the taste of those very cherries baked in a kuchen, she described them so often. Poor mothers, but lucky offspring, eh, Theodore?" She looked up into her husband's face and patted his arm. "Oh, this is exciting! You two may remember your passage over, but I was only a baby."

From Antwerp to Brussels, from Brussels to Paris. It was Theodore's string-pulling and money that had won them hard-to-come-by reservations at the Hôtel Meurice on the Rue de Rivoli; but from Brussels onward, Edward's superior French came to the fore. He was the one who dealt with officials and tradesmen if their hired guide happened not to be at hand. Having spent three idyllic summers at that tree-shaded house of their grandmother's in Alsace, he spoke with a near-native accent. The first time he had to step in to take over an exchange from Theodore, he enjoyed showing up his brother.

When they got to Paris, it gave him still more pleasure to lose himself in the busy, crowded city yet not feel lost. By then, he had forgotten that he was reading window signs and newspapers in French; he simply took in their meaning. And although he could not follow all the local dialects or slang in the streets, the more accustomed he became to listening, the more he caught of conversations around him. He resumed his morning walks. At first, he did what his Baedeker recommended, strolling down the Rue de Rivoli and along the Champs-Élysées. He walked through the Tuileries Garden and on the quays by the Seine. He watched the crowds gather at the Champs de Mars to enter the World's Fair; he bought a posy for Sophie on the steps of the Church of the Madeleine. Once, he crossed the river to walk in the Luxembourg Garden. Gradually, as he gained a sense of where things lay in relation to each other, he left the Grand Boulevards and let his feet go where they would.

One morning, on a side street near the Parc Monceau, he paused to watch workers fitting in the last stones on a block still being re-paved in the run-up to festivities planned by the Third Republic for the end of June. A stoop-shouldered man with a bristling gray beard and a wooden peg leg was watching, too.

"The past is no good, *monsieur*," remarked the man. "Paris is an old tart, but she holds up her stockings with a gay garter, eh?" He gestured toward the pavers and around at a bench set under a tree newly encircled with a painted rail over an iron grille. "No vestige of the siege."

"You fought, *mon ami*," said Edward.

"*Oui, monsieur.*"

"*Moi aussi.* A different war."

"For a soldier, *monsieur*, they are all the same."

They watched a minute or two more in companionable silence. The veteran made some remark about the street as it had been thirty years ago. A waiter stood impassively in the door of a café.

"Will you join me for a coffee, *monsieur*?" asked Edward.

The veteran accepted with pleasure. Edward ordered him a brandy to go with the coffee. They talked a little of wars, of cities, of the changes the veteran had seen in the neighborhood. When Edward walked on, he felt lightened in some way. He enjoyed recounting the little incident to Sophie in his mind; but somehow, when he rejoined the family, it was too elusive, too hard to put into words what was special about it. He kept it to himself.

CHAPTER TWELVE

M. Bouguereau

Short and stout, William-Adolphe Bouguereau exerted gravitational pull as he moved through the studio; no one had to look to know exactly where he was. While the students worked on, or pretended to, he made a methodical progress through the room, pausing at each easel with Miss Richardson in his wake. Little disturbances arose as stools were shifted to make room for them or students stepped out of the way.

"A good thing we're this far across the room," Jeanette whispered to Emily beside her. "Maybe I can still shade the curve of this shoulder."

"You can always turn it front to back if you want, and he'll pass you," Emily whispered back.

Jeanette was nettled by the suggestion that she might wish—or need—to avoid criticism. It was true that she felt rushed trying to ready her piece in the instructor's presence, but comparing her sketch to Emily's work emboldened her. There was no doubt of Emily's delicacy of touch and exquisite rendering, but her own figure had more vigor.

"*Pas mal, pas mal,*" she overheard, somewhere to her left. Not bad; keep working. Well, that wouldn't be much help, but neither would it hurt—unless there was, perhaps, a note of sarcasm in M. Bouguereau's voice?

A cool morning illumination from the skylight threw no strong shadows to help with the modeling, but enough for the shoulder and curves of the spine. She already had a passable foot; she was good at feet.

M. Bouguereau came nearer. Jeanette tried to work faster. A few stations away, he sat down on a woman's stool. He frowned; and while he rumbled something inaudible, his thumb made a decisive gesture downward, as though he were rubbing something out or smearing in a contour. He looked up from under bushy eyebrows to ask the student whether she understood.

"*Oui, monsieur, merci,*" she said, frowning intently as she looked back and forth between her work and the model.

"*Bon.*" He slapped his knees and rose to move on to the next easel.

When M. Bouguereau finally reached Emily, he bowed slightly with a hand at his jacket button. "*Mlle. Dolson.*"

"*Bonjour, monsieur,*" she said, softly, keeping her eyes down.

He turned to her pale drawing. Mmm, beautiful as always, but . . . In a corner of the page, he sketched in a quick study of the underlying musculature of a shoulder, followed by an adjacent rendering of the visible flesh. Jeanette looked from its perfect accuracy to her own work, which now appeared unsupported and false. He was telling Emily she must study anatomy. For half a smug instant, Jeanette prided herself that anatomy lay ahead as part of the Vassar art curriculum, then remembered with a lurch that she was cut off forever from what had been hers. Where in Paris, she wondered, could a woman receive instruction in the bones and muscles of the human body? She must begin by asking Emily to let her copy those two instructive little illustrations; but before she had time to follow her train of thought, she was being introduced by Miss Richardson as a student who had joined the class the day before.

"*Monsieur!*" she said, with her heart in her throat, all but bobbing a curtsy.

The breadth of M. Bouguereau's wide shoulders pushed into and occupied all the space in front of her easel; the fibers of his dark suit, a bit too tight where only the top button of his jacket was fastened over the waistcoat, were imbued with cigar smoke. His silvery, reddish-brown hair had receded from the temples, but it was still thick where it was combed back in waves; his brown beard and mustache were bushy and full, touched at the ends with gray. He had a face that could be avuncular and bland as it was now, but she had already glimpsed it sharpen several times that morning. Indeed, his eyes briefly assessed her as penetratingly as they regarded the model. It made her uneasy. But his rosy face when he turned to her drawing betrayed nothing.

"The work of one day? *Bon. Vous avez talent,*" he told her, after a silence. She had talent. When he had moved on, Amy Richardson pressed Jeanette's arm. "Good show," she muttered.

* * *

"*Monsieur*," called La Grecque, loudly, when M. Bouguereau finally stepped away from the last student. In liltingly Italianate French, she begged him to remember how long she had held position that day. Past the break. He would use her again sometime, eh?

As she had the day before, she came out of her pose with catlike stretches, only today they were slower, more sensual. Her head rolled before she closed her eyes, arched her back, and lifted her elbows wide, displaying her breasts to the full while she held the back of her neck with strong fingers. Her nipples were erect. She fell back and pulled the tissue up to cover herself, looking down at herself from one side to the other as she adjusted the cloth.

"Or perhaps my little girl. She is four years old, you know. She learns the trade. You still paint little girls, *n'est-ce pas?*"

"Signora Antonielli!" exclaimed Miss Richardson.

M. Bouguereau, who for a moment had parted his lips as if to speak, pressed them together angrily. His silent stare from under drawn brows held La Grecque and the whole room motionless, until he said coldly that he did not take the Erinyes as a subject and began making his dignified way through the students. Never taking her eyes off him, the model stepped into her slippers and down onto the floor. She started to call out something as his broad back neared the door.

Miss Richardson hissed at her to shut up, as she hustled her in the direction of the changing corner. La Grecque shook her off and flounced toward the screen. Miss Richardson hurried after M. Bouguereau into the corridor. An excited, polyglot hubbub erupted in the room.

"Do things like this happen often?" Jeanette asked Emily.

"Of course not! Poor Amy."

"Damn Antonielli!" cursed Amy, when she came back into the

room. "Of all the masters to choose for such a performance. Damn, damn, damn." Jeanette was taken aback by the force of her anger but found the swear words dashing. "I try to help her. I give her extra work—the whole day—because she *is* good, and what does she do? Makes it necessary to fire her on the spot and impossible ever to hire her again, that's what. Oh, hell, now listen to her howl." Strangled, frustrated sobbing came from behind the dressing screen. Miss Richardson's eyes narrowed and her mouth set hard. "Well, it's her job or mine, and I can tell you this, it isn't going to be mine."

"Why do they call Antonielli La Grecque if she is really Italian?" Jeanette asked Emily, later, as the classroom emptied.

"Because of her classic good looks and the way she wears her hair. She has posed for some of the best artists in Paris for their big mythological pictures. I suppose this will be my last picture of her," added Emily, looking down at her unfinished drawing.

"At least it has a nice little anatomy lesson on it," said Jeanette, wistfully. "Where can we study anatomy?"

"You could do what the Countess did," said the woman on the other side of Emily as she gathered up her things.

"The Countess?" asked Jeanette.

"A star student in the class for the full nude," said Emily. "Countess Marie Bashkirtseff."

"Had you heard?" went on their neighbor. "She bought herself a skeleton and hired a medical student to tutor her! Dissects her own cadaver, they say."

"It's an idea," said Jeanette later, recounting her day to Effie. "Not the cadaver, obviously, but the medical student as a tutor. Emily's brother has a friend who might be willing to lend us a textbook or something. He even has a skeleton." She sprawled back on their sofa. "Whew, I'm tired. Miss Richardson fixed on me as the rawest recruit to fill in as model for the afternoon—dressed, I promise! But, of course, nobody stayed. I had no idea how draining it could be to sit still for three hours." She yawned. "What did you do after you dropped me off?"

"Well, I went to the reading room in the Galignani Library, and then I paid some calls. At the embassy first. You know, just a formality: I left both our cards. You may hear from General Noyes." (The American ambassador was from Ohio.) "And I paid a visit to the McAll Mission, which a friend at the Children's Aid Society suggested. Here, some pamphlets I picked up. And you remember that your mother and Cousin Maude both wanted us to call on Mrs. Renick?" An eagerness came into Effie's voice.

"The one from Columbus that Mama knew, and her brother is a judge in Cincinnati; Papa knows him," said Jeanette, dutifully remembering, while she flipped without interest through Effie's religious tracts and booklets. "Mr. Renick did business with Uncle Matt."

"More with Harold Vann's father, I think. Marius Renick. He's a banker."

Jeanette closed her eyes and suppressed another yawn. She was not usually so completely bored by social rounds and family connections, but at the end of a long, exciting day in the studio, they seemed as far removed from anything that mattered as a Protestant missionary society did. Without opening her eyes, she tried to show half-hearted interest.

"Was Mrs. Renick at home when you called?"

"She was! And she's the last word in elegance, in spite of being confined by a leg and a back brace. She was thrown by a horse in the Bois de Boulogne—"

"An elegant way to cripple yourself."

"You sound like Adeline."

"Don't flatter me."

"I wasn't."

Jeanette's eyes widened at an unaccustomed acerbity in Effie's voice. "You must have liked Mrs. Renick."

"I did," said Effie, accepting Jeanette's conciliatory tone as apology enough. "She's very gracious, and the house—no, I can't do the house justice, nor Mrs. Renick either. You'll just have to see them for yourself. Which you will, and your mother will be glad to hear it." Effie grinned. "We have our first dinner invitation. She wants us to meet some visitors from the States, a family named Murer."

CHAPTER THIRTEEN

A Dinner Party on the Rue de Varenne

After the Murers' names were published in the *American Register*, which listed the Americans arriving in Paris each week, Sophie received a note from Mrs. Marius Renick, inviting her to call one afternoon at the Rue de Varenne. The families were acquainted. Cornelia Mattocks Renick was Edward's age, the daughter of a newspaperman who had spent a few years in Cincinnati before starting up his own paper in Columbus. Cornelia and Edward had known each other in elementary school, and Sophie knew one of her sisters-in-law from club work. As for Marius Renick, Theodore had occasionally done business with his bank in the past and wanted to pay a visit to his office on the Rue Lafitte to introduce Carl to him.

"Why don't you two go while Sophie pays her call," suggested Edward. "Eddie and I can take in the zoo."

"But you knew Cornelia Renick, didn't you?" said Sophie.

"Only as children. And she invited you, not me."

"Or if Carl is going to meet Mr. Renick, perhaps you should—"

"Why blight his chances by dragging along the sad uncle?" said Edward, more tensely.

"Go to the zoo, a good plan," interposed Theodore. Edward's constant self-deprecation irritated him.

It worked out well. Edward and Eddie came back in high spirits with tales of sociable kangaroos who boxed with zoo visitors and an ostrich that pulled a cart. Moreover, whether thanks to Sophie's call or Theodore and Carl's office visit, a card was delivered to the hotel a couple of days later, inviting them all to dinner. "There's more than one kind of zoo," Edward confided to Eddie, though in fact the idea of dinner at a private house in Paris appealed to his secret sense of himself. And he remembered liking Cornelia.

Marius Renick had begun his career in Ohio, but soon moved back East to work at his grandfather's mercantile bank in New York. He had helped to expand the business greatly and had converted a comfortable living for himself into a considerable fortune by financing what he called back-fillers—local railroad spurs, reinsurance schemes, secondary reuse of industrial by-products. With the bank's money, he was canny. With his own, he regularly took a flier, less for the thrill of quick gain than to keep his nerves keen to what was afoot and to scare his cousins; it made him sharper than his competitors. Sending him abroad to head up a new European branch of the bank temporarily resolved rivalries within the family, but everyone had expected him to return to make a bid for the bank presidency. And then he found the house on the Rue de Varenne.

"A seventeenth-century palace," Cornelia delighted in telling people, "complete with an eighteenth-century duchess."

The duchesse de Mabillon had indeed been born in the 1790s, in London, where her parents had fled during the Reign of Terror. She and the duke, whom she had married in exile, had not taken possession of the house, which was hers by inheritance, until after the overthrow of Napoleon Bonaparte. Then they unboarded the windows, evicted squatters, and weathered the vicissitudes of subsequent regimes while the house slid further and further into decline, the more so after the duke's death, when their son preferred to expend what was left in the family coffers on an equally decrepit patrimonial château in the country and on horses. The duchess, who disliked both rural discomfort and her daughter-in-law, remained ensconced in urban decay on the Rue de Varenne until some accident or fate brought Marius Renick to her drawing room one day. A few months later, on the strength of a ninety-nine-year lease, she had withdrawn into one wing of the house and removed all her belongings to the attic.

Before installing their own furnishings, the Renicks had brought in plasterers, painters, paperers, regilders, and city water. Outside they had brickwork repointed, stucco reapplied, slate work repaired, and all the copper on the roof replaced. If the duchess avariciously marveled at seeing them spend so much on her property or raged that new American money found it so easy, she never betrayed more than ironic resignation. Years of penury and danger had taught her to draw strict boundaries and honor them. She never gave the Renicks' servants orders, not even the gardeners; nor did she ever let any of the Renick household into her own quarters. Only as a way of keeping her eye on what her tenants were doing did she occasionally accept an invitation to tea; and once a year at Christmas, she condescended to include them in a gathering where the food was scanty and bad but the complaints epigrammatic.

"I'm absorbing her every snobbery to rebuff Newport at need," claimed Cornelia.

The duchess, of course, would not be at the Renicks' dinner for the Murers. Knowing that Americans loved to dine with even the most minor European nobility, Cornelia considered inviting a Norwegian count and his wife, a soprano, who both spoke tolerable

English. It would help with the seating chart, but she decided that Theodore and Sophie would be even more pleased if they were able to bring their younger son—so awkward to travel with boys unless you had a tutor. If she placed herself at the hostess's corner instead of at the head of the table and included children, she could work off the Monroes as well, another business obligation of Marius's. Then with Edward Murer already on the list, to add funny Miss Pendergrast and Sarah Palmer's daughter would require only one extra man—Hippolyte Grandcourt. There, he would do nicely, provided he wasn't conducting that night. A bachelor of sixty, he had dined off stories of the musical world for forty years and for forty years had done well by himself and his hostesses. Luckily, he was available.

The Murers were the first to arrive. It was to be an early supper, not only for the children's sake, but also to give the older guests time to put in a late appearance at the Opéra or go to a *café-chansant* if they wished. The Murers' carriage, hired for the evening, turned around the circular drive and deposited them at the front door. For a moment, they caught a glimpse of a last brilliance in the treetops behind the house, but the shadowed daylight lingering over the round lawn and graveled driveway in front faded into dusk under the covered entry porch.

Sophie had tried to describe the place, but nothing prepared Edward for his sense of dislocation and wonderment when a footman admitted them to the house. Golden light swimming through windows at the far end of the entry hall gave the ducal magnificence of pale walls and elaborate gilt ornament an air of enchanted removal from the everyday world. Whenever he had read fiction or history, in order to visualize aristocratic European settings he had drawn unconsciously on wisps of boyhood memories, all of them bourgeois. From now on, his mental images would have to be drastically revised and enlarged.

The wide hallway led between doors, mirrors, and tall porcelain vases on gilt stands all the way to double doors opening onto a back terrace. Midway to their right rose a broad, curving staircase, lit by candles in tall torchières. At the top of the stairs, the butler waited outside the salon to announce them.

"Mr. and Mrs. Murer?" he asked, merely to confirm what he knew must be true. (Hastings, hired away from an English family who had mistakenly counted on family loyalty to outweigh the lure of salary, was the key to Cornelia's success in running a perfect household.)

"Yes," said Theodore, pleasantly, remembering not to use his customary *ja*. "Good evening."

"Sir."

Hastings ushered them into a large room, the long south wall of which was punctuated by French windows leading onto a wide balcony over the back terrace. Marius Renick stood near the door to receive his guests and conduct them to where, on a straight-backed Louis XIV sofa, Cornelia sat erect in her brace, a radiant presence in the dwindling natural light. Theodore bent over the hand she held out to him and, without hesitation, raised it to his lips. Sophie sat down where Cornelia patted the sofa beside her.

"Edward, my dear, if you weren't looking so sleek, I would say we were a perfectly matched pair of old crocks," she exclaimed, holding out her hand to him. "Wherever did you get that walking stick? If you say Cincinnati, I may have to consider reemigrating."

"Good evening, Cornelia." Edward squeezed her hand sympathetically before releasing it. "We were sorry to learn about your fall. The cane? No, not Cincinnati. I found it at a shop on the Rue Auber, next to the one where you sent Sophie to look for fans."

"Isn't that place a gem?" said Cornelia, turning to Sophie and unfolding a confection of embroidered ivory silk, lace, and feathers. "This came from it; I hope you discovered your heart's desire."

Cornelia set about charming Carl and laughing with young

Eddie before sending the latter off to a corner of the drawing room with her own son for the boys to amuse themselves.

"Miss Pendergrast and Miss Palmer."

"Oh, you gentlemen must help me," said Cornelia, in an undertone.

Edward and Carl instantly faded back, but stood nearby at attention. Their duty was clear.

As soon as she saw Mrs. Renick, Jeanette was mortified. Adeline had warned her that fashion was shifting in Paris. Not a bustle was left; and with them had gone voluminous skirts, ribbons and bows, panniers and ruched trains caught up in the back. "Jeanette's best dinner frock from Vassar should do for any entertainment likely to come her way," Sarah Palmer had retorted. "Well, at least until she has had time to study what's new," said Adeline. Jeanette's best meant a full-skirted, garnet-and-gray-striped silk with a ruffled hem. When they got it out with the Renicks' dinner in mind, Effie had the idea of taking the skirt off the waistband and pleating it so that when it was resewn, all the garnet was overlaid with gray and the silhouette was slimmer. They had pinned an artificial rose at the waist to cover an unfortunate bunching. But the striped bodice and ruffle remained, and here and there garnet streaked the edges of pleats that hung wrong. How Jeanette wished now that she could have paid a dressmaker to make it over properly!

Mrs. Renick's dress was smoothest Prussian-blue satin over a pale sky-blue satin underskirt, the kind that required hanging space in a huge closet and skillful ironing. A plunging neckline opened out from a V to peaked lapels in the paler blue; it was filled with ivory lace, which rose to frill a standing collar and frame the back of her head. Matching lace fell softly from her three-quarter-length sleeves. Tiny self-covered buttons down the front emphasized the dress's symmetries and Mrs. Renick's erectness in her brace. The overall effect was opulent and assured, a dress for neither afternoon calls nor the theater but precisely for a dinner at home. Jeanette felt gussied up, down at heels, and out of date all at the same time. It didn't help that the handsome young man with the wavy blond hair standing to one side contrived to make wearing impeccable evening clothes look offhand.

"Miss Palmer is from Ohio," said Cornelia to Sophie, when introductions were made. "Theodore may know her father. Judge Palmer is active in Republican politics."

Both ladies had immediately perceived Jeanette's discomfort and remembered what it felt like to be self-conscious at a party; both set about to be kind. From her presence in Mrs. Renick's house and Jeanette's own manners, Sophie was assured that she was someone suitable for Carl to know, if unlikely to attract him; and Cornelia thought she saw a spark of something interesting. Before there was time for conversation to encourage her, however, Hippolyte Grandcourt was announced.

Grandcourt was the professional master of the grand entrance. Just as everyone turned toward the door, his face lit up and he strode vigorously forward into the room. ("*Strode,*" Effie would always say afterward, "that's the only word, *strode.*")

"My dear Mme. Renick." A flourish, a bow, a kiss of his hostess's hand, and Grandcourt paused briefly to catch Cornelia's eye before straightening up to sweep everyone into his gaze. "*Chers amis*, you must all hear this," he said, in a mixture of French and French-accented English.

Grandcourt crossed the large room to the Renicks' piano with the familiarity of long use. He adjusted the piano stool, flapped back the tails of his jacket, and sat down, half facing his audience. An arch of one eyebrow invited them to listen. His right hand hesitantly picked out a few notes, paused, then repeated them more strongly. "Ladies and gentlemen, I give you 'The Beggar's Polka' by Jacques Offenbach!" He swung around to thump out the melody at a jaunty beat, with the left hand joining in for a full improvisation on the theme.

"This may be the only drawing room in Paris to hear it tonight, but on the street—!" He held up his long right forefinger for emphasis. "On the street, it is for sale by the very beggar of the title— *vraiment!*—in front of Offenbach's own Théâtre Bouffes." He threw back his head to show his profile as he laughed loudly at the joke, then looked around at them confidentially. His hands played on softly.

"We are walking the boulevards one night, the good Offenbach and I. A beggar approaches. Offenbach has no coin to give him; I reach in my pocket. 'No, no,' says he. On a scrap of paper with a pencil stub, he dashes off a few bars, adds a title to the top, and signs his name at the bottom. 'Voilà,' he says, handing it to the mendicant, 'give this to a publisher in the morning and he will pay you two hundred francs.' We walk on; he hums out his new little piece; we are both much amused; but the laugh, it is on the composer. This mendicant, this poor man in rags, he is no beggar, *mesdames et messieurs*—he is a modern man, an entrepreneur!"

Grandcourt drummed the keys.

"Tonight on the Champs-Élysées, as I am coming here, the street musicians are out in force. A tune sounds familiar—and there he is, our mendicant, with a companion to play the accordion, and two pretty girls to dance while he himself hawks a stack of freshly printed sheets. *Oui!* He put the tune up to bid, he tells me, sold it for a thousand francs, and retained the rights to sell it on the street. I have it here. He cost me a franc, after all, and another for his autograph."

From inside his jacket, Maestro Grandcourt produced a rolled-up sheet of paper and carried it over to present to Mrs. Renick. Beaming, she clasped it to her bosom, while he sat down in the seat on the other side of her from Sophie—which, until a moment before, had been occupied by Effie. Long years of living in Maude Hendrick's company had taught Effie the skill of vacating a seat before anyone else noticed it was needed.

"Well, I call that a treat!" said Effie, joining Edward, Carl, and Jeanette behind the sofa. "You must sketch M. Grandcourt at the piano, Jeanette, for a letter home."

"Do you draw, Miss Palmer?" asked Carl, politely.

"Yes, I . . ."

"Oh, Jeanette is studying with the best teachers in Paris. At Julian's Academy!"

"A school for lady artists?" grinned Carl.

"For artists." Jeanette was annoyed, not only with Cousin Effie, but with Carl for putting her off on the wrong foot.

"The Académie Julian is a proprietary school, Carl," said Edward. "It has gained quite an international reputation."

"You know it, then, Dr. Murer?" asked Jeanette, turning gratefully to this reserved gentleman, whose face, despite darker hair and a trim beard, bore a family resemblance to his nephew's.

"I've only read about it. I envy you the opportunity."

"I'm going to be studying, too," said Carl, "though nothing so fancy as art. Vats of chemicals and modern manufacturing. Lord, and all in German!"

He plunged into a comic account of his upcoming year. At first, Jeanette tried to inject the occasional remark to establish herself as a serious student, too, but made little dent. She fell back on laughing at his jokes, despising him as conceited, and trying to hold herself at the angle that would show her at her prettiest. It would serve him right to know that the lines and shadows in his uncle's face piqued far more interest than his fatuous good looks.

* * *

"Mr. and Mrs. Monroe. Miss Monroe. Miss Rose and Master David."

Hastings announced the arrival of the last guests. Mr. Monroe was dressed *de rigueur* in black evening clothes; but with his sandy gray hair and light eyes, he appeared as opalescent as the rest of his family. His wife was decked out in pearls; the older daughter was borne before them as if on display. Lila Monroe was an auroral vision of pale gold chiffon and evanescent pink silk, of bare shoulders rice-powder white, and blond hair held softly in place by mother-of-pearl combs. The quiet set of her mouth and her languid, unseeing gaze—it took her half a beat to meet the eyes of anyone to whom she was introduced—gave her the stillness of something costly and un-touched. She could afford to be remote because no one in the room, in any room, could ever doubt her worth.

No one, perhaps, except Eddie Murer. At fourteen, he was still immune to ingénues of seventeen. Seeing his brother Carl's entranced expression, Eddie rolled his eyes. Jeanette wanted to annex him im-mediately. If she couldn't hide behind the curtains or simply go home, she wished she could at least join the children's table—though that would put her with David and Rose, two other inhuman exha-lations wafting across the room. The best she could do was slip behind Cousin Effie to hide. A moment ago, she had been feeling superior to Carl; now he was a prize that she had just lost. Edward was touched more by the dismay in Miss Palmer's face than attracted by the bisque-china loveliness that had inspired her jealousy and captivated his gaping nephew.

To Carl's credit, until he was struck dumb by Lila's entrance, he really had been doing his best to amuse Miss Pendergrast and Miss Palmer. He knew it would please his mother to see him socially at ease; and the chance to talk endlessly about himself, though he would never have put it that way, made him expand with good feel-ing. Now it fell to Edward to pick up the slack; they could not all stand staring mutely while Cornelia greeted her new guests. "Have you been to the World's Fair yet, Miss Pendergrast?" he asked.

"Well, no—"

"I want to see the art exhibitions," said Jeanette, turning a brave face to him (and her back on Miss Monroe). It was rude, she knew, to interrupt when the question was put to Effie, but she was desperate and couldn't bear that dithering, abashed simper of Cousin Effie's just now.

"My younger nephew, Eddie, would tell you the sculpture of a rhinoceros rearing up at the entrance to the Trocadéro was the best thing at the fair. It's life-sized and lifelike, too—in fact, livelier than the real feller at the zoo, who just snoozes in his cage."

"Did you see the exotic displays, like the Japanese and the Persians?" asked Effie, eagerly.

"Not yet. Perhaps—Carl?"

To his astonishment, Edward realized he had been about to propose getting up a party, but by then Carl had sidled away to be introduced to the beauteous Lila. Edward was saved from himself by Hastings, who, having notified the kitchen that the last guests had arrived, came in to announce that dinner was ready.

Edward was not sorry to find himself seated between comfortable Sophie and harmless Miss Pendergrast. Across heaps of fruit, flowers, and candles down the length of the table, he could watch the more entertaining side: Mrs. Monroe, Grandcourt, Miss Palmer, Carl, and pretty Miss Monroe. It was quite clear that Carl would devote the entire evening to Miss Monroe if allowed; but when Cornelia turned from Theodore on her right to Mr. Monroe on her left, Lila turned, too, obedient to convention or to a silent command from her father. Back and forth the conversation turned in ten-minute intervals, through course after course. After julienne soup came a choice of *filets de soles à la Normandie* or lobster rissoles. A menu card at each place gave the more inexperienced the chance to rehearse their decision before flawlessly trained footmen on each side of the table presented platters. The second time Carl was forced to turn to Jeanette, she was smiling animatedly and began recounting a story Grandcourt had just told her. Carl, who was committing to memory the next thing he wanted to say to Miss Monroe, missed the premise and had to ask her to start over. The story fell flat for both of them. They both absent-mindedly tore at their rolls, leaving heaps of crumbs on the table-cloth.

"Bread crumbs make good erasers," said Jeanette.

Carl stared at her blankly.

"For pencil or charcoal. They don't damage the surface of paper."

What on earth was she talking about?

"Most of us use india rubber," she went on, desperately. "It's cleaner and less wasteful of the good bread, as Mr. Ruskin would say."

Oh, thought Carl, artists. "You could use the bread when you're sketching in the park and feed the pigeons at the same time." He grinned smugly, thinking he had made a brilliant comeback.

A third course (*filets de boeuf à la jardinière* or ham and peas), then ducklings with compote of oranges or *soufflé à la vanille*. Carl was slow to turn toward Jeanette. His natural amiability had been winning over Lila, who rewarded him by opening up delicately. With an abstracted look of contentment, Carl reached forward to break off a bunch of grapes to go with his duckling. Jeanette picked up the gold grape shears laid for that purpose and expertly snipped first a cluster, then a single, thick-skinned grape, which she proceeded to peel.

"So that's what those little scissors are for!" said Carl. "You probably even know what to do with the seeds."

Jeanette ate the grape and discreetly disposed of the seeds into a corner of her fist in the correct manner. He smiled appreciatively. "Are grapes a regular part of the dinner table in *Circleville*?" he teased.

"At Vassar College," said Jeanette, and immediately wished she hadn't.

He looked at her quizzically as he tried to work something out. "I thought Vassar was for brains, not a finishing school." Jeanette reddened. Carl frowned. "And if you go to Vassar," he said, slowly, "what are you doing here?"

"I *went* to Vassar; I don't any more." Carl, who had perhaps drunk more wine than was good for him, failed to pick up the warning signs in her face and voice. He waited for her to say more. Blinking back tears of frustration and shame, Jeanette bit the inside of her lip. Couldn't he see that if she had graduated, she would have said so, and no other explanation—bad grades, lack of money, family obligations—was any of his business? A sudden squall of angry pride overtook her. "You are sitting next to a very dangerous woman, Mr. Murer. I was expelled."

"Expelled!" Carl's disbelieving exclamation caused a startled silence to fall over the room.

Before she could stop herself, Jeanette icily dropped the explanation: "For helping my roommate elope."

"Gardiner McLeod's daughter," squeaked Effie, in consternation, to no one in particular.

Everyone slipped glances at everyone else.

"Couldn't have happened to a more deserving old sinner," snorted Mr. Monroe, at last.

"Look, Miss Palmer, I'm sorry." Carl was abashed by what he had precipitated.

Cornelia felt her dinner party disintegrating and appealed mutely across the table to Hippolyte Grandcourt. He who had never failed a hostess yet, nor disappointed an audience, stepped into the breach. He was wise enough to pick up the offending term lightly.

"When I was young," he said to the company at large, "there was a composer named Dutoit. A talented man at melody, full of grandiose ambitions. He took it into his head to write, as his magnum opus, an opera based on Cervantes' divine *Don Quixote*. For the libretto, he chose the episode in which the beautiful Moorish maiden, Zoraida, has eloped with a Christian galley slave. Now, the soprano he had in mind . . ."

Off went Grandcourt, telling his tale in a voice that projected the whole length of the table while retaining an easy, conversational tone. As he elicited a final, general laugh, he met Cornelia's worshipful eye and released the other dinner guests to focus all his attention on Jeanette. With a blithe comment to Theodore, Cornelia restarted conversation at her end of the table. Lila turned to Carl, her eyes sparkling with suppressed, malicious glee. Mrs. Monroe nervously returned to Mr. Renick, Sophie to Edward. To the delight of Lila and Carl, Mrs. Renick held the pattern longer than was conventional. During ices, however, seeing that she must rescue Effie from Mr. Monroe, who was trying to worm out more of the scandal, Cornelia changed partners again. Edward could now attend to Miss Pendergrast with the soothing demeanor he brought to his patients, and Carl gamely tried to recoup his standing as a good fellow, if not with Miss Palmer, then at least in his own eyes. "You can probably tell me which are the best pictures to see at the Louvre," he said.

Grandcourt's ministrations had restored Jeanette's equanimity, but not to the point that she could pretend nothing had happened. "The *Mona Lisa* is universally admired," she replied in such chilly tones that Carl made no further attempt to converse. They both knew their only real obligation was to make no further trouble. This was best accomplished by the slow, wordless eating of an excellent black currant sorbet.

At the end of the evening, while the guests were headed downstairs to their carriages, Cornelia put a hand on Edward's sleeve to hold him back.

"Edward, dearest," she said, with a conspiratorial gleam in her eye, "could I ask you to do me a favor? We had already arranged for Albert, our driver, to take Miss Pendergrast and Miss Palmer home, but after the poor girl's embarrassment at dinner, a little additional chivalry seems called for. Would you accompany them, there's a dear? Albert can then take you on to your hotel or anywhere else you want to go."

Edward was oddly pleased, both to be asked and to be able to show a little kindness. "It would be my privilege, Cornelia."

"Good, then make it look like it was your own idea."

CHAPTER FOURTEEN

The World's Fair

I n the hall below, Jeanette and Effie were just leaving. "May I see you safely to your door, Miss Pendergrast?" asked Edward, as he caught up with them.

"Oh, no need, Dr. Murer," said Effie. "Mrs. Renick has ordered her carriage for us. That is . . . I mean . . ." She slid into confusion as it dawned on her that the offer had been made, not as a practical matter, but as a compliment.

Edward was accustomed to helping customers out of self-imposed difficulties. "It would be my very great pleasure," he said, gravely.

After her embarrassment at dinner and the need to keep up appearances for the rest of the evening, Jeanette wanted only to escape home and die, but she tried to stand a little straighter. Silently she begged Cousin Effie please, please to quit dithering.

"Why, I call that handsome of you, Dr. Murer!" said Effie, bashfully.

By now, the other Murers had assembled in a staring knot behind them.

"I'll meet you at the Ambassadeurs," said Edward. Before they had a chance to ask questions or propose alternative plans, he was helping Jeanette and Effie into the carriage.

Inside, Edward leaned back into the shadows, almost invisible in his black clothes and top hat. Jeanette was glad of the covering darkness, glad not to have to meet his eye—although, she thought bitterly, his thin reserved face contrasted favorably to that horrid Carl's beefy father or pudding-faced Mr. Monroe. Edward sensed energy in the two forms opposite him. Miss Palmer was tense, pulled back against the seat. Miss Pendergrast was perky, poised on its edge; and once her tongue was loosened by excitement, she chattered. Eventually, with some kind prompting, Miss Palmer was brought into the conversation to recount one of M. Grandcourt's anecdotes. It involved Rodolphe Julian's exploits as a wrestler in a circus while he was a student at the École des Beaux-Arts, and her voice eased in the telling. By the time the carriage turned onto the Rue Jacob, Edward had decided to act on his earlier impulse.

"Miss Pendergrast, would you and Miss Palmer do me the honor of joining me tomorrow on an excursion to the World's Fair? It's crowded on Sunday; but, Miss Palmer, you are busy on weekdays, and—"

Effie squeaked. Jeanette, unable to bear her havering, spoke out of turn. "That's very kind of you, Dr. Murer. Thank you very much."

"It's ridiculous that we haven't gone yet!" chimed in Effie.

"Then that's settled. If you prefer to attend divine services in the morning, we can make it an afternoon visit only, but there's plenty to do all day; I'd be happy to pick you up after breakfast."

To Jeanette's astonishment, Cousin Effie said, "Oh, I think the good Lord can accept wonderment at His creation as praise."

"That's the spirit! The gates open at ten; let's say I'll be in a cab at your door at nine thirty."

* * *

"Cousin Effie, I believe I'm chaperoning *you*!" exclaimed Jeanette, when they got upstairs. She fell backward onto the bed. "You've made a conquest."

"Go on," said Effie, turning pink. "Dr. Murer is a real gentleman, though, isn't he."

"The nicest person there," agreed Jeanette, closing her eyes as she dissolved into tears.

"What a thing to say when Mrs. Renick was your hostess!"

Jeanette rolled onto her side and made an effort to hide her misery. "And M. Grandcourt," she said. "Mr. Renick, though—you hardly notice him, do you?"

"Oh, I think you'd find that Mr. Murer and Mr. Monroe noticed very little else," said Effie. If life in New York City had taught her anything, it was to locate the center of power in a room.

"Not that he or Mrs. Renick will want to see us again—ever." Jeanette buried her face in the counterpane. "Oh, Cousin Effie, I'm afraid I spoiled everything for you, too."

When they were little, when their nurse scolded and they were afraid of their mother, the Hendrick children had always run to Effie to hide tearful faces in her black skirts. She had no power to intervene with the authorities that governed her life as well as theirs, and her efforts at giving comfort were clumsy; but until about age twelve, when they learned to see her with dismissive adult eyes, they depended on her. She came now and sat down on the bed beside Jeanette with her hands in her lap, looking straight out. "I don't think it's so bad as all that. Anyway, it won't change things much for me if I never see the Renicks again."

"Well, it might change them for the better if you did!"

"It might. And, of course, dear, it probably would be better not to mention being expelled from Vassar in future—"

Jeanette bit a wad of bedding and squeezed her eyes tighter shut.

"—but from my side of the table, you looked pretty and vivacious all evening." Effie turned sideways and touched a tentative hand to Jeanette's shoulder. "I was proud to be with you, that's what."

Jeanette lay weeping softly. Then, like her Hendrick cousins, she wriggled closer to put an arm around Effie's waist and pressed her head against the older woman's side until she gained control of herself. When she sat up again, wiping her eyes, she did not have to do anything more to express her gratitude.

"Time for beauty sleep," said Effie.

"It's *you* we have to make beautiful tomorrow!" said Jeanette, in a half-sobbing laugh.

At the Place de la Concorde, Edward had himself let out to walk through the tree-filled Champs-Élysées. A chestnut allée led to the grounds of the big outdoor *café-chansant*, Les Ambassadeurs. In the leafy night garden within the café's enclosing hedge, tiers of gas globe lamps hung luminous enough to glow through the shrubs and lower branches of trees. Strains from an orchestra playing a popular tune carried out over a clamor of laughter, voices, and glasses clinking. The smell of alcohol, tobacco, and eau de cologne diffused into the night. Out in the shadowy expanses of the park, the subtler fragrance of linden trees and lilacs hinted at something desirable, elusive. The lovely phrase came to him, *passer la nuit à la belle étoile*: more of a whisper in French than in English, to spend the night under the stars. For a moment, Edward wished he could follow the genial drift of dreamers and strollers among those more mysterious trees, but the blatant entertainment of a *café-chansant* was one of the sights of Paris they had promised Sophie. He paid his entrance fee.

"Uncle Edward!" said Carl, who was on the lookout. "Come on. We have a table and champagne."

They threaded their way among scores of tables set out behind more densely packed rows of seats. On a garishly lit stage sat two rows of ornamental young women in short-sleeved, low-cut evening gowns, who watched the performance or the customers and whispered behind fans.

"Not one of those girls can hold a candle to Miss Monroe," said Carl.

"Better for your morals and pocket to think so," replied Edward.

Out front on stage, a coarse-featured woman, highly made up and buxom, strutted, bobbed, and gesticulated suggestively while she belted out a rollicking song. With each verse, the general-admission crowd swayed and joined in ever more lustily at a refrain about cracking walnuts. As they approached the Murers' table, Edward was glad Sophie spoke little French—though from the look on her face she knew very well that the lyrics were risqué. At the same time, she seemed at ease among the well-dressed clientele at the tables around them. Good old Sophie: no prude, nor for that matter really a snob. Her wholehearted enjoyment in the evening was at one with his sense of mild adventure.

"Here you are, *liebken*, sit down," she said. "Now what was that all about?"

"What was what all about?" said Edward. "Is that ice cream you've got, Eddie?"

"Vanilla—and my first champagne!" With a broad grin, Eddie held up a tulip-shaped glass.

A waiter appeared at Edward's shoulder and filled one for him from the magnum Theodore had ordered.

"*Merci*," said Edward. "*Santé*," he added to Eddie, lifting the glass.

"Well?" demanded Theodore.

Edward met his brother's eyes coolly. Sometimes when he thought Theodore was pulling rank as the elder, it helped to remember that he had killed men in cold blood, whereas his brother never had. It put an edge to the deliberate reasonableness with which he answered, "Cornelia asked me to escort Miss Palmer and Miss Pendergrast home. So I did."

"She saw that you were the man for wounded ducks," said Theodore.

"In her exact words, she said she thought a little chivalry was called for."

"Chivalry!" hooted Carl. "Toward that pair of horrors?"

"They are not horrors," said Edward, "and I didn't see one of them forget herself at table."

"Then you didn't hear Miss Palmer blurt out that she was a dangerous woman. She might have been laying a trap on purpose for a fellow to trip over."

"A fellow can be tripped up, Carl, but not a man of the world."

Carl stared in disbelief at the uncle who had taught him how to fish and throw knives, but whom he tended to patronize mentally, having witnessed too much of Edward's fastidiousness at the store and too many of his breakdowns. Tonight his reproofs were coming out of unsuspected regions of experience. *"Touché."*

Edward lifted his glass in salute.

"Well, well," said Theodore, looking uncertainly from one to the other. "So Eddie," he went on, turning to his other son, "now that you have seen the famous *café-chansant* for which you are much too young, and tasted your first champagne, for which you are also too young, and eaten your ice cream, are you ready to go back to the hotel, eh?"

"Oh, Pop, can't I watch the clowns? Please, sir, just a little longer?"

A pair of comic dancers had come onstage at the conclusion of a set by the star chanteuse. The noise level in the audience rose as hundreds of spectators turned to talk among themselves. Theodore chuckled.

"Ja. Poor clowns. They will be glad of the attention. Turn your chair around and you will see better. Then, Edward, perhaps—"

"I'll take him back," volunteered Carl.

"Look, I want to get up early tomorrow," began Edward.

"Carl is right," said Theodore, holding him back with a look.

Later, when the boys left, jostling and punching each other on the shoulder, Theodore watched them indulgently. "It is good to be young and good for brothers to do things together. They walk down the Champs-Élysées in Paris and a few blocks along the Rue de Rivoli—it is something they remember the rest of their lives. You and I, Edward—"

"Carl won't remember anything from tonight except Miss Lila Monroe," said Edward.

Sophie laughed. "Carl falls in love easily, but not yet hard. Still, why not dream moon dreams in Paris? You should fall in love yourself, *liebken*."

In the synthetic gaiety of the surroundings, the triteness of the suggestion fell as a false note in Edward's ear, especially from Sophie, who should know him better. He hid behind gallantry. "You are already taken, *madame*."

"She reserves a little corner of her heart for you," said Theodore, looking at his brother shrewdly.

"Where it is very peaceful," said Edward, returning the look steadily. "But you inhabit the mansion."

The next morning, to be sure of avoiding the family, Edward left the hotel for breakfast. On the street, the air was cool and surfaces damp with collecting dew; over the occasional swish of a vehicle on the wet asphalt, he could hear birdsong in the trees of the Tuileries Garden. In the space of two blocks, he met a man still in evening dress, walking with the precarious precision of inebriation; two yawning girls in limp finery; a uniformed footman walking a standard poodle on a leash; and three Arabs in full desert attire— enough, thought Edward, to make a man from Cincinnati count as a full-fledged flâneur in his own eyes. He stopped at a tobacconist to buy a newspaper and tickets to the fair, then selected a café notable for its brass and marble, where he could read in mirrored splendor. Before going in, he tipped a *commissionaire* to bring an open four-seater around at nine.

At nine thirty, on the Rue Jacob, the ladies were waiting for him, unpretentiously punctual. Effie's face lit up when she saw him, and even more so when he conducted her to a stylish landau: She was sure it would raise her and Jeanette in the estimation of the ever-watchful Mme. LeConte. Jeanette, still tired after a bad night's sleep, was more subdued. She had overcome her initial reluctance ever to get out of bed again, much less meet someone from the night before, only by yielding to Effie's excitement as the course of least resistance. Also, her mother's voice reminded her that she was the one who had accepted the invitation.

Once they left the claustrophobic side streets, the carriage sped alongside the quay. As they neared the entrance to the fair, however, traffic slowed almost to a standstill.

"Do you mind walking from here?" asked Edward.

"Heavens, no!" said Effie. "We'll be on our feet all day, anyway."

"But the crowd—?"

"I'm sure it's no different where you come from," said Effie. "A straight back and a firm step, that's all it takes!" Her eye fell on Edward's bad leg. Too excited to be daunted, she added brightly, "Or, I guess, the rap of a good walking stick to clear the field."

Jeanette froze, stricken, but Edward was only amused. He thought he had never met anyone so guileless as Miss Pendergrast. With the ivory knob of the weapon in question, he rapped for the driver to halt, then helped the ladies down and offered his arm to Effie.

The Great Exhibition Hall built specially for the fair covered several square blocks; its walls of bluish glass reflected changes in sky and atmosphere. At its main entrance, burgundy-red doors set in highly ornate iron frames admitted visitors into a deep foyer from which arches led into long avenues of galleries devoted in turn to agriculture, manufacture, education, and art. If she and Effie had come alone, Jeanette would have propelled them to the fine arts section at once, but the Grand Vestibule itself contained dazzling displays of luxury goods that slowed most visitors. Beside a life-sized equestrian statue in bronze, which commemorated an imperial visit by the Prince of Wales to India, two storys of slender columns and latticework rose to onion domes.

"Inside that pavilion," said Edward, "they've got a display of treasures the prince brought back with him."

"Oh, may we take a look?" begged Effie. "I'm like a crow with a piece of shiny tin when it comes to glitter, Dr. Murer—I just can't resist it." In her perennial black, amid all the peacock colors around them (malachites from Russia, huge vases of lapis lazuli), she might suggest a crow; but the yearning in her face was not acquisitive, it was a longing to admire. The only jewelry she ever wore was a gold locket containing a picture of Polycarpus and a lock of his hair. "Of course, if you two—"

In answer, Edward steered her toward the pavilion. Solemn-faced attendants in turbans greeted them silently. Inside, a respectful hush prevailed in the presence of so much wealth: silken draperies, carpets underfoot, velvet cushions on which rested coils of pearls, huge rubies and emeralds encircled by diamonds, sapphires, amethysts, gold, brassware.

"I feel like Aladdin in the den of thieves!" said Effie, happily.

"Wrong country," teased Jeanette.

"Den of thieves is right," said Edward.

"Oh, you two," said Effie. She dawdled, admiring all the riches, but kept moving. "What next?" she asked, when they emerged from the pavilion.

"May I suggest the Avenue of Nations?" said Edward. "We can dip into some of the exhibits there, then come back up the length of the fine arts galleries at our leisure, Miss Palmer."

Although they knew they would soon give up trying to see everything, they began with the first exhibit, a full-sized house with a Queen Anne façade. One room had high wainscoting and Chippendale furniture; others held other styles of furniture sold by England to the world. It was all very pretty and very forgettable until they came into an up-to-the-minute chamber decorated by James McNeill Whistler. Tones of mustard yellow dominated, enriched by the luster of gold, softened and harmonized by the use of buff, and brought to life by touches of ochre. *Dandified* was Edward's reaction, but he could see that the ladies had other thoughts. Jeanette had never been so engulfed by a color. It made her impatience with drawing lessons worse. She wanted to apply paint to canvas, pigment to ground. It was more than the superb balance and blending of related hues; it was the subtle effects of texture and lighting, the contrast of effulgent gleam to matte finish. And the minute Effie entered, she felt an upsurge of delight, a leap of the heart. How Polycarpus would have hated it! How indignant Maude would be. Fashionable Adeline would falter before it, doubting whether she could bring it off—but not Effie. "Oh, my. Well, I am glad to have seen this while I'm fresh," she said. Speculating on how to achieve similar effects on a tight budget, she bent and stood on tiptoe to examine every detail, intending to remember them all.

After that, the fair became one sensation piled on another, a jumble of goods and revelations. Despite the sound-absorbing wood, plaster, and cloth of the displays, the endless tramp of feet and sound of voices roared and echoed throughout the huge hall, loudest in the long corridors but audible in even the quietest, most obscure corners of the least-visited exhibits.

At the end of the Avenue of Nations, Edward proposed that they take a break. It was a relief to step outside and leave the hall behind. Not only their heads but their whole bodies felt lighter in the pleasant late-spring air. Lawns and trees separated the hall from big restaurants on the edge of the grounds and offered breathing space. The brasserie to which Edward led them fed a thousand at a time.

It was noisy, too, but its pastry buffet offered a tempting array of choices always with more chocolate, more whipped cream, and strong dark coffee. A half hour later, they reemerged fortified to tackle the fine arts galleries.

They started by trying to look at least quickly at every painting in each gallery. Effie took a straightforward delight in scenes of places she would never visit. Edward enjoyed the landscapes, too. Jeanette was trying to observe, learn, sort, and analyze, but had to give up. Much too soon, she found herself becoming dazed again, then slap-happy. In the Austrian section, in front of a colossal history painting—thirty feet long, eighteen feet high—Effie was ready to sink down onto a bench and dutifully study its many, many, many details, but Jeanette giggled. Catching Dr. Murer's eye and seeing that he, too, somehow found the challenge funny, she shook with laughter. She could stop herself only by biting down on her fist. "It's really good, only, only—"

"Only!" agreed Edward, and laughed out loud with her.

"We'd better just find the gallery with M. Bouguereau's paintings," said Jeanette, stumbling backward between gasps. "He's my teacher, and I do want to see them."

They had to search through several galleries, stopping occasionally along the way. With a dozen canvases hanging, Bouguereau turned out to be one of the better-represented artists. Full-length portraits. A Virgin with the Infant Jesus and Saint John. A Pietà. A very pretty, very naked maiden who faced the viewer with a naked cherub on her shoulder. "Fondant," Jeanette overheard someone say. She bridled and then looked again at the nude; *fondant* was apt, not that she would admit it out loud.

Ahead lay many more French paintings, and then the Italians and the Russians. As they came into the next-to-the-last section, British art, even Jeanette was past caring. Seeing the fatigue in her companions' faces, she said, "I can't look at another picture either.

We'll just have to cross the Channel someday, Cousin Effie. Oh, no, wait—I take it back. Please, I must look at this one. Have you ever seen anything like it, Dr. Murer? Is it wonderful or ghastly?"

What had snapped her back to attention was a six-foot-high painting of two life-sized figures: An elongated, barefoot woman in clinging draperies stood with an open book in her hand; her lips parted slightly as she stared fixedly over her shoulder. Behind her a man half reclined on a bench under a bower—no, in the low, twisted branches of what? a vine?—a split hawthorn tree in profuse bloom. *Edward Burne-Jones, The Enchantment of Merlin*, read the label. Around the woman's head coiled snakes or a strange cap. The more Jeanette looked, the weirder the picture became. It was flattened and decorative like a tapestry design. Jeanette was deeply attracted and repelled at the same time.

"I don't know the story," said Edward.

"It's from King Arthur," said Effie. "Viviane was an evil young sorceress who apprenticed herself to Merlin and cast a spell on him to make him fall in love with her. Then she trapped him inside a tree and kept his book of magic all to herself."

No fool like an old fool, thought Edward, studying the wizard's regretful, stupefied face. It was the face of an ascetic sensualist who, once having broken his own discipline, would yield again despite knowing the costs.

"Funny," said Effie, with a frown. "He doesn't look like Merlin. He isn't old enough—just middle-aged."

Frizzy wisps of unkempt gray hair escaped from under the figure's turban. "To her, he must seem very old," said Edward.

"But Merlin should have a beard."

Jeanette squirmed at Cousin Effie's obtuseness. "Notice how the white hawthorn flowers clustering around his head are open," she pointed out as civilly as she could. "They surround his face with a kind of hoariness, like the traditional hair and beard of an old man, but the buds and blossoms around hers are only half opened. That's a good symbolic touch."

"She hasn't triumphed over him yet," said Effie. "She's still half afraid."

"Angry, too," mused Jeanette. "It makes you wonder whether she loved him at least a little."

"Cornelia," said Edward, a week later when he called on Mrs. Renick once more before leaving Paris, "I want you to look after Miss Palmer and Miss Pendergrast."

"Have you seen them again, my dear? It was so sweet of you to take them home."

Edward told her about the visit to the World's Fair. The three of them had enjoyed it so much that he had taken them and Eddie to the Cirque Fernando on Montmartre.

"A very different wooden O from Shakespeare's Globe, I hear!" laughed Cornelia. "Is it really built in the shape of a circus tent?"

"It is, and painted gaudy colors. The French should be told about boiled peanuts."

"And did Mlle. La La hang by her teeth from the trapeze?"

"She did."

"Oh, Edward!" exclaimed Cornelia, clapping her hands together, "why didn't you take *me*?"

"It never occurred to me that you hadn't gone. An equestrienne like you should see the riding. Why hasn't Marius taken you and the children?"

"Oh, Marius is the dearest man in the world, but he has no taste for anything vulgar. And, of course, it would be impossible for me right now—but I'm going to ride again, Edward, I am, and walk all over the place. It's too tiresome being hobbled. What I need is an extra pair of hands and feet—what do you think of Effie Pendergrast, besides as an object of your most darling charity?"

"I think she's very sensible, Cornelia," said Edward, although it was clear from the way he said it that other people might disagree.

"Just what I thought, too! I can see her becoming indispensable. But what about her charge, Sarah Palmer's Jeanette?"

A gleam came into Edward's eye. "At the Palais du Trocadéro, when we came to the statue of the elephant—"

"Our little artistic know-it-all told you it was no good."

"No! It isn't any good, by the way, not compared to my rhinoceros. No, what she told me was about the time a circus came to Circleville. She and her sisters climbed out onto the roof of their house so they could watch with field glasses while the elephant was being given a bath at the racetrack."

"And you remembered the time we went down to the wharves and sneaked onto the showboat to watch the horse act rehearse," cried Cornelia, clapping her hand and whooping.

"You'd like her, Cornelia, she's a girl after your own heart."

"Well then, my dear, maybe we should let her into the club." Maybe, she thought, you already have.

CHAPTER FIFTEEN

Paris in Summer

Ten days after the party, Mrs. Renick invited Effie for morning coffee. "Oh, my," said Effie. Jeanette was relieved; at least she had not spoiled everything.

When Effie arrived at the Rue de Varenne, Hastings showed her up immediately to where Cornelia was positioned on a chaise longue in an informal sitting room, if any room hung with an eighteenth-century pastoral tapestry and carpeted with a twelve-foot Savonnerie carpet could be called informal.

"Oh, how kind of you to come, Miss Pendergrast. A quiet little tête-à-tête is just what I need this morning to rescue me from fretting over this silly piece of needlepoint. Either I'm cross-eyed or it's askew." She set the embroidery aside. "Do sit down. I call this room my Poutery. Did you know that *boudoir* comes from the French word for pouting? Well, it does—so like the French, so wise, to have a room where a woman may withdraw to sulk in peace. But I'd much rather talk than pout."

"May I see your work?" asked Effie, who was itching to get her hands on it.

Cornelia had guessed she would be and handed it over (in her experience, there was nothing like an opportunity to give advice to break down social inhibitions). "It's the rabbit's head. Doesn't it look wrong?"

Effie's fingers moved rapidly and her tongue clicked. "It's an extra stitch on this row that's throwing off the developing pattern," she said. "Would you like me to rip out for you? My cousin Maude Hendrick always has me do it; she finds ripping tiresome."

"It is, so I wouldn't dream of asking a guest to do it." Cornelia took the work back and hid it. "Instead you must tell me how you are occupying yourself in Paris."

Effie described spending mornings at Galignani's reading room and investigating shops and department stores. What gave most shape to her days, she said, was the McAll Mission, where she had agreed to teach English in a class for little girls to make them more employable. She also helped set up halls for prayer meetings and expected soon to receive an assignment in a neighborhood health clinic. To Cornelia, the mission work sounded dismal, but it confirmed her hunch about Effie's abilities. The next week, she invited her again for morning coffee and did not deceive herself that she was being charitable.

For a while, Effie continued to accompany Jeanette to and from Julian's; but the streets were well policed, and after Jeanette discovered that another American in her class lived nearby, Effie left them to themselves. They were sometimes joined on the walk by a Polish woman named Sonja Borealska, who lived farther south on the edges of Montparnasse and painted in the class for the full nude.

Sonja was in her midtwenties, tall, big-boned, and forceful. Her clothes were the most disgraceful of anyone's in the school, and many students tiptoed around her on account of her temper; but she and Amy Richardson were friends. Miss Richardson had introduced Jeanette to her one day when they all happened to run into each other in the *passage*. "Sonja Borealska has a real future," she said, afterward. "Quite worth getting to know." And Effie unexpectedly liked her—probably, thought Jeanette, because in addition to her native Polish, Sonja spoke English (as well as French, German, Italian, and, so everyone said, Russian, though she would not admit to it).

Walking with other students pulled Jeanette deeper into school gossip and caused the world outside Julian's to dwindle in importance to her. Although she still checked the mail every day hoping for letters, news from Circleville and Vassar came to seem very far away. Her own weekly letters home were filled with school anecdotes and marginal drawings of what she saw around her. The need early on to admit that she had been assigned to draw instead of paint had been embarrassing, but she quoted Miss Richardson on how everyone else at Julian's expected to spend at least two years drawing. *Some professional painters even come back for a month of practice from time to time,* she wrote. *I guess I'm a very small frog in a very large pond.* After that, she strove always to write in a happy, confident tone and impress the folks back home with her sophistication (her account of the dinner party was a masterpiece of judicious selection).

It genuinely helped her morale that Emily Dolson also worked with pencil, not brush. As so often happens after a first accidental placement, they continued to set up next to each other at the beginning of each week. Emily had little standing among the other students; her circumscribed work inspired no emulation, and she was not gregarious. Nevertheless, Miss Richardson occasionally set up on Emily's other side with the familiarity of a friend. When Jeanette asked how long they had known each other, Emily said, vaguely, "My brother and I met her when we came to Paris a couple of years ago."

As a spell of hot, dry weather set in late in June, the fourth-floor studio grew stifling. By noon, the streets below felt blessedly cool in comparison. Jeanette and Emily took to walking a few blocks south at midday to a public garden at the Place Louvois, where water cascaded in a fountain. *It's one of the civilized features of French life*, Jeanette wrote home, *that you can eat your bread and cheese on a park bench and nobody thinks the worse of you.*

One day, when Miss Richardson was along, Jeanette spotted strawberries at a fruitier's stand.

"We grow those at home, and I haven't seen any since I left Ohio! My treat."

"They cost a fortune."

"Just this once, Miss Richardson. They won't get any cheaper."

"Then I'll buy a pot of crème fraîche, and do call me Amy outside class. If we're going to dip into the same jar, we'd better be on first-name terms."

Later, when they had eaten, she said to Emily, "You're still as flushed as the berries, my girl. It's too hot. Why don't you take the afternoon off? You can work this evening when it's cooler."

Emily sat wilted against the back of the bench. "Evenings," she murmured, keeping her eyes on the fountain, "that reminds me—

would either of you be interested in getting up an informal anatomy class?"

"Sorry, not I," said Amy. "I'm working with Sonja Borealska on sculpture."

"Well, I would," said Jeanette. "Does this mean your brother's medical-student friend, the one with the skeleton, is willing to take us on?"

Emily nodded. "His name is William Winkham, and he has a problem about housing just now—only temporary, but he needs a place to store the skeleton. He offered to give us lessons in exchange for a place to put it. Robbie is willing, but only if there is at least one other girl to make it proper."

"Robbie?" said Amy. "Offering to house a skeleton and turn home sweet home into a teaching studio?"

"No-o-o," said Emily, "not exactly. He isn't keen on cluttering up the sitting room with a skeleton or having girls underfoot. Not that he's ever really home in the evening."

"Just as I thought. Colossally selfish, that brother of yours, like all good-looking men."

It was a line that Jeanette thought her cousin Adeline would appreciate, but it was all too clear that Emily did not. "What about our room?" she proposed. "We've got a worktable and an alcove where the skeleton could stand, and we face south, so it's light well into the evening. Of course, it's hot."

"Everywhere is," said Emily, her face beaming with gratitude. "It could be ideal."

Ideal, it was not. With better ventilation than the studio, the room on the Rue Jacob cooled off overnight and was generally pleasant by morning; but that evening when Jeanette got home, it was airless. Effie's black dress clung to her back.

"A skeleton? Oh, I don't know," she said. "What will Bootsie?—well, more important what will Mme. LeConte—? We must ask her first."

"Can't. I've already made the arrangements. They're coming tonight."

At eight, prickly with the heat and on the defensive, Jeanette went down to the courtyard to greet her guests. A short, intense man in a flat cloth cap carried something like a hat rack trussed under canvas. With him were Emily and another man, tall and languid, who must be Robert Dolson. The resemblance between brother and sister was unmistakable—though how cruel of Nature to make him so handsome and her so shy! In an evening coat from a previous generation and a much-brushed beige top hat worn at a tilt, Robbie Dolson strolled as if he owned the world. Emily must have accepted his opinion, for Jeanette had never seen her happier.

"For one of my stripe to be servant to a ministering angel sits strangely, Miss Palmer," said Mr. Dolson, with a bow and a flourish of the topper, "but so you find my unworthy self—at your service."

"I'm being selfish," laughed Jeanette. "It's very good of Mr. Winkham to give us lessons."

Before they could enter the house, however, Mme. LeConte appeared in the door of the *portière*'s office to demand what was going on. Jeanette tried to explain. Mme. LeConte frowned skeptically: The premises had no license as a teaching establishment; the other tenants must not be incommoded. She pulled aside an overlap in the canvas. *Non, absolument pas!* she shrieked. What could *mademoiselle* be thinking? This was a decent house. M. Mort must be removed immediately.

"You don't mean to say you never tipped Cerberus first? No wine-soaked sops, no coin?" muttered Mr. Dolson in Jeanette's ear. "Well, you are the tyro, aren't you?"

Jeanette burned at the sarcasm.

"What am I to do now?" fretted Mr. Winkham. "Look, Dolson, if only for tonight, couldn't you—?"

"No, Winkie lad, sorry; I've told you. Oh, but see here, there must be a way. Come along, Miss Palmer, introduce me to your three-headed dog. Bound to be a closet or cupboard we can commandeer. M. Mort, she called him? Very well, Mortimer shall be housed."

With all the ease and arrogance of a young milord, but in fluent French, he apologized for the inconvenience, complimented Mme. LeConte on her house, and worked his way around to the subject of broom closets. Mentioning a consideration, he held a hand open behind his back. Mr. Winkham sighed and slipped him a franc. With little more wheedling, Mme. LeConte agreed to hold the abomination overnight.

Anatomy lessons might have ended right there had it not been for Sonja. The next day, after Jeanette had recounted the previous night's debacle during the walk to Julian's, Sonja followed her up the stairs on the Rue Vivienne.

"Amy, *ma chérie*, we change courses," she announced. "A skeleton in my own studio? It is too good to refuse. We shall show the Countess that she is not alone in obtaining such a treasure. You and I, we model in clay from bones—from bones! Emily and Jeanette draw. Maybe, this Mr. Winkham, he will allow me to cast the skull." She fingered the air. "Oh, I cannot wait to touch over its contours."

Sonja's studio was an ancient shed in a squalid yard reached through a series of connecting yards off the Boulevard du Montparnasse. Its original purpose was forgotten. Some years back, the current owner had salvaged glass from an industrial exhibition, knocked holes in the walls of a warren of workshops and two-story warehouses, and, after installing windows along with a few furnishings, rented out spaces to artists as studios. Sonja's was the most dilapidated: The stucco had broken off most of its soft, old bricks; the roof leaked at one end; the wind, whistling through cracks at the windows and doors, was a trial in winter. But it was her own; it was cheap; and she cherished a disheveled, squat willow beside it that a basket weaver had once kept pollarded.

"If there is a willow, there must be a hidden spring," observed Robbie Dolson, the next evening. He and Mr. Winkham had retrieved the skeleton from Mme. LeConte and brought it around with Jeanette, Emily, and Effie.

"True," said Sonja, from her doorway. Her honey-blond hair was swept up carelessly. Her sculptor's smock, stained red with clay, did not hide that she wore loose trousers. Her feet were in clogs. "It is why the floor stays damp."

"And why," said Mr. Dolson, "a trickle perpetually oozes down that noisome gutter, I suppose. Good lord, have Haussmann's sewers not reached this far?" A shallow depression, unevenly bricked, carried runoff from one yard to the next; it did not bear close investigation. "Really, Emily, I don't think you should—"

"Please, Robbie, it's just for a few weeks."

Emily so seldom contradicted him that Robbie Dolson lifted his eyebrows questioningly. Her look was beseeching. He patted her arm. "Well, Wee Willie, what do you say? Are the girls safe?"

"Barring an outbreak of cholera."

Dolson stared at Mr. Winkham for a moment, then burst out laughing. He saw that the joke was on him, and it transformed his face. There were amber lights in his gray-green eyes. Sonja, however, glared belligerently, as though she, too, were having second thoughts—in her case about admitting them into her domain.

"I say. That starry-crowned Minerva above you," said Robbie, at sight of a fragment of glazed ceramic bas-relief, perched at a slant on a ledge over the door. "Where on earth did you find it?"

"In the weeds."

"Here? Marvelous! We must have a treasure hunt some day. She's quite fitting, you know—patroness of arts and trades."

"We do know; and we are also quite up on Diana, Proserpine, and Juno," said a new voice.

"And Hecate, Miss Richardson—Medusa? Winkie, my lad, these are sacred precincts from which my unhallowed masculine feet had best be off. Since yours remain, be good. Miss Pendergrast, keep an eye on this fellow." Effie, who had effaced herself as usual in the presence of a forceful man, giggled in delighted alarm. "Mlle. Borealska, your servant.

"I'll be back for you at nine," Robbie added to Emily, in a solicitous undertone. He bowed slightly to Jeanette, glanced a challenge to Amy Richardson, and left without a backward look.

Sonja gestured for the rest of them to enter and grabbed up the stand, which she carried one-handed at a tilt like a lance. "Mind the step."

"Mind my skeleton!" said Mr. Winkham.

If the stone floor did not exactly weep moisture as Sonja had implied, it did have a cool luster, except where it was topped by runners of straw matting. There were bricks and planks stacked against the walls for building catwalks in the wetter months, and rough bins to store canvases sat permanently on wooden pallets six inches off the ground. Sonja led the way to the north end of the shed, where a wide double window and a skylight let in the summer evening sun. She set down the skeleton beside a couple of wooden crates for Jeanette and Emily to use as stools. Nearby, on a heavy, tarpaulin-covered table, stood two lumps, wrapped in damp towels.

Cousin Effie, who had straggled behind the rest, studying sketches pinned to more straw matting on the walls, picked up a linen strip as though to begin unwinding it. "May we peek?"

Jeanette hissed a wordless warning to her to put it down. Too late: Sonja had seen. Yet something in Effie's undisguised curiosity amused Sonja.

"Why not? But let me." The fingers of Sonja's big, strong hands worked delicately to remove the wet toweling without disturbing what was underneath.

"You have the hands of a surgeon," said Winkham. "Ah, no," he emended, as a portrait bust of Amy Richardson emerged. Even in its highly unfinished state, a mercurial flash was discernible in the face as though something had just caught the sitter's eye. "You have the hands of a genius."

On evenings when Mr. Winkham was free to give a lesson, Jeanette and Effie met him and the Dolsons at the Luxembourg Garden after a six o'clock dinner for the walk to Sonja's studio, where Amy would already have shared supper with Sonja. Robbie Dolson seldom accompanied the group farther than the park gate at the Rue d'Assas, but when he did, he monopolized conversation. Robbie was a writer, at work on some mysterious magnum opus of undisclosed scope and genre, who in the meantime supplemented a meager inherited income with freelance articles on Parisian life for the popular London press. Although he kept Emily on his arm, he seemed to enjoy making Jeanette laugh, and she was more than ready to listen to his gossip from the *beau monde* or a café where daring poetry was read and incendiary, scabrous songs sung.

Mr. Winkham had ambitions to lecture on medicine as well as become a practicing physician. It was his conviction that workmen's institutes in London could do much to combat vice and disease by teaching the poor to understand their bodies and honor how nobly and intricately they were made. He had jumped at the chance not only to house his skeleton for a few weeks but to try out his skills as a teacher. He was happy to begin by explaining how bones and muscles worked if that was what the ladies wanted. Entrails, too, he thought important—how could they portray the body cavity if they had no notion of what was at work inside? (They voted him down.)

They started by measuring individual bones and worked out ratios. They twisted Mortimer into different positions and thumbed through a textbook Mr. Winkham brought along to clarify his explanations with engravings. Exhilarated by having Mortimer at her disposal, Sonja disappeared from her painting class for a few days at the beginning of July. When the others next arrived one night, they found all twenty-odd bones of the left foot and ankle laid out neatly on the table.

"What have you done?" demanded Mr. Winkham, angrily.

"Posed a practical problem for the evening's lesson."

"But it's all in pieces!"

"With the other foot intact as a model. Here I have beautiful copper wire, very pliable," said Sonja. "We shall reassemble the foot, bone by bone. I promise, the foot will safely articulate each natural movement."

"That may well be, Mlle. Borealska, but you never asked permission!"

"Sonja," Amy said, "I regret to say it was just like you to disassemble someone else's property without asking. Nevertheless, Mr. Winkham, wouldn't you say now that the best thing all around is to put Humpty Dumpty back together again?"

"Death's left foot lay a-lying on the table," sang Jeanette.

> *a-lying on the table,*
> *a-lying on the table.*
> *Dear Wee Willie, we are willing now and able*
> *to put him right again.*

Mr. Winkham turned on her furiously. "This is not some silly girl's school!"

Jeanette winced.

"Winkie," said Emily, with conciliating softness, "it will be all right. We won't leave until it's all put back together. Sonja really is very good with her hands."

Mr. Winkham swallowed his anger as if he knew he must accede. "Very well, ladies, start with the toes. There's one for each of us," he said, curtly. "Pick up a distal phalanx. I see, by the way, Mlle. Borealska, that you have laid everything out with taxonomic precision."

"Naturally. This is a scientific demonstration, not a parlor game."

"The devil it is."

Later, when she had a chance, Jeanette said, "I should not have called you Wee Willie, Mr. Winkham. I'm sorry. You don't like that nickname, do you?"

"No," replied Mr. Winkham, disarmed by her forthrightness, "Of course, with a name like mine—William Winkham? I ask you. And me being short—well, inevitable, I suppose. It's all right coming from Dolson, but—" He broke off. "I don't mind plain Winkie so much: We all got stuck with something—Dolson was Dolly at school."

"He wasn't!"

"He was."

"Do you ever call him that?"

"Not often."

Somehow their brief conversation put the two of them on a different footing, more trusting, more confidential. Jeanette came to think of him as Winkie, a friend, and not merely an appendage of the Dolsons.

"Oh, he's worth a dozen Robbie Dolsons," agreed Amy, when Jeanette said something about him later, "not that it will ever do him any good."

"What do you mean?"

Amy hesitated before answering. "Maybe that some people are born to be taken advantage of, that's all."

As August approached, talk turned one night to where it would be best to spend the month.

"All of Paris empties," Amy explained.

"More likely it'll be stuffed to the gills," said Jeanette, "what with the World's Fair and all."

"Tourists don't count."

Even Sonja was locking her door behind her and decamping. "I go to Italy."

"Italy! In August? You can't," said Amy. "It will be boiling hot, and pestilential. It will make Paris seem like the Arctic by comparison. You'll catch Roman fever. Nobody goes to Italy in August."

"Thus it will be cheap. Somnolent peasants will pose without knowing it, and no bustling Englishmen to spoil the view."

"It's the sun will spoil the view, my girl. Glaring down white and reflecting off every surface. Even under an umbrella, you'll have to squint to see a thing. Impossible to paint."

"Where are you going, Amy?" asked Jeanette.

"Back to Brittany, of course. I must have the sea for at least part of the year, you know."

"Artists congregate in Brittany more thickly than in Julian's ateliers," said Sonja to Jeanette and Emily. "Gray studies of gray beaches and low, gray waves rolling up onto the gray shore. A stalwart woman with her sturdy back to us peers out to sea, dressed in drab olive—"

Amy threw a balled-up muddy rag at her.

"Robbie wants us to go walking in Switzerland," said Emily. Mr. Winkham looked around at her sharply.

"Do you?" asked Amy.

"It's sure to be sublime," said Emily, without sounding convinced.

"Sublime is forty years out of date and exhausted by Turner," said Amy.

"Are you sure you have the strength for mountain climbing?" asked Mr. Winkham.

"I must, Winkie, or I'll slow Robbie down," said Emily. "If I don't go, neither can he."

"Why not?" asked Jeanette.

"Because he has to look after me," said Emily, as though it were obvious. "I couldn't stay in Paris by myself."

"You *could*," said Amy, who lived alone, "or you could go visit cousins back home in England."

"There aren't any we haven't quarreled with."

"What about coming somewhere with Cousin Effie and me?" asked Jeanette. "We could get up a ladies' party. What do you say, Cousin Effie?"

"My, it would be good to get out of this heat. A city is always hot at the end of summer; you have no idea what New York can be like."

"Amy, how expensive is Brittany?"

"It all depends. Pont Aven, where I'm planning to be, is not bad, and the farther inland you go, the cheaper the lodgings."

"Could the three of us get a cottage?" asked Jeanette.

"Detached? Maybe. More likely rooms to let in a farmhouse."

"You girls could go sketching and I could keep house," said Effie, wistfully. Her voice gained strength as the beauties of the plan revealed themselves to her. "And, then Mr. Winkham, *you* could go hiking with Mr. Dolson! Anyone can see you're particular friends." Winkie opened his mouth to say something, but Effie prevented him. "It would do you both good—fresh air, manly company. Miss Richardson, if you come in with us, too, and share the rent, it won't cost a thing. Do you suppose we can find a place with a goat? I've always wanted a goat, such sweet faces, though not a billy; they smell."

"A goat is not guaranteed in Brittany, Miss Pendergrast, but all too likely," said Amy. "There would certainly be barnyard fowl pecking at the door."

"Which would mean fresh eggs!"

"It was just an idea," said Jeanette, alarmed to see Cousin Effie's tether slipping loose.

"But a jolly good one," said Amy. "Let's give it some thought."

"Oh, there's no need to think," said Effie. "I always find that when the right idea pops up, the decision has already been made."

CHAPTER SIXTEEN

Going Down to Brittany

I don't think Amy was glad that Emily's brother rode down with us to see her settled, Jeanette wrote home in a letter about the party's train trip to Brittany, *but honestly he was a big help. He did things like lift everybody's overnight gear into the luggage racks, and at stops, he fetched refreshments. All day long, it was the funniest thing how he kept pulling maps and books out of his pockets.*

Robbie Dolson could discourse on a wide range of topics, but he could also listen when he chose. He questioned Jeanette on life in small-town Ohio as if she had come from somewhere as remote and bizarre as the outback of Australia, with opossums for kangaroos.

"You certainly needn't travel to Pont Aven for the picturesque," he said. "Why ever did you come to France at all?"

"To learn to paint what I see, of course!—and what I think."

"Now, that is very interesting—though a word of advice: Spend no more than a year or two at Julian's, or you'll lose your originality."

"Hear that, Emily?" said Amy, without looking up from her book.

"Emily's originality is irreducible," said Robbie. He leaned back, stretched out his legs, and closed his eyes.

Dismissed! thought Jeanette. Yet later, while the others were dozing, Robbie looked across at her. "Originality is the very deuce," he mused, as though there had been no interruption in their conversation. "It's all that matters in the end, all that wins one a place in history, but you never know whether your glittering brightness is the real thing or fool's gold. As true for us writers as for you painters. Why do you suppose we do it?"

"Because if we don't, we'll always be wishing we were," said Jeanette.

"It's certainly the only way to be with people who halfway understand. Not that most of one's acquaintances don't turn out to be lackwits or drones."

"I feel guilty saying it, but do you know something? When I went to the World's Fair and saw all those hundreds of contemporary paintings, after a while they began to look alike. Not the subject matter, of course, but technically."

"Subject matter, too. They run in herds."

Jeanette grimaced. "What's worse is how you sometimes get fooled into thinking they are realistic when they're not true to life at all. The funny thing is, here I am trying to acquire those very same skills and practicing on all the same subjects."

"Strange girl to be so candid."

The women had decided to wait until they reached Brittany before breaking the trip. It was six o'clock when they reached the hill town of Vitré, where Amy had reserved a couple of rooms. Everyone was tired; the sky was overcast—not heavy with storm, but low enough to make gray stone buildings and timbered gables more glum than quaint. Against such a sky, the half-ruined castle high on a precipice remained gloomily romantic, but what Jeanette really wanted was a hot meal.

At their hotel, a small one on a side street, the landlady regretted that her house was almost full. Perhaps if *monsieur* would accept a small room under the roof? He would.

"I have a view of the castle!" Robbie reported, when they gathered again downstairs. "Well, a view of a bit of the tower. If I lie prone across the foot of the bed, I can see it out a window under the eaves.

If someone were signaling with a lantern up there, I'm sure I'd know it. The room must usually go to pirates, smugglers, or spies."

Amy cut short his description. "Let's eat," she said.

Next day, Jeanette woke up early, very early, to a hint of dawn where the shutters were slightly ajar. Slowly and carefully, she peeled back the covers so as not to disturb Cousin Effie and tiptoed to the window. It must have rained overnight, for the world smelled wet; overhead the pale sky was clear. She slipped into clothes—at dawn the stealthy spy crept forth, she thought, smiling to herself.

In deep shadows below overhanging gables, a steep, crooked street climbed to an open square where a moss-furred, utilitarian fountain trickled. As Jeanette approached, the first sunbeam touched it. Mist floated off tiny bracts. She paused, captivated by the miniature world of sunlight, green growth, and water particles. A few yards away, a flock of sparrows, twittering softly, popped out one after another from a heavily branched vine surrounding a door. Taking fright, they disappeared into the leaves again, diving with a beat of wings. As she walked on, she tried to take in everything—the sound of a dog barking, cooking smells, dark crimson dabs of geranium petals in window boxes. At the top of the hill, she leaned on a wall to look over pitched roofs and chimney pots down to the sheen of the river Vilaine where it reflected the sunrise. Narrowing her eyes to reduce visible detail to abstraction, she analyzed the scene into simple areas of light, medium, and dark. If she expanded the range of tones to five—white, ash, medium gray, charcoal, black—how much would that help? In this light, not much. Next, what was most important in what she could see? What would Mr. Dolson call an original view? Straightening up, she made a circle of her thumb and forefinger to frame compositions. After weeks of focusing only on the human body, it was liberating to embrace the larger world.

A memory of Effie's Dr. Murer floated across her mind. They had been looking at landscapes in the Russian galleries at the World's Fair. "After this, if I never go to Russia, I'll still feel like I've been on the steppes," he had said, with a quiet conviction that moved her. He was nice. She had the feeling he was the sort of man who would know what mattered even if she could not have said what she meant by that.

The journey by rail on the second day was less than half the length of the first; but at Quimperlé, they had to wait from noon until six thirty for the horse-drawn diligence, which would take another four hours to reach Pont Aven. The good news, said Amy, was that it would deliver them to the very doorstep of the Hôtel des Voyageurs, where they had rooms reserved for their first night.

In Quimperlé, Amy proposed that they stroll around the market to pick up a picnic supper to eat along the way. "The diligence shakes, but the road is surprisingly good."

"One up to Napoleon III," said Robbie. "However tinselly and factitious the late emperor's reign may have been, he understood roads."

"Marius Renick helped finance the gravel crushing," said Effie.

"Good lord, Miss Pendergrast, the journalist's bonanza," said Robbie, as he took her by the elbow.

Amy drew Jeanette aside and fell back a few paces. "Are you two actually acquainted with Marius Renick?"

"A little. Mrs. Renick had us to dinner when we first arrived in Paris—my parents know her brother back in Ohio." Jeanette was not about to go into the details of that horrible night. "She's taken to inviting Cousin Effie for morning coffee."

"You do know that they have one of the best private art collections in Paris."

"No, I didn't! I mean, there are Watteau panels in the dining room, but I thought they belonged to the house, and some gorgeous modern things in the salon. I did notice those."

"Yes, and bless your compatriots for buying from living artists. Not everyone does. She collects artists themselves, too, by the way, everyone from painters to actors to writers."

"I sat next to Hippolyte Grandcourt at dinner," said Jeanette, unable to resist the pleasure of name-dropping.

"Did you, indeed. Lucky girl," said Amy. "Well, in addition to whatever they display as decorations, there is reputed to be a gallery well worth the visit if ever you are asked. And if you are, and if you are invited to bring a friend, do remember who told you about it."

In the diligence, Jeanette sat by the window and watched as the long summer's evening waned. Conversation flagged. A golden haze spread like a thin varnish over a slanting heathland and hovered in the air, brightest where it was closest to the ground; it made the shadows more, not less, impenetrable. Scattered sheep, their backs dirty and nubbly, were virtually indistinguishable from the coarse heather and broom. If there was a farmhouse tucked in somewhere out of the wind, no gleam of oil lamp nor trace of smoke betrayed it.

"I don't think I've ever been anywhere so remote," she said, dreamily.

"That cannot be true, Miss Palmer," said Robbie, without opening his eyes. "America is the land of wide, open spaces and trackless wastes. You can't fool me."

"It's not just distance; it's something about emptiness and secrecy and time," said Jeanette. "This is an old landscape."

"Druids," said Effie.

"Very poetical," said Robbie, still with his eyes closed.

Sunset faded into the late, northern dusk. Dusk deepened to a summer's night of pale stars. The passengers, including Jeanette, nodded off.

A rattling plunge jerked her awake as the coach pitched into a steep declivity. Louder than hoofbeats and the creaks of the vehicle as it strained against its brakes came the tumult of a river in a rocky course. "Thank God," said Amy, "we must be starting down Toullifo Hill. That will be the Aven you hear. We drop plumb into Pont Aven."

The coach clattered down between two stacked rows of houses and into the main square, which, despite the hour, was peopled with shadowy knots of villagers—men here, women there, their hands busy with knitting and their winged Breton coiffes like giant white moths in the darkness. Outside the Hôtel des Voyageurs, men sat at little tables, men in straw hats or berets. Their corduroy smoking jackets and velveteen waistcoats showed faintly brown in the light of two oil lanterns: the artists "thick on the ground" against whom Sonja had railed.

From the doorway, a magisterial woman in kerchief and coiffe bent to say something to a guitarist on a bench against the wall. He laughed and struck a chord. As Robbie jumped out of the coach to hand down each of their party, the guitarist strummed insistently faster and faster, louder and louder. Robbie lifted Jeanette's hand in sportive exaggeration. Saucily pointing her toe, she sprang down lightly with a twitch of her shoulder. The next instant, she felt a fool when he helped Emily down gravely. Jeanette stepped to one side but stood with her chin up, still hoping she looked pretty. After a final chord, the guitarist thumped out a hollow rhythm with his fingers on the wood. "Miss Richardson!" called an American who stood talking to someone at the nearest table.

"Charlie Post, as I live! Don't tell me Rag-Tag and Bobtail are back, too. Nobody warned me you lot were coming."

"Where else would any of us be in summer, Miss R? I'm at the Gloanec. Regular supper and drink for me, thanks, and stagger up to bed on the premises. Ragland and Nagg, with their dour Presbyterian views on liquor, took a shanty below the quay. I've got my big canvas in their shed. Dolson, what brings your disreputable carcass this way?" Mr. Post, a sandy-haired American of about thirty, looked inquisitively at Emily. "That's not the famously guarded family jewel, is it?"

"Don't be offensive, Post," said Robbie, coldly, and made no introduction.

"Do I detect a midsummer frost?" asked Mr. Post, raising his eyes to the sky and holding out his hands palms upward. "Weather may be warmer a bit south; I'll be off."

"Who was that?" asked Jeanette, as soon as he was out of earshot.

"A most dissolute beast," said Amy, though clearly she liked him. "Mr. Dolson for once is right. Miss Pendergrast, you must flap your apron and shoo Post away if he ever comes sniffing at our door. But he has an enviable talent for rendering water and wet surfaces."

"Chic tricks," said Robbie. Then, as though sparring with Amy were not worth the trouble, he slipped Emily over to Effie's side. "Excuse me. Must circulate if I'm not to sleep on the ground." He sauntered over to an acquaintance as if to prove that this was his world as much as Amy's, in which claim the smell from little glasses of curaçao and absinthe concurred.

Mlle. Julia, as the landlady was universally called, greeted Amy and led them inside. She did not mind that Amy's party was looking for cheaper lodgings this year; she had no trouble filling her rooms, and the more the artistic community thought of the Voyageurs as its center, the better for business. She suggested a farm that had, in the past, provided a meal and a bed to travelers on the old highway west to Concarneau. Little traffic used the road any more, and she thought that Mme. Gernagan would be happy to let a couple of rooms for the month. Meanwhile, they must partake of a late supper in the common room before bed.

"Well, that was easy," said Robbie, coming in behind them. He swung a leg over to sit on the bench next to Emily. "Found a bunk."

"We may have found a place for the month, too," said Emily, and told him about the farm.

"Oh, no, it won't do at all," said Robbie. "I know the sort of place.

There will be a loft upstairs under the eaves with three wide beds and everyone sharing, including the passing drover. Still, you must go see it for local color."

"We shall certainly go," said Amy.

"Whereupon you will see what I mean, Miss Richardson."

The next morning, Jeanette had to admit to herself that she hoped Robbie Dolson would not turn up before they had seen the Gernagan farm; but just as they set out, he did, tousled and much in need of a cup of coffee. A quarter of an hour later, they headed west over the main bridge beyond the market square. Outside town, the road sank between banks deeply shaded by old oak trees until it came out onto open land that tilted toward the sea in long slopes. They found a roadside shrine they had been told to watch for and soon drew alongside a walled farmyard where a cart gate was open.

"Entry through straw and manure," said Robbie.

"We'll try the front," said Amy, unlatching a gate in the wall. Its hinges were rusty, but it opened. A flagstoned footpath ran up to the front of the house, where a thick rose vine was trained over the front door.

"How pretty!" exclaimed Effie.

There was no knocker. Robbie beat his fist on the heavy wooden door. No one answered.

"Try again," murmured Emily.

When still no one answered, Robbie said, "Too bad," and turned to leave.

Effie was about to follow submissively, when Jeanette insisted, "We should try around back."

"This way," said Amy, and took the lead.

Around the corner in an older wing of the house that faced the service yard, the upper half of a kitchen door stood open. From inside came a woman's voice singing and the smell of packed earth, wood smoke, and something Jeanette could not quite identify. She sniffed: vinegary old apples. Amy tugged the rope of a thick brass bell. At its clang, a plain young woman in ordinary clothes with a baby in her arms appeared at the door. Amy explained their errand. The woman introduced herself as Mme. Gernagan; she would be happy to show them rooms. When she opened the lower half of the door, they saw a toddler holding on to her apron skirt.

"*Bonjour*, tot," said Amy, in a friendly, matter-of-fact way, and lightly tapped the top of the child's head. At once, he leaned harder against his mother, chewing a ball of the apron.

Inside, it was clear that the family lived, ate, worked, and slept in the kitchen. The first thing to catch Jeanette's eye was a fire burning even in summer; but as her eyes adjusted to the dimness of the room, she saw an enormous, intricately carved box bed with three tiers of bunks. Near it in a wooden chair sat a tiny, very old woman in Breton dress, from a spotlessly white winged coiffe and earrings down to gray socked feet that would slip into sabots when she rose. Gazing at the newcomers intently, she spoke in Breton to Mme. Gernagan. Jeanette thought a weariness came into Mme. Gernagan's face as she respectfully hushed her what—her mother, mother-in-law? More likely her grandmother-in-law. Mme. Gernagan said something more, and the old woman slapped her knees. The little boy ran to her.

Beyond the box bed, deep in shadow, a steep stair led upward. In the loft, explained Mme. Gernagan, shifting the baby to her hip, were beds that had always harbored foot travelers. One corner of Robbie's mouth lifted into a told-you-so sneer. "*Mais, suivez-moi, s'il-vous plaît.*"

Amy shot him a glance: So there.

Mme. Gernagan led them into the newer wing's sitting room, where stout furniture and several crackled but still colorful pieces of Quimper ware spoke of considerable peasant prosperity once upon a time. Use of the room would be included in the rent, and the neglected front door, which opened into it, would give the tenants a separate entrance. The party clumped up a bare wooden staircase directly into a bedroom out of which opened a second; they were furnished with plain iron bedsteads and simple wooden chests and chairs. The larger bedroom, through which the chimney ran, had a fireplace; the ladies could have a charcoal brazier there if they wished to do their own simple cooking. It also contained a very steep staircase into an attic under the eaves. While Amy discussed the practical arrangements and terms, Jeanette climbed high enough to peek into the attic. It had a fully planked floor and was largely empty.

"Take a look," she said, coming back down. "I think we could use this space if anybody needs privacy."

"In fact," said Amy, who took her place on the ladder, "if we move two mattresses upstairs and take apart the bedsteads, we can clear out the big sunny room for a studio."

"Rot," interposed Robbie Dolson. "Emily, you can't stay here. Think of the sort of traveler who might stop on the other side of the wall."

"Looser morals among your chums at the Voyageurs and Gloanec than here, Mr. Dolson," said Amy.

"It's quite a solid wall, and I doubt anyone will come," said Emily in a soothing voice.

"Oh, my, just look at that garden!" said Cousin Effie.

Jeanette joined her at the window. A back garden was enclosed by the wings of the house and stone walls. Directly below were cutting beds. Knobby hollyhocks climbed hand over hand up spires; beside them marched regiments of gladiolus with triangular pennants of cream, peach, and red. Next came rows of zinnias and dahlias, hot golden marigolds, abundant pink mallows, and a few frothy stocks still holding on at season's end. Beyond the flowers and easily reached from a kitchen door was a potager laid out in onions, cabbages, lettuce, and herbs. Farther still, outside the back wall, an orchard of fruit trees grew on the lower slope of a steep hill that would hold the afternoon sun.

"Oh, Robbie, it's my motif," said Emily.

Amy came over and peeked between them. "Not to mention fresh salad straight from the garden and milk pure from the cow. Just what you need, Emily, to buck you up."

"Mr. Dolson, do come look," said Jeanette, turning to him.

"You can't be deserting me, too," he said, pleading with soft eyes.

For an instant, she wavered, then shook her head and laughed. "I fear you are faced with three ladies in love."

"In love but not, alas, with me," said Robbie.

"A goat!" exclaimed Effie.

"I beg your pardon!" said Robbie, in mock indignation.

"A goat!" repeated Effie. "There's a goat in a pen nibbling on the bean vines through the fence!"

"Trumps," said Amy, and went over to Mme. Gernagan to complete arrangements for a four-week stay.

At the window, Robbie spotted Effie's goat. "Endless entertainment, Miss Pendergrast; I congratulate you," he said. A wistfulness crossed his face as he continued to survey the scene below. "The view out a window is always a vexed invitation, isn't it: a barrier and a call. Emily, if you must—"

"Already done, Robbie, my boy," said Amy. "Anyone can see you're champing at the bit to be off to Switzerland."

For a moment, he looked as if he felt challenged to object but backed down quickly. "Too true, Miss Richardson, and why not, with matters so satisfactorily settled here."

He took Emily by the arm. As he did so, he just brushed Jeanette—deliberately, she thought. Their eyes met. Restlessness and intelligence. He looked as though he still might say something more, but his expression went sad instead, sad and then remote. By evening, he was gone.

CHAPTER SEVENTEEN

Pont Aven

Why don't you like Robbie Dolson?" asked Jeanette.

"Now there's a long and dreary tale," said Amy. Seated on a camp stool in front of a portable easel, she was concentrating on a distant headland. "Ah," she breathed, with satisfaction, when a faraway cliff face loomed forward, brightened by a patch of watery sunlight. "Just the highlight I need."

While Amy changed brushes and took up a new color, Jeanette, who was sketching her at work, paused to decide how much of the surrounding landscape she should include in her own picture. They had placed themselves on a hillside above a field where a man, a woman, and three children were harvesting grain. Below the harvesters, scrub brush dropped to the water's edge with Amy's headland out on the horizon. *Pace* Sonja, the scene was not all gray shoreline.

"Is it just the way he sometimes takes Emily for granted, or the way he's moody?"

"Still on about Mr. Dolson, are you?" Amy turned toward Jeanette. "You wouldn't be the first, you know, and you won't be the last. But I warn you, the most he will ever bestow on you or anyone else is that great charm of his—which, as you have just observed, comes and goes. He is not a generous-hearted man."

He can be in the right circumstances, thought Jeanette. She might as well have spoken aloud.

"Oh, Jeanette, don't do this to yourself. Robbie Dolson knows whom he adores, all right; he sees Inamorato in the shaving mirror every morning."

Jeanette felt sheepish. In her current favorite daydream, Robbie handed her down out of the coach in front of the Voyageurs to an admiring welcome from the assembled art colony of Pont Aven; she shone with the glory of being the first woman to win a major award at the Salon; he insisted on keeping her on his arm. When they quarreled, as they sometimes did, her wit matched his. No doubt her mother would point out that she exalted herself in all her day-dreams, but then, who didn't?

"He wouldn't see anything in me, anyway—an American girl from nowhere. It's not as though I were an heiress."

"Oh, I'll grant our Mr. Dolson this much: He'll never marry for money—he has too high a regard for his own ability to get by on nothing a year. Not but what it's Emily paying dribs and drabs out of her lunch money that keeps his line of credit open with his tailor and tobacconist. He has probably even borrowed from Winkie."

"Amy, that's not fair! Winkie lives right on the brink of disaster and Robbie knows it. He wouldn't."

"Well, only in sums too trivial to make him a sponge. Neverthe-less, I ask you: If one of them were likely to borrow from the other, which would it be?"

"Put that way . . ."

Amy turned back to her board. "As I said, Robbie doesn't really care for money. He likes being a touch raffish. You may have noticed the antiquarian flavor to his style; he's the last man in Paris to nose out frippery instead of buying cheap off the rack."

"Aspiring to English eccentricity at a young age?"

Amy glanced over her shoulder again and stuck out her tongue. She was hiding something, but Jeanette let it drop. Perhaps once upon a time Robbie had broken Amy's heart—yet Jeanette doubted that was it, or not the whole story. They worked on in amicable silence until the noon Angelus tolled faintly from several directions and the family below broke for their midday rest.

"Drat!" said Amy. "Gnat in the paint." With the wooden tip of her paintbrush, she pricked the insect out.

Jeanette mentally doodled a cartoon of a giant bug trying to pull its feet out of gluey goo while her *artiste* flung back arms in open-mouthed indignation. She stood up and stretched. From its cool nook among rocks where a small stream splashed down from the hill above them, she fetched their lunch basket and investigated its contents. "Cousin Effie has given us two hard-boiled eggs apiece," she said, "and some cheese. Brown rolls—oh, good, with butter in a cabbage leaf and a knife. There's something wrapped in another cabbage leaf—gooseberries!"

"Good show. She does very well by us, your cousin. Do you think she enjoys keeping house?"

Jeanette thought about it as she handed the basket over. "Yes, I think she *is* having a good time. She never complains about what they serve us at the *pension*, not even the gristly stew, but she had years of planning the meals with my aunt Maude's cook. She enjoys being in charge again here. Hand me your cup; I'll fill it."

When Jeanette brought back their water, she stood for a moment, letting her eye follow a snaky irregularity through the heath below the grain field. Halfway to the sea, a fingerlike boulder thrust up.

"Amy, had you noticed that boulder? Could it be a menhir?"

"Too isolated, I should think."

"There's a path to it." Jeanette squinted, straining to read a slight misalignment where the edges of bushes folded over against each other instead of blending seamlessly. "Or maybe it's a stream. When they're done cutting, let's go explore."

Jeanette was ashamed to admit that she wanted to take a break from endless artistic application. Maybe the problem was that she had not yet found her subject. Amy had come to Brittany with ideas in mind from last year. Emily had set right to work on the gardens and, perhaps thanks to her smattering of Welsh, was allowed by ancient Mme. Gernagan to sketch in the kitchen. Jeanette sketched the farmyard and gardens, the streets and church in town, the water mill clacking, women scrubbing laundry in the river. She put such scenes in letters home, but they were only what everyone drew or painted in Pont Aven. She set down her sketchbook.

"I'm going to climb the hill a way."

"Anything wrong?" asked Amy, over her shoulder.

"No, but I want to get something straight in my mind."

Hopping from rock to rock, Jeanette followed the stream up. Near the crest of the hill, it issued from tangled brush. She bent down and forced aside a low-spreading branch with her shoulder. Behind lay a pool of dark water, receding under a low arch in the hillside. Only near the lip, where the stream escaped into its channel, did the water seem to move at all. She pushed in closer and dipped her fingers. The water was cold. Our very own natural treacle well, she thought.

She turned around to run down and tell Amy but caught her breath at the view. From this height, the full mouth of the Aven estuary could be seen widening out into the ocean. If the sun had been bright and the air crisp, she might have flung her arms wide and shouted. Instead, haze softened the rugged landscape and lifted land and sea skyward; distance paled into silvery blue. She crossed her hands to the knobs of her shoulders. Her mind hovered. She began the descent, letting her feet find their own way down. When she reached the point where the bay dropped from sight, she scrambled.

Her excitement induced Amy to follow her back up the hill.

"Here," she said, at the brushy edge of the pool. She broke some branches and pushed back the resisting bush.

Amy whistled. "Coo, this *is* a find. The stones seem deliberately set. I wonder about that arch." She crouched to try to see better.

"Do you think it might really be a holy well?" asked Jeanette, kneeling beside her.

"I doubt it. The way the locals tend shrines, if this were known to cure warts or reflect your true love's face by the light of the midsummer moon, there would be offerings, little strips of cloth tied to the branches."

"We'll work magic anyway." Middle finger to thumb, Jeanette flicked a shower of droplets at Amy. "I'll asperse you—"

"Wretch!"

"—if you sprinkle me." Jeanette squealed and backed out of the bush, shielding her face as Amy splashed back vigorously. Jeanette pulled out her handkerchief to dry herself and, laughing, handed it to Amy.

"I'll tie it to the bush, as a first offering. There," said Amy. "It will help us find the place again. Come on, let's climb to the summit."

"Do you have time?"

"Oh, all work and no play makes Jill a dull girl. Besides, the better you know a place, the better you paint it. It has to seep into your bones."

They climbed up a stone ledge scoured bare by wind and rain.

"Some of your countrymen live here and paint all year," said Amy, looking out. "I can see why; I almost could."

"You wouldn't find it gloomy in winter?"

"Perhaps—though wait until you see a Parisian winter for everlasting gloom. No, it wouldn't be the weather." Amy's gaze pulled back from the sea to the land below. Somewhere, invisible from this vantage point, her reapers were hard at work again. She turned back to Jeanette with her customary briskness. "No, too isolated. I need the stimulation of other artists—the whole, big, difficult rough-and-tumble of Paris—and Julian's help. Come on, girl, once more into the breach."

CHAPTER EIGHTEEN

Second Interlude: Switzerland

After leaving Paris, the Murers went to London, then back through France to Zürich and on to the little town of Romanhorn on the Swiss side of Lake Constance. There, Edward kept Theodore company at a resort hotel while Sophie crossed the lake with Carl and Eddie to visit her native Bavaria. At the ferry dock, Theodore took his wife's hands in his: "If you wish, Sophie, I will come with you, after all."

"No, no, dearest. This will be an adventure for the boys and me. They are half Schlegel and should see where the Schlegels lived; but you full-blooded Murers, you stay here. A couple of days' rest will do you both good."

"You and I, we are as much Franck as my sons are Schlegel," chuckled Theodore after the boat left, "but let a woman reason like a woman."

The brothers found it liberating to wear straw hats and ramble together alongside the sparkling, white-capped water of the lake, free of skirts, offspring, and schedules; they sat at ease under umbrellas on the flower-decked hotel terrace. High summer in Cincinnati was hot and muggy. Here even on the brightest days, although the air might shimmer in the sun, it was always fresh and the breeze was cool. Eyes closed, Edward felt like a transparent glass retort filled with a gently volatilizing liquid.

"I can't remember when I last felt this carefree," said Theodore, scanning the sails of pleasure boats on the lake with satisfaction.

He lit a cigar. Edward wished he hadn't. Its acrid pungency curled through the pure air, tainting the sweet smell of grass and flowers. It diminished ever so slightly his feeling of lightness. He opened his eyes.

"Will you go to Kiel, do you think?" asked Theodore, hunched over, puffing to set the tobacco burning evenly.

"*Jawohl,*" growled Edward.

Theodore chuckled and sat back, his cigar hand dangling away from Edward. After the boys and Sophie left, they had gone on speaking mostly English—Edward from second nature, Theodore out of a proud allegiance to his adopted country. English made them less self-conscious among the hotel staff and other guests; it also exempted them as Americans from any little frictions of region or class.

"It was strange to be in Paris again," mused Theodore. "All the new boulevards, the Opéra at night as bright as day, all the clearances. I am all for progress," he added quickly in a warning tone. (Asphalt! Electricity! Cincinnati Light and Power, thought Edward.) "Don't get me wrong."

"I won't," said Edward.

Theodore shot him a sidelong glance, snorted, and puffed on his cigar. He resumed his musing tone. "The first time I went to Paris, Papa and I paid a call on a distinguished colleague of his, a member of the Académie Française perhaps. Such men had apartments in the Louvre then. *Ja,* it is true, a privilege. I remember the place as vast, but not what you would call palatial—the opposite, if anything. Broken cornices, the gilding tarnished black, moldy tapestries to cover dampness in the walls—"

"Must have been hard on the books."

"I don't remember any books or bookcases. No, the French don't read; they go to the theater. Of course, some wings of the building were better maintained than others. There were squatters on the worst floors and on the roof, too—under trees no less, spindly trees but trees. I remember their feathery leaves; they must have grown in cracks and gutters. Well, to get to where we were going, we had to wind our way through a maze of tall crumbling houses and dark little shops; here and there an old town house of some *grand seigneur.* All of it crammed between the Louvre and the Tuileries. Splendid squalor. Hard for me now to separate the jumble in the streets from the jumble in the hallways. But we found the right apartment. Papa was made welcome, and the professor led me to a tall window. So tall that window was, and glass all the way to the floor! I was afraid I would fall out if I moved an inch, but he pointed and said to me, 'Observe closely the window over there, *mon petit*, and you may see the queen.' I have forgotten his name, but while he and Papa talked revolution and chemistry, I kept watch for the queen of France."

"And did you see her?"

"*Ja!* At least, I saw a lady come to her window and pull aside the curtain. She seemed to be looking down to where some boys were playing a noisy game on the cobblestones below. She watched them, and I watched her. She tossed them something—boiled sweets I have always thought, though I can't remember why. Queen Marie Amalie."

Edward studied his brother, who had fallen silent, one hand resting on his ample middle, the cigar hand dangling out of sight. Theodore's eyes were following something inconsequential in the distance—a shorebird in flight, a sail on the lake—while his mind went in search of something else much farther away and far more elusive.

"You never told me that story before."

"What?" said Theodore, coming to himself again. "No, well, hardly a story. Besides, it was chemistry and reform that won out. We Murers are republicans. Still, the old professor was right: All children are royalists; they love their kings and queens. And when we get old, we grow nostalgic. I do not mind that my first Paris has been swept away, but I should not like the same for Kiel."

"Surely Kiel will not have changed so much as all that, not like Paris."

"A seaport for the Prussian navy now? Fortifications, big warships under construction? Pah. Poor pretty little Kiel. And think of the effect of even subtle differences—the present obliterates not only the past, but memory. Can you really remember Walnut Street as it was when you were growing up?"

True. Edward had watched the old street fill up, improve; it was hard to recall it at any one stage. But their old house . . . "The house," he said, with assurance.

"*Ja, ja.* Mutter never changed a thing, nor Papa after she was gone." Theodore took a puff on the cigar. "But Kiel: all my old friends, all the old associations—gone or betrayed, or, worse, turned traitor. Graybeards! It is a golden time, youth. When is the world ever more real, eh? You measure the rest of your life by it."

Edward huddled down into his chair. Youth, war, Mutter gone when he got back, Marie. He shut his mind against the abyss and looked out only at the clear light on the lake.

Theodore shifted uncomfortably. "I am tactless," he said, but his guilt was laced with irritation.

"Oh, no, it's real, all right, the past," said Edward. "Nothing more so."

He regretted the bitter outburst; at the same instant, a memory floated up, of a boat-building shed down at the wharves in Cincinnati. He and his friends—Cornelia among them—had monitored the construction of the big *Floating Circus Palace* showboat, right up to the day of its launch. "Do you know what was golden for me?" he said. "Not young manhood; earlier. Our second or third year in America. The summer when some of the boys and I went exploring everywhere. That was the summer Cornelia Mattocks played with us. I'm glad you looked up Marius Renick. It was good to see Cornelia again."

It was, and he looked forward to seeing her the next time he was in Paris. First, he must go to Freiburg-im-Breisgau with Carl and settle in with Cousin Paul Murer and his wife, Anna, and yes, perhaps go north to Kiel; but eventually, soon, he would go back to Paris, alone.

CHAPTER NINETEEN

Breton Seas

To give Effie a break from cooking and keep in touch with the close-knit artistic community, the four women ate occasionally at the Voyageurs, where everyone gossiped and opinions were strong. The company was largely male, but Amy held her own. She would lean on her elbows and call out a jolly rejoinder to some comment down one of the long communal tables. Nor was she the only woman to hold forth. Most notably, there was a middle-aged Anglo-Irish lady, Miss Mabel Reade, who painted; her voice boomed. Her sprightly younger sister, Miss Isobel, kept house and worked intricate handcrafts with seashells and feathers. Miss Isobel soon adopted Effie as a fellow worker bee. "We're toilers in the vineyard, cogs in the wheel, Miss Pendergrast, but the wheels couldn't turn without us. A privilege, a privilege, to foster genius, but no need for us to miss out on a little *fun*."

Midway through the month, the weather turned so uncharacteristically hot and sunny that one day they ate their breakfast outdoors. Amy leaned back and clasped her hands over her head behind her.

"A bright day should stimulate one, but I feel downright lazy."

"All work and no play," Jeanette quoted back to her, "makes Jill—"

"—as dull as Jack," murmured Emily.

"Emily Dolson! I didn't know you had it in you," laughed Amy.

"What we all need is a day by the water," said Jeanette. "Amy, what about that cove below the grain field?"

"Rather a long a walk in this heat," said Amy. "Let's go see what Rag-Tag and Bobtail are up to. If we feel like going on, there's a footpath below the quays that leads on down the estuary. Will you join us, Miss P?"

Effie, of course, would. A half hour later, the four of them were in the village on the way down to the boats. As they passed by the Reade sisters' lodgings, Miss Isobel was at an upstairs window. "Yoo-hoo!" she called, and waved. They waved back.

As expected, Ragland and Nagg were at easels on the low flats by the waterfront a few yards from the old building that they had rented. They had improvised a tent roof out of worn-out sails and broken spars to cut the glare on their canvases.

"Where's Post?" asked Amy.

"Inside," said Ragland, jerking his thumb toward the open door.

"You know how he abominates high contrast. Post!" shouted Nagg. "Are you decent, man? Ladies!"

"I fry in the fires of my genius or bake in this oven you call a home," roared a voice from inside. "Where are the cracks and breezes that turn it frigid in winter, I ask, and do not know the answer. I burn, I burn. Do not waste my time with women unless they are sluts."

"Charlie Post, you pest and bother, it's Amy Richardson. I'm here to give you a crit, and you are going to give my friends—"

"Miss Richardson, is it? That's different," said Post. He appeared at the door, grinning. His filthy smock was open and his sweaty shirt unbuttoned. "Why didn't you say so?"

Emily tugged at Amy's sleeve and whispered, "Robbie wouldn't . . ."

"Bosh," muttered Amy, from the side of her mouth.

"Brava, carissima." Post leered at Emily, hiding behind Amy's back. "I see you have brought *la dolce Dolson* with you."

"And Jeanette Palmer. Good morning, Mr. Post," said Jeanette, brightly, stepping forward to shield Emily. "This is my cousin, Miss Pendergrast."

Mr. Post squinted menacingly at Effie. "Are you a genius or a duenna, Miss Pendergrast?"

Something she had been groping for ever since they arrived in Pont Aven fell into place for Effie. "Post," she said, slowly, ignoring the unbuttoned shirt. "Why, I know who you are! You're Mr. Moyer's friend. You paint water."

"Holy smokes—a clairvoyant. You can't mean Frank Moyer?"

Effie nodded. "In New York."

"Frank Moyer!" whooped Post. "Haven't seen him in a donkey's age. What's he up to? Still hewing wood for his Hedleyship on Tenth Street? Come in, come in."

"He's engaged to Miss Whitmore," said Effie.

"The blackguard. May the engagement be long or wisely broken."

"Why?" asked Jeanette. "What's wrong with Mr. Moyer?"

"Nothing, Miss Palmer, but Susan Whitmore is much too good an artist to be lost to wifery. Spare us Moyer babes mewling and puking in their mother's arms." He ushered her past him.

Jeanette involuntarily wrinkled her nose. Windows and a skylight installed by Ragland and Nagg provided light but not enough ventilation. The shed had once been a mackerel warehouse, and the smell had sunk into the boards. Over the fishy substratum floated a fresher brew of pipe smoke, dirty laundry, and turpentine. One cot was made up; another was not; the working space of each man was marked off by an easel and worktable; a carved chair in a corner was heaped with various props under a banner inscribed *Omnium Gatherum.* Dominating all the clutter and reek was a giant canvas, its back to the door, stretched and nailed to a braced wooden frame. On an easel at an angle to it stood a smaller canvas of the same proportions, longer than it was high. But what caught Jeanette's full attention while the others talked was a third small canvas, smaller still, propped against the wall, face out: dark rocks and a pebble-strewn beach in the foreground with water curling around the base of a boulder. One long, low, crested wave spilled forward all across the middle ground. Near a distant horizon hung a sickle moon.

She moved to where she could see all three versions at once. Post's prattle stopped while his eyes followed her. From talk at the Voyageurs, she knew that the larger tableau on the easel would depict the same subject, as would the huge work in progress: fanatical renditions of the same, the same, the same. The wonder was how he explored the scene anew each time. The breaking wave, the advancing flow, the white reflection of the moon in a pool so close to the picture plane as almost to spill out—in each redaction everything in the picture came forward, while all the yearning that gave it meaning was distilled into the retreat of the thin sickle moon.

When she looked up, Mr. Post was watching her silently. His face had come to rest in a precarious poise. A desolate, wintry pallor belied his sprinkle of summer freckles. When she met his eye, its gleam sharpened defensively to an ironic glint. No, this matters, her answering look told him; I see it, and it matters. She also saw that its pursuit could break a man's heart.

"*Cherchez le demi-teinte!*" proclaimed a stentorian female voice from the doorway.

A spasm of irritation crossed Charlie Post's face. Recovering, he thrust out his palette, held his paintbrush high behind him, and gave an exaggerated jump. "Carolus!" he cried. "Do I need to explain that Miss Reade is an acolyte of Carolus-Duran's?"

"No, you don't," declared Miss Reade. "They've heard me praise him and seen my work. Could have saved myself twenty years of misguided effort if I'd known the master sooner. Well, he has put me on the right track now. Shan't ever paint like you, Post, and don't want to—but, you girls, pay attention to what this young dog does. *Post finds the halftone.*" Post bowed. "When Isobel saw you out the window, I told her 'Isobel, your hat.' And here we are."

A half hour of shop talk followed as the ladies examined the men's various canvases. Back outside, they gathered between Ragland's and Nagg's two very different takes on Pont Aven in the sun. Post looked at each moodily, with little interest. He pulled Jeanette aside. "If you could choose a vantage point this morning, Miss Palmer," he asked in an undertone, "what would it be?"

A light answer would have sufficed, but an image half-formed in Jeanette's mind. "An interior," she said, "a corner of the studio. Rooms reveal so much, Mr. Post."

"Thank you," he murmured. He caught up her hand and with soft, moist lips kissed the palm.

Hastily, she pulled her hand free, hoping no one had noticed.

"Off you go now, girls," ordered Miss Reade. "Isobel and I are poaching Miss Pendergrast for ourselves. Came after you for that very purpose."

Gratified to be wanted, Effie went off with her new friends while Jeanette, Amy, and Emily continued down the river.

When they turned into a long inlet that wound a half mile or more, they lost sight of the wider estuary. It ended in a strip of gray sand, beyond which pebbles spread smoothly back through a band of boulders. The big stones were streaked with salty flood lines where tidal waters must rise during storm surges, but today all was calm and flat. Across the cove, steep cliffs were reflected almost perfectly.

"I think we've found it," said Amy, and no one had to ask what. Of one accord, they deposited their things by a rock and took off their shoes.

As Jeanette peeled back her black stockings and looked at her feet in outdoor sunlight, she was shocked by their smooth, thin-skinned translucence. They always used to be brown by the middle of the summer, and the soles were thick and tough from going barefoot when she was out of her mother's sight. Now on the pebbly beach, she wobbled. A stone jabbed painfully into her arch, but then her toes dug into wet sand and grasped. Holding her skirt and petticoats up, she took short, searching steps into the water. It was warmed by the sun; a tiny wavelet ran over the tops of her feet onto shore.

"I've never been in the ocean before," she said, staring down in fascination.

Amy and Emily exchanged a look behind her back.

"This hardly counts as the open sea," said Amy.

"Ohio is landlocked in a very *large* continent, where," said Jeanette, turning around, "we do have swimming holes and boys who tease." She kicked expertly, sending a low, well-aimed splash against their shins.

"Not again, damn you!" cried Amy, jumping back. "You have a mania for drenching people."

Emily, who had been trudging against the water, pushing it to make it surge and swirl, stood very still. She looked around.

"There are no boys here to tease, and none likely to come." She turned to them with her face glowing and whispered in low, wicked urgency, "Amy! Jeanette! Let's *bathe*." Without waiting for an answer, she waded splashily out of the water.

Jeanette looked at Amy. "Shall we?" she asked. She meant, yes.

"Emily, we don't have any bathing togs," called Amy.

"We can wear our shifts." On the beach now, Emily beckoned them toward their deposited bundles.

"No," said Jeanette. "Skinny-dipping!"

"Shameless American," said Amy.

"Oh, come on. What could be worse than wet underwear on the

way home? Emily's right: No one can see up into this cove." Jeanette was already unpinning her hat.

Despite being sure they could not be seen, they retreated behind the head-high boulders to take off their clothes. With mixed feelings of trepidation and daring, they helped each other undo buttons and laces in the back. "Don't look," they demanded, while egging each other on.

"All valuable combs should be carefully stowed," warned Amy, taking down her braids.

"Hairpins and hatpins, too," said Emily.

Covering themselves with their arms, they peered around the boulder one last time to make sure of their privacy and gave each other sidelong glances. They began at a tiptoe and then dashed around the rock, shrieking. Emily first: elfin, white, and pear-shaped. Amy's waist was small, her thighs sleek. But what Jeanette was mainly aware of was her own thighs jiggling, of feeling silly and excited at the same time. When she uncrossed her arms to keep balance, her breasts bounced. She high-stepped into the water, her whole body free to bend and feel the air and sun and water against her skin. The warm shallow water sloshed and sprayed. She floundered to where it was deeper and fell forward. Her feet left the bottom just before the slope fell steeply away.

"Oh!" she panted. The frigid water stung; it knocked the breath out of her. "Oh, oh, help! Oh, I've never been in water so cold. Oh!"

She flailed wildly to get back into the warmer shallows. As soon as she could, she stood up, wildly chafing herself for warmth. Emily and Amy hooted.

"You should feel the water off Blackpool," called Amy.

Amy waded out deeper and dived forward. She was a strong swimmer. Unlike many sailors, her seagoing father could swim; and unlike many fathers, he had taught his daughter the practical skills he would have taught a son. She struck out into the middle of the inlet. Jeanette had learned from other children only how to stay afloat and dog-paddle. As her feet and shins got used to the cold, she waded deeper again. With a shudder, she crouched to submerge herself, all but her head, and ventured into the deeper, colder water but quickly thought better of it. She rejoined Emily, who was floating on her back in the warmer water with her hands, palm out, beside her face. Her pale skin just below the surface of the water appeared brownish green. Her long hair floated out around her.

"Ophelia," she said, rolling unseeing, blank eyes up to the sky. Her mouth was slack, half open.

"Don't, Emily! That's macabre!"

"It's an allusion."

"It's still macabre. If you want to be weird, be enticing, be a mermaid."

Emily drew her legs together and swayed knees and ankles while she settled onto the bottom. She leaned back on her elbows. Jeanette, who had been holding her chin above water, decided it was no good taking her only swim in Brittany without ducking under all the way. She shut her eyes, held her breath, and dropped down. Her breath escaped in a trickle of bubbles. Cold water tickled in over her scalp; it lifted her hair. She shot back upward in a churning commotion, gulping and laughing. By now, Amy was on her way back. When she reached waist-deep water, she stood up and pushed forward, taking heron strides from the hips.

"That's better," she said, and headed for the shore.

At the boulders, Amy dried her hands and face with a petticoat and patted herself over lightly; then, laying the cloth on a sun-heated rock that rose like a beached whale, she pressed her hands down and sprang up onto its back. Jeanette followed. After lolling a little longer, Emily came out, wringing her hair, and climbed up beside them. The lightest of breezes raised goose bumps on their arms and thighs until the sun began to warm them again.

"I'm going to be a limpet," said Emily, draping herself face down over the rock, with her hair spread over her.

Jeanette perched on the whale's nose, hunched over her drawn-up knees, to watch tiny crabs in a tidal pool below.

"You two are merging into the landscape," said Amy, who was squinting past them to the opposite shore of the cove. "Your skin has blue tones."

"Nymphs in Arcadia," said Emily, sleepily.

Jeanette leaned back in a coy studio pose.

"No, no," said Amy. "Real nymphs are more aware of water and trees than of men. Blend again."

Jeanette looked down at herself. "The interesting thing is, we don't look like nymphs at all, do we?" She flexed her feet back; her calves had a walker's pronounced muscles. She relaxed them; her thighs went soft where they spread over the stone. "I'm plump—and, Emily, you're too thin; you need feeding up."

"I'm pounds heavier. Miss Pendergrast has been seeing to that."

"You are both beautiful."

"You're the beautiful one," said Jeanette, tilting her head back to look back over her shoulder. Amy no longer had the lissomeness of girlhood, nor were her regular features and thin mouth remarkable in any way; but her skin was clear; she was graceful and strong.

"Did you hear about the time the Countess took home some of the girls?" asked Emily, her cheek still against the warm stone, her eyes closed. "She stripped off her clothes and lay back on her couch—"

"Oh, jiggerums, yes," said Amy. "*Here is beauty!* they say she proclaimed."

Jeanette swung around with her knees still up and turned disbelieving from one to the other.

"She did," insisted Amy.

Jeanette sputtered with laughter through her hands.

"She claims we all cover up our nakedness because we are ashamed of our imperfections," said Emily, with her cheek on the stone, her eyes still closed.

"Who can resist the temptation to show off a perfection?" mimicked Amy, reclining on her elbow with a hand languidly gesturing in the air. She lifted her chin. *"Shame disappears in the presence of supreme beauty; the ideal impresses the mind only with admiration."*

They all three exploded. Emily kicked her feet up and down.

"I hope her mama," began Jeanette, and broke off, choking. "I hope her mama has hinted to her about other reasons." She wiped a stinging tear from the corner of her eye. "All the same, she has a point. It is why we idealize from the model. Nobody's perfect."

"Which Sonja denounces as all wrong," said Amy. "Draw what you see; depict reality with all its cross-grained flaws. I say, will you two hold still while I make a quick sketch?"

While Amy slid down to get her pocket sketchbook, Jeanette glanced around nervously to make sure they were still alone. Emily clenched. She's going to go shy, thought Jeanette. To prolong the moment of ease and hot sun, Jeanette crossed her arms over her knees again and lay her cheek against them, saying comfortably, "Not too long, Amy, or we really will get sunburned."

"A few jottings only."

It worked. Although Emily's face, hidden in her hair, was unreadable, her shoulders and torso went slack again.

"Sit up and look out to sea, Jeanette. Thanks."

Nearby the air seemed clear, but out toward the horizon, distances were hazy, humid. The week's hot weather would end in rain—soon, Jeanette supposed, tonight, tomorrow—but not now. It was still too bright for Mr. Post. Her hand remembered the press of his lips; her stomach tightened in revulsion (or titillation?). She tried to push away thoughts of him; daydreams didn't help, too pallid. She found herself wondering whether Charlie Post ever painted the sea on dark afternoons when storm threatened. If so, would his sun behind clouds suggest promise or menace?

"I've had an idea," she said, aloud. "What would you think of drawing empty rooms as portraits?"

"Why?" asked Amy.

"Because people hide," said Emily.

"And rooms reveal—but an empty room also hints; it's suggestive. I guess what I'm really wondering is how we choose our subjects."

"When a subject is mine, I'm not there at all, only the picture," said Emily, without looking up.

Jeanette looked around at her, then met Amy's eye. "Oops, sorry. I moved."

"Doesn't matter. Inch way over to the edge and stare down. Lovely. You were saying?"

Seaweed oscillated in the pool below Jeanette; the little crabs scuttled; a wave slopped over the rim. "Well, just now you wanted to draw us, Amy, but I don't feel any desire to tackle the pool below me even though I could stare at it for hours. Emily's right that a picture should seem as much outside as in you, but it's inside, too."

"Sometimes I start composing a picture and find I've done something else when I finish—" said Emily.

"Happens to all of us," said Amy, matter-of-factly.

"—because other things have crept in," said Emily, "invisibly."

"Oh, lawks!" cried Jeanette, scrambling to her feet. "I'll tell you what's creeping in, it's the tide! Our clothes!"

Sure enough, water had crept around the base of the boulder, almost surrounding it entirely. They tumbled down its sides as alarmed as if they had heard someone approach. In their haste to pull on garments—some wet, some dry—they blundered, fumbled with each other's laces, missed hooks and buttons. Their skirts and sleeves twisted into maddening snarls.

"Don't put on boots yet, we're going to have to wade to the path," said Amy.

"Can we go through town like this?" asked Emily.

"Amy, is that tall boulder the one we saw from the grain field?" asked Jeanette.

"It's a menhir," said Emily.

Jeanette shot a smug I-told-you-so glance at Amy, who shrugged: "If anyone knows, Emily does. We'd better reconnoiter."

They forced their way up through scrub bush. When they reached the stone, they could see a mowed field above them where the grain was piled in neat shocks.

"We have walked into your picture, Amy," said Jeanette.

"So we have. Come on, then, let's climb to the top. Emily, you can see Jeanette's mystery well, after which we'll sneak our disgracefully disheveled selves home the back way."

That night, although Jeanette had seen each of Emily's Pont Aven floral studies as it was completed, she asked to look through them as a group. Emily worked in layers of tiny watercolor strokes that caused light not only to reflect forward off flowers but to pool behind them; shadows receded under foliage. She sometimes painted rows of the cutting garden from almost ground level. The effect was the opposite of Charlie Post's oncoming wave: Her pictures withdrew; they occluded. And yet, the more Jeanette looked, the more she knew that the work of both artists responded to a disconcerting power more felt than understood.

Mr. Dolson warned against losing originality. Amy said you had to spend time in a place to know it well enough to paint it. It was half enticing, half frightening to realize that you must also plunge past what you knew into what you could only sense. A conviction came to her that her hunch was worth pursuing: Empty rooms could express much about people's hidden lives. And it came to her also that sometimes you had to take a chance on qualities that you sensed hidden in people, too, people like the Dolsons or Charlie Post—or, oddly enough, Effie's Dr. Murer.

CHAPTER TWENTY

Paris, Early Autumn 1878

Parisian artistic life would not revive until October, when the École des Beaux-Arts reopened. Nevertheless, the Académie Julian started up again in September, and Amy had duties. It was time to return to disciplined work.

Early on the damp silvery morning of the party's departure, Jeanette took one last walk up through the orchard. In late August, branches were heavily laden with fruit; and on a tree that Mme. Gernagan had called a Belle d'Été, she found a few oblate apples perfectly ripened. When she rolled one back on its stem, it dropped into her hand. A prickly acid under the skin stung her gums and tongue, yet the juice was sweet, with an aftertaste of cloves. For a moment, she rebelled at the thought of leaving Brittany, the farm, the studio where she and Amy and Emily had worked so happily. She looked higher at the sweeping hillside, which blocked the horizon, then turned to gaze down on the farm buildings and the straight rows of vegetables and flowers in the angle framed by house and barn. Next year, she vowed, next year she would be back—not in Ohio, here. And next year she would be painting in oils.

Mr. Dolson and Mr. Winkham met us on the platform when we got back to Paris, Jeanette wrote her parents. She did not mention that when she waved from the compartment door, the men's eyes remained fixed solely on Emily. *I asked Mr. Dolson whether he had gathered enough material in Switzerland for an article, and he said, "Easily a thousand words a day in my diary, and more packed into the cranium." Then he told Emily that an article called "Dispatches from High Places" would feed them on caviar all fall. "And dispatches from low?" asked Amy. "Always an inspiration, Miss Richardson," he said. Then he and Mr. Winkham whisked Emily away.*

After being made to feel invisible on the train platform, Jeanette was glad to return to Julian's Academy and find that she was no longer the new girl but a regular, chatting away with the others about vacations. She was content—until Emily arrived with a palette and bundle of paints and brushes.

"Robbie gave me money to buy supplies," beamed Emily. "I took it for a sign."

Amy and M. Julian had long been urging Emily to take up oils; and after seeing her dense watercolors in August, Jeanette had joined them. It didn't change her own need to master drawing techniques, but it was a jolt to see Emily pulling ahead.

"Tell you what," suggested Amy. "As the weeks go by, the floor will be littered with mostly spent tubes of paint. Collect them, and I'll teach you some exercises in color gradation. It's never too early to start mastering the tonal scales in color; they are fiendishly hard."

At noon, Sonja stormed in. "I will hear of your stay in the gray lands later. Welcome back and all that. First you hear my news or I explode. What do you suppose awaits me when I return from Italy? Seven paintings in my studio ruined, *ruined* from a new leak in the ceiling. I demand satisfaction, and that pig, my landlord, tells me to buy a bucket to put under the drip. *Deduct the cost from the rent,* he says. He says the paintings were always unsaleable and thus worth nothing."

"He said they were worthless?" exclaimed Jeanette.

"Damn his eyes," said Amy.

"Perhaps you had better just move," said Emily, with the resigned look of someone who had done it often.

"No. I stay, but I deduct the rent entirely."

For Cousin Effie, the return to Paris soon brought a welcome resumption of invitations to morning coffee with Mrs. Renick. One morning, as she came into the Poutery, Cornelia said, "Darling Effie, look who's here!"

Effie stopped. Her cheeks turned pink. "Dr. Murer! Oh, my."

Edward rose from a chair beside a low table on which stacks of fashion magazines lay mixed up with sheet music and newly bound novels, one with a silver paper knife stuck in it as a bookmark. In an open gilt-paper box, chocolate bonbons nestled individually in gold tissue paper. Perhaps owing to his recuperative year spent with Sophie, he felt at ease amid this feminine clutter. He also perceived his effect on Effie. He was glad, very glad, of a chance to resume his acquaintance with her and, as he hoped, Miss Palmer. At the same time, the reticences that had kept him a bachelor in Cincinnati warned him now to tread carefully.

"Effie, dear," said Cornelia, patting the seat beside her, "come show us what you've brought. Effie has been to the Bon Marché for me, Edward, to pick up samples of lace. And Edward has just been telling me what it's like to live in the land of half-timbered houses and cuckoo clocks."

"If the Brothers Grimm weren't dead, I'd expect to see them coming down the street any time to collect folk tales," said Edward.

While Cornelia fingered pieces of lace one by one and spread them on her knee, he went on with his description of Freiburg. The center of town was far more medieval than either he or Carl had been prepared for, while the industrializing suburbs were rawer and newer. "It's been a dye-making region in a small way for centuries, and people are used to seeing colors run in the rivers from time to time, but they complain now when arsenic kills the fish."

"Arsenic!" Cornelia looked up.

"A by-product of the alizarin dyes that give you all your vivid new reds. It's in the effluent."

"Oh, it shouldn't be. What a waste! Surely there is some way to recover and reuse it—make rat poison or something. We must tell Marius. That's the sort of out-of-the-way scheme he loves."

"It's what Carl has in mind, too."

"And where is your golden-haired nephew, by the way?" asked Cornelia. "You didn't bring him along this morning."

"I left him in Freiburg, pegging away at his coursework; he's going on a sales trip soon with one of the cousins. But I've waited a whole lifetime to come back to Europe, Cornelia, and I don't want to spend my whole stay in a dye works. I missed Paris."

"Oh, so do I, Edward! Every day I miss it, and I *live* here. Trapped, trapped." Cornelia rocked from side to side in her brace. "Tell me exactly what you are going to do this very afternoon. I'm going to close my eyes and imagine myself walking every step of the way with you."

"This afternoon? I thought I would go to an organ recital at the Madeleine. It's only the assistant organist, but—"

"Oh, he's supposed to be *wonderful*! He's new, you know."

"I didn't."

"Well, he is, and he composes."

"That much I did know. He's put something of his own on the program."

"I can't bear to miss it. Promise me to come back with a report. Come tell me whether I should invite him to play at one of my little musicales."

"Cornelia, how much can you move?"

"Oh, Edward, I can walk from one side of the room to the other, using two canes. Up twenty-eight steps into the Madeleine? No, not if that's what you're thinking. And I certainly won't be carried up by footmen in public like some painter's dummy or a rag doll."

"So you really don't get out of the house, do you."

Cornelia sighed. "Not much. Into the garden mostly. Marius had a backstairs lift installed for taking me up and down in my wheeled chair." Mischief came into her eye. She held down Effie's hand and lowered her voice as if she were telling a secret. "And now once a week I'm making the most marvelous escape. It was dear Effie's idea."

Effie made a noise of modest protest and smiled into her lap. The points of her cheeks went pink again.

"It *was* your idea, and I'm nothing but grateful! Effie pointed out that I might be able to handle the reins of a trap, Edward. I couldn't ride, but maybe I could drive. And, of course, she was right—I can! The first time we went, Jacques, the footman, wheeled me out to the stable. I can't tell you how wonderful it was to smell horsiness and hay and stable dust again. I can still feel the tickle of soft hairy lips taking sugar from my hand."

"You were thrown from a horse, weren't you?"

"I was. Dear sweet Flora, it wasn't her fault at all. Some duffer let his mount dash across our path, and Flora reared in a panic. I would have kept her, but Marius was too upset. I can't tell you how much I miss her. Anyway, now when we go out, Albert, the coach-man, brings the trap around to the front door. He and Jacques lift me up onto the driver's seat, Effie gets in the back, and off we go, Albert, of course, at the reins. He takes us through all the traffic— I am not a complete idiot; I would never have attempted to drive through Paris in all my daring days. But when we get to the Bois de Boulogne, Albert hands the reins to me and takes up his post on the footman's stand, Effie comes forward, and off we go, trot, trot, trot, ever so free and debonair. I wave to all my friends; I'm seen around and about; I'm not forgotten. It's a grand jollification, isn't it, Effie? What an ingrate I am to want more." Sadness came into Cornelia's voice. "But I do—so much more."

"Cornelia," said Edward, gently, "may I ask the nature of your injury? I don't mean to pry or be indelicate, but . . ."

"Oh, ask away, Edward! I'm not one of those women who's afraid to say *legs* in mixed company. Besides, you have seen the offended member muddy and scabbed. Now, don't blush, Effie; you may have never climbed trees with this man, but I have. It was my knee, Edward: torn ligaments and a fracture—the head of the fibular bone."

Edward nodded. "That can knock you back, all right. Knees are intricate. Even after the bone knit, you found your foot gave way under you?"

"Suddenly, without warning! My back was hurt, too. No broken bones, thank goodness, but I jarred myself badly when I hit the ground, and I must have wrenched something."

Did they—? wondered Edward; and blocked the word.

Unaware that she was answering his unspoken question, Cornelia ran on, "They gave me laudanum at first, bless them; it does dull the pain. Well, I don't have to tell you that, you're a druggist. You know the dozy haze it puts you in . . ."

He became very still, listening behind a polite mask.

". . . as though nothing . . . in the world . . . matters at all." Cornelia's voice trailed off in a singsong. She snapped back. "Edward, I won't end up one of those invalid ladies with the drifting stare. The world is much too much fun to leave behind."

"Were you able just to quit?" asked Edward, enviously.

"Luckily, yes. Oh, but why not? I was always plumped up with cushions and hot-water bottles and had nurses to order around. Two months, and then came the crutches and trying to walk. When my foot gave way one time too many, the doctor strapped me into this contraption of his to keep me supported and rigid. You are frowning."

"I'm a druggist, Cornelia, not a surgeon, and I'll assume your man is the best in Paris."

"He is, but, but—? Go on."

"Well, it's just that from my experience—" He remembered from years back the pressure of Sophie's hand behind his elbow, guiding him; a fleeting memory of touch. Too personal. He changed tack slightly: "From what I saw in hospitals after the war, it was the stubborn ones who wouldn't stay in bed who mended fastest. I'd have said you should be moving around as much as possible. Restricted muscles wither."

"That's what I said!" Effie nodded vigorously.

"And didn't I see it when the cast came off. Ugly, blotchy, flaky, shrunken; you've never seen such a hideous—well, that's stupid of me. You've seen far, far worse. But you're right: I should be moving; I *know it*! It's just that Marius is so afraid for me. Never mind. It's your turn, Edward. You were shot in the leg, weren't you?"

"Leg, lung, and rib." He spoke dispassionately, as if merely stating a fact. Yet a simple assent would have been more to the point; he knew it was his analogous leg that interested her. It was not that he longed for sympathy over his wounds; he had had more than enough of that through the years. To state the extent of his injuries was an excuse, a sop to his pride, the old rationalization for his weakness.

"Rib and lung! My dear, no one ever told us."

"It was a long time ago, and ribs heal. So do lungs, more than you'd think," he said. "But, yes, I took a bullet in my leg, and it shattered some bone."

"And *you* walk freely."

"Well, it's a different injury. But if you're willing to try exercise, Cornelia, I'd certainly talk to that medical man of yours."

The two women exchanged a wordless, excited look. Cornelia bubbled. Pure champagne, thought Edward, and Miss Pendergrast is fizzing like soda pop. Obviously, they were up to more than drives in the park.

That afternoon, Edward attended his recital. He arrived early enough to play the sightseer and walk through the variegated marble splendors

of the Church of the Madeleine. Neither an aggressive freethinker
like his father nor an indifferent one like Theodore, Edward had
turned resolutely away from philosophic and religious speculation.
But he had always liked to hear mysteries embodied in music, and
he was finding in Europe that he responded to the buildings in
which it was played: churches, opera houses, and halls. The neoclas-
sical Madeleine, built in his century and dedicated to a redeemed
sinner, was confident and opulent. With a dose of irony, he liked it.

After the concert, it was almost too good to be true to walk out
onto the side porch in the late afternoon and see the last of the flower
sellers loading buckets of unsold roses and bronze chrysanthemums
into handcarts while across the street lavender shadows played
against mellow stone. A few blocks away, the harsh white glare of
the electric light about which Theodore was so enthusiastic would
soon come on to bleach and harden everything in sight; but for now,
trees on the Rue Royale led gold and russet to the Place de la Concorde. Up and down the sidewalks, women in black coats with a
touch of fur at the throat and men in top hats dodged among one
another in long lines like notes on a staff. What a pity it was for
Cornelia to be shut away from this liveliest, loveliest of cities! More
than a pity, damnable. He remembered them both with the gravel
stings in their hands and muddy knees. She was always laughing,
her hair slipping free out into a fuzzy nimbus from whatever braid-
ing or ribbons her mother had used to try to control it. Good old
Cornelia. As he started down the church steps, he supposed that he
ought to have invited Miss Pendergrast to come along to the concert;
she was the sort who enjoyed any outing. But no, truth to tell, he
was glad he had obeyed his instinctive caution with spinsters.

Pulled toward the Place de la Concorde, he crossed traffic and
continued on the western side of the bridge over the Seine. A cluster
of young men leaned at their ease on the balustrade and discussed
where best to watch the sun go down. The Seine turned to a molten
sheen overarched by a blazing sky would be a sight worth seeking

out, but looking at a bank of low cloud in the west, Edward thought the day would not end in fire. As he turned eastward upriver, his heart leaped; for there, with the sun still in the sky, a pale golden moon was rising. Just as he had at the rail of the *Nordland*, he blinked back tears, yet to anyone who had felt as deadened as he had for so many years, there was no inward regret at finding himself moved, only gratitude that he could feel beauty.

At the entrance to the Tuileries Garden, a woodsy-sweet roasting smell hung where a mother and two children were buying chestnuts from a street vendor. Inside the wall of the park, the central gravel path held the waning light while the surrounding grass gradually faded from wan green toward no discernible color at all. In the basin of a big fountain, a pair of silhouetted ducks glided at the apex of an ever-broadening wake. A few people dawdled along the paths or sat under the ranks of trees on either side of the park. The tree trunks were strictly aligned, very French; but wind and rain had stripped their leaves in scattered patches, and a few trees were almost bare. The naked upper branches reached toward a primordial wildness having little to do with parks or men. One lithe young tree, which must have been planted to replace a victim of the 1870 siege, had attained height but not girth. Its skeletal twigs probed an invisible chaos; it seemed inimical to man, or not so much hostile as heedless in its dark energy. The trees at Shiloh had been like that. With a blink of the eye, Edward dismissed the fancy; the tree fell into place in a formal row that led to a creamy hemispheric wall. Above the wall, the mass and irregular roof of the burned palace blocked the far end of the garden. No queen of France to watch for now. In the growing dusk, golden lights pricked out the Rue de Rivoli to his left. Edward whistled a measure from the afternoon's concert. At the *rat-a-tat-tat* of a drum being beaten to signal the closing hour, he felt a momentary urge to flout the martial-sounding order. As a boy, he might have hidden for the fun of climbing over the fence later. The middle-aged man decided to go in search of coffee and brandy.

He came out on the Rue de Rivoli, where a young woman in a small hat perched forward over curls stood under a streetlamp. Her eyes met his; she yawned and immediately held a prettily gloved hand to her mouth. So natural a gesture, so public a slip in decorum amused him, and he raised a hand to tip his hat. She winked and tilted her head. His hand hesitated; blood rushed to his face at his mistake. She turned away, perhaps herself inexperienced enough to be embarrassed, more likely already seeking a better prospect. Completing the tip of his hat with a flick, *adieu*, Edward was glad that Carl had not been present to see his blunder. He took a seat at a sidewalk table and sipped his coffee and brandy, watching the crowd with skeptical new eyes.

When he was done, it was still too early to dine. He felt dissatisfied. Sophie and Cousin Anna constantly reminded him to take his meals regularly and he knew he should, but he rejected food as a corrective to the uneasiness that had crept into his evening. His limbs wanted action. He returned to the Meurice and asked the concierge to recommend a fencing studio.

It was an odd preoccupation to have lodged in his brain, fencing, and he knew it. As a boy, he had learned the basics from Theodore, who in his university days in Kiel had excelled at the sport. He remembered the salute, the *en garde* position, a few parries and ripostes—enough to have led him to accompany Carl one night in Freiburg to watch Young Paul fence at a club for soldiers and students, where dueling scars still conferred glamour. He hated everything having to do with real officers' real sabers; but when he saw the young men in their warm-up exercises and ritualized practice with foils, he began to wonder whether the discipline might help his stiffness and pain. If only to slake his curiosity, he thought he would experiment here in Paris, where he could make the trial away from the eyes of anyone he knew.

* * *

The *salle d'armes* to which he was directed proved to be a ground-floor establishment at the back of a courtyard near Les Halles. As he approached the door, out came two men, laughing and talking. They had the easy gait and glowing faces of healthy men who had just exercised hard. They nodded with a slightly distracted friendliness and held the door for him.

By gaslight inside, brown-speckled mirrors and stained wallpaper gave the impression of a place long in use. Thumps, stamps, whining clinks, and shouts rang out from beyond a partition behind a reception desk. Chalk dust and sweat permeated the air, interpenetrated by a heavily perfumed Turkish cigarette being smoked by the desk attendant. It's going to be my lung, not my leg does me in, thought Edward. The attendant assured him he could be supplied with instruction, he had come at a good hour, the master could work him in at once. All the necessary equipment could be hired on site; there was a charge for each broken foil, of which there were likely to be a few each lesson. If *monsieur* would step this way.

In the dressing room, Edward was given a wadded buckskin jacket, sweat-stained and greasy from use, but the flannel shirt to go under it and a pair of linen trousers were freshly laundered. So was a hand towel to take with him to wipe his face. Bath towels were ready for later, when Ahmed would be available to give him a rubdown (*monsieur* should take advantage). The old man who ruled the dressing room knew his business: The trousers were just the right length and fullness to give ease of motion; the shirt was comfortable at the neck. In trading the confinement of collar, cuff, necktie, and suit for such freedom, Edward felt he was putting on a disguise.

Back out at the desk, the clerk introduced him to the *maître d'armes*, M. Pierre Artaud, who assured him that nothing could better reinvigorate him than the noble art of fencing. To commence, they would warm up *monsieur*'s muscles and then see what he remembered.

After a few stretches, knee bends, and arm rotations, M. Artaud took down a mesh-visored mask from a line; inside were tucked wide-cuffed gloves. *Monsieur* should always use these sets bound in red; the others belonged to regular clients. Below hung foil after foil. The one M. Artaud handed to Edward was light and springy, far lighter than the sabers that officers carried into battle in 1861. It could break as the attendant had warned, but its springiness demanded panache.

Edward stepped back and came to rigid attention as he had in the Ninth. With his mask held up to his chest, he flourished his weapon through a salute and begged the honor of a lesson in arms. M. Artaud returned the salute with solemnity and proceeded to bark out a series of commands: pronate, supinate, advance, retreat, lunge. Edward maneuvered the blade through basic positions and took up stances, learning in only a few minutes how tiring it could be to maintain the balance of a long foil against gravity. Although he knew he ought to take as detached an attitude as his examiner in a diagnostic session, he was annoyed when the blade wobbled. When he made mistakes, he leaped to try again before Artaud could correct him.

"*Bon, monsieur.* Now we cross swords—only briefly, only to touch steel, no follow-through."

It was not a match, but every cut or thrust made by Edward was quickly deflected. When it was his turn to demonstrate ripostes, he could not remember them. The approach of the foil point to his mask frightened him. Yet against all reason and growing breathlessness, he threw himself into trying harder. No good. He felt weak; everything flew out of control.

"*Arrêtez!*" M. Artaud called a halt and stepped back calmly, breathing normally.

Edward gasped for air. He coughed; his right arm and both knees trembled. It brought back the rout and confusion of defeat in war and how sick even the work of victory had made him, scavenging and stripping bodies after a battle with the reek of metal, gunpowder, and death in the air. (When he had taken his first sword out of the dead hand of a Confederate officer and tossed it on a heap of gathered weapons, the clank seemed to be all that chivalry amounted to.) He could hardly register what M. Artaud was saying.

"Here is what I can do for you, *monsieur*. Your hands are good. With them, I see, you habitually make precise and controlled movements. You must learn to rely on them, not your arm, to control the blade, though the arm needs strengthening, too, a matter for barbells. Your eye is good, but you must learn not to flinch when the point comes near, also to be aware of a wider field of vision. Your lame leg will be no obstacle to attaining flexibility, precision, and speed. *Bon*, I shall turn you over now to an assistant to teach you a routine warm-up."

An hour and a half later, Edward left in a haze of exhausted wellbeing, all memories of the war forgotten. He had worked out, taken a lesson, bathed, and been worked over with oil by the Algerian masseur who manned a table in the dressing room. Emerging into the semidarkness of the courtyard, he headed for the gaslight marking the street. He was tempted to hail a cab back to the hotel and fall into bed, but a tightness across his temples and the clap of his belly warned him instead to eat or he would wake with a pounding headache at the very least. Luckily, Les Halles was full of unpretentious restaurants and cafés catering to those who worked in the nearby wholesale food markets. He had not gone half a block before he came to a brasserie called Les Vosges and saw two peasant farmers enter, one with downy goose feathers clinging to his trousers. Edward followed them. He was feeling unequal to the elegance of the Meurice, but by the look of these two men, they might have worked on Gran'marie's farm in Alsace.

Inside, similar customers stood at a bar with tall glasses of beer or sat with food in front of them, four or six to a table, talking politics or leaning back to laugh at a jest. Four men in a corner were playing cards. The atmosphere was something like that in Edward's Cincinnati eating house, but he could expect better food. Soon, he was provided with soup, beer, a wedge of pâté, and crusty rye bread. The soup was only cabbage soup with pork and vegetables—only soup? One taste and he realized it was the *potée* of his childhood, transformed by godlike hands into ambrosia. In a flood of contentment, he decided to invite Miss Pendergrast and Miss Palmer to a play.

CHAPTER TWENTY-ONE

Moving Day

Quick, Cousin Effie, put your coat on," said Jeanette, banging the door violently one evening, a few days after Edward's arrival in Paris. Boots, who had been pouncing at yarn dangled for him by Effie, swerved under the sofa. "We're going to La Poupée en Bas for supper for a council of war: Sonja's landlord has given her two weeks' notice to vacate her studio."

"Two weeks' notice! Oh, dear. Is that legal?"

"You know Sonja," said Jeanette, shaking change out of the ginger jar. "She doesn't have a lease, and she hasn't paid the rent since she got back from Italy."

"She ought to take him court."

"Why? She wouldn't win."

"Because the law drags things out, that's why. It would buy her time to look for a new place. Shoo, Boots, out you go." The cat, who was slinking back toward Effie's abandoned ball of yarn, made a sideways dive, hopped languidly onto the windowsill, and stepped out as though he had meant to leave all along.

"The owner is planning to pull the building down. We've got to find somewhere for her to go right away. Amy is unhappy with her place, too, and said she might go in with Sonja if they find something good."

La Poupée en Bas was Sonja's discovery, a supper club organized by women artists whose studio windows overlooked a back courtyard where the kitchen of an Italian *ristorante*, Les Deux Hélènes, received deliveries. *They engaged the owner of the restaurant to supply them with simple boxed lunches and daily dinners for a flat fee,* Jeanette had written her parents the first time she and Effie were taken there. *They all knew her because she used to be a model—a really good one, too, who commanded top fees. What she said, though, was that beauty fades, while people always need to eat and drink, so she lived with her mother and saved up until they could open a tavern. Mama Elena used to do all the cooking, but then the daughter, La Belle Hélène, married a cook from their home town in Tuscany. Nobody could believe it because he's so ugly and she's so pretty.* She thought it better to leave out that everyone also said that Agostino sweated in the kitchen and flavored the food with yearning. *The artists call their club La Poupée en Bas—the Doll, or the Mannequin, or the Model Downstairs—because it's in a kind of half-basement out back below the restaurant. They put a lay figure in a chair by the door, and somebody really good painted La Belle Hélène's face on it. The walls are splintery, and the soft bricks in the floor are worn down into powdery hollows. You feel like you have to duck where the ceiling is low, and you can look right up to the beams and the underflooring of the main story. But the subscribers whitewashed the walls and put blue-and-white checked table cloths on secondhand tables to make it cheerful, and the best thing about it (besides the food!) is that they hang a rotation of their own paintings, drawings, and prints every month.*

When Jeanette and Effie arrived, Amy was seated at a table near the back across from Sonja, who was sprawled half-turned in a tilted chair, her elbow propped on the top rung.

"Ah, Miss Pendergrast, you come, too. Good," she said. "One moment, please." She turned back to finish recounting to a woman at the next table the particulars of her case, freshly indignant over every intransigence on the part of her landlord and relishing every insult she had hurled at him.

"Emily's not here," observed Jeanette, a little disappointed. Emily had said she must consult Robbie first.

"Inconvenient to His Nibs, no doubt," said Amy, dryly. She nodded toward a sideboard, where a vat of soup and platters of meat sat next to a round of cheese in muslin and a bowl of fruit. "Better hurry before it's all gone."

While Effie ladled up creamy soup for them, Jeanette leaned across the sideboard to study a small canvas.

"Who did that wonderful still life of eggs in a copper bowl?" she asked, when they sat down.

"Louise Steadman," said Amy. "Good, isn't she?"

"Exquisite contours, as Emily would say. You know what we should do? Set up studies from a dairy shop: eggs, those big mounds of butter, and round cheeses—think of all the fat shapes."

"I can tell who's hungry," said Amy.

"No, really, think of the curves and closely related tones," insisted Jeanette. "What is in this marvelous soup?"

"Your eggs and cream in wine and beef broth," said Amy.

"We can never go back to America, Cousin Effie," sighed Jeanette.

"It may be required if ever you want a studio," said Sonja, gloomily. "None is to be had in Paris."

Sonja had assumed that she would hear of something that night, for the members of La Poupée en Bas always notified each other of any openings in their buildings; but by October everyone who was going to move that fall had already done so. On their way to the sideboard, a few women did stop by with an address to try or the name of someone else to ask. After one such visitor, Effie asked Amy in a low voice, "How is that name spelled?"

"Are you keeping a list, Miss P? Good show."

"Well, it's going to take some legwork, you know."

"Cousin Effie, what about Miss Reade and Miss Isobel? Could you ask them?"

"There's a thought," said Amy. "No telling what that pair might come up with. Sonja, you remember that I told you about Mabel Reade—Irish woman, older? The one who began studies with Carolus-Duran? She recently moved across the river to be in his vicinity: Nôtre-Dame-des-Champs."

"Too expensive for you and me, even on the sixth floor."

"Nonsense. There are all sorts of things around there from palaces to ant heaps."

"You never know what you'll find till you look," said Effie.

"No cold feet, you swine."

"I told you, Sonja, no promises."

Effie visited a few places with Sonja to get a sense of what she wanted. She sent a note to Miss Reade; she checked at agencies; she put the problem to Mme. LeConte, the *portière* of their *pension*.

"Sonja isn't looking for a *pension*," said Jeanette.

"Of course not, but the porters all know each other; and one thing leads to another."

Effie walked block after block, climbed dusty staircases to look at dirty rooms, and nosed out obscure back alleys. She investigated a Right Bank neighborhood near the Place de Clichy to check out comparative values. "It's closer to where Miss Richardson is now, which she might prefer." Under false pretenses, she talked her way into one apartment and studio near the Reade sisters' building on the Rue d'Assas just for the pleasure of sighing over its view of treetops in the Luxembourg Garden. With her bad French, no one knew how she managed it all, but she did. She found time, moreover, to stop in for morning coffee and report to Cornelia on her progress. "Darling Effie, you must write all this down," said Cornelia, more than once. "You could sell it to the newspapers." Sometimes Edward was there. When he was not, Cornelia regaled him later with heightened versions of Effie's accounts. "You must not dream of returning to Germany," she said, "until we know how it turns out."

On Wednesday of the second, fateful week, Effie arrived midday at Julian's, greatly excited. It seemed that Miss Reade had a friend whose upstairs neighbor might move downstairs if the two ladies could find someone congenial to sublet the cheaper studio and apartment while they tried out their shared living arrangement. The upstairs tenant would be home late that afternoon and was willing to show her place.

"It's on an impasse off the Rue Madame. If Mlle. Borealska will just come take a look at it on her way home before she does anything foolish . . ."

"I doubt that Sonja is here today," said Amy, shortly.

"You don't mean she's off signing a lease!"

"I have no idea what Sonja Borealska is doing. Why I ever so much as hinted I might go in with her is beyond me. But I can promise you one thing: She never signs leases."

"What about this, Cousin Effie," said Jeanette, as worried by Amy's irritation as by Effie on one of her flights, "I'll meet you at Galignani's reading room after the first break this afternoon. We can scout out the apartment. If it's any good, we'll track down Sonja somehow."

The Rue Madame began near the mismatched towers of Saint-Sulpice and ended at the Rue d'Assas. Throughout the area, buildings were fast filling in what remained of the semirural garden plots, work yards, and vacant land that had characterized the district not many years before. Having mastered its intricacies during the last ten days, Effie could go straight to the address on a dead-end half-block. The *portière* sent them through an archway into a narrow passage between the building and a high wall.

The studio block was ten or twelve years old. Its burnish of newness had worn off without acquiring charm, unless a few scars and gouges where it had been hit by Prussian shells counted as marks of history. Pigeon droppings stained the walls and had been allowed to pile up in ragged pyramids along the base of the building—an authentic Sonja touch, thought Jeanette, stepping carefully to avoid dirtying her shoes. When they came out into a little courtyard, they could see better over the wall beside them: Splay-fingered, brown leaves of two tall chestnuts were visible along with the half-bare limbs of a few apple and pear trees. An entryway door opened into a stairwell that reeked of turpentine, linseed oil, and possibly urine. At each floor landing, the jambs and entablature of the door frames dwindled in width and decoration. The fifth-floor fixtures were strictly utilitarian and the hallway was painted an olive that must have been nondescript even when it was fresh. Yet any doubts about the place were banished as soon as Mlle. Tourneau, the tenant, admitted them to the apartment.

Even on a dark day, cool light emanated from the studio on their right, abundant reflected light that could come only from a very large space with many windows. Behind Mlle. Tourneau, a corridor ran past a couple of rooms, back to a daylit kitchen. Mlle. Tourneau explained that she used one as her bedroom and the other as a dining room, but they could both be made into bedrooms if one ate in the studio. There was running water. Outside a studio window, the treetops next door became part of a wider view. There was far more greenery here, and more variety in the building types and rooftops than on the Rue Jacob.

Ah, oui, the orchard was very beautiful, agreed Mlle. Tourneau, and showed them a downward-angled landscape she had painted from that very window. She came to the point: Did they think Mlle. Borealska and Mlle. Richardson would want the apartment? Someone else was coming to look this afternoon, too. With a start, Jeanette realized what Mlle. Tourneau had just said.

"If our friends don't want it, we do," she said firmly, in French. "Miss Reade will vouch for us."

"How could you commit us to a higher rent like that?" expostulated Effie, when they were back outside.

"At worst, it's only six months, Cousin Effie. We'd find a way. We've saved thirty francs a month over what we had planned just by living in the *pension*."

"And spent most of it, too! Oh, dear. Well, something would turn up, I suppose, or . . . What am I saying! You make me sound like Mr. Micawber, Jeanette."

"Don't worry. Sonja and Amy will take it."

They found Sonja; she saw the apartment; she took it. In the past, she had repeatedly refused the commission for a portrait of two children, offered as what she knew to be charity by an exiled friend of her father's. On the spot, she decided to accept it in order to get the advance. "Better to sacrifice my pride than sleep in the rain this winter," she admitted. "And such light!" When Amy saw it, her earlier dissatisfactions with her own place became unbearable. She agreed to share the rent as soon as she could give notice.

By the time Effie sat with Cornelia and Edward in the Poutery on Friday to report on the dénouement, she was pink with the triumph. "We're going to have Mlle. Borealska out in time to beat her deadline tomorrow. She has borrowed three handcarts for haulage and the girls are festooning them like carnival floats. Why don't you come, Dr. Murer? It's going to be like a carnival."

"Edward Murer," said Cornelia, "if you don't go and come back with a report, I shall never let you into my house again!"

*　*　*

The next day at noon, Edward had a cab drop him at the corner nearest the rather dubious address Effie had given him. From there, he went on foot, relying on what he could remember of her instructions. He put a question or two to strangers, and the sixth sense acquired by walking as much as he did got him the rest of the way. His top hat, frock coat, and elegant cane were out of place in such a knockabout neighborhood, but his quiet self-possession deflected attention. He was ignored as someone who might be coming to inquire about a piece of work.

As he came to a roofed passage under a building, he almost asked a man sitting with a newspaper in a recessed doorway whether he was going the right way, but there was no need. Through the arch on the other side stood Miss Pendergrast's carnival carts, their long shafts up in the air and crêpe paper rosettes tacked around their rims. A few boxes were stacked near the open door of a dilapidated outbuilding. Over the sound of voices, a hammer banged in nails to close up a crate. Inside, half a dozen women and several young men were packing up the last of Sonja's belongings. Jeanette, who was helping Amy wrap up some small sculptures, saw Edward before Effie did. She smiled. Among her friends in all this activity, she was far more animated than he had seen her before. It made her pretty. "Cousin Effie," she called, and guided Sonja over to meet him with Amy and Emily in tow. "You must meet Cousin Effie's friend, Dr. Murer."

"I own nothing, nothing," moaned Sonja, after introductions were made. "How can there be this chaos?" Edward was amused by the genuine perplexity on her face.

"A little crockery, a teakettle," said Amy, mimicking her moan. She still held last summer's terra-cotta bust of herself ready to wrap in a canvas rag.

"A saucepan, spoons," crooned Jeanette.

"A broom, a mop, a pail," keened Emily, in a thin wail.

"They laugh at me. I tell them this is all I own, and it is true. A little crockery, a broom. Except, of course, tools of my trade."

"Profession; we are professional artists, not artisans," corrected Amy. "But of such tools, there are rather a lot, and some of them very large."

In the crates she used for furniture, Sonja had put her scanty wardrobe, the bits of costumes she had acquired for models, and the few domestic implements her friends teased her about; but then there were all the paints and canvases, the stretchers, her turntable and finished terra-cotta pieces, a tub of clay. The plan had been to set off at noon, but the work of loading carts had not even begun.

"How do you do, sir? My name is Dolson," said Robbie, who had pushed off from the wall to follow Emily over. He held out a hand. He was at his most golden and innocently insolent.

Edward took the hand. "Murer," he said. He was not fooled; this man Dolson was complicated. As Effie joined them with a dot of pink pleasure in each cheek, the shade of insolence melted out of Robbie's face, to be replaced by merriment. Edward lifted his hat.

Jeanette had not missed the instant of scrutiny and veiled challenge between the two men nor the contrast in their demeanor when Effie arrived. She wondered which face she would rather paint. Dr. Murer's was the darker, the more forbidding (something very wrong there, or pained), but kinder; an imposed stillness over turmoil. In Robbie's case, you would need to catch a different kind of shadow, like bruises under the bloom of a piece of fruit.

"I'd say we're ready to start loading the carts," said Amy, to cut short any further chitchat. Slow as progress had been that morning, without her habit of taking charge, everything would have taken four times longer.

"Not without a break first," said Robbie, always ready to contradict her. He took Emily and Jeanette each by an arm. "Fortification required before heavy lifting. Midday repast, everyone? *Le déjeuner?* Come along, Wee Willie, mustn't miss lunch.

"Our bonnie lad's strength exceeds his height tenfold," he said to Edward. "Allow me to introduce you. Winkham is studying at the École de Médicine. I believe you practice in the inspiringly named Cincinnati?"

Edward met short Mr. Winkham's long-suffering eye and liked him. "The *Doctor* was conferred on me by customers," he said, as they shook hands. "I'm a dispensing pharmacist."

"Do more good than many a quack with a diploma," said Winkie. The two men fell easily into discussion of botanicals and synthetic alkaloids as they walked among the others.

The break ran longer than intended. Fourteen people walk slower than one; fourteen diners talk as well as eat. By the time they returned to the studio, two hours had elapsed. In the interim, the windows of the building had been boarded up from inside and Sonja's padlock had been replaced by a new one. There were indignant calls for a mallet—"Two can play at this game!"—but Robbie stepped forward and crouched in front of the door. He took the lock in his left hand to test its weight and wiggled the fingers of his right hand.

"Ah, Jasper," he said, with satisfaction, invoking the old reprobate who had taught him to poach. Without looking around, he held his hand palm up behind him. "Emily, dearest, a hatpin."

"I haven't got one."

Jeanette saw Emily's face close but was too excited to care. "Will this do?" she asked, pulling out one of hers. She felt the same gleeful recklessness as on the night she had impersonated Abigail McLeod— a compound of fear that they might be caught at any moment and an unquestioning certainty that it was in a good cause.

"Winkie, keep a look out," said Robbie over his shoulder as he probed the lock delicately. Already he was absorbed in listening and feeling for subtle adjustments in its tumblers. Mr. Winkham and one of the burly sculptors slipped away to post themselves at the two approaches to the yard.

It was a stout padlock but simple in its mechanism; no trouble at all. Not to an experienced housebreaker, thought Edward. He knew that in principle, as a man of property, he ought to side with the landlord; as a longtime boarder, he did not. Men who profited on sties like this had to take their lumps, especially if they allowed rain to damage the means of a tenant's livelihood. Moreover, license must be granted to anyone who could sculpt a portrait as alive as that bust of Miss Richardson. He was less sure about a license to pick locks, but Dolson did the job too quickly to allow time for scruples. The lock came off; the door was opened.

"Women inside, men out," ordered a stonecutter whom Sonja had enlisted to help pull the carts. Edward's seniority and limp exempted him from the human chain that quickly formed to bundle out Sonja's possessions helter-skelter, but he took up a position beside the cart and pitched in to help straighten and pack things in more scientifically after they were hastily deposited.

From his watch post, Winkie gave a whistle and came hurrying back. His face expressed regret at ever having gotten mixed up in this prank. "Two henchmen with staves," he reported to Robbie. "We've got to get Emily out of here."

"That way," nodded Robbie, in the direction the other guard was watching.

Too late. A man in a hairy checked suit and bowler hat with two toughs at his heels was in the yard. Robbie ducked inside to guard Emily as Sonja came to the door of the studio. Disdain rather than fear pursed her mouth. With her chin in the air, she pushed up a sleeve, sniffed loudly, and deliberately turned her back again, as if daring her antagonists to try to stop her from returning to work. She looked like she might duck around again to throw the first punch. Edward admired her courage and theatrical instincts but agreed with Mr. Winkham: With women involved, things must not be allowed to get out of hand.

"*Bonjour, monsieur,*" he said, pleasantly, coming forward from behind the cart. He halted at a little distance, which compelled the landlord to divert his eyes from the doorway. As Edward suspected, the presence of someone like himself was a surprise.

"*Qui est-ce c'singe à soie?*" one of the muscle men muttered. Who's the swell?

Edward explained with deliberate calmness that he was a visitor to Paris who had heard through a friend that Mlle. Borealska was moving; he had been invited to come along to help. He had seen her work for the first time today. She was very good. It must have been a privilege to provide space to so talented an artist.

The landlord grimaced derisively. He had buildings full of talent such as this. Edward lifted his cane and pointed it over the man's shoulder toward the wall of studio windows behind him. He bobbed the point of the cane lightly, controlling it with his forefinger and thumb: There, there, and there? he inquired.

A henchman shifted his staff from one hand to the other and started forward. Immediately, Edward swung the tip of the cane around at him and drilled him with a hard stare. Behind him, the burly stonecutter shifted weight. The landlord stretched out an arm to stop his men. A little bullying, a little rough stuff to force payment or confiscate goods was one thing. It was quite another to come up against a bigger crowd than he had bargained for and to find this *type*, someone entirely outside his reckoning. With a last warning gaze at the subordinate, Edward lowered his cane and said politely to the boss: "You were about to remark on your many tenants . . . ?"

"Cuckoos and cheats, most of them," grumbled the man.

"But not Mlle. Borealska. I was on the point of offering her two hundred francs for a terra-cotta bust." An astonished murmur ran through the yard. It was not a princely sum at a time when a new canvas by Meissonier sold for thirty thousand, but it could cover several months' rent.

Only Sonja frowned. "If you think I pay *him* out of these two hundred francs, save your money."

"On the contrary, *mademoiselle*, I was going to suggest that he negotiate to settle your differences by retaining a piece of your art. As an investment, I assure you, *monsieur*. I believe this lady's work will rise in value—though not the water-damaged pieces, of course."

The two men stared at each other. The landlord backed down, then reasserted himself. "If I wished to be a honey pot, I'd never lack for flies," he grumbled. "They all try to barter their *crottes* for rent. I could open a gallery."

"Which might prove amusing. But come now, admit that you would not be in this business if you did not care a little for artists— and you and I, *monsieur*, we could not stay in business at all if we did not know when to cut our losses."

Whether a change in Edward's tone was persuasive or the landlord had already arrived at the same conclusion, he suddenly gave way altogether. *"Eh, bien, Cosaque, va-t'en avant le coucher du soleil,"* he said, insulting her with the familiar *tu*. He turned heel. Be gone by sunset.

"Long before sunset!" Sonja jeered to his back, then added resentfully to her friends, who were crowding out: "Does he call me a Cossack, *me?*"

"Sticks and stones may break my bones, but words can never hurt me," said Amy, giving her a prod in the back. "Let's finish up."

"That was brilliant, sir," said Robbie, reemerging from inside with a congratulatory hand held out to Edward. "Picking a lock is as nothing compared to picking a man's pocket in broad view."

It was not lost on Edward that under the cover of witty self-deprecation, Dolson was being offensive. Nor was it lost on Jeanette. It exasperated her that Robbie seemed to go out of his way to provoke people when he could be so likeable, but her overriding reaction, like everyone else's, was admiration for Dr. Murer's cool handling of the landlord.

"Oh, I'm so thankful you prevented trouble, Dr. Murer," said Effie. "What a bad turn that could have been!"

"Is it true you want a sculpture of mine?" asked Sonja. "Or was that bluff? In either case, I thank you."

"Not bluff at all. I do want one—and for the two hundred francs I named. If you agree to part with it, I would be honored to buy your portrait of Miss Richardson."

"The bust of me!" exclaimed Amy.

"The one you were holding when I arrived," said Edward. He turned back to Sonja. "It's a remarkably lively piece, and I think it would please a friend of mine. Cornelia," he added to Effie in an aside.

"Mrs. Renick," Jeanette mouthed to Amy.

"I give it to you. No, no, I *give* it to you," said Sonja, who saw that Edward was about to insist on paying. "It is only a study. You consider it, and if you desire later, you buy something else or commission a new piece."

"Well, that's very handsome of you," said Edward. "My friend has been following your saga, and I think she will treasure the piece."

"My face in Mrs. Marius Renick's collection?" murmured Amy. "Well done, Sonja. For your work to be seen there is worth far more than two hundred francs."

"Dr. Murer," asked Jeanette, boldly, "do you think Mrs. Renick would like to have the artist and model deliver the piece?"

Effie yelped at her forwardness, but Edward thought it an excellent idea. "Now, Miss Pendergrast, you know how much she enjoys diversion of any sort. I think such a call would be most welcome."

After that, the removal, which had always been planned as part escapade, part parade, turned into a high-spirited celebration. From a corner heap, Sonja produced a papier-mâché mask of Minerva to adorn the broom and set it atop one of the carts. The mask had a diadem of silver stars, and Emily brought out matching spangles for the ladies to wear. Other bits of costume were also distributed— Jeanette threw a glossy, if moth-eaten, satin shawl around her shoulders; Robbie donned a tricorn hat with a plume. Edward accepted a comically large rosette for his lapel. When they were ready to go, Sonja took the lead, bellowing a Polish marching song. Her burly friends pushed and pulled the carts-turned-float through the streets of the Left Bank. Along the way, a number of tagalongs and extras fell in, including a concertina player. When he launched into an Offenbach galop, Robbie took Jeanette by the hand to pull her in among the livelier members of the group, who were dancing variations on the can-can. He kicked high. She pranced and lifted an ankle to shake. Effie was not one of the dancers, nor Edward, who escorted her with a formal gallantry. But if he did not join in, he smiled broadly at the revelry; with that much approval to go on, Effie grinned, too, and marched along at her ease.

When they reached the impasse on the Rue Madame, Miss Reade was ready upstairs with a dozen bottles of Beaujolais. Miss Isobel had festooned the studio in paper chains. For the six-month trial, Mlle. Tourneau was subletting the apartment furnished, and from somewhere, platters of charcuterie, loaves of bread, and cheeses had appeared to be laid out on the dining room table. Sonja insisted that Effie and Edward go straight up and claim the sofa: "Miss Pendergrast, you find the apartment, and Dr. Murer, you save the day. We make you king and queen of the fête." Everyone else carried up something, and a few of the new neighbors pitched in. Hauling everything up five flights of stairs was harder work than packing had been, but it went much faster. It was all done in less than an hour, whereupon a violinist from the building added his fiddle to the concertina. There was more impromptu dancing in the large studio and loud song. But as darkness fell, Amy lit candles and the mood became more sentimental; the fiddler's tunes turned gypsy. It had been, as Effie had promised, a regular Latin Quarter ball.

"Oh, my dear," said Cornelia to Edward, when she heard the story the following Monday, "how can I ever thank you for including me in the sequel?"

"You can give me an expert opinion on what sort of piece to commission."

"Oh, that's easy: You must have her do portraits of darling Effie and Miss Palmer."

※

CHAPTER TWENTY-TWO

The Treasure Room

Cornelia formally invited Sonja and Amy for the following Sunday afternoon. In honor of the occasion, Amy insisted that Sonja look respectable. "For the Faubourg Saint-Germain, *oui*," agreed Sonja. She was too tall and brawny to borrow clothes easily; but from her own trunk, she produced the nondescript brown cashmere dress trimmed in braid and jet buttons in which she had arrived from Poland four years ago and even the yellowing corset to wear under it. A friend from La Poupée en Bas lent her a high-crowned, brown felt hat trimmed in pheasant feathers. Altogether, she looked rather haphazard but imposing.

As for Jeanette, this time she could visit the Renicks secure in the knowledge that what she wore was perfect. Not only did Effie now regularly bring home Cornelia's discarded fashion magazines, but she also spent a lot of time window shopping or browsing in the big department stores on her way to and from McAll Mission halls and Mrs. Renick's Poutery. Moralists inveighed against buying frenzies induced by the seductive displays of goods in the huge emporia, but a New Yorker on a tight budget and hardened by exposure to

Macy's was in no danger. Effie came closest to losing her head one day in the Bon Marché (her favorite store because many on the staff spoke English) when she spotted a ready-made navy blue jacket on a sale rack. It closely resembled an illustration she and Jeanette had admired in *La Mode Illustrée*. A rip in the jacket shoulder greatly reduced the price. Even then, rather than buy wildly, Effie persuaded a sales clerk to hold it a few hours until she could hurry Jeanette over to approve it. Jeanette did so, enthusiastically; and with repair by an in-house seamstress and a skirt and bodice run up from the yard goods department, she found herself provided with a smart new outfit for daytime.

To Jeanette's embarrassment, Emily was not invited to the unveiling. "Why should I be?" asked Emily. "I am neither the sculptress nor the model nor a friend of the Renicks. Very few people even know I exist." As a matter of fact, Cornelia had heard a lot about Emily from Effie; and Mr. Renick, who had many sources of information, had made inquiries. Miss Richardson was as safe as houses, and Mlle. Borealska came of good family with connections to minor nobility. More than one member of the Polish exile community predicted that sooner or later Sonja Borealska's disregard of convention would make her notorious; but so far, as the ninth child of eleven and a woman who showed no designs on eligible men, she was too insignificant to be ostracized. The Dolsons were different. There was nothing definite against him in police reports, but Robert Dolson was known to keep shady company. Journalists often did, of course; and for that very reason, Mr. Renick was firm about which ones he let into his house. A banker could not be too careful.

Edward arranged to pick up Sonja and Amy in a carriage first, then Effie and Jeanette. Ever since they had met at the Renicks', Jeanette had thought of him as Effie's Dr. Murer and a friend of her parents (technically untrue but close enough); nor did Effie's reports of him from the Poutery do anything to change her mind. Then in the previous week, after Sonja's moving day, he had taken her and

Effie to Corneille's *Le Cid* at the Théâtre de l'Odéon, where Effie had kept a copy of the play open on her lap to help with the dialogue. Judging by his absorption whenever Jeanette glanced at him, Dr. Murer needed no such crutch. Once he caught her looking at him and half smiled inquisitively. She shook her head and turned back to the action on stage. Later, when it was Jeanette's turn to hold the play, he missed an exchange and leaned toward her. Correctly reading his intent, she silently passed him the book. That night, as she drifted off to sleep rehearsing the evening and embroidering on it, the little moments between them came up over and over again. Over the next few days, Dr. Murer's confrontation with Sonja's landlord likewise grew longer, with variations and ever-more-melodramatic outcomes. Now, by the wide-awake light of day, when he handed her into the carriage, she met a pleasure in his eyes with pleasure of her own. She was very aware of gathering up her new skirt and stepping up buoyantly.

To Edward, she looked no older than when he first had first seen her in May, yet less touchingly gauche, more polished. Paris was working its reputed magic. Ever since the theatrical outing he, too, had had a sense that they were inside a new pale of acknowledged acquaintanceship—not courtship, but even as he tried to deny it, he had to admit that he had wished all along to court her company. Since the night he had found Marie's photograph dead to him, returning health had enabled him to resuscitate a sentimental flicker of affection for his dead fiancée's memory and the happiness they might have shared, but he no longer deceived himself. His early attachment was fixed in ghostly lines, unchanging except to fade molecule by molecule as surely as the silver iodide of the tintype. Miss Palmer was vital. Her limbs had volume; they occupied space; and when she moved, the air took on her scent. She was not the primary reason he had been on his guard to avoid anything more than courteous relations with Miss Pendergrast, but she undeniably made him more aware of just how tactfully he must tread.

Inside the carriage, Effie sat beside Edward and sensed the currents. The effect of pretty young women on men of all ages was not news to her, nor the nullity of being middle-aged, homely, and poor. All the same, she had come out to the carriage cheerfully thinking of Dr. Murer, a man her own age, as her friend from the Poutery, while the three students were set off in her mind as "the girls." She might not often have let herself stray into speculating on what it would be like to go home, not to New York City, but to Cincinnati, as a married woman with a house of her own; she might have every reason to be well content with the platonic friendship of an old maid and old bachelor unlikely to last more than the few weeks of Dr. Murer's visit to Paris; nevertheless, it was cause for chagrin to be forced to revise her assessment of his inclinations.

At the Renicks' house, a junior footman wanted to take the battered, striped-silk hatbox in which Sonja carried the portrait bust, but she would not relinquish it. Up the grand staircase she marched with an alarmed Amy on her heels. Right past Hastings, who waited at the drawing room door. Straight in to where Mrs. Renick was seated on her sofa halfway across the room. Sonja deposited her hatbox on the floor, curtsied deeply, and proclaimed, "Mme. Renick, I am Sonja Borealska." Without waiting for an answer, she dropped to her knees and sat back on her heels. From beside the sofa, Mr. Renick silently signaled Hastings to send the others in unannounced. From the musty, faded plush depths of the hatbox, Sonja lifted out the bust swathed in a clean silk scarf.

"Now you take the box," said Sonja, grandly, indicating it with her head to the flustered junior footman, who had followed the guests into the room, unsure whether he was wanted. "Burn it; it has served its last purpose."

"Come closer, everybody," said Cornelia, as she began carefully to unwrap the clay bust. "*Mademoiselle*, you must sit here beside me." Cradling the back of the portrait head in her hands, she tilted it to examine the face. "Oh, Edward! it is as alive as you described it—and almost as beautiful as the model." She looked up at Amy, who stood with Jeanette at one arm of the sofa. "Forgive me, Miss Richardson; I spoke too freely; that was personal. But, oh, how I am carried away! Mlle. Borealska, the skill of your fingers catches the brilliance of your insight. Thank you, *thank you*, for parting with this. I couldn't have done it in your place. Jacques—" The head footman, who had been waiting inconspicuously, brought over a side table on which sat a revolving sculptor's chassis. With gloved hands that were practiced in dealing with precious objects, he set the bust on the turntable. Mrs. Renick winked her thanks at him in a glance. "Dr. Murer tells me you are primarily a painter, *mademoiselle*," she said to Sonja, without taking her eyes off the piece, "but it is obvious that you also love this medium."

"It is only a maquette, *madame*. Hollowed out, but not fired— air-dried."

"Yes, I can see that." Cornelia turned the piece, lightly fingering it. "I adore enameled earthenware, but the play of light over bisque is more revealing. And *this*—!"

"If you wish, I make you a more permanent cast and fire it. This clay is too impure for the kiln."

"No, no! I love its soft spontaneity."

Cornelia revolved the turntable inch by inch to examine the piece from different angles. From behind the sofa, Mr. Renick leaned forward intently. "I think we must show them the treasure room," he said, quietly.

His wife nodded wordlessly, her eyes still on the sculpture. Then she looked up. "But first, we must see what else they have brought. You did all bring samples of your work, didn't you?"

Jeanette had brought a few figure studies from class, which demonstrated her progress since May. To avoid showing even draped nudes to Dr. Murer and Mr. Renick, she let portraits from the afternoon sessions demonstrate her progress in class. She had also included a drawing of Amy at work perched on their hill in Pont Aven and another of her at her easel in the Gernagans' upstairs room.

"I can see that you loved that room. How perfectly you handled the last reach of the sunbeam into the farther corner!" said Cornelia, pausing to smile over the picture. "And is this Mlle. Borealska's famous willow? My, my, it does have character!—or have you given it a personality?"

"No, no, she does not impose. It is potent, that tree," said Sonja. "It has a wild heart."

"If you beat a child with a willow stick, it will stunt his growth," said Cousin Effie.

There was a brief moment of paralysis while everyone looked at her, not knowing how to respond. Jeanette felt an all-too-familiar inward constriction and then, from practice, turned back to her drawings and simply continued in a slightly forced voice. "I thought you might like to see some more of what Sonja abandoned."

A cartoon of Mortimer treading a catwalk. A quick sketch of Amy carving her bust of Sonja. A more elaborate study of a cluttered corner of the studio.

"You have a gift for rooms, Jeanette," said Cornelia, "especially studios."

"I keep thinking that when I go back home, I won't be able to make people understand what it's like here unless I can make them feel the inside of the rooms!" Jeanette eagerly pulled out two sheets from deeper in the portfolio. "Here's one of my things set up in our front dormer, and here's what we see out the window. And here's a watercolor of Cousin Effie on the sofa with Boots. You see? She found this mustard-yellow folding screen with the Japanese bamboo pattern at a flea market; it's broken, but we hide the smashed part, and it has made all the difference in the room."

When Cornelia had seen every picture, she looked up at Mr. Renick. "Why don't you show them upstairs while it is still light enough, before tea is served. Darling Effie can keep me company—unless, my dear, you want to see things again?" If Effie would usually have preferred to be part of any party and look at precious objects rather than stay behind to converse with someone she saw several times a week, nothing in her habits or experience would have allowed her to say so. Today, in fact, she was grateful.

The way to the Renicks' treasure room led through a long picture gallery hung with landscapes by the Dutch Masters and the latest depictions of Parisian life. Edward paused in front of a picture of sand dunes with the roofs of a brick town in the distance; it might have been painted on the very coast of Belgium that had welcomed him back to Europe. Above it hung an even earlier Flemish Nativity set in what appeared to be the ruins of a stone hall. An ox and ass stuck their heads through broken windows. Outside, just visible, stretched a tiny landscape of green hills with patches of woods and a road winding to a half-timbered village. Struck by a look on Dr. Murer's face, Jeanette stopped beside him. What could account for such longing? "Do you know what I love?" asked Edward. "It's that glimpse of what's outside the window. There's a whole world in that tiny landscape. If you could get into the picture and walk up that road, you'd be bathed in clear sunshine and a world new made. It would smell of grass and flowers."

Meanwhile, a different painting had brought Amy to a halt. "I say, sir, can that be a Rembrandt?"

"*Rest on the Flight into Egypt*," said Mr. Renick, "his only nocturnal landscape. This, of course, is a copy, but from his own studio, I believe."

The others joined them. To Edward, the effect of the night scene was the opposite of his Flemish Nativity. Here, one would not venture out into the dark shadows but take refuge beside a campfire in the lower left of the picture. Its blazing heart of flame held his eye. Jeanette, too, saw tenderness around the fire and mystery in the shadowy trees beyond it, but her eye was pulled upward to the cool, silvery light of an unseen moon emanating from behind a bank of dark cloud, transcendent.

"Someday," began Jeanette, without thinking, then paused.

"Someday?" prompted Mr. Renick.

Hoping not to sound presumptuous, she went on: "I'd like to copy this picture."

Mr. Renick made a half bow. His face remained as impassive as always, but Jeanette caught a pleased glint in his eye. "Of course, you must copy it when you are ready, my dear. We shall be glad for any of you to work in the house. Apply for appointments with Hastings.

"And now, before the light fails—"

Mr. Renick led them up a back staircase to a bedroom rendered highly adaptable to his purpose by a vogue in the previous century for bedroom alcoves, embrasures, and little rooms of all sorts. A dressing room or small study had become a secular chapel for a carved altar, Flemish triptych, and painted wooden statue of an angel. A shallow closet with the door removed now housed a variegated marble column on which sat an alabaster bust of a lady. Above and behind her was mounted a monochrome enameled Madonna and Child.

"Luca della Robbia," said Mr. Renick, gesturing toward it. "Our only example of his work, but we also have an Andrea della Robbia and several polychrome pieces from their studio."

"And this?" said Sonja, letting her gaze fall back reverently to the alabaster sculpture.

"Florentine; fifteenth century; artist and subject unknown."

"May I?" asked Sonja. Her arms were at her side, but her hands were cocked at the wrist.

"Of course," said Mr. Renick, watching her keenly.

Sonja's kid gloves were disgracefully spotted, but they had once been fine and were delicately thin. Her fingers in them ran lightly over the smooth, barely modeled planes of a face elegant, aloof, serene. The archaic smile was almost Attic; the almond eyes were suggested largely by thin crescent lids.

"If I try for this pure simplicity, ideal, so perfect," said Sonja, "I fear a blank. Ah, but Lucca della Robbia: the face he models has more detail. For this nineteenth century of ours, so nervous, so full of change and quickness, clay must portray movement, a moment, nothing ever exactly the same, but true, true." Sonja took the tour out of Marius Renick's hands. All the while she talked, she bent, examined, and measured things with her eye. Perfectly capable of wresting back control if he wanted it, Mr. Renick seemed instead to enjoy viewing his own collection through the prism of Sonja's idiosyncrasies.

"Enamel finish, does it not make a piece fine, debonair? Dr. Murer, you tell me the other day you investigate glazes in Germany, yes? A revival of pottery, it will be a good art to take to the wider audience of this democratic age. Many people should own beautiful things."

"Would you consider undertaking glazed terra-cotta portrait plaques yourself?" asked Mr. Renick. "I have a son and daughter . . ."

Sonja pursed her lips in thought. "In this I am not specially trained. Never have I fired glazes. Perhaps I could line up time at a kiln, but—" She lifted her shoulders, unsure.

"Perhaps you will do me the honor of giving it a try on Miss Palmer and Miss Pendergrast first," said Edward.

"Us!" exclaimed Jeanette.

"To be honest, I feel I owe it to Mlle. Borealska's former landlord—"

"To that *crétin* you owe nothing, nothing!"

"Well, but I owe it to you, *mademoiselle*, for making this day possible. Let me commission a pair of portraits, just among friends. If you will notify me when you are going to fire them, it will be my great pleasure to come watch and I might be of technical assistance. I return to Freiburg this week, but I'll go with a lighter heart if I know there's something special to bring me back to Paris."

CHAPTER TWENTY-THREE

Noggins

On Monday at the studio, Emily set up in a back corner, an oddly distant vantage point for someone who always made highly restricted studies. Jeanette put herself at an angle she preferred, closer to the model; but at the first break, she asked, "Is everything all right?"

"Almost," said Emily. "Not quite."

The next day, Emily was still withdrawn when the two of them walked to the Louvre for a half day of copying drawings in the Department of Prints, something they now did regularly on Tuesday afternoons.

On Wednesday, Jeanette climbed the last staircase from the Rue Vivienne to an excited buzz in the classroom. It quieted when she came through the door.

"Jeanette, how could you?" demanded Amy.

"What?"

"This," said Amy.

She jerked a magazine open, face out. Inset into a double column of type was a cartoon—a lady artist under a tree recoiling from an insect stuck to her canvas, Jeanette's cartoon from Pont Aven. Her own work in print! Jeanette's tiny clap of pleasure sank into bewilderment—how?

"Let me see that," she said. *Noggins*, it was called, a magazine in English. Her eye skipped up to the opening paragraph:

From the Continent comes word of a dire new contagion. Emanating from the capital of all that is fashionable, the fever has now spread beyond the environs of Paris. Fair ladies, beware, for the malady is very catching—and, gentlemen, oh, be warned of how very fetching it is upon 'em! If not checked, this infectious mania must soon cross the Channel. Indeed, an incipient outbreak among Albion's daughters abroad has been witnessed personally by Your Very Own Correspondent on a recent holiday excursion to Brittany. Out with the telescopes, on the alert! First symptoms of the bewitching disorder are a palette, a paintbox, and a deliciously coy straw bonnet.

A satire of women artists painting out of doors: The resemblance of the cartoon lady to Amy was enough to explain her anger. When Jeanette came to a paragraph about an American naive waxing lyrical on a train, her face flushed. "Robbie Dolson wrote this, didn't he?"

"Who else? Don't pretend you didn't know about it—you must have supplied him the cartoon. It's yours. That's me. I was there when you drew it, remember?"

"But I didn't give it to him! I gave it to Emily. She had painted a bee on the lip of a gladiolus trumpet—don't you remember that, too? We swapped." Jeanette skimmed the rest of the article. "You don't suppose she gave it to him on purpose for *this*," she said. "How could he write such an insulting piece about his own sister?"

"How could he use your work without permission? If what you say is true, that's what you should be worried about. It's flat stealing. And for your reputation, you do want to control where your work appears, you know."

"Where's Emily?" asked Jeanette, fiercely.

"Well, if she knows this hit the stands yesterday, she's hardly likely to come here today, is she?"

But Emily did come. Once Amy had explained, in French, that Jeanette was a victim of piracy and not the perpetrator of the offense, the magazine passed from hand to hand again for everyone to take a second look. They debated the cartoon's merits as a drawing, as a joke among friends, and as a likeness to Amy. Everyone agreed that Emily had been either a traitor or a fool to let her brother publish a friend's work without asking.

Emily seemed to expect the worst. At the midmorning break when the room was half empty, she crept to her easel, hidden under the hood of a cloak. She was so drained of color that she had never appeared mousier or more unwell.

"Has Amy seen it?" asked Emily, barely above a whisper.

"If it's *Noggins* you mean, yes; she brought a copy to class."

Emily hung her head. "Robbie showed it to me Monday night. He—"

"Don't try to make excuses for him, Emily! There aren't any good enough. And I should warn you that Amy is just as mad at him as I am."

"She would be." Emily stood bent over her stool, silent for a moment. "Do you know why Amy hates Robbie so much?"

"No," said Jeanette, taken aback by the non sequitur. "And I've asked!"

"We were all three good friends at first. She used to encourage me."

"She still does when you let her."

Emily clutched herself under the cloak. "She and Robbie would wrangle tongue-in-cheek. Beatrice and Benedict. I suppose she was in love with him; most people are." Her soft voice grew lower. "Until he called her a second-rate talent who substituted plod for genius."

"How could he!"

"She was stung to the quick. It hit home."

"Emily! That's a horrible thing to say!"

"Well, it's true. But she'll have her successes all the same. She'll be in the Salon, if not next spring, then the year after that. M. Julian will see to it. And so will you, and so will everyone else in this room, every single one of you. But I won't. *There will be two more revolutions in taste before she finishes a single canvas*—oh, yes, I heard someone say that the day M. Bouguereau complimented me. *Comme Ingres*, he said, but it doesn't make any difference. He won't sponsor me, and everyone despises me. And now this, this—!" She bit her lip.

"Shhh, stop it! They're coming back in."

Emily's face crumpled, and she leaned over, flattening her hands against the stool. Her shoulders heaved. "Now you hate me, too; I won't have any friends left. I'll—"

Seeing Amy in the doorway, Jeanette signaled alarm.

Amy came directly over. "Emily Dolson, we'll worm the whole story out of you later, but for gawd's sake, buck up now," she said. "The less this *Noggins* nonsense disrupts the class, the better."

"I think she ought to go home," said Jeanette over Emily's head to Amy.

"What do you say, Emily?"

Emily nodded.

"Well, be back here tomorrow or you'll lose your nerve altogether," said Amy. "I mean it: Be here."

"I'll go with you," said Jeanette.

"No, they'll only hate you, too." With her head down, Emily brushed past Jeanette and Amy.

But Jeanette grabbed her coat and followed. When they reached the street, Emily leaned against the door lintel and said in a choked voice, "Life is so cruel."

"Emily—"

"Cruel."

"If you mean the class . . ."

"Oh, they'll never understand what I do, or care. No, it's being poor and working hard with nothing to show for it, and then something happens and we have to leave. And yet sometimes the work is good, his and mine, both of us. We have to keep at it, don't we? We have to make it come out right, otherwise how do we know who we are? That's what you said this summer. You said something like that in Pont Aven."

"Hush, Emily, not on the street."

Emily hung her head, weeping.

"It is hard," said Jeanette, soberly. She took Emily's arm. "Which way?"

Emily started south, and they walked toward the river in silence.

No one had ever known exactly where the Dolsons lived, only that they picked up their mail at a stationer's shop on the Île Saint Louis. Near a bridge to the island, the Pont Maîre, Emily said, "Thank you, Jeanette. I'd better go on alone from here." She sounded calmer. "Don't worry. I'm not going to jump in the river."

"I'm still coming with you."

"No, if Robbie is at home—"

Jeanette's suppressed anger flared. "Then he'll just have to explain himself in person."

Emily clutched her arms under her cloak and, without speaking, turned to cross the bridge. Jeanette stuck doggedly with her. As they passed under an archway into the courtyard of a mansion once grand but now neglected, Emily gave Jeanette one more beseeching look.

"Go on," said Jeanette.

She turned her key. The door opened into an ill-lit room with moisture-blotched murals and flaking gilt. The ceiling was far too high for the room's width, which was narrowed by a gimcrack partition wall that cut its one window in half. Robbie rose from a couch. His hair was tousled, his beard unshaven; his generously cut dressing gown of blue velvet was rubbed bare in places.

"Emily, my dear, at this hour? Unwell?" His expression of concern congealed to hostility. "Ah, Miss Palmer. To what do we owe the honor of this invasion of domestic privacy?"

"To *Noggins*, Mr. Dolson. Amy Richardson brought in a copy this morning."

"How quickly is fame bruited abroad! You don't look pleased."

"And you don't look apologetic."

"I don't apologize for work that pays my bills."

"What about my work, my bills?"

"Oh, please, don't quarrel, please don't!" sobbed Emily. "I can't stand it. I can't, I can't."

"There, there, dearest, no more." Robbie drew her to his side and blocked the way into the apartment. His face became dangerous. "Miss Palmer, I must ask you to leave."

Shaken, Jeanette left. On the way back to Julian's, she was still angry with Robbie but also stunned by his animosity. He often slid into dismissive boredom, but such rancor was something new.

Walking steadied her nerves; and somewhere along the way, a thought of Dr. Murer floated across her mind—Dr. Murer with his inquisitive look, his air of courteous attention. The contrast to Robbie could not have been greater. Dr. Murer wanted the portrait plaque of her; he was coming back to Paris for it. She soothed herself with thoughts of seeing him again.

Jeanette took home Amy's copy of *Noggins*, showed it to Cousin Effie, then tore up Robbie's article and threw the magazine away. Behind her back the next day, Effie bought another copy.

"Oh my, you just can't think what trouble this has caused," she said to Mrs. Renick on Friday. "Jeanette is still furious, and Emily hasn't come back to class."

Cornelia skimmed the article Effie had brought, laughed, and flipped through the rest of the issue. "Heavy-handed waggery seems to be the magazine's style. The girls shouldn't take it so seriously," she said. "Of course, plagiarizing the cartoon is a different matter." She made a mental note to tell Marius that he had been right about Mr. Dolson's character. "Still, you know, Jeanette does have a gift for caricature. There was that skeleton on Mlle. Borealska's catwalk, I remember. Darling, darling Effie, here's an idea! Why don't you two collaborate on illustrated articles? Two American ladies in Paris? Artists and how they live? If the New York papers wouldn't run them, surely a Cincinnati or Columbus paper would. They couldn't say no, not to Judge Palmer's daughter."

"But I can't write!"

"You're always telling me stories, Effie dear. Put them down on paper."

"But it would be so *public*."

"Use pseudonyms."

On Saturday, a note arrived at the Rue Jacob, a note in jade green ink on expensive cream paper. *If the company of a chastened sinner is not wholly repugnant,* wrote Robbie, *I beg to be allowed to treat you and Miss Pendergrast to luncheon at the Café Tortoni, where atonement could take the form of the best ices in Paris. But no iciness from you, please, please, please, dear Miss Palmer. The prospect of spending time in the company of your meltingly sweet self would so restore me and ease Emily's return to Julian's.* He suggested a Tuesday, before Jeanette and Emily went for their regular afternoon at the Louvre.

Jeanette balled up the note and slammed it into the wastebasket.

"Who was that from?" asked Effie.

"From the insufferable Robbie Dolson. Emily must have let him know about the atmosphere in class. Someone should also tell him that drollery and blackmail don't work together."

Effie fished the note out of the basket. She shook her head. "He is an impertinent piece of mischief. Though give him the benefit of the doubt, Jeanette—maybe deep down inside he's ashamed of himself."

"He wouldn't be so horridly facetious if he were."

"Oh, I don't know. Pride is sometimes a hard thing for a man to swallow. In any case, why not take the invitation at face value?"

"I believe you really want to go, don't you?" exclaimed Jeanette.

Effie ducked her head. "Well, it might be our one chance to go to Tortoni's."

Jeanette was disgusted, but curiosity about what Robbie was up to nagged at her. After fighting it all evening, she finally gave in and wrote him a curt note of acceptance.

The next week, Jeanette and Amy tried to act as if nothing had happened when Emily returned to class, hangdog and coughing. The disdain shown her by the popular clique made them tacitly rally to her side. By the end of a week, the *Noggins* offense had been forgotten by everyone but Jeanette, and Emily was snubbed only out of habit.

At noon on the appointed Tuesday, Cousin Effie joined Jeanette and Emily at the Rue Vivienne to walk the few blocks to the Boulevard des Italiens. Mellow October had given way to overcast, raw November, lessening the appeal of ice cream, but Effie beamed.

Some way from Tortoni's blue-striped awning, Robbie stood with his shoulders hunched against the weather, apparently examining the notices posted on a cylindrical Morris column. In the dispiriting gray daylight, he looked less a dandy from a bygone era than the shabby inhabitant of some other *arrondisement*, as handsome as ever but careworn—more than careworn, shopworn. A couple turned to go into the café just as Robbie came forward; the cut of the gentleman's overcoat and the sleekness of the lady's furs showed up a grease spot on his lapel. It's the wrong setting for him, thought Jeanette, not in the least bit charitably. As if he could read her mind and resented it, Robbie said, coolly, "I think not Tortoni's, after all. Too crowded for those with work to do later. Another time, Miss Pendergrast, when you and I can while away an afternoon? So much more agreeable. Besides I have made a discovery."

Jeanette stopped dead. Emily bit her lip. Ignoring them both, Robbie insinuated Effie's arm through his and smoothly headed her into the flow of pedestrians. Then he looked over his shoulder and cocked his head. Jeanette started to stalk away, but that would give him too much satisfaction. Worse, it would leave Cousin Effie with him unchecked. "Come on," she said, harshly, to Emily.

In a block or two, Robbie led them around a corner to a newly opened patisserie called Le Petit Honoré, which had a few tables, a dazzling display case of baked goods and sweets, and a short luncheon menu. Throughout the meal, Emily stared at her plate and ate little, while Effie—who had reason to feel let down, but who was also wise to the importunities of poverty—laughed at Mr. Dolson's jokes and made the effort to chatter away. At first, Jeanette indulged her anger but gradually suppressed the worst of it in order to be able to eat (as Robbie had so rightly pointed out, there was the rest of the afternoon ahead). When Robbie's attention to jollying Cousin Effie effectively foiled her every attempt to confront him, she pulled out a little pocket notebook and below the edge of the table made a rapid sketch to catch his expression.

"You're pinning my soul to paper, aren't you, Miss Palmer?"

"Only Lucifer could do that, Mr. Dolson."

"Has done, I think you mean. What would you say I received in return?"

Something genuinely haunted lurked in the shadows and weary lines around his eyes. No distant amber lights in their gray sea-green depths today. On the surface he was all suave irony; below dodged an arrogant furtiveness, a reliance on his ability to escape; deeper still lay a bleak watchfulness completely outside Jeanette's experience. Robbie Dolson was utterly unreliable, utterly selfish, and she knew it, yet all of a sudden she found herself still half hoping he would live up to the promise that was part of his peculiar appeal. What sad bargains, what compromises, had he had to make, she wondered. Nevertheless, she was not in a forgiving mood.

"The Devil is prodigal in his gifts, Mr. Dolson, but you are fishing for compliments. Here's the best I can do." She propped up her sketchbook on the table.

Robbie clapped his hands once, loudly, and rocked back in his chair. "Me to the life!"

"As drawn by a featherbrain from Hicksville?"

"What? Ah, so *that's* the rub, my dear. But surely you weren't really rankled by my fictional ingénue."

Jeanette hesitated. To admit she had been offended was to risk looking humorless and vain; to back down was to injure her sense of herself. "I trusted you when we talked on the train last summer, and you made me look silly."

He shifted uncomfortably. "Well, I could say you now know better than to trust me again. Oh, but no one else could possibly associate you with that particular jest; put it out of your mind. You are hardly a featherbrain, nor even an ingénue. In fact, we are destined to be partners in crime. Listen——" He leaned forward and dropped his voice. Hardly aware that she did so, Jeanette leaned forward, too. "I understand that you were more than a little vexed about my borrowing your cartoon."

"Borrowing?" Jeanette sat back, disbelieving.

"All right, purloining if you prefer. Unforgivable liberty, dastardly deed, haste and a deadline, mea culpa, mea culpa. No, but that article can be a breakthrough for you as well as for me. Anonymous, of course, we shall use a nom de plume; neither of us wants to be known primarily for trivialities. But I want you to come in with me on a series of regular little feature columns. 'Unexpected Paris'; 'Off the Boulevard Beat'; 'The Paris Nobody Knows'——I'll come up with the right column title." (Effie stiffened, opened her mouth to say something, and shut it again.) "Meanwhile, we start right here, right now; you can use this sketch. Go ahead, add in a detail or two of decor. I do up a few paragraphs on the soon-to-be discovered sensation among the more knowing Parisians at midday——"

"It would not be anonymous if your caricature were the focal point of the illustration, Mr. Dolson," said Jeanette. She was aware of Effie's agitation but chose to ignore it as she tried to sort through her own puzzlement.

"Clever girl. Not me, then—use that modish Parisienne by the window; it's a better idea anyway. Why don't you put in a bit of the lettering backward to identify the spot?"

Toying with her pencil, Jeanette was silent. She knew she was in the right and he was in the wrong, yet somehow he was gaining the upper hand. She made an effort to sound worldly and bantering.

"Well, supposing we did go in together—just supposing—what other sorts of things do you plan to write up?"

"Oh, any little sight seen serendipitously will do. Behind-the-scenes oddities like the dismantling of the World's Fair—there's an opportunity missed, but you see the point. No, wait: In fact, that one can still work. I'll trace what happened to some extravagant *objet* from the exhibition."

"The head of Bartholdi's Lady Liberty."

"Too obvious."

"Jacquemart's rhinoceros?"

"Splendid! I told you we were meant to collaborate. You do a witty illustration; I shall sparkle. Once we're known, we'll be invited everywhere—to restaurants, to theaters, to gallery openings, just you watch."

In spite of herself, Jeanette had fallen for a moment into playing along with him, but she had not forgotten the intensity with which he had evicted her from his and Emily's lodgings. Also, something besides the sheer effrontery of his suggestion perplexed her. "Why me?" she asked. "You have an artist in the family. Wouldn't it be easier to coordinate the pieces if you and Emily worked together? More lucrative, too: You could keep both fees in the family."

"Money, money. Oh, you Americans."

Far from cowing her, his rebuke put her back up. "Why me and not Emily?" she persisted.

"Oh, well, then, if you must—and who is fishing for compliments now, my dear Miss Palmer? Dash and speed. Emily, darling, your gifts are not those of the cartoonist, are they?"

Without lifting her eyes, Emily shook her head. Jeanette felt cold in the pit of her stomach. Which was Robbie dismissing—Emily's work or hers? There was something unpleasantly close to what Amy always said, both in Emily's meekness and Robbie's way of undermining his sister's confidence. But it also might be that he was enticing her into something from which he shielded Emily, something fit only for a vulgar American.

"Anyway," he said, abruptly sitting back and sounding bored, "the editors liked your bit; that's why they ran it. But if you don't want to . . ."

Cousin Effie squirmed harder in her seat.

"I'll have to think about it, Mr. Dolson; but if you can use this, it's yours," said Jeanette, determined to prevent one of Effie's wild shots. She tore out the sketch she had been working on while they talked. It showed a table by the window with a bit of backward lettering as ordered. A modern young woman and a dandy sat across from each other, arms crossed over chests, heads turned away, noses in the air. "And now, I think, my time will be more profitably spent in the Louvre."

Outside, Jeanette rounded on Emily. "What is going on?"

"Oh, Jeanette, Robbie is quite desperate to get this column accepted or to find some other source of regular income."

"I thought he'd sold his long story about the Alps."

"He did, but he's . . . he's run into difficulties of some kind. I don't know. It has happened before; and when he's distracted by worries about pennies and farthings, he becomes . . . temperamental. The worst is, he can't get on with his real work."

Real work, the big project into which you poured all of yourself that mattered. For a moment, Jeanette wished Robbie nothing but time to work, unbroken time, time free from all outside demands, from fits and starts and interruptions. If he was the genius Emily and Winkie believed him to be, he deserved it. And even if he was not, it was still what any artist or writer needed in order to achieve something good. "How much are his worries worrying you?" she asked. Like Amy, she sometimes wondered why she felt protective toward Emily, but they both did.

"I cope," said Emily, and closed into herself.

"Mr. Dolson was about to tear up that sketch of yours," Effie told Jeanette that evening, "but I stopped him. I told him he should add a caption—something like this. *She: Why did you bring me somewhere nobody knows? He: You'd better eat fast before* tout le monde *arrives.*"

"You gave him a caption?"

"You gave him the picture." Effie's face was alight with the eager, wide-eyed chipmunk look that made her chin disappear.

"As a taunt, Cousin Effie! I didn't really mean for him to use it."

"Now don't be angry, Jeanette. I couldn't sit by and let him tear your picture up. Besides, if all goes well and he gets it published, I have an idea." Jeanette glared, in no mood for one of Cousin Effie's ideas. "It was really Mrs. Renick's. She suggested that you and I collaborate on some stories for American newspapers."

"You never told me that."

"Well, it seemed so unlikely, I let it go. But this afternoon, while Mr. Dolson was talking, it came to me, thump, just like that: ladies' magazines. A story about your class at Julian's or living in a *pension* or visiting a butter shop—there are all sorts of things we could do. And it came to me clear as day that two samples of your work in print would be better than one for showing editors."

"But I don't want to be a cartoonist."

"You won't be. We'll submit a regular drawing, but it will help if you can show that you've already been published. People are cowards; they want someone else to give a stamp of approval before they commit themselves to anything."

Jeanette thought a moment. A way to add to her and Effie's purse without their having to fall back on family charity appealed. Even small sums would help. "If Robbie peddles that picture and it's accepted, I wonder whether he'll pay me this time," she said, slowly.

"Ah," said Effie. "Well, I admit I pointed out to him that you had given him the cartoon free and clear—which you did, you know. He isn't obligated. But then again if he's smart and wants more of them, he'll pay you this time."

An image of an attenuated, sinuous dandy a lot like Robbie lolling on the blocky back of Jacquemart's rhinoceros sprang fully formed into Jeanette's mind. She pulled out her notebook from the World's Fair. Working quickly in her broadest cartoon style, she copied and distorted a sketch of the sculpture, then placed her dandy on top. It pleased her. If Robbie wanted dash and speed, voilà!

"Cousin Effie, what if I made Robbie a running character? Not so much a series of jokes as comic decorations like this." She held up the drawing. "If each picture put him in a different pose with an item or two out of his piece—well, it would be easy to do. I'll send him this for bait. I know what the next one should be, too. And, if he doesn't want it, it will do for you and me. What do you say we join Amy at next Monday's slave market?"

CHAPTER TWENTY-FOUR

Models

One of Amy's weekly duties as *massière* was to hire models. She could stay a week or two ahead by booking the reliable, expressive models who posed in one atelier after another at Julian's, but new faces and new physiques were always desirable. While she lived in northwestern Paris, she made a point of passing often through the Place de Clichy, where models on the Right Bank congregated to look for work. From the Rue Madame, she must revise her habits. Eastward in Montparnasse, models gathered at the foot of Rue Nôtre-Dame-des-Champs, but that was the wrong direction for heading back over the river to Julian's. For the time being, she was exploring a third major venue, the gates of the École des Beaux-Arts, where Mondays saw the biggest crowds of job-seekers.

"I wish you wouldn't call it a slave market," fretted Effie, as she and Jeanette fumbled tiptoe down the staircase from their rooms to meet Amy the next week. In the brown darkness, a shoulder and hip sliding down the cold wall were almost as much guide as the feeble light of their candle.

"It's just studio slang," whispered Jeanette. "You don't have to come if you don't want to."

"It's ugly slang. Dear Polycarpus died to put an end to such things."

Talk about firing cannons to kill gnats, thought Jeanette, grumpily, although deep down inside she knew that she used the term to tease Cousin Effie.

They crept silently through the lawyer's antechamber on the floor below and down into the stale, darkened chill of the rest of the house (with windows shut against the weather, the *pension* smelled of mice and mold). Outside, they could breathe easier again, although they remained silent in the prevailing predawn hush. Mist from the river drifted in wisps over dark paving stones, wet where street cleaners had hosed them down. The narrow strip of sky above the center of the street was still dim. As they walked along, each footstep on the pavement, each creak of a handcart or clank of a bottle sounded separately and was magnified by an echo. Butchers, bakers, and grocers grunted *bonjours* to each other as they took down shutters or rolled out awnings; a few nodded to Effie and Jeanette. A block or so on, they turned into the Rue Bonaparte to reach the square in front of the church of Saint Germain-des-Prés and found Amy standing at the stall outside a *crémerie*, drinking chocolate from a white china bowl. "Join me?"

"Please," said Jeanette. "It was too early for breakfast at the *pension.*"

"Well, feed up quickly. I've got to hire people today."

Mingled among the local inhabitants and delivery men passing by were others: gymnastic young men in light clothing that showed off their bulging muscles; striking older men with military bearing and pronounced features; women in the native costumes of many regions of France and Italy; bold, pretty girls; eleven-year-old boys with cigarettes dangling from their lips. As Jeanette, Effie, and Amy joined the movement toward the river, a young man pulled astride them and tipped his hat. "Poaching, Richardson?"

"Rescue work, I call it," answered Amy. "Give a model a chance to pose to talent for a change."

He laughed and walked faster.

"Who was that?" asked Jeanette.

"Lad in Cabanel's class at the Beaux-Arts."

Near the school's high, wrought-iron gates, street and pavement became crowded. The young men strutted more obviously; the military men stood even straighter. Some models talked among themselves, but most tried at the very least to appear interesting. The more animated called out, flirted, or struck poses.

"Oh, the poor old soul!" said Effie, fumbling in her pocket for a coin. An old man in rags sat on a mat, propped against the stone wall with his head bowed, eyes lowered, and hand out.

"Put your money away," said Amy. "Week in and week out, old Frederic there is Lazarus outside Dives' door or Job or Priam in his sorrow. He's posed for every painter in Paris and never missed a day's work in twenty years as far as I know. Can't think why he's out here now—though it is a thought. If he's available, what do you say, Jeanette—fancy tackling Gerontius? We haven't had his type since you arrived. Oh, lord!"

Amy clutched Jeanette's arm. Too late. Jeanette wasn't quick enough to help her merge into a crowd around the corner. A woman was pushing a solemn-faced four-year-old toward them. It was La Grecque.

"*Buon giorno*, Miss Richardson. Am-ee," she said.

Amy or *amie*? Jeanette wasn't sure. So as not to seem too inquisitive, she smiled down encouragingly at the little girl, who responded with an unnerving glare. La Grecque said something to the child in Italian. The little girl twisted her whole body around, no! La Grecque jerked the child's arm and rapped out a firmer order. The child screwed up her face in a pout. At another jerk of the arm, she glanced up at her mother's menacing scowl, went limp, and then suddenly spread her legs apart. She cocked her head and rested her cheek on her hands, smiling a beatific smile.

"You see? She is perfect for your class: obedient, beautiful," said La Grecque, picking up the child. "You hire her, *non*? You no take the bread out of my little cherub's mouth again, eh, Miss Richardson? Her papa—"

"Her papa? Which papa? Twenty papas in Paris that wretched child has, and none!" roared a voice. "Away with you, Antonielli, you blackmailing bitch. *Va-t'en.*"

La Grecque clutched the child closer, whirled on the speaker, and spat. "You, at least, I cannot accuse of fathering children, M. Post," she snarled.

Effie gasped.

"Andrea," Amy began, but La Grecque stormed away, carrying the little girl, who stuck out her tongue over her mother's shoulder. Amy shook her head regretfully and turned to the newcomer. "Well, Charlie Post, of all people."

"Your humble servant, Miss Richardson. I hope I did right."

"I hope you did, too. Can't be helped in any case. Now explain yourself: You're the last person I ever expected to see in Paris. What brings you here?"

"The very question I ask myself: Post, you son of a gun, what brings you to Paris? The road, I think. Made the mistake of stepping out onto it. All roads lead to Rome, they say; but those who say it are liars, fools. At the very least, out of date. All roads lead to Paris these days, Paris, glittering capital of the world once more. Prussians take note: *La ville lumière* is queen of cities, not Berlin. To be more precise and prosaic, Ragland and Nagg came up on business, and I seem to have tagged along."

"You do, indeed; and here you are, at the crack of dawn, looking to hire a model, something else I would never have predicted. Very early hours you're keeping, Mr. Post."

"There I think you are wrong. I believe I'm up late. The model part, though, that's very perceptive of you, but wrong again, wrong, wrong." He rolled his head from side to side as he spoke. "Sometime 'long about four, I got this idea that a nymph, a naiad, a spirit of water would be found here. My art would take a whole new direction. Figurative from this moment forward or symbolical or something. It seemed important to stay up and meet my fate. Thoroughly bad, four-in-the-morning sort of idea. Deluded. Look around you: No nymph, no naiad, not a muse to be found. All hacks. Unless—unless, perhaps, it is *you*, Miss Palmer," said Charlie, turning to fix his gaze on Jeanette. "I remember you; you are the discerning girl."

To her surprise, Jeanette was not in the least disconcerted. She met his bloodshot eye. Underneath his alcoholic haze and ironic disillusionment prowled the keenness he had exhibited in Pont Aven, only frightened now, beaten down. "I'm not a muse, Mr. Post, and you don't need one," she said. "It's the sickle moon you must not lose sight of."

He took her hand between both of his. Remembering the press

of his lips on her palm the previous summer, she pulled back hastily, but not before he had kissed the gloved fingertips and mumbled,
"Discerning girl, discerning girl, bless you." He stepped back,
yawned extravagantly, and said, "I'm in my cups. Should be in bed.
'Night, all."

As they watched Post totter off unsteadily, Amy said, "Whatever
were you thinking, Jeanette? The sickle moon indeed."

"What will become of him?" asked Jeanette, with her eye still
on Charlie Post.

"Paint a great picture and hang himself, I'd say."

Cousin Effie shook her head. "Hanging takes a special kind of
willpower. He'll die of drink."

"You're heartless, both of you!"

"Forget Post; we're here on business," said Amy.

Old Frederic, as it turned out, was between major engagements
and happy to sit half a day for a week. While he and Amy negotiated
a fee, Effie took notes on the going rates. "So that's the full figure
taken care of," said Amy, as Frederic enfolded himself in a wide cloak
and headed off across the river.

"May we do a child's face for contrast in the afternoon?" asked
Jeanette.

"Not Andrea Antonielli's cherub, if that's what you mean. But
you're right, a future of children's portraits looms large for most of
us. We'll scout the fringes. Bound to be some other poor girl with
a baby."

Sure enough, hanging back at the edge of the crowd toward the
river stood a forlorn girl, maybe sixteen or seventeen, cradling an
infant in her arms under a shawl. With a little gentle questioning,
Amy drew out her story. As a newcomer to the city, she had felt lucky
to model privately for a painter; she cooked for him a little; she kept
house; they kept company. Now there was the baby and, and . . . she
found herself without his support. Oh, yes, she knew what she was

doing; she could sit very still. The baby was so good a baby, very quiet.

It was only her face that was needed, explained Amy. Suppose she were paid a daily five-franc fee and, for every afternoon that the baby was quiet enough to sketch him also, a bonus of another two francs. But only if he was quiet!

Worship replaced tension in the girl's face as she received Amy's directions for finding the atelier and three francs in advance to buy food.

"We can't have her passing out this afternoon. Between our class and the class for the dressed model, we can give her two weeks' work in a warm studio with her clothes on," sighed Amy. "It's something, anyway. The baby, of course, is too young to be trained; one must hope it sleeps a lot."

"Oh, he'll sleep, all right," said Cousin Effie. "She'll put poppy syrup on his gums."

The girl with the baby proved to be only a so-so model, slumping all afternoon in maternal dejection and mortal fear that the baby would move. Only Emily responded with a notable study. Having requested a child, Jeanette felt obliged to skip her Tuesday at the Louvre and sketch the baby from a series of angles around the room. Her drawings did not add up to anything worth showing M. Bouguereau, but she was pleased with the set for reference.

"It is well you think about what makes the good model," said Sonja, late in the week, "for now it is time for you yourself to sit. We must not forget the good doctor in Freiburg who awaits his portrait medallions. Tomorrow you and Miss Pendergrast walk home with Amy; we eat at La Poupée en Bas and begin."

In mid November, with Christmas packages to be assembled and overseas shipping to be paid for, a Friday night dinner at La Poupée was as much indulgence as Jeanette and Effie could allow themselves, but it was all the more welcome for coming when early darkness and drizzle had increasingly confined them to evenings at the *pension*. Effie had begun spending more time with fellow boarders after supper in the parlor, where a coal-burning stove was lit for a few hours; but Jeanette preferred to wrap up in shawls and work by the light of an oil lamp in their unheated room. She lied to herself that she enjoyed the romance of the garret.

On Friday night, when Jeanette, Effie, Sonja, and Amy arrived at La Poupée en Bas, fire in charcoal braziers was blessedly knocking the chill off either end of the half-subterranean room. The subdued amber glow of oil lamps added an illusion of warmth if not exactly coziness to the deeply shadowed room. (*There is no word for* cozy *in French,* Jeanette had observed in a letter to Becky, *and with good reason.*) Throughout the meal, a Milanese *cassouela* suffused the air with a meaty odor, fragrant of rosemary and bay, while feminine voices kept up a pleasant hum. It was tempting to linger.

"Who will fetch coffee?" asked Amy. "Jeanette, you're the youngest."

"No," proclaimed Sonja. "We have no time." Her chair grated as she pushed herself to her feet. "Amy, you will make us your admirable coffee at home."

"Oh, bother, Sonja. There is admirable coffee here already made."

"And paid for," said Effie.

"Three against one." Jeanette rose to head for the coffee urn.

Sonja stopped her with an imperious gaze. "These two stay behind. You and I go. Cold air will knock sleep out of you. We work."

Outside the damp cold was silvery; shadows were invisible rather than black. A mizzly evening, as Amy would say. Gauzy aureoles burred the lamp globes overhead; a little light filtered down to the wet pavement.

"I love the way edges and distances merge on a night like this," said Jeanette.

Sonja gave a short grunt and shouldered her way off among pedestrians. On the back streets as well as the arteries, people were making their way home or running a last domestic errand; they paused to gossip at food stalls or to buy a newspaper. Feeling only well fed at first, Jeanette came more awake as she hurried to keep up with Sonja. The walk was a counterpoint to the Rue Jacob at dawn, and through it for Jeanette ran the novelty of being somewhere at night without Cousin Effie. "Remove your hat to pose," said Sonja, in the apartment vestibule as she carelessly flung off her own baggy beret.

While Sonja lit lamps near a tall stool, Jeanette turned back a corner of damp sacking from over a wooden tub and poked at the block of cold clay inside. More solid than flesh, it gave only slightly, yet it was pleasantly smooth. With a wire scoop, she cut out a lump the size of a small egg, rolled it around in the cup of her hands, and pressed.

"Tell me about Dr. Murer," commanded Sonja. "What is he like?"

"You've seen him."

"But not so much as you. And it is your portrait he wants."

"Your work, you mean."

"No. If it were my work he wanted, he would ask what I offer to sell."

Jeanette squeezed the softening clay and smiled to herself. She was not sorry to be standing in deep shadow outside the lamplight.

"Over here now, please." Jeanette held on to her ball of clay while Sonja positioned her on a stool. "What about him would you say is most salient?"

The sidelong, inquisitive look Dr. Murer had given her when he caught her studying him at the Odéon flashed into Jeanette's mind; she felt him beside her on the tour of the Renicks' art collection.

"There's something mysterious about him," she said, slowly. "You don't exactly notice him—not at first, anyway. But when you do, he's more *there* than other people. At the same time, I think he's always holding something back."

"He is a man of business."

"It's not that—and I don't think he's an ordinary businessman, Sonja."

"So his clothes proclaim him, very conventional."

Jeanette shook her head, disagreeing, and then remembered to hold still. "Not an ordinary Ohio businessman, not like my father—nor my Uncle Matthew in New York City, for that matter."

"A better tailor."

"Maybe that's it," said Jeanette, though she didn't think so for a minute. "There's something else. He doesn't push forward—except when he has to, and then when he does, he's almost scary. Remember with your landlord?"

"Could I forget? He is a swordsman, this Dr. Murer."

"I don't know about that."

"I do." Sonja correctly took position, *en garde*, and extended her arm. Whisk, whisk, her hand cut through the air with an imaginary blade. "So he scares you?"

"No! Just the opposite! I think I'd trust him anywhere. He holds back, but underneath he's the kindest, most observant man I've ever met, Sonja. I think maybe he's unhappy. I've seen him look at paintings. It's not the way a painter does, nor a collector, nor a connoisseur either; but he sees things, and he's not afraid to say what he thinks—only, only you sense there's lots more going on than what he says out loud. He wants something."

"Imagine now: Dr. Murer is coming through that door."

For an instant Jeanette glanced over at the dark doorway into the corridor; she smiled involuntarily, a warm, quick smile. "You're the artist, Sonja! This is your commission. Show him what you see."

Sonja *was* an artist, and she had seen a lot. On that first night, however, her task was to study Jeanette's head as a three-dimensional object. She sketched the face from different sides to learn its bone structure and proportions. The next day, when there was plenty of light, she posed Jeanette and Effie side by side to think about her medallions as a pair. She had them look at each other, look away, face in pure profile, look out at three-quarters. She told them to look happy, to look sad, to look angry. She found that when Effie talked about Boots, her face became affectionate; when she did needlework, it was serene. With Jeanette, Pont Aven brought animation.

"I shall say to you *Pont Aven* at the beginning of each session," said Sonja. She also mentioned her patron every once in a while in an offhand way, always taking her subjects off guard.

The next few weeks fell into a pattern: Effie sat on weekdays and Jeanette spent Saturdays at the studio, where she posed for Sonja and was coached through color exercises by Amy. Emily joined the coaching sessions for the first couple of weeks; but as autumn wore on and darkness closed in, she grew increasingly pinched and pasty. She stopped coming. "I'm not sleeping well," she admitted to Jeanette. "Chloral helps a little, but it makes my throat worse." Meanwhile, pellet by pellet, bits of potter's clay were added to Sonja's sculptures and smoothed by her sensitive fingers into forms, planes, and finally the likeness of living flesh.

It was Sonja's genius to make for Edward two faces that balanced each other as surely as the masks of comedy and tragedy, while at the same time conveying the warmth of an intimate friendship. Effie she portrayed in a mood of quiet tenderness, gazing down gently as though something in need of protection lay in her lap. Jeanette's face was alight with the pleasure of looking up at the mention of something she loved. The two portraits were less lively than the bust of Amy, for they were intended to be glazed, a process that would reduce the nuance of light across the features and make them speak less to a particular moment than embody an essence. But the essences Sonja chose to emphasize were generous to the sitters and to the man who would own the finished pieces.

Pellet by pellet, bit by bit, days on the drying rack, and then in December a first firing in the kiln of a friend who turned out commercial terra-cottas.

"So," said Sonja, jubilant when no crack appeared, no blemish in the surface. "It is time for Dr. Murer to return if he wishes to attend the glazing."

✖

CHAPTER TWENTY-FIVE

Medallions

Edward's interest in ceramic glazes dated from a time in his youth when he occasionally lent a hand at the kiln to a potter in Cincinnati. They had talked of running experiments on graduated variations in pigments and the temperatures at which components were fused into glass but had never carried out the project. Early in his stay in Freiburg, when he was casting about for something to do, Edward had mentioned it to Cousin Paul, who viewed any interest in colorants as normal and provided him with laboratory space in the Murer dye factory. On the train back to Freiburg from Paris in October, something he had read in a paper on benzene isomers resurfaced in Edward's mind as a question about the molecular structure of oxides used in glazes. As soon as he was back in the laboratory, alongside the empirical tests already under way, he set up some new, more theoretical experiments.

One day, with mounting excitement, he realized that a certain line of inquiry just might lead to new products for insulating porcelain electrical fuses and the like. He made notations. He stared at them and thought some more. While he wrote out assumptions and the relevant formulae more fully, he mentally designed ways to check his idea. He set up preliminary tests to scotch the hypothesis at the beginning if it was untenable, but the results suggested that, on the contrary, he ought to go on.

He flirted with the idea of renting a full workshop and buying equipment but was brought back to earth by the realization that he could spell out everything on paper: initial hunch, preliminary confirmation, hypothesis precisely stated, tests to be run, and possible applications. He could send it all to Theodore, who would understand every aspect and could set trained scientists at Murer Brothers to work on it. Edward hated letting go of his beautiful scheme, but it was no good playing the amateur if it had the potential he thought it did. He drew up a proposal, made a fair copy, and posted it to Cincinnati.

Two weeks later, by return mail, came a congratulatory letter from Theodore. He had already assigned men to the project and would consult with lawyers about patents. He proposed a closely held joint-stock partnership; he foresaw the Cincinnati power company as their first customer. A twinge of jealous exasperation ran through Edward's pleasure as Theodore rolled on. He had known when he wrote that he was relinquishing control of the project but had not foreseen how totally detached from it he would feel once it was out of his hands.

He showed the letter to Carl, who looked up midway through reading it. "What exactly is this all about, Uncle Edward?"

"Here's the proposal."

Carl switched to the rough draft and picked his way quickly

through Edward's formulae, interlineations, and emendations. His immersion in chemistry classes at the *Hochschule* made the technicalities and speculations immediately comprehensible. "This is brilliant, sir," he said, impressed back into the childhood honorific not only by the science but by his uncle's grasp of commercial practicalities. He finished reading his father's letter and looked up, grinning. "Pop's really running with it! Well, and no wonder—this could be a gold mine."

"It won't revolutionize an industry."

"No, but it could launch Murer Brothers into a whole new field."

The prospect of a material success and his increased standing in his brother's and nephew's eyes gratified Edward, but the whole episode also stirred a restlessness he couldn't shake. He wanted either real work or real leisure. Travel might answer. Come January, he and Carl should go to Italy, maybe as far as Greece.

Then came the summons from Sonja in mid December. With the help of Cousin Anna, he and Carl had long since sent home a Christmas package containing gilded gingerbread, beer steins, and a wooden cuckoo clock. Now it was time to think about his German hosts: French toys, ladies' fans, French brandy. "I'm going to make another quick trip to Paris," he announced, and cabled ahead to Mlle. Borealska and Cornelia.

Edward arrived in Paris a few days before the Renicks set off to spend the holidays in Provence. Cornelia invited him for a scratch lunch and asked Effie to bring Jeanette. "I don't know what we'll serve," she said, "but Cook will manage something."

Serious women students at Julian's scorned their flightier sisters who missed class to attend luncheons and teas or visit the dressmaker; but as Christmas drew nearer, everyone loosened up, and Jeanette was too excited about the medallions to care anyway.

"Too right," agreed Amy. "I'll tell you what: Sonja has to make arrangements with Dr. Murer about the firing. We'll invite him for tea that afternoon and you can join us. You, too, Emily—you must see Sonja's masterpieces."

When Jeanette slipped out on Wednesday, she bounced down the stairs, swinging gaily around the posts at each landing—to leave before the noon break and alone was as good as playing hooky. And it was Christmas. On the wide, tree-lined sidewalks of the Boulevard Montmartre, temporary tables and stalls in front of the posh shops and fashionable cafés hawked everything from handkerchiefs to oranges (all through December Paris gutters smelled of orange peel). *Bijoux*, bibelots, music boxes, and puppets. The blasé reserve of passersby gave way to pleasantries with strangers in front of a blanket on which tumbling puppies for sale entertained gratis. The queue at the omnibus stop responded jovially when the conductor of Jeanette's bus swung to the ground and handed down a woman as gallantly as if she were a queen. He beckoned the new riders aboard with broad gestures and droll expressions. As Jeanette stepped forward, he cocked his head suddenly, a lovelorn Harlequin to her Columbine. She bobbed a mock curtsy, then did a double take. She knew his face from somewhere—but where? He met her confusion with a knowing wink and struck a contorted pose.

"Ah, monsieur, vous avez posé chez Julian!"

"Oui, oui, mamma-zella." He rolled on in a patois she could not understand. It didn't matter; she had to move forward anyway. The bus was crowded, but someone made room for her on the bench, from which she could watch out the window as the conductor jumped on and off, directed foot traffic, collected fares, and turned the ride for his passengers into a pantomime performance.

"Au revoir, monsieur, merci," she said, smiling, as she stepped off the bus. He staggered, a marionette unstrung by adoration.

When Hastings showed her into the salon, she was startled for the second time in an hour to recognize someone: not Dr. Murer (her eyes had sought him out; she was expecting him), but Hippolyte Grandcourt. Immediately, she became more demure. Edward, who had quickened at the sight of her animation, wished he knew what she had been about to say. Grandcourt had the charm and presence of mind to ask.

"It—it was nothing. Oh, well, only that the conductor on my omnibus was so comical. When I got on, he looked down at an angle like this—" She sparkled again as she mimicked his atelier pose. "I *knew* I knew his face from somewhere—and then it came to me. He had once been the model for a *concours* at Julian's. I see the winning picture every day. I asked, but I couldn't really understand his answer; he spoke a sort of gabble."

"All the streetcar conductors in Paris speak gutter Italian, *mademoiselle*; it is a *mafia*," said M. Grandcourt. "They come from Italy to be wrestlers or models or both; and when they tire of it, they obtain for each other jobs on the omnibus lines. I shall tell you a story about one of them, and then I must take my leave. *Eh bien.* Up to the moment when the Third Republic was declared, the world was at this man's feet. Today he is clean-shaven and carries himself like anyone else; but for years, his mustaches were long and waxed to a point; he leaned over his legs when he walked as if he were about to fall, yet always with an air of command. He bore, you see, an uncanny resemblance to the emperor, Napoleon III. Now consider this: No one asks an emperor to pose for his portrait hour after hour, certainly not on a horse—nor on a saddle flung over a barrel. Am I not correct, *mademoiselle*, about the barrel?"

"*Oui, monsieur*," said Jeanette, laughing.

"Ah, but someone must sit on it—and sit and sit. An empire requires portraits! There must be portraits, portraits, portraits for every official purpose. For the most part, copies, of course, but also new depictions for new occasions; and our friend, he made a living entirely by posing as this one man. He becomes an expert on the imperial wardrobe; he had regalia made for him by a tailor on the appropriately named Boulevard des Italiens."

"Not the man who also makes ladies' riding costumes?" exclaimed Cornelia.

"The very one. You know him? You have been in his shop?"

"Often, in my riding days."

"Ah, mais oui, madame, hélas." A look of sympathy was chased by a wicked gleam in M. Grandcourt's eye. "He is now appointed to His Excellency, the emperor of Brazil. A shop that sells court regalia and ladies' riding costumes: surely the scene for an *opéra bouffe.* But you must be asking yourself, *madame*: How could a future bus conductor afford such things? The answer is simple: He commanded the highest fees in Paris because he was unique.

"Eh, bien. One day he gets wind of a reception to be given by one of the glittering new men, an art dealer, an ardent Bonapartist. Now our Italian who wears the *cordon imperial* across his chest by day is by night a socialist of the reddest dye. He decides to play a prank and enlists the aid of two friends on the omnibus line. From somewhere they borrow the caps and capes of gendarmes to wear over their bus uniforms.

"At the gallery, in the public rooms there is candlelight, much candlelight but many flickering shadows, too. It is not so easy to make out a face as one thinks. Our three farceurs enter; a hush falls over the room. The crowd falls back. Guests press against each other to bow or curtsy and make way for the emperor. He trips forward on his short legs with that strange gait of his and shifts a sly glance from side to side but says nothing—all perfectly in character, I assure you. From the next room, the host bustles forward in an ecstasy of adulation—the supreme moment of his career—only to realize at the last moment when he makes his salutation that, *zut alors!* it is the blasted *sosie*, the mannequin, the double—or as you might say, Herr Dr. Murer, the doppelganger. What to do?"

"He should have unmasked the fraud and joined in the laugh," muttered Edward, inexplicably nettled to have been recognized as German. He felt soothed when Jeanette met his eye and nodded.

But it was the suppressed mirth between the Renicks that caught Grandcourt's attention. "Oh, ho, M. Renick, *madame*, I believe it is you who must finish the story."

"We don't know the end," said Marius Renick, whose lips were twitching.

"Oh, but Hippolyte, you are right: We were there!" chimed in Cornelia. "And we were duped—duped!—along with everybody else in the room!"

Grandcourt beamed.

"As I remember," said Mr. Renick, "Naudet escorted the emperor into a side room for a private supper and that was about all that happened."

"It was all that happened, but confess, my dear, how we all waited—and waited and waited and waited. We were dying for another glimpse. But then somehow word went around that His Excellency never mingled at such impromptu appearances—"

"A rumor no doubt hastily set going by Naudet and the gallery staff," said Marius.

"*Bien sûr*," said Grandcourt, whose eyes twinkled at the unexpected confirmation of his story. "Meanwhile, in a storeroom, your infuriated host bundled the imposters into stockboys' smocks and shoved them out the back door onto the alley. He could not bear, you see, to lose the momentary prestige of an imperial visit. But, of course, the truth got around."

"We never heard it!" exclaimed Cornelia.

"You do not ride the omnibus, *madame*."

"Oh, *maestro*, neither do you."

"*Non, c'est vrai.* I myself heard the story at Compiègne from the emperor, who loved it. He had his spies, you know. But now that your luncheon guests have arrived, *madame*, I must take my congé. *Mesdames et messieurs, joyeux Noël à tous.*"

* * *

What seemed to constitute a scratch lunch for Cornelia was informality (there was no hint of the leftover or random in the food). Conversation was general or flowed naturally.

"I'm looking forward to seeing what Miss Borealska has done," Edward said to Jeanette seated beside him.

"She told me that you had sent her a formula for the glaze."

"A bone white, warmer than della Robbia."

"I saw a sample. It's lovely, but I have to admit I was surprised that you knew how much whites differ."

"Family trade, dyes and pigments. Why surprised?"

"I guess I don't imagine most men paying the least attention to fine discriminations in color. I know my father wouldn't." With a shiver of pleasure at flirting with an older man, she cocked her head pertly and ran on: "M. Grandcourt probably does."

By the logic of the analogy, Edward ought to feel even older; but to the contrary, he threw off feeling his age at all. By the time the lunch was over, it was somehow assumed that Jeanette and Effie would spend the afternoon with him, shopping for his German relations, after which they were all due at the Rue Madame at five o'clock.

"I have serious toy purchases to make, Cornelia," said Edward. "Where should we start?"

"That's easy, and if it weren't impossible, I'd come with you for the pure seasonal joy of it. Go to Au Nain Bleu on the Boulevard des Capucines."

It was a large store, where it was a pleasure to look through the eyes of a child for a while. Jeanette assured Edward that any little girl would pine for one particularly elegant set of dolls' china, and Effie was bewitched by a furry Puss-in-Boots with a long feather in his peaked cap. Edward ordered the china, the cat, and several other items on which they all agreed, to be gift-wrapped and delivered to his hotel. Afterward, as they strolled, it was a toss-up which were more worth noting: the crowds, the street stalls, or the window displays (Jeanette's favorite was a jeweler's gold-and-crystal Cinderella coach pulled by a pair of diamond-collared white ermines).

"Would it spoil appetites for tea if we ate an ice cream at Tortoni's?" asked Edward. He could tell by their reactions that he had said something either very right or very wrong.

"Tortoni's or else we know the most diverting little pastry shop," said Jeanette. She told him the story of *Noggins* and Robbie's idea of atonement.

"Sounds like the bounder deserves showing up," said Edward. "Tortoni's it is, and we'll hope pistachio is on today's menu."

While they sat over their ice cream (as good as reputed), Jeanette told him how the idea for a series of articles for ladies' magazines had sprung from Robbie's delinquency.

"But, oh my, it's harder than I thought," said Cousin Effie, shaking her head. "We've had plenty of dandy ideas, but I just can't seem to get anything on paper."

"Instead of trying to be entertaining like Dolson," said Edward, "why don't you dwell on the practical side? Guide the American visitor."

"Oh, *ouufff.*" Effie made a blowing noise she had picked up from Mme. LeConte. "There are plenty of wiser heads than mine for advice."

"You could certainly write the book on how to find cheap lodgings in Paris," said Jeanette.

Effie's eyes became fixed on a distant point while her spoon dangled against her ice cream dish. "The Lady Artist's Guide to Living Cheaply in Paris," she rapped out slowly. She looked from one to the other, her eyes alight. "Living quarters, laundry, where to eat breakfast, where to buy supplies, how to hire a model, the omnibus system, where to see fine art for free."

"Where to sketch outdoors safely," said Jeanette.

"The Hôtel Druout for auctions, street markets," said Effie, "where to find tea at wholesale prices."

Edward made a few suggestions and Jeanette furnished illustrative anecdotes, but it was clearly Effie's brainstorm. Later in the afternoon, when they had walked some more and it was time to head across the river for tea, Effie wanted to take an omnibus—"In the spirit of the thing"—but Edward overruled her in the name of Yankee pragmatism. They took a cab and stopped by Julian's to pick up Amy and Emily.

At the Rue Madame, on the stairs to the studio, Edward suddenly found himself apprehensive, half afraid of disappointment. Until this moment, he had assumed that the medallions would delight him in the same way as the bust of Miss Richardson. He had never contemplated the effect of a failure—a dull portrait or an inaccurate one.

Sonja was waiting for them, a glowering Amazon. In her eyes, Edward realized, he was on trial. He suspected she was worried less about the quality of her work than about his ability to give it its due. He met her eye steadily as he unconsciously guided Jeanette. Jeanette was aware of his touch yet also felt utterly invisible as she sensed the tension between him and Sonja.

"Thank you for letting me come," he said. "I have been looking forward to this day."

"Come in. I show you the sculptures."

"Shouldn't we have tea first?" asked Amy.

"No, in which case, we sit around pretending to enjoy. We get worst over first."

"You mean the best," rebuked Jeanette. "But you're right. We can't wait."

They gathered around the worktable where Sonja had propped up the medallions on crude wooden stands, covered by muslin veils.

Two lamps were lit somewhat away from them. "You must stand there and there," Sonja directed Jeanette and Effie, placing them so that each stood behind her own hidden portrait. Amy and Emily hung back. Without further ado or fanfare, Sonja pulled away the cloths.

A lump rose in Edward's throat. It didn't matter. If the onlookers saw him moved, they would consider it as a tribute to the artist's skill, as in part it was. He looked from the portrait of Jeanette to find a hushed attention in her face. Effie was fidgeting, looking down modestly, overcome by embarrassment. Edward had foreseen that the pieces could be beautiful in themselves. What he had not foreseen was how much a portrait sculpture could communicate thoughts and emotions. When he first saw Miss Palmer's image, it seemed to greet him with a sunny pleasure; but he also took in the air of quiet solicitude that enveloped the second portrait. Miss Pendergrast with her rabbity chin and old maid's ways would be easy to mock, but Mlle. Borealska had done no such thing. She had revealed to him a dimension of Effie's worth that he had not until this moment recognized.

"They are more than I knew how to desire," he said, softly. "No wonder the Lord God chose to work in clay if mortal fingers can achieve so much. Are you sure you want to glaze them, after all?"

"Ah, yes," said Sonja, earnestly. "They are made with glazed surface in mind. Half baked, they lose half their beauty."

"Surely not half," said Edward. "Already these have souls. It seems almost presumptuous to offer congratulations, Mlle. Borealska, but I thank you with all my heart. It will be a privilege to own such beautiful things."

"Well done, Sonja!" said Amy. All this American emotion was beginning to make her uncomfortable. "Now if everyone will excuse me, I'm going to make tea. I'm famished. Emily, you can help cut sandwiches. Sonja, you did pick up a *gâteau*, didn't you?"

"Of course, and pastries. On the table."

Amy and Emily returned from the kitchen laden with a big cobalt-blue earthenware teapot, a jug of cream, and platters of finger sandwiches, tiny tarts, and an iced cake. Planks on trestles draped with a tablecloth already held silverware and a collection of blue-and-white cups, saucers, and plates, most of it fine porcelain (Meissen, Spode, some Chinese), though few pieces matched.

"I'm afraid everything is chipped or cracked, Dr. Murer," said Amy, pouring out the first cup for him as the guest of honor. "I know it's silly to collect broken china, but it's great fun to find usable pieces in whatnot bins and pick them up for nothing."

"Street markets, bazaars, and bric-a-brac shops!" said Jeanette, pointing a finger at Effie. Effie grinned back.

"Miss Pendergrast is going to write a guide to living cheaply in Paris for people like us," Amy explained to Sonja. "She cooked up the idea this very afternoon."

During tea, conversation became general. To illustrate his experiments, Edward brought out a couple of sample tiles from a flat leather wallet in his pocket. Only Sonja among them was doing any serious work in clay, but they were all interested. Effie especially, with her love of pretty things, caressed the smooth, glassy surfaces. For a while in the mellow semidarkness of the room, camaraderie lowered the barriers of sex and patronage to admit Edward into the group as one of them.

A knock sounded at the door. "That will be Robbie for me," said Emily.

"Wee Willie Winkie!" they heard Amy say. "Come in, come in. The pot's gone cold, but I can have another made in a jiffy. There's lovely chocolate *gâteau*."

"I can't stay, I'm afraid, Miss Richardson. Dolson sent me around to pick up Emily, but I'm on duty at the hospital tonight."

Mr. Winkham came to the studio door behind Amy, still in

his overcoat and turning a shabby top hat in his hands. "Evening, all," he said, and nodded specially to Edward, who had risen. "Dr. Murer."

Emily was already on her feet, too. "It was a lovely afternoon," she said, in a slightly constrained voice. "Thank you for including me. Sonja, the medallions are beautiful."

"The medallions!" said Amy. "Winkie, it will only take a minute. You must at least come in and see them."

Mr. Winkham held back, then changed his mind. "Ah, yes, well, I should like that."

He sounded preoccupied but walked to the worktable where the sculptures sat, still lit by their oil lamps. He studied them in silence. "Remarkable," he said. He gave Sonja an upward glance. "Good bones beneath the skin."

Sonja clapped him on the back. "You will be the more glad I dismantle Mortimer when I do your portrait, Mr. Winkham—not your face, but every knuckle of your surgeon's hands."

"Oh, Winkie, you should let us all have a go at it!" said Jeanette. "Hands are so difficult."

"Sit down and have a cup of tea, Winkie," ordered Amy. "Eat a sandwich. Make Emily eat a few more, too."

"Well, if you put it that way. Will you eat another, Emily?"

"If Robbie is expecting us . . ."

Winkie shook his head. "Said he had to see a man about a dog. You're not to wait supper."

"That settles it," said Amy. "If I know you, you *will* wait—but not on an empty stomach, my girl. Nor will you go off to hospital without your tea, Mr. Winkham. Sit down."

When the party broke up for good a quarter of an hour later, Winkie stood to one side with Edward. "I wonder if I could have a word, a bit of advice. None of my business, really, but Dolson sent me instead of coming himself because—Ah, well, no, as I said, none of my business. It's just that I worry about Emily." Winkie's eye went to her across the room.

Edward remained silent and waited. He knew that those who needed to get something off their chest were more likely to keep talking if not interrupted.

"Not that she complains, not to me anyway. I try to keep an eye on her, but what with one thing and another . . ." As Emily approached, tying a scarf over her small felt hat, Winkie looked down at nothing in particular and muttered, "Ah, well, no. None of my business."

"Nor mine, but if ever I can be of any service . . ."

Jeanette saw Dr. Murer listening to Winkie with grave attention. He was an observant man, she had told Sonja. As if to prove her point, he came across to her with the same inquisitive lift of an eyebrow that he had given her at the Odéon.

"You caught me," she admitted. "I would have eavesdropped if I could—but, no, don't worry: I won't ask. Tell me instead how long will you stay in Paris after the firing."

"Not even a day, sorry to say—I can't miss any of *Weihnachten.*" His face changed. "Miss Dolson is lucky in her friends."

A little quiver of pleasure ran through Jeanette; he meant her as well as Winkie.

"Well, now, I think we'd better be going, Jeanette," said Effie, joining them.

"You will allow me to accompany you home, I hope, Miss Pendergrast."

"Oh, we've taken enough of your time for one day, Dr. Murer. You've given us a lot of pleasure—I don't know when I've been shopping for children like that!"

"I shall enjoy the company of the originals even more than of the medallions."

When he left them at their door on the Rue Jacob, he wished them good night and a Merry Christmas.

"*Au revoir?*" said Jeanette.

"*Au revoir,*" said Edward.

Au revoir, not *adieu.*

⁂

CHAPTER TWENTY-SIX

Winter's Cold, 1878–1879

*D*r. *Murer went back to Germany the day after the medallions came out of the kiln,* Jeanette wrote her parents on Christmas Eve, *and we haven't seen Sonja since then either. She is all caught up in Christmas in the Polish community (which I find funny, considering Sonja, but Cousin Effie says is only natural). Amy has gone to England to spend the holidays with her father for the first time in three years. In fact, it is getting a little lonesome around here. I don't know where the Dolsons are. Last week, I invited Emily to bring her brother to a party for waifs and strays that we are having at our* pension *tonight. She didn't say yes and she didn't say no, so I went by their apartment on the Île Saint Louis yesterday, but no one was home. I left a note at the stationer's where she receives her mail, just in case.*

In fact, the Dolsons' porter had grumbled about rent cheaters, and the stationer said that the Dolsons had not picked up their accumulation of bills and duns for a couple of weeks. He complained that he hadn't been paid his December fee and charged Jeanette a sou to add her note to the pile.

The tenants who were remaining at the *pension* over the holidays, along with a few other foreign students and neighbors who were alone, attended midnight mass together at the eleventh-century church of Saint-Germain-des-Prés around the corner. Afterward, they all returned to the Rue Jacob to share a traditional *réveillon* feast of twelve cold dishes and sweets. To be out so late among the many worshippers and families headed to similar feasts throughout the city felt very French.

The next morning, Jeanette presented Effie with a framed picture of Boots. Effie reciprocated with a white collar embroidered in her delicate stitches, which Jeanette wore in honor of the day when they attended the Christmas Day service at their own Protestant American Chapel on the Rue de Berri.

Back at the Rue Jacob, after a dinner provided by Mme. Granet, the landlady, they finally opened their Christmas presents from home. Judge Palmer, who had been told about the ginger jar, sent them a check to replenish it for January. He also sent an affectionate letter to Jeanette with the news that Adeline and Harold Vann would be traveling from New York to Paris in May. *It's no good your leaving before they arrive,* he wrote; *you must stay al least until midsummer.* As far as it went, that was good news, but it jolted Jeanette to be reminded that she must do something soon to impress her father with the need for at least another full year. She could hardly begin on Christmas afternoon, so for the few hours until darkness, they went for a long walk in a quiet, closed-up Paris.

As they drifted homeward again at dusk, around the great fountain basin of the Luxembourg Garden, the sky beyond the broad steps on the western side was a smoldering red band beneath dark clouds. "I should have signed us up to serve dinner at a mission hall," said Cousin Effie.

"Next year, we'll plan better," said Jeanette, determined to be there.

In Freiburg, far from being homesick or lonely, Edward was smothered in family. Under the cover of the many crates and boxes he had brought back from Paris, he smuggled in the medallions without having to explain them to Cousin Paul and Cousin Anna or, worse, put up with impudence from Carl. There were parties and music, peals of bells from the cathedral and other churches, a fall of crisp fresh snow to set off the dark evergreens of the Black Forest, and, most evocative of all for Edward, a hushed parade through the darkened house on Christmas Eve to the Christmas tree, twinkling with small candles on the dining room table. The ceaseless activity carried the danger of overwhelming a man who habitually required a certain amount of solitude, yet Edward threw himself into it with a show of willingness that fooled everyone else and felt genuine even to him much of the time. It was a true joy to have tastes, smells, and sounds confirm memories from his boyhood. In Freiburg, these had a fullness they had lost since he came home from the war to find Mutter dead. Yet as 1878 was rung out, 1879 rung in, and still they had not reached the feast of the Three Kings, he felt a headache coming on.

Inevitably, on the sixth of January, it felled him. He awoke to find Carl dressing by the light of a candle. He squeezed his eyes shut again and shrank against the pillow, unable to bear either the feeble flame or the motion of turning his head away. Recognizing the symptoms, Carl extinguished the candle. Downstairs, he explained to Cousin Anna that tea was needed. She said she would steep it herself and gave orders to the cook for toast.

A little later, Edward heard the tread of someone trying to be silent and a slight rattle of china. He knew he should ready himself for a maid but was in too much pain; he only wanted her to go away. To his relief, it was Carl carrying the bed tray. As a nurse, Carl had learned a calm matter-of-factness from his mother. It was not the same as Sophie's deep, sympathetic understanding, but it sufficed. In response, Edward did not resist when Carl slipped a hand under his shoulder to raise him against the backboard. He eased the throbbing base of his skull gingerly into an extra pillow provided by Carl.

He sipped the milky, sweetened tea uncomplaining, though he thought it tasted strange. Slowly, he chewed, stopped, and chewed again a small bite of toast; he let the dissolving pulp sit on his tongue; he swallowed.

"I'll be all right," he croaked, with his eyes closed.

When Carl checked back after his own breakfast, he found that Edward had eaten most of one slice of toast and drunk much of the tea in his cup. He was asleep again, and his brow was smooth, though in the semidarkness, his face looked sunken and chalky.

At midmorning, Anna knocked on the door of the sickroom. She brought a second pot of tea on a tray and poured him a fresh cup. With a weak smile, still recumbent (he was too used to being nursed to feign strength he didn't feel), he asked her not to sweeten it this time. It was honey, she told him, and he would probably want it again, for she had infused good Friesian tea with willow bark against the headache.

Edward rubbed a hand across his closed eyes and fingered his left temple. His limbs felt flaccid; a tightness lingered against his skull; yet the worst pain, which had felt like stone being drilled, was gone. He struggled upright against the pillows and dutifully drank some more, then drowsed again. By lunchtime, he was up and around— drained by the aftereffects of his migraine but able to escape suffocating domesticity indoors by walking in the garden behind the house. Over the next couple of days, Cousin Anna's knowledge of traditional cures gave them something to talk about. He thought some of her herbal concoctions worth noting down to test, but her remedies of garlic wrapped in red flannel to press against a sore throat and the like he dismissed as superstition.

Twelfth Night had come on a Monday. On Friday, he went back to the laboratory. It was drab and the gloom of the dark northern European winter oppressive. On the rare occasions when the sun shone clear, he took walks outside town where snow in meadow and forest was white. Clean cold air with a resinous tang did his lungs good; he breathed in deeply whenever he detected the right mineral iciness. But too much of the old city was choked by ever filthier, churned-up mud and ice; murky daylight could hardly make its way down past roofs to the streets. In the new industrial districts, factory smoke turned fogs an ugly sulfurous yellow; they stung the eyes and tasted nasty. The prevalent damp cold made his leg ache. Vague dissatisfactions and regrets kept him off stride, and through them crept tentacles of longing, longing for laudanum.

It would be easy to get. All he had to do was walk into a pharmacy or, for that matter, ask Anna if she had some in her medicine chest. Even if Theodore had warned Cousin Paul and the others against its dangers for him, surely no one would object to moderate use. Cousin Anna would probably enjoy administering carefully measured doses, just so, according to some strict regimen she would devise. It shook him to realize that submitting to a scheme of hers would probably be safer than trusting to his own diagnosis and restraint. Gritting his teeth, he set himself to abstain.

He kept doggedly to his experiments. He resolved to work out with Indian clubs at the *Turnhalle* regularly and kept to a schedule for a while. Once, he let Carl talk him into going back to Young Paul's fencing club, the *Fechtverein*, instead. Carl and Young Paul knew nothing about his lessons in Paris and were impressed by his handling of a foil in their warm-up exercises; but from the minute they entered the building, Edward had disliked a smell of puerile aggression and arrant militarism that contrasted to the bonhomie in the sweat of M. Artaud's establishment. A rising sense of savagery and futility in himself drove him to leave early.

Throughout this period, he left the medallions under his bed. The uppermost part of his mind clung to the belief that they would console or inspire him; deeper inside, he doubted it. Toward the end of January, when he finally put hope to the test, his fingers slid over their perfect creaminess. He balanced Miss Palmer's portrait upright against his knee, and briefly his heart ached with pleasure at the trusting appeal in her sculpted expression. He set the piece down and picked up its gentle mate. As he studied them, their power ebbed; they were only clay images glassed over. Although he told himself that sculpture was more permanent than tintype, that these betokened flesh and blood very much alive in Paris, no distant vitality reached him. His spirits sank lower; he put the portraits away before disappointment spoiled them for him forever.

On a night soon after, Carl cursed when he came home: "Dash it all, it's cold."

"Italy," replied Edward, hollow-eyed.

He had known one recent morning that he must get away when he found he was turning in at a pharmacy door. He had forced himself to walk on instead to the train station. Paris beckoned, of course; but Paris, too, would be cold and overcast. Cornelia was not there to call on. He had no errand. No, that was not true; he very much had an errand, one he shrank from pursuing. The last thing he wanted was for Miss Palmer to see him like this. He felt too seedy to think it through, but he knew he wanted warmth and light. He wanted color. He wanted to revive. Greece, Cyprus, Algeria all occurred to him, but all involved travel by sea. No relief could be bought at the price of seasickness. He inquired about trains to Rome.

"Italy?" asked Carl.

"Every educated gent sees Rome," said Edward, trying to maintain the illusion of a light touch.

"But what about the *Hochschule* and chemistry?"

"You're not sitting for a degree."

Although Edward could not bring himself to plead aloud for help, his eyes did, and the circles under them. As soon as Carl understood that his uncle really meant to go, he jumped at the chance to be released from classes. "Leave it to me," he said.

* * *

Paris was as cold and overcast as Edward feared—dark when Jeanette set out for school, dark when she came home. As she crossed from the Right Bank to the Left in the evenings, a weird, electric glow arched over the city behind her; ahead, gas streetlamps studded the murk like weak stars in a lower, brooding firmament, but none shone overhead. Snow rarely fell; rain often did—icy rain that slashed down hard or clammy drizzle that hung around for days. Yet there was also a silveriness to the fog when the sun shone pale behind it, and a luminosity in stone buildings under the city grime. Over and over again these beauties made up to Jeanette for numbed cheeks and chilled fingers. (*A muff*, she declared in a letter home, *is the greatest invention of man*.) She was blessed with good health; and although she caught a head cold from Cousin Effie in January, she shook it off in a few days.

Effie's sneezes turned into a sore throat, which kept her house-bound for more than a week longer. Mme. LeConte kindly brought up soups and lent her a charcoal brazier for their unheated room. As Effie convalesced, she fussed over three sample Lady Artist's Guide pieces—how to find a studio, what to look for in a *portière*, and how to hire a model—which she planned to show Mrs. Renick when the family came back from Provence: "It was her idea, after all."

"Not entirely—you thought of doing them as a Lady Artist's Guide. But she might have an idea about a publisher."

In the middle of January, Emily returned to classes, looking less hounded and underfed. She and Robbie had been in Belgium, she said, without spelling out any particulars. Whatever their errand had been, it must have solved their money worries; for she paid the high weekly fee to take her through the rest of the month, and her shy smile was almost exultant as she handed Jeanette a heavy enve-lope. It clinked with the weight of coins and contained a note:

My dear Miss Palmer,

Most dashing of collaborators—behold enclosed the well-earned reward for your talent and toil: five francs apiece for the Quarrelling Couple and the Rhino. In short—as bully Bottom would say—our play is preferred. Or should I say, our jests. We are in Noggins *for February and March, dear lady! If you will but pen our handsome lad into a mad mannequin scene at the Beaux-Arts gates, we cannot 'scape April as well.*

Your ever grateful and obedient partner in drollery,
  R. Dolson

"What cheek," said Amy, but Jeanette hugged Emily.

That night, after she had grinned at the note, Effie said, "This should make Cousin Joseph very proud, and Sarah, too."

"Mama does believe in self-reliance," said Jeanette, weakening inside a little at the hope of pleasing her mother.

"With two publications and a third in the offing—? Of course, she'll be tickled pink."

"But what about this piece on the models' market? You've already done one, and . . ."

"Oh, it's too different from anything Mr. Dolson will write to matter."

"Very well, then! Here are five francs apiece for pin money—mine for me as the artist; yours for you as the agent."

"Not equal shares!" said Effie.

"It's what every bloodsucking parasite of a gallery owner charges," said Jeanette, doling out the coins.

"Well," said Cousin Effie, a little flustered, "all right then, just this once."

Effie deposited her five francs in the ginger jar, but Jeanette splurged at an art supply store. To her ever-growing collection of scavenged paint scraps, she added a large tube of lead white, a few new brushes, and a stack of cheap pasteboards so that she could continue practicing Amy's exercises in juxtapositions of color and paint mixing at home.

With Emily back in town and Sonja turning again to graphic work, Amy suggested Saturday sessions at which the four friends could pose for each other. The first week, when Jeanette set off for the Rue Madame, she took a little time to dawdle and enjoy the street despite a freezing fog. At a grocer's window, bunches of leeks hanging upside down caught her eye: Roots were spread out like frothy fringes above white stalks; these, in turn, descended to spreading skirts of green. They looked like some exotic flower. How French! She almost laughed out loud at the thought of startling Circleville some day by *arranging* fruits and vegetables. At the studio, Amy came to the door wearing a loose wrapper without stays or corsets under her painter's smock; her hair, usually coiled and pinned tightly, was braided loosely at the nape of her neck. It was like being back in Pont Aven. In the studio, the coal stove was lit.

"Heat—what bliss!"

"The Witkiewicz children pay for it," said Sonja. "The count, their father, approved my portrait of his wife. Now he tells me to paint *les enfants* but insists that my studio be warm for them. You supply coal, I tell him; I supply stove."

"You didn't!" exclaimed Jeanette.

"She did," said Amy. "But not until she had told him Polish children should be indifferent to cold."

"They should," said Sonja.

"What did the count say?" asked Jeanette.

"Purchase coal."

A few minutes later, Emily arrived, bringing with her the warm, buttery smell of baking. "These are just out of the oven," she said, holding out a paper cornet spotted with grease. "*Pains au chocolat.* We can save them for elevenses . . ."

"Not if they're hot right now, my girl," exclaimed Amy. "I'll make coffee, and we'll have a second breakfast."

"No time," objected Sonja. "Set them beside the stove to keep warm."

"And be tantalized all morning? Not on your life." Amy whisked the bag away and headed for the kitchen.

"Robbie refilled my housekeeping fund, and I thought I might as well stand us a treat before he dips into it again," said Emily, as she shed a fur-lined mantle. It dated perhaps from the forties, and the fur was worn in spots; but it was warm and somehow suited her.

The second breakfast cost them half an hour. Nobody but Sonja minded, and she was pacified when Amy said, "Pose me first. I'll pose you last, and you only have to sit for an hour."

Jeanette followed Amy in a standing pose. When it was Emily's turn in the afternoon, Sonja told her, "For your face, so pensive, so delicate, I have special use. I embark this spring on allegories. Here, sit." She placed a straight chair on top of a crate for a model's throne. "Now hang your head down to the right, please. Lower shoulders."

"What thoughts shall I think?"

"Deep regrets or sorrow," ordered Sonja.

Emily's face saddened.

"Not sorrow, secrets," suggested Jeanette. She thought Emily should not brood like that for an hour and a half; feigned emotion bled too easily into the real thing.

"What on earth *are* you thinking?" demanded Amy, as Emily turned enigmatic.

"*I tell my secret? No indeed, not I. It snows and blows and you're too curious: fie!*"

"Good lord!" said Amy. "Did you make that up?"

"No, it's by Christina Rossetti."

"Come buy, come buy," said Jeanette, throatily.

Wicked stealth crept across Emily's face though she kept her head turned down. *"We must not look at goblin men."*

"We must not buy their fruits," said Jeanette.

"Who knows upon what soil they fed / Their hungry thirsty roots!" they chanted together, and burst out laughing in spite of Sonja's instructions.

"Christina Rossetti in America?" said Amy.

"Well, we can read, even in the backwoods. I'll have you know that *Goblin Market* was passed around the dormitory after hours all one semester," said Jeanette, forgetting that she had vowed never again to allude to Vassar. "We'd whisper *Come buy, come buy* whenever we were warned against the big, bad world."

"Such warnings, pah," said Sonja.

"They are not altogether misplaced," murmured Emily, wistful again.

Three days later, on their Tuesday afternoon walk to the Louvre, Jeanette said, "The goblin men, Emily, is it you or Robbie they're after?"

"Poor Robbie. Pirates and smugglers after him, I think, or miserly usurers; but he escaped."

"He seems to have gained the upper hand. You certainly came home from Brussels flush with gold."

"Enough for now."

"And the goblin men?"

"Oh, Jeanette," said Emily, wearily, "they tempt you with luscious fruit and honey from a rock—with visions and when those grow dark, oblivion."

CHAPTER TWENTY-SEVEN

Third Interlude: Rome

Rome, the red-rose dusty city, was nothing like the halls of white marble that Edward had hoped he would find. The hills were hillier, the surrounding folds and flats of the Campagna more barren, broken at intervals by the ruins of medieval saints' shrines and relics of the ancient empire. He had come a long way to lose his craving for laudanum only to find it lurking in the dinginess of the Eternal City. He promised himself a day at a time that if nothing improved, he could take a dose; day by day, he succeeded in postponing surrender. He counted the hours. He also adjusted his expectations of what the city should offer as he and Carl explored it. And from the beginning, there was sunshine—such sun! It floated at noon, when the Alban hills swam azure on the distant horizon. In the late afternoon, it glowed in every shade of ochre from yellow to tan to darkest red. As surely as the Black Forest firs bristled in dense endurance against ice and snow, Italy's conical cedars and open umbrella pines promised the return of summer. Not that there were never cold or rainy days; there were, and then Edward's leg ached. But almost from the start, entire days could be spent out of doors, resting against a sun-warmed stone wall or sitting at an open-air café, or strolling in the vicinity of the Piazza Colonna where well-dressed men seemed to have nothing to do but devote their time to genial idleness. It was a wholly new experience for Edward to welcome ease as natural. He might have accused himself of lotus-eating had he not awakened one day toward the end of their second week glad to greet the morning, satisfied with the previous day, unafraid of the day to come. Neither lotus nor poppy conferred such a solid sense of well-being. He wondered for a moment how long it could last and knew in the next it was better not to ponder the question.

Carl had booked them into a hotel safe from bedbugs but well shy of opulence. His apt choice for two unpretentious American bachelors of adequate means impressed Edward favorably until he realized that their arrival had been duly noted by the American colony in Rome. They were taken up as indispensable commodities: unattached gentlemen. Had he been alone, Edward might have declined all the invitations. But knowing that he was a dull dog as a companion for Carl, he made an effort; and if he listened more than he talked, so much the better for the other guests and his hostesses. Carl came back late one night looking self-consciously pleased with himself and tried to slip into bed without arousing attention. The moon shone in through the shutters, which Edward had left open, and betrayed him. "So now you know," said Edward, from his bed. His own initiation had been with a prostitute, too, a scrawny, bitter camp follower; it was a scene too hurried, coarse, and sordid to afford much pleasure in recollection except at the revelation of entry into a woman's soft moisture. He hoped the Italian had had more leisure and a greater willingness to lead sensually. "Remind me in the morning to warn you against the clap."

Despite his own widening circle of friends and activities and Edward's contentment with what he called plain loafing, Carl never altogether neglected his uncle. He bought a Baedeker and showed a willingness to visit churches, monuments, museums, and recommended vistas on the principle that a man might as well get the benefit of the Old World charm he had paid to come and see. As January flowed into February, that charm came to include burgeoning verdure, the first flowers, and the fragrances of spring. Given the drabness they had first encountered, they were both astonished by the beauty—Carl with naive enthusiasm, Edward with an almost disbelieving gratitude. They had both read enough to know that they ought to have expected it, but nothing secondhand could prepare them for what they saw and smelled and felt in their blood. The insides of churches and palaces came to seem cold and clammy by contrast to the sweet air found in gardens or on drives to villages in the hills. They went to Florence; they went to Naples.

Edward would have gone on to Provence if the Renicks had not returned to Paris in mid February. After the acute phase of his nervous attack passed, he still tired easily and without warning. He was sometimes unaccountably jumpy. The first time he realized that Cornelia must have left Marseilles, he felt a panicked need to follow her to Paris as if she would otherwise be lost to him forever, as if Jeanette Palmer and her friends would be lost, as if he would be cut off from the new life he was groping toward. Habit enabled him to bite his tongue. Gradually, the waves of sudden desperation, the feeling that he was on the brink of losing something immeasurably precious, ceased as he got used to the sense of time outside of time during this Italian interlude. It was better still when thoughts of Jeanette Palmer arose in his mind, unbidden, and he could look forward calmly to seeing her again.

March unleashed an ever-mounting exuberance in nature; April promised to be better still; but Edward and Carl both began to stir. Italy was splendid, but it was not where they belonged. They needed to move on.

"Well, what shall it be? Freiburg? Vienna?" asked Edward, one day.

"You know something, Uncle Edward?" said Carl, "I'm thinking Cincinnati. If you ask me, it's about time to book passage home. I can't see going back to the *Hochschule*, but I'm turning into mush."

Edward was momentarily taken aback until he realized, with a wondrous lightening of spirits, that Carl's desire to go home made no difference to him. He could do whatever he wanted. And he wanted to return to Paris.

CHAPTER TWENTY-EIGHT

Carolus-Duran

Effie was fully recovered from her cold by the time the Renicks returned to Paris in mid February and was again invited to spend mornings tête-à-tête at the Rue de Varenne. (Cornelia's fashionable friends never paid calls before lunch.) On milder days, she assisted Mrs. Renick on slow walks around the extensive garden behind the house. She ran errands or played social secretary, helping to write out invitations and the like. Without a clearly defined position in the household, she became a fixture. Footmen stood straighter when she passed, and the parlor maids dusted more vigorously if she was sent to fetch something from a room where they were working; but she never trespassed on the prerogatives of Hastings, Cornelia's lady's maid Bette, or the housekeeper. Indeed from all the servants she learned a great deal about negotiating her way through the city.

"You're very wise to pick their brains," said Cornelia, one morning. "What odd corners they will send you to for your Lady Artist's Guide! Speaking of which, where have you sent the three samples you showed me?"

Effie mumbled something about nowhere yet, she wasn't sure, they weren't ready to show.

"Nonsense, they're marvelous. I feel quite able to hire a model, now. I'll tell you what. Send them to the New York *Weekly Panorama*. The editor is an old friend; use my name. I shall write him you are bubbling over with other ideas."

That night, Jeanette helped an excited Cousin Effie put together a packet. And then toward the end of the month, while they waited to hear from the *Weekly Panorama*, Effie brought home other news closer to hand: Carolus-Duran was to begin painting Mrs. Renick's portrait in March. Owing to her infirmity, moreover, he would go to her house rather than she to his studio.

"She's having a dress made to his orders, and gloves and everything. Oh, my, it's quite a to-do."

"Cousin Effie, could you wangle me an invitation to sit in on a session?" begged Jeanette. "Tell Mrs. Renick I promise I wouldn't get in the way; I'd hide behind a curtain or anything."

"Well, I, I . . ."

"*Please*, Cousin Effie."

Effie, who could seldom bring herself to ask personal favors, would probably never have worked up the courage; but Cornelia invited Jeanette unprompted. She was to come in the early afternoon of the second Tuesday in March, the fourth sitting.

On the magic Tuesday, when she arrived, Mr. Renick was just on his way back to the bank after lunch but delayed his departure long enough to escort her up to the gallery where the sitting had begun. At their nearly silent entrance, a young man with a heavy dark mustache and short beard started to rise from his chair off to one side. Mr. Renick stopped him with a curt shake of the head. At the far end of the gallery, Cornelia sat facing them on a settee, dressed in yards and yards of gold satin trimmed abundantly in lace. Clustered at her breast was a corsage of crimson roses; behind her hung a dark red velvet backdrop. She wore a long, dark rose glove on one hand; the other held its mate in her lap. M. Duran retreated several steps and leaned back to study her; under the redoubled force of his gaze, even Cornelia seemed to stop breathing. Dexterously, he exchanged one brush for another in a sheaf he held splayed out under his palette. He loaded it and lunged forward to touch in a new color.

Off came Jeanette's right glove as she pulled out her pocket sketch-book and the pencil she always carried at the ready. She opened randomly to an untouched page. As she kept her gaze on the three figures, her hand worked rapidly, semiblind. A quick curved line for M. Duran's shoulder; downward plunge for his upper left arm; round sweep for his huge, tilted palette (he must be strong to hold such a monster); twitchy little zigzag for the ruffle at his wrist. (Ruffles!) On to the other visitor: beard over sloping chin, raised knobby knee, extended long leg. Now back to the main figure. Jeanette's heart beat a little faster as she raced against the moment when the com-position would change. She badly wanted the romantic profusion of M. Duran's bushy black curls, the confidence running through his powerful, broad shoulders.

"The hidalgo puts on a good show," murmured Mr. Renick.

"He paints a good portrait!"

"He does, which is why I hired him."

Unless M. Duran's ears were extraordinarily good, he could not have made out the words of their whispered exchange, but the slight stir caused him to look over his shoulder. Jeanette hurriedly slid her sketchbook back into her pocket. An intelligent flash of the painter's dark eye registered his surprise at seeing Mr. Renick again, though he had presumably been warned that a young art student, a friend of the house, might appear. He lowered his palette. As he did so, the young onlooker shuffled awkwardly to his feet.

Cornelia came out of her pose, rotated her shoulder with a flirta-tious cock of the head, and winked at her husband. Her gaze shifted to Jeanette's hidden hand. "I saw you, my dear. You were sketching—just like Mr. Sargent."

So the tall, young man who managed to loom and efface himself at the same time was John Sargent! Everyone in Paris knew he was Carolus-Duran's star pupil, with a painting of his own in the last Salon, no less. Other art students spoke of him with awe shading into envy, but Jeanette had never met him. Nor did she give him much thought now, except to register peripherally for Amy's benefit that his pointed-toe shoes matched those of the master exactly; for even a rising star fades in the light of the sun.

And M. Duran outblazed even Mrs. Renick. A Mephistophelian arch to his eyebrow and a pointed beard above his wide collar hinted at danger within the effulgence; anyone could see that he had a temper. Jeanette's feelings were too mixed to sort out: admiration for his work, chagrin at the mention of her sketching, and naive excitement at being in the presence of someone at the height of fame, especially someone so handsome. Mr. Renick escorted her across the room, delivered her up, and withdrew, saying he really must be off. As introductions followed, Jeanette managed to suppress what Aunt Maude denounced as gush, but just barely.

"Now, Mr. Sargent," said Cornelia, "my vanity insists on seeing what you have done with me." The young man handed her the sketchbook readily, unencumbered by false modesty. "Oh, my goodness! This is beautiful—not me, *it*."

"It, it w-would be my honor to, to present it to you," stammered Mr. Sargent.

Mrs. Renick clutched the sketchbook to her heart, then turned it outward for M. Duran and Jeanette to see. "You must be a wonderful teacher, Carolus."

A bow acknowledged the compliment with pleasure. "Perhaps. But it was not I who taught John how to draw. That he learned elsewhere. How well I remember the day he brought his portfolio to my atelier! Not a man present will ever forget our astonishment."

He turned to Jeanette. "Is it true, *mademoiselle*, that you also were sketching?" If her hot face had not given her away, Jeanette might have lied. How stupid to have given in to the impulse! Her one chance to meet Carolus-Duran and what must she show him? Squiggles— squiggles in competition with a near-perfect drawing. M. Duran was genial at the moment, but his eye betrayed a ruthless, professional efficiency. He would make short work of a talentless amateur.

"I was only taking down an impression, a sort of souvenir—" No. No girlish apologies, no excuses; it only made things worse. Jeanette handed over the open sketchbook.

The drawing was distorted, silly. Mr. Sargent almost tipped out of her picture; Mrs. Renick's hair might have taken flight. Yet the firm strokes for the master were confidently placed. They widened and tapered like the cut of knife in clay; they had energy.

"Virile," said M. Duran, while Mr. Sargent, mouth slightly open, looked over his shoulder. "May I?"

Without waiting for permission, M. Duran flipped back to the dirty-edged pages at the front of the sketchbook. Some held first drafts of cartoons; some idly recorded a detail from a lunch table. "*Evidemment vous avez talent et esprit, mademoiselle,*" said M. Duran, "but from so slight a sample, I can tell little more. Perhaps you will show me a larger portfolio?"

"Do you mean, *monsieur*, that you will give me a critique?" asked Jeanette, in hopeful disbelief.

"No, *mademoiselle*. That I do only for my pupils, but I will evaluate your work to see whether there is a place for you among them. You wish to paint, do you not? And Rodolphe Julian tells you to draw, draw, only draw. Perhaps out of class, you paint, in the Louvre—not yet? No, but at home, in the studio of a friend, you put brush to canvas."

Jeanette blushed and looked down.

"I am right. *Bien.* If I can teach you, I will. If you are not ready, I shall waste neither my time nor yours. Bring examples of your work to my studio on Thursday; I shall be in between nine and eleven."

From the Renicks' house, Jeanette walked to the Louvre, loving every tree and streetlamp, every shop, every passerby, every fluctuation of light on the swollen river hurtling by in its spring floods. She passed under the arch to the Place du Carrousel and saluted Victory driving her chariot on the arch at the Tuileries end. A short time later, she slipped in next to Emily on the bench at a work stand in the print department; but after she had spilled out her story, it was impossible to settle down to copying. She went out into the galleries to search for paintings by the artists Carolus-Duran had praised while he painted—Velázquez, Titian, Rubens. In front of a Rubens, she remembered the well-dressed copyist she had seen there on her first visit to the Louvre. Her heart stopped. Could that have been Carolus-Duran himself? It could have been, might have—must have been. From now on, as far as she was concerned, it was; she would count it as an omen.

That evening, Jeanette went through her notebooks and finished drawings to put together a portfolio. She would take it to Julian's for Amy to review her choices, but she also had another idea. Cousin Effie had kept up with the Reade sisters ever since their return from Pont Aven. "Do you suppose Mabel Reade would give me advice? She studies with Carolus-Duran."

"Oh my, yes indeed, she does! She has been most interested in anything I can tell her about Mrs. Renick's portrait. Let's invite her to tea tomorrow."

Effie sent an invitation by messenger to Miss Reade and Miss Isobel for Wednesday afternoon. Before they had gone to bed, they received a counterinvitation to come to the Reades' apartment on the Rue d'Assas at the end of the school day—a much better arrangement, for the sisters had both the room to entertain and a maid.

Miss Reade's large studio overlooked the Luxembourg Garden and doubled at one end as a sitting room. It was furnished with shabby, well-built furniture. Miss Isobel's shell sculptures mingled with bric-a-brac on side tables; peacock feathers filled a brass vase; a threadbare carpet of Turkish weave lay at the sitting-room end, but the rest of the floor was bare, the easier to be swept out. Altogether, the place had a knockabout comfort overlaid with frilly, fussy touches.

At the working end of the studio, a large canvas, blocked in and partially worked, stood on an easel. In the innermost corner, away from the light of the windows, hung pictures in darker tones with more emphatic highlights than she used now, rather busy pictures; they clustered above a jumble of framed and unframed canvases stacked against the wall, three and four deep.

"There you have B.C.—Before Carolus," said Miss Reade with a dramatic thrust of her arm toward the rejects. She swept on around to the easel and the nearer paintings, which hung in honor. "And here you have A.D.—After Duran. Night and day. Mash and distillation." (The Reade family's money came from whiskey.) "Ought to destroy all the old stuff, but somehow can't."

"Memories, sister; dear, dear memories of places and people," piped Miss Isobel.

Miss Reade disagreed. "Egoism," she said. "Extension of the beloved self. You, too, Isobel; you like seeing pictures of yourself young. Take my advice, Miss Palmer, and prune regularly. Everything not indispensable is noxious, says Carolus. Applies to life as well as art. Now let's see what you've brought."

The next morning, to avoid fiddling further with the portfolio, Jeanette and Effie gave themselves an unusually leisurely breakfast and leafed through all the morning newspapers downstairs in the *pension* dining room. Nine to eleven, M. Duran had said, but they thought it might be a mistake to arrive on the stroke of nine. Although by that time artists all over Paris, and especially art students, would be hard at work, they did not know the master's habits. Accustomed as they were themselves to an early start, they were left with time on their hands. Back upstairs, Jeanette touched up her hair, changed her mind about how to place her hat, changed it back. Cousin Effie brushed cat hair off her coat only to pick up more when she shooed Boots out the window. Jeanette untied a perfect bow in the ribbon and rifled through the contents of her portfolio. New doubts assailed her about her choices. She slammed the portfolio shut and retied the bow sloppily.

"Come on, let's go," she said. "I can't stand it inside any longer. If we make a detour around through the Luxembourg Garden, we should get there at about the right time."

The garden was one of their favorite places, somewhere they could go at any time of day or evening and feel they belonged. This morning, as they turned in the gate, young mothers and uniformed nurses were already pushing perambulators or holding the hands of toddlers. An old gentleman, with his hands resting on a cane between his knees, sat on a bench with his eyes closed to let watery morning sunlight hit his face. Purple, gold, and white crocuses bordered beds of yellow daffodils. It all should have calmed Jeanette, but halfway to the main fountain behind the palace, she suddenly decided they had pushed their luck. "Well, then, let's cut over this way and head on out," said Effie in the placating tone of someone humoring an overwrought companion.

By nine thirty, they had reached Rue Nôtre-Dame-des-Champs. They were not alone. To Jeanette's dismay, as they approached the handsome façade of No. 58, a well-dressed gentleman was already entering the house while three carriages stood parked at the curb, their loitering drivers deep in conversation with—oh, no, Robbie Dolson.

In a fury, Jeanette marched up to him. "What are you doing here?"

"Why, Miss Palmer, always a pleasure! Surely you know that, of all places, Carolus-Duran's studio is the place to be on a Thursday morning. Of course, you do: Here you are. Or did you think you had a private audience?"

"Why did you come?"

"Oh, well, because, for my sins, I am a journalist and must cover whatever is happening."

"Not this, not for *Noggins*."

"Well, I do sell to other periodicals, you know. Nothing if not versatile, this lad—although, dearest collaborator, how brilliant! After all, our dandy Peregrine does go *partout*." He took her by the elbow and started her up the front steps.

She pulled back, resistant. "I don't think I want—"

"No cold feet now," whispered Effie, on her other side. Effie's curiosity was whetted by the traffic, and not even Robbie's behavior could dampen it.

Nor, on second thought, would Jeanette let him ruin her chances. She jerked free of him and climbed the steps.

At the front door, a servant was posted to receive and direct visitors to a large front room on the ground floor. It was strewn with thick Persian rugs and hung with tapestries and pictures. Some dozen people circulated to examine M. Duran's paintings, while more clustered in front of a full-length portrait mounted in the middle of the room. Its subject, a fashionably dressed lady, let fall a fur-trimmed evening cape as though she might step out of her frame to join her admirers or disappear behind one of several tall potted palm trees in the room.

"Why, it's as elegant as a hotel lobby or a fashion house!" exclaimed Cousin Effie as they stood on the threshold.

"May I use that?" said Robbie.

"Shhhh!" hissed Jeanette.

"Mais elle a tout raison, mademoiselle." But she is so right. Horrified, Jeanette turned to face the smirk of a man who had arrived behind them, a boulevardier in his thirties, dressed in a well-cut English suit of subdued gray-and-brown checks.

"Martineau, *mon ami*," said Robbie, somewhat wryly. "May I introduce Miss Pendergrast and Miss Palmer from America."

Cousin Effie ducked and grinned. *"Enchantée,"* said Jeanette, anything but enchanted to have had Cousin Effie's stupid remark provide a bon mot to be repeated all over Paris.

At sight of the new arrivals, Carolus-Duran crossed the room, his teeth shining in a wide smile. On his own ground, he appeared even more astonishing than at the Renicks' house. The boots in which he stepped lightly were made of sueded kid, supple enough for a dancer's shoe; their cut above the ankles hinted at the equestrian sports at which he excelled. His striped trousers were, if anything, tighter than the pair he wore on Tuesday; instead of the roomy work jacket of two days ago, he wore a short velvet smoking jacket, soft yet cunningly shaped by a tailor to show off his lithe torso. His collar was wider, his cravat looser. A gold bracelet shone out from under his ruffled cuff as he extended a hand to lift Jeanette's fingertips and conduct her into the room.

"Vous êtes venue, mademoiselle," he said, and took her hand in both of his. She had come. Good. Did she know these gentlemen?

Reluctantly, she introduced Robbie as the brother of a fellow student at the Académie Julian. She regretted that she did not know M. Martineau.

Ah, but M. Duran did. He spoke in a tone that implied it was better that she should not, although he and M. Martineau exchanged civilities. With a cock of his famous eyebrow, he bowed the two men on into the room. A moth's kiss brushed over the back of Jeanette's hand. For an instant dark eyes avowed his deepest wish to attend to her and her only, immediately, at once. Ruefully they added, what could he do? Such a crowd! So many demands! He would be with her as soon as he could, he said. In the meantime, she should put him to the test by examining his work. Before she could reply, he was off to the far side of the room to attend a white-haired gentleman.

"Well, it's certainly a privilege just to look around!" said Cousin Effie.

Jeanette thought it should have been, but she was overwhelmed by the artificiality of the open house made worse by the need to avoid or thwart Robbie Dolson.

They soon learned from overheard comments that the featured portraits would be sent to the Salon this year. "Maybe that's why there are so many people here today," said Effie.

While Cousin Effie surveyed their fellow visitors with a surreptitiousness that fooled no one who happened to notice her, Jeanette kept her eyes fixed only on the walls even while she was careful to maintain a distance from Robbie. Studies for the portraits that had won M. Duran his large clientele were hung along with some landscapes, the head of a gaunt man asleep, a copy of a Rubens—not her Rubens, but surely her omen! She swung around to search out M. Duran again. It thrilled her to think he must still explore, must still copy in the Louvre sometimes. His work was the work of a colorist, a man who took sensual pleasure in the act of painting. In that moment, she knew to a certainty that he loved, really loved his art.

"Well, look at that, he's selling on the spot," said Cousin Effie.

M. Duran's hand was, in fact, slipping something into his jacket pocket while the white-haired gentleman took down a small, unframed study of a nude with coppery hair.

"One of the naughty ones," Effie continued in a stage whisper.

"Shh. It's just a study like a thousand others," said Jeanette. But Robbie and M. Martineau were watching, too, with malicious enjoyment. They smirched the sale with a touch of the sordid. Jeanette felt an irrational pity for the little nude when a servant appeared discreetly to wrap it in brown paper and string for the white-haired gentleman to carry away with him. She turned away and moved off, not wanting either M. Duran or Mr. Dolson to know she had witnessed the transaction.

"Ah, mademoiselle, maintenant."

In trying to make herself inconspicuous, she had drifted toward a screen where, suddenly, M. Duran was beside her, kindly but brisk. Obviously wanting to be quick about it, he conducted her behind the screen to a worktable on which artist's paraphernalia had been pushed more or less neatly to one side. Effie scurried in behind them. Jeanette set down her portfolio and opened it to a full-length figure study.

"*Vous êtes heureuse, mademoiselle,*" said M. Duran. She was lucky— lucky to be at the beginning of her career when she might devote herself entirely to her ideals. Impatiently, he dismissed the crowded room behind them. He turned a few pages without comment. When he came to her sheet of baby's faces, he smiled and glanced at Jeanette. You have seen the portrait of the boy that goes to the Salon? he asked. *Bon.* To catch a child's expression, the tenderness of its skin in the delicate envelope of air surrounding it, ah, *tres important et tres difficile.* He looked at a couple more drawings, then reached for the little oil sketch on the bottom, a view out the back window of Amy and Sonja's studio. But she had not done this *chez Julian.*

"*Non, monsieur.*" It was done in the studio of a friend who had given her a few lessons.

Evidently, she was a good teacher. "*Vous êtes contente?*"

"*Oui, monsieur. Non! Non, je ne crois . . .*"

He smiled at her confusion. She was right to be loyal to her friends, he said, but it was equally important to serve her talent. Yes, he could teach her. Her drawing was strong enough to support paint-ing now, although she must continue to work on it with Julian to perfect her technique. His ladies gathered at No. 11, Passage Stan-islas, at eight in the morning. He would advise the *massière* of the class to expect her. *Au revoir, mademoiselle.* Until Monday.

He bowed slightly from the waist to her and to Effie (the first indication he had been aware she was present). When he was gone, Jeanette felt shaky inside—exhausted and elated at the same time. Her hand trembled as she straightened her samples slowly and retied the ribbon. "Oh, my." Effie, who had watched and listened only half understanding what was said, understood enough. When Jeanette turned to meet her eye, Effie neither dithered nor gaped after

Carolus-Duran. Instead, she stood calmly with her face composed and looked at Jeanette with pride. "I knew you needed to come to Paris," she said.

"Oh, Cousin Effie!" cried Jeanette, leaving the portfolio on the table to throw her arms around her cousin in a burst of tears.

Effie returned the embrace with a quick pressure. "Oh, my. Well."

"I know," said Jeanette, wiping the corner of each eye with the back of her gloved hand while she squeezed Effie's hand with the other, "this is not the place for demonstrations. But, oh, Cousin Effie—I am so glad you were here."

In her present mood, Jeanette could almost forgive Robbie Dolson for coming. When they reemerged from behind the screen, she felt as light-footed as the master himself. She was an initiate now; she pitied all outsiders and mere visitors, the petitioners and customers who packed the studio more densely than ever. In a moment she would have made her way through them out into the glorious day— glorious whether the sun shone or not. Robbie pushed out of a slouch against the far wall to cut through the crowd. She could not hold back a broad smile; he brightened in response.

"I see something splendid has happened," he said. His barely concealed taunts from earlier were replaced by an eager friendliness to all appearances genuine.

Jeanette warmed to him. "The best possible news. M. Duran says I am to join his class next week!"

"Oh, well, this does call for celebration. Congratulations, Miss Palmer!"

"We are just on our way to coffee," said Cousin Effie.

"With a shot of brandy, I hope," said Robbie.

Jeanette suddenly craved something hot, filling, and restorative— no, not brandy. "*Café au lait*," she said, "or chocolate. You are the sophisticate, Mr. Dolson, but I want fatness, butter, cream."

"Then I know just the place. Emily will be delighted at your news. I beg permission to be the one to tell her."

"As if I could stop you two sharing anything!" laughed Jeanette.

"Did you notice," said Robbie, outside, as they descended to the pavement, "how truly pell-mell the mob in there was? High and low, all sorts mixed together. Take the errand boy gawping at the nudes, for instance—how often is he let into an artist's studio? The *beau monde*, of course, in the person of Martineau. But that beautiful woman hidden under a veil—did you see her? The burning question is, how does Carolus induce such a *belle Parisienne* to rise in time for a midmorning call? I was speaking to her carriage driver when you arrived—the one, yawning. *He* isn't used to such hours."

Jeanette stopped on the sidewalk. "You *are* thinking about a *Noggins* piece, aren't you?"

Robbie shrugged his shoulders.

"No, Robbie; no, please. I can't start work under Carolus-Duran by drawing him or his private studio into a cartoon. You must see that I can't. I won't."

He seemed moved by the use of his first name; his face softened. "If you put it that way, my dear, of course not. You shall do nothing of the sort."

"And you won't either."

"You cannot believe for a moment that Carolus-Duran would mind a little more publicity? Oh, well, have it your way. No matter. Paris of the thousand beguiling nonces will toss us something equally diverting soon enough. Has Emily told you, for instance, about the new organ grinder on our block? I'm thinking of tackling the question, where does an organ grinder procure his monkey's fez? But for now, coffee, coffee."

CHAPTER TWENTY-NINE

A Loan

Robbie led Jeanette and Effie to a nearby café at No. 23, Rue Brea. M. Cagniard, the owner, offered felicitations when he learned that Jeanette had just been accepted as one of Carolus-Duran's pupils. His celebrated neighbor was a great master, a veritable genius, *et très gentil*.

At Robbie's request, he gave them a table large enough for Jeanette to open her portfolio and show him her work while they drank their coffee. When Robbie had gone through all the drawings, he said, "I'm glad to have seen your serious work. I never had before, you know. You're rather wasted on cartoons."

"I'll take that as a compliment, Mr. Dolson," said Jeanette, retying the portfolio, "but now I'll need cartoon money all the more with double tuition to pay."

"Carolus-Duran would be easy to caricature."

"No! I told you: We just can't."

Even as she spoke, the need to come up with a hundred francs in a hurry almost overwhelmed principle, but Jeanette quashed her fears. After that, she knew she talked too much. It was partly that Robbie paid such flattering attention, partly the lingering exhilaration of her triumph. Outside, she parted from him genuinely grateful for his having enlarged and extended her happiness, but once he was on his way, she came back up hard against the demand for tuition.

"Oh, Cousin Effie, how am I going to pay M. Duran? You told

me to put all the *Noggins* money in the ginger jar. Why didn't I listen?"

"Well, if you hadn't bought paints, palette, and brush then, you'd have to now."

Effie's words were meant to be charitable, but they only reminded Jeanette of all the other expenses that lay ahead. Her mind raced as they walked home arm in arm. She tried to think of something she could sell, work she could pick up—she knew a girl who tinted photographs in the evening; maybe she could do that. "I wonder if I could stall the *massière* or pay by the week."

"Offer to pay a deposit," said Effie. "Take whatever is in the ginger jar."

"But that's supposed to be for emergencies and pleasures—yours as well as mine."

"This is both."

Jeanette gave Effie an affectionate tug as thanks, then sighed. "That would leave the rest of the tuition to worry about. What if I couldn't come up with it?"

"You'd have to drop out for a while."

No, thought Jeanette obstinately, no. She bit her lip. There had to be some way to find the money for at least one month's tuition, now; there had to be. Finally she said with a sigh, "I'll cable Papa."

"Cables cost money."

"I can't help it. Even with a cable, there's not much time. Today is Thursday; payment is due Monday."

"Maybe you should start with M. Duran this summer."

"Cousin Effie, he said to come next Monday! By next summer he won't remember who I am!"

They walked on in silence. And then Effie made one of her brave, fantastical flights. "I'll just have to withdraw a hundred francs from my account at the bank tomorrow to cover the first month."

"But you can't! That's yours," protested Jeanette, genuinely shocked.

"To do with as I please," said Effie. "And it will only be a loan; your father is sure to repay me."

Every prudent scruple about money ever instilled in Jeanette, every ounce of family feeling told against taking advantage of Cousin Effie's straitened means; and for the rest of the day, she resisted. But once the offer had been made, no other solution suggested itself no matter how much more they talked. After supper, back upstairs in their cold room, Jeanette sat on a chair at the window, twisted around to rest her chin on her forearms across the back of her chair. She searched the street and rooftops as if another answer might lie out in the darkness.

"I wonder what I have that a pawnbroker would give me a hundred francs for. Nothing. And even if I wanted to go to a moneylender, I wouldn't know how."

"Mr. Dolson would," said Effie, with a chuckle. "He could probably supply you with names, addresses, and warnings against the worst screws."

"You think I should—?"

"Hush, now; of course not. I didn't mean *ask* him."

Jeanette said nothing but only continued to stare out the window.

"Let me tide you over a few days, Jeanette," said Effie. "I have a lot invested in your success."

A tear came to Jeanette's eye. "Has the adventure worked out for you, Cousin Effie? The whole thing, I mean—coming to Paris?"

"How can you even ask after today?"

"But what if I don't succeed?"

It was Effie's turn to pause. The deep, protective shadows in the room invited confidences. When she spoke, her words came almost in a whisper: "It will still have been worth it to me. I have come back to life. When Polycarpus died, I thought all I had left to look forward to was endless years of helping in the Hendricks' nursery and waiting on Cousin Maude. You may think running errands for Mrs. Renick is much the same—"

Jeanette shifted in her chair. Privately, she did.

"—but there's all the difference in the world. Mrs. Renick treats me as a friend. She thanks me and never criticizes. And I could say no to her any time I wanted and walk out of her house and still be in the most beautiful city in the world. And there's the McAll Mission and the church. I suppose I should think of New York City as home now, but it never really was. Anyway, I want to be here in Paris on the day when you have a picture in the Salon—you and Miss Richardson and Mlle. Borealska."

Jeanette sobbed into her forearm for a moment and then crossed the room to lay her face across Effie's lap. She was also half frightened by the strength of her own desire. "I've never wanted something so much in all my life," she said.

CHAPTER THIRTY

Where the Light Falls

On Monday, with Effie's loan in hand, Jeanette went to M. Duran's atelier for women on the Passage Stanislaus. The *massière* proved to be a smartly dressed woman named Lucile Dobbs. She was handsome in a chiseled way, with luxuriant auburn hair and a sensual mouth that hung open slightly as though she took in information from air passing over her moist lower lip. "Carolus says you have studied at the Colarossi or something," she said, as she took down Jeanette's name in a sloping hand and recorded the first month's payment.

"The Académie Julian."

Miss Dobbs shrugged as if the two establishments were interchangeable. "Then you know the routine. Set up wherever you like; it's first come, first served here." Her eye was already on the week's model, who stood in the doorway.

"One thing, Miss Dobbs," said Jeanette. "Is there someone I can send for a *bienvenue?*"

With a roll of her eyes and a much put-upon look, Miss Dobbs called out, "Rosalie!"

A *bonne*, whose young, pretty face was frozen into hostile correctness, answered, *"Mademoiselle?"*

Miss Dobbs told her curtly that Mlle. Palmer had an errand for her. Jeanette apologetically handed over some of the few coins found in the ginger jar.

"Ah, Palmer!" boomed Miss Reade. *"Bonjour, Rosalie."*

Rosalie thawed. *"B'jour, ma'amoiselle."* She bounced the fist with the coins and nodded to Jeanette before disappearing again.

"Dobbs been rude?"

"I wouldn't say *rude.*"

"Then you are too well brought up to be truthful. Pay no attention; the rest of us don't."

As Jeanette set up beside Miss Reade, she noticed at once that there were fewer easels than she was used to at Julian's—also that everyone came stylishly, daintily, or expensively dressed. She was going to have to pay attention to cuffs and collars even if she could never again buy new clothes on the tight budget she and Effie had worked out.

After requesting the model to bare her shoulders and let down her hair, Miss Dobbs announced to the class that they would be working from the head alone this week. She looked down at her class book as if she had already forgotten Jeanette's name, introduced her brusquely, and left. Before long, she returned, a step or two behind Carolus-Duran. Anyone not at her station hurried into place.

"What luck!" whispered Jeanette.

"Not luck, your arrival," said Miss Reade. "Watch."

In his loose working smock, Carolus-Duran swept to the center of the room, his dark eyes flashing from one student to the next. A few were favored by a wink or a nod; no one was left out. He bowed to the model and turned to greet the class.

"*Bonjour, mes filles*," he said.

"*Bonjour, mon maître*," they chorused.

He beckoned to Jeanette. Excited and self-conscious, she edged forward until he took her hand and turned her to face the class. They had met Mlle. Palmer, *n'est-ce pas? Bon.* Now to show her what was done here. An expectant semicircle formed behind him where Miss Dobbs had set a primed canvas board on an easel. Keeping Jeanette beside him, he now spoke to her as if there were no one else in the room.

"There are many valid ways to paint," he said, in French. "I do not attempt to teach them all, only those I understand. If you can study only one artist, *mademoiselle*, study Velázquez. Meanwhile observe me."

With a few masses smudged in by deft fingers, he achieved a minimal charcoal sketch of the model's head. He held out the stick of charcoal in front of his eye to take a measurement with his thumb just like a beginner. He put in another touch or two; then, using some bread crumbs that Miss Dobbs held at the ready, he rubbed back to the white ground for a few highlights. "*Merci, ma chérie*," he said, glancing up at his assistant with a disturbingly improper intimacy.

While a mollified Miss Dobbs applied fixative to the sketch, M. Duran began pulling tubes of paint out of a large pocket and asked Jeanette for her palette. On it, he laid an arc of a dozen colors—silver white, yellow ochre, raw sienna; on through several reds; cobalt; a transparent viridian green; and last near the thumb hole, bruxelles brown and ivory black. "These are the colors I habitually use myself," he said. "I recommend them to you while you learn the method of this atelier. But in time, you will discover the ten to fifteen colors that best enable you to express the world as you see it. Then you must school your hand to reach for them as if by second nature.

"Now for the least underpainting. Study where the light falls and where the shadows lie. We commence by indicating the darkest masses." Jeanette was familiar with the use of thin brown to compose a picture, but never had she seen work so broadly or so fluidly achieved. From a few swirls of a wide brush, the waves of the model's hair on one side of her face emerged.

"The background is laid in even more broadly, only be careful that it is very thin and transparent where it touches the head. *Bon.* Now the shadows of the face . . ." M. Duran fell silent a moment as he shaped contours and the rest of the hair. "In the beginning, you will use thinner brushes to touch in details to the underpainting, but in time you should be able to go straight to color at this stage. Either way, what is most important now is to find the *demi-teinte generale.* Half close your eyes, *mademoiselle*; regard the model. Somewhere on the scale from the lightest mass to the darkest lies the central tone most characteristic of the face in general. Do you see it?"

"I-I think so."

"Good. That will be the tone in which to paint most of the features no matter which pigments you use, with gradations down to the shadows and up very slightly for the highlights. As our time is limited, let me demonstrate what will become possible for you with practice."

He began to paint in colors, using smaller brushes. In less than an hour, the portrait was finished, a fresh and beautiful likeness. His dazzling display of virtuosity had been accompanied throughout by instructions that clarified miracle after miracle. At each step, Jeanette was sure she understood what was done; but after a while, it all began to run together. At the thought of facing her own blank academy board, she wilted. Amused by her all-too-visible consternation, M. Duran assured her, "You will learn."

He stood back to look at his own work. If a body could be said to strut while standing still, he strutted. "*Pas mal, eh?*" he exclaimed. "*Bon!* I leave you to it." With a flourish, he returned Jeanette's palette to her. If she could have afforded to replace it, she would have preserved it forever, allowing every scrap of remaining paint to dry hard.

That night, she returned from Julian's to the Rue Jacob intending at least to paint a little picture of the palette with the colors set out in M. Duran's order. She would write a rhapsodic letter home and decorate it with a watercolor copy. She was met by a telegram from her father: NEVER BORROW.

"I've had one, too," said Cousin Effie, guiltily wringing a handkerchief. Hers read, THANK YOU STOP NO MORE LOANS STOP FULL REFUND WIRED TO BANK. "Oh, dear. I hope I haven't caused trouble."

Over the next three days, Judge Palmer's disapproval weighed heavily on them both. Whenever her father was operatic in his complaints, Jeanette could be sure that his mood would change; but these telegrams had been grimly terse. She wrote a quick letter home the first night and began a second, longer one the next day. In her classes, she tried to focus all her attention on her work and leave off arguing mentally with her family, but she went back to the *pension* each night dreading to find a summons home to Circleville.

On Thursday morning, M. Duran came in around eleven thirty to criticize the pupils' work, with a day left for corrections. (Mercifully, he passed over Jeanette's clumsy first attempt.) Afterward, instead of leaving at once as M. Bouguereau always did at Julian's, he dismissed the model and rested an elbow on her tall stool. Leaning casually against it with one foot crossed over the other ankle, he took out a cigarette from a flat, gold case. "You don't mind?" he asked and, without waiting for an answer, lit up.

For a quarter of an hour, between long drags and exhalations of smoke, he lectured on what he called the sympathetic imagination.

To paint with insight and individuality, the painter must draw on personal experience and interpret a client's character or create figures for a dramatic picture. Women with their intuition were lucky, he said, but they as much as men could benefit from conscious exercises. He would give them an assignment. Over the next two weeks outside of class, they were to paint a picture based on the birth of Moses, illustrating the role of one of the women in the story: Moses's mother, his sister Miriam, the Pharaoh's daughter, or even one of her attendants.

He walked us through the story, Jeanette wrote home that night, *and made us imagine each step by comparing it to something in our own lives. For Pharaoh's daughter, he asked us whether we had ever found a lost child or some baby animal that we wanted to take care of. He told us to remember how it felt to hold a baby sister, and I could remember Mattie right after she was born, how soft she was, and how she smelled milky warm. He told us if we thought through all the possible moments in the story, there would be one when we'd say,* I can just see it! *and that's the one we should choose. The funny thing is that what came to me most vividly was playing hide-and-seek down by the Scioto River one time when Sallie was running along bent over beside some bushes.* I can just see it! *I said, so Miriam following the baby in the reed basket is what I'm going to do.* She decorated the page with a baby's face, a bulrush, and a quick sketch of a girl running at a crouch. *What was most inspiring, though, came at the end of the lecture. He said if we consulted our own experiences and feelings honestly, then even if we chose the same subject, all our pictures will be different, for each of us has an imagination that is hers alone. Do you know what I think I'm going to learn from M. Duran? Not technique, but how to know what I should be painting and how to do it my own way.*

Her letter crossed in the mail with one from her mother, which arrived on Monday. Sarah Palmer was scathing. She called Jeanette reckless and selfish. *You betray a heedless disregard for Cousin Effie's welfare,* she wrote, and elaborated. She decried her eldest daughter's sense of her own importance at the expense of her sisters; she rebuked a feckless attitude toward money that approached dishonesty. The charges were worked and reworked, in a small intense hand, front and back for two full sheets. Sickened by shame as she read, but also by frustration, Jeanette had to force herself to finish the letter. Then she was angry.

Over the weekend, she had devoted many hours to pencil sketches for her Moses composition. At Amy and Sonja's studio on Saturday, Emily had agreed to pose for the figure of Miriam; and since it was necessary to work fast, even Effie had agreed that time spent on Sunday afternoon in their own room on a biblical study could, at a pinch, be considered observing the Sabbath. A finished charcoal study was ready to be copied into an underpainting, but now she almost hated it. Although she had always known her execution would be the worst in the class, she had cherished hopes of original-ity. Working on the assignment had felt like an immense step for-ward. Her mother's scorn robbed it of all value.

She put her head down on the table and sobbed.

Very quietly, Effie pulled the pages of the letter out from under her hand and leaned over to read them in a small pool of light from the oil lamp. As she read, she made little bleating noises. "Oh, dear," she said, "oh, dear. It never occurred to me that Cousin Joseph would have any difficulty . . ."

"He didn't. Mother loves to think of us as paupers for no good reason," said Jeanette, into her arms. "It suits her sense of pioneer virtue, and it means she doesn't have to grant Papa what a big success he has made in the world."

"Jeanette! Don't talk like that about your mother! It's disre-spectful."

"Well, it's true."

Effie was not entirely convinced. Her lower jaw wobbled as she tried to pull her thoughts together. She put a tentatively consoling hand on Jeanette's shoulder. "All the same, I, I must write Sarah and apologize. I have written Cousin Joseph, but I must let her know that it was I who pushed you."

"It won't make any difference, and you didn't," said Jeanette, still pressing her eyes into her forearm. "Mother hates it that I'm here. She hates that I can draw. She'll hate it if I learn to paint well. She hates *me*."

"Now, Jeanette, calm down. That's going too far." Sarah Palmer did not hate her daughter any more than Maude Hendrick had hated hers when *her* girls came running with the self-same wail to Effie, but the vehemence of Sarah's letter was worrying. As family factotum, Effie preferred never to take sides; but she had done so in a big way when she enabled Jeanette to come to Paris, and the loan only compounded that first transgression.

"Mama only wants me to do things she thinks will be a credit to her." Jeanette wallowed a moment longer in her misery, then sat up heavily and sighed. "All the same, she's right—I shouldn't have borrowed from you. Papa's mad, too, or I would have heard more from him by now. I shouldn't have got you caught in the middle, you of all people, Cousin Effie." She took Effie's hand and laid it against her cheek.

The show of loyalty turned Effie fiercely partisan again. "Well, I didn't know then and I don't know now what else you could have done in the short term! That's why I backed you."

"You *did* back me, Cousin Effie, and I'll never forget it," said Jeanette. "I'll just have to figure a way to earn the money myself. I'll drop out from M. Duran's class after this month if I have to." She picked up her drawing ruefully. "I meant to send this home when I was done with it, but I guess that's no longer a good idea."

"Actually, I think you still should, Jeanette."

"Whatever for?"

"Because it will be much more dignified to keep on showing your folks that you are proud of your work. Besides, even if Cousin Joseph has been silent, he'll want to see it, and so will Sallie and Mattie. And so will Cousin Sarah, I think, even if she won't admit it."

"All right. But I won't write her back; I refuse to answer that spiteful letter."

"Not in your present mood, dear. Later."

Jeanette made a face. "What I had better do," she said, "is start a cartoon of Peregrine Partout with an organ-grinder's monkey. Even this light is good enough for that, and I'm going to need every penny I can lay my hands on."

Nevertheless, she wrote her father again very humbly. She promised to stick to a budget and try to find a way to repay him the hundred francs. *I have sold another cartoon with Mr. Dolson. And since you have already paid for a term at the Académie Julian, I can continue there no matter what.* She enclosed the drawing of Miriam and added, *I hope this will prove to you that even one month with M. Duran has not been wasted. Oh, Papa! you don't know how much I want to learn to put my heart into pictures!*

Jeanette's letter had the intended effect. Judge Palmer sent her a check to cover the rest of the spring at the Atelier Carolus-Duran. *Just between you and me,* he wrote, *after you met Theodore Murer at the Renicks' house last spring, I bought some shares of Cincinnati Power and Light. They pay a good dividend and are rising in value. I don't see why you shouldn't benefit. We'll call it a finder's fee and keep it between ourselves; but in return, Jeanette, you must write your mother a kindly letter.*

"Oh, how like Papa to turn around a hundred and eighty degrees!" beamed Jeanette.

"But he's right about your mother, too. You must write Cousin Sarah soon," said Effie.

"If only there were something to say."

"She's a proud woman, Jeanette, and you've got that same streak of pride if only you knew it. You've both got your backs up."

Jeanette's face tightened until she remembered her vow never to be irritable with Cousin Effie ever again. "An exercise in sympathetic imagination?"

"It wouldn't hurt."

CHAPTER THIRTY-ONE

Edward's Return to Paris

Edward's announced intention to remain behind in Paris after Carl returned to America set off protests from Murers on both sides of the Atlantic. Cousin Paul and Cousin Anna wanted to know what was wrong with their house. Had the laboratory space been too small? In Cincinnati, Sophie was, if anything, more alarmed and Theodore more indignant. Edward knew all too well why the family united to treat him as an invalid; but if Italy had taught him anything, it was that a gentleman could lead an orderly life of leisure and be none the worse for it—much the better, in fact. He was determined to live where that was understood. It was time to set himself up again in a place of his own.

"He means some *pension* like Mrs. Wiggins's boardinghouse, stinking of mice and cabbage water," grumbled Theodore.

Sophie reached for the letter. "He speaks here of an apartment."

"What a cuckoo! An apartment would mean staff. Can you see Edward's hiring, much less managing, servants?"

"There was Hans."

"Hans was an apprentice pharmacist, not a valet."

Yet who could force Edward to stay in Freiburg or return to

Cincinnati? Carl needed no companion on the voyage back to America (if anything, he would have to be dispatched to Europe again to fetch Edward home in the event of the worst). Nor was money an issue. As Theodore had spent the last decade pointing out, Edward could afford to live anywhere he wanted. Now he knew where that was: in Paris.

Darling, darling Edward, how delightful, wrote Cornelia, when he sent her the date of their arrival in Paris and his plan to see Carl off. *Please bring your nephew by for a last inspection—I must see what a year abroad has done for him, and Marius will want a report on your cousins' dye works.* She saw no reason to add that, other than having precipitated Jeanette Palmer's unfortunate outburst, Carl himself was a near blank in her mind, one of the many interchangeable young men assigned to the middle of her seating charts. She invited them to lunch with a mother and daughter who would be sailing on the same ship.

The lunch was pleasant. Afterward, when the two ladies had been sent off with cheery promises to meet next day on board, Carl proposed a walk. "You know what I'd like, Uncle Edward? This being my last full afternoon on land and all, I'd like to just saunter up the Champs-Élysées and then maybe climb Montmartre. They say you get a view out over the whole city up there."

They took a cab to the Arc de Triomphe; and from there, strolling just as Carl wished, they meandered off onto side streets lined with young trees and handsome new apartment buildings. Looking up at a row of second-floor balconies surmounted by Beaux-Arts friezes, Carl said, "I can see being willing to live in an apartment if it were one of those." The odd thing was, so could Edward. It surprised him to like the newness, the decorous symmetry of the buildings in these preserves of the modern commercial class. The district had no history. Perhaps that was what he liked about it; it was what he wanted in his own life: all future, no past, and a certain level of comfort. Not luxury, he didn't need that, but no more shadows and dust, no more meanness.

After Edward saw Carl onto his ship at Le Havre, he spent a couple of nights at a seaside hotel just to prove to himself that he was at his ease alone and then returned to Paris. Not to the Meurice, where he and Carl had stayed, but to a room in the hotel near M. Artaud's fencing school where he had stayed the previous fall. "False economy, my dear," chided Cornelia, when he visited her in the Poutery. "What you really need is chambers at the right sort of club, the kind they have in London."

"I can make do where I am for a while."

"No, Edward, not even for a little while. You need a good suite of rooms at the very least. You may shrink from the fuss of house-keeping, but you will want to spend some evenings at home, and an uncomfortable chair in a shabby bedroom won't do."

"Agreed, but if I take a suite, inertia might keep me in it. What I want is a place where I can put a bookcase and hang some pictures—"

"Plaques, you mean?"

Edward half smiled evasively.

Cornelia gave him a meaningful look. "If it were lodgings in the Latin Quarter you wanted, you could engage Iphigenia Pendergrast as your agent."

"I'm not a lady artist."

"No. Oh, but I almost wish I were! Has anyone told you that your brilliant idea paid off? The New York *Weekly Panorama* bought her first article and engaged her to write a whole series of columns."

"Well, that is good news!" said Edward, breaking into a real smile. "She deserves some reward in life."

"She does, she does. They also bought a sketch by Miss Palmer to make into a signature decoration." She paused to see whether

Jeanette's name would provoke a further reaction, but when none was visible she went on. "Now tell me, my dear, what do you have in mind? It's really very clever of you to see the danger of making yourself half comfortable. Not many would if I didn't. Have you called on General Noyes at the embassy, by the way?"

"Not yet. Theodore did last summer." Edward's face fell. He felt inadequate at the mere mention of the indefatigable ambassador: Cincinnati lawyer, war cripple, former Ohio governor, presidential crony. He was a high-ranking officer in the Union army who had continued his command after the amputation of a leg, not a corporal who went to pieces over a broken tibia.

Cornelia read his expression but refrained from observing that comparisons are odious. "Don't put it off too long, Edward. If you are going to be part of the American colony, it pays to observe the civilities. Besides, all the young men who work there are in lodgings; they hear about vacancies, and so do their wives if they're married. And I'll ask around."

The threat of becoming an object of interest to the wives of American diplomats and bankers spurred Edward on. He was always more resourceful and businesslike than his worried family gave him credit for, at least when he was well. He resumed fencing lessons and let it be known among the regulars that he was looking for a place to live. He called on a stockbroker he had met in Rome, a chess player who collected botanical prints. He looked into resources for research at the Jardin des Plantes and lectures at the École de Pharmacie. He paid the required call at the American Embassy and joined a club, the Cercle des Etrangers, Voyageurs, et Explorateurs, where he could dine, read in the library, or play billiards.

By the middle of April, he had accomplished what no one would have predicted: He had rented a laboratory near the Hôpital Beaujon on the Rue du Faubourg Saint-Honoré, put together a daily routine, and sublet a furnished apartment off the Boulevard Malesherbes, where there was room for a few things of his own. He had always barricaded himself behind Mutter's dresser; now he meant to buy something beautiful.

"This room expresses your personality perfectly, Cornelia," he said, as his eyes swept the Poutery when he came to tell her about the apartment. "I think of myself as someone who likes to travel light, but I'm mostly a stick-in-the-mud."

"Next you'll be telling me you must find a house of your own!" laughed Cornelia. And perhaps a wife, although she did not say so out loud. Cornelia was, first and foremost, a hostess, and a realist when it came to old bachelors. "Who will look after you?"

"Did I tell you about taking Carl into Alsace to hunt up my grandparents' farm? Probably not; it was last fall. We found the place easily enough. Near Colmar, right across the Rhine from Freiburg, and still in the hands of cousins. It was much as I remember it—"

"—only smaller."

"I'd have sworn that avenue of poplars ran a half mile at least, but it's only eight trees on each side. Also the cousins are peasants— rich peasants, but peasants, not a bit like Gran'marie. She had a butterfly's touch and the lightest step. We got a mixed reception at first."

"City folks in city clothes."

"Worse than that, German industrialists. But we played up being from America, and they thawed—took us around the place and hunted up everyone who remembered Gran'marie."

"All with reverence and affection, I'm sure, but I also see that you're teasing me, Edward. What does all this have to do with how you'll manage in Paris?"

"Everything. A few of the old farmhands were still on the place; but when the Prussians invaded in 1870, some of the families fled. I got wind of a couple I'd known as a child, whose daughter now runs a grocery store in Paris. The old folks live with her. I looked them up in December and again last week. Turns out that a grand-daughter Marianne, who was in service as a parlormaid, had married the estate carpenter just before their employer went bust. They're both out of work and willing to come to me for a year."

"A carpenter, Edward, how original! Ten times more valuable than a gentleman's gentleman—provided he learns to brush your suits. But now this matters: Can this Marianne cook?"

"As well as her mother."

"An ambiguous reply. If she fattens you up, she has my blessing. Now, tell me exactly where the apartment is."

"Up by the Parc Monceau."

"Not on the Left Bank?" Cornelia had expected—and half hoped—to hear that he'd rented somewhere halfway between herself and Jeanette Palmer.

"It's near my new laboratory. I want to do some real work, Cornelia. I investigated setting up on the Left Bank near the medical faculty, but I'm most comfortable around practical men. The laboratory I took is in a new building with different kinds of workshops."

"One of those big buildings with big steam engines in the basement?"

"Exactly. I'm surrounded by other little chemical research laboratories and manufacturers of specialized tools for the hospital. And I like being to be able to walk to the Madeleine. M. Fauré is always worth hearing."

Cornelia saw that he was not teasing her now, but deflecting her from the personal. For the moment, she amiably followed his lead. "Did I tell you that I had Maestro Grandcourt bring M. Fauré around last winter? Which reminds me—they will both be at my big garden party next week, and you must come, too. I usually give it at the end of May when the irises and roses have begun, but this year I'm using it to steal a march on the Salon. We'll unveil my portrait that day while it can still make a splash. Once the Salon opens, everyone will be too glutted with new art to be impressed.

Le tout Paris will be here, or at least everyone who will hobnob with mere rich Americans, which luckily includes most of the more interesting people. The worst snobs and bores always declined, so we quit inviting them."

"Which now they regret."

"Oh, no, not they—nor do we! But—" She leaned forward, eyes shining, and whispered conspiratorially, "if the sun is out, take a look on the second floor of the duchess's wing and you may see light winking off her opera glasses. We do still invite the duchess. She never comes, of course—but she spies. Now, Edward, although you are neither a snob nor a bore, you are nevertheless wondering whether you can skip this mob scene."

"I don't relish crowds, Cornelia."

"Superior people seldom do—no, I mean that, although, on second thought, it isn't true: Carolus adores crowds and so does M. Grandcourt. Anyway, listen to me. All our young artistic friends are invited—Mlle. Borealska and Miss Richardson and, of course, Jeanette Palmer. We must make a to-do over Mlle. Borealska because she has had a painting accepted for the Salon. And guess who else is coming? Sophie Croizette from the Comédie Française is bringing the ineffable Sarah Bernhardt just to prove they are friends, which, by the way, they are and have been ever since school. Mlle. Croizette has one of Miss Bernhardt's paintings in her dressing room next to a sketch by Carolus. I know because I've seen it. Now, you must come see *them*."

"I have seen them both, Cornelia."

"On the stage, you mean. Not good enough. Meet them in person. Write home, *I met Sarah Bernhardt and Sophie Croizette*, and they'll all simply swoon in Cincinnati. Sophie is Carolus's sister-in-law, which is why she will come. A few years ago, he painted a marvelous portrait of her on horseback."

"I remember," said Edward, slowly. It was in one of the magazines he had brooded over in the back of the drugstore. "By the seaside."

"You actually saw it? Where?"

"Only an engraving, but it was very striking."

"Not as striking as the flesh-and-blood model! And that was no studio pose, by the way. She rides as well as Carolus, which is saying a lot. I used to ride with her," added Cornelia, wistfully. She shook off self-pity. "Now, never mind about the crowd; it spreads out thin over the grounds except near the refreshment tents and the music marquee. Oh, and I'll give you permission to use the secret side garden. Everyone should have a secret garden, and I do—off the library. When you go downstairs today, tell Hastings to show it to you. In return, you must stop by the Madeleine sometime between now and then, and pray for good weather."

CHAPTER THIRTY-TWO

A Garden Party (1): Who Met Whom

Edward, who knew he had no special line to heaven, did not pray for sun; but April in Paris can, if it chooses, be lovely on its own, and it chose to be balmy for the party. Cornelia was credited with audacity amounting to genius for staging a garden party weeks before anyone else dared try. On the ten-acre grounds, budding spring leaves were tinted as delicately copper, rose, and blue-green as the last of the winter hazels were yellow. Hundreds of forced flowering shrubs advanced the season by weeks. In the downstairs hallway, a dozen full-sized gardenia bushes were in headily fragrant bloom.

The party was to begin at two, at which hour the least fashionable of the Renicks' guests would begin arriving in order to enjoy every bit of entertainment provided. Jeanette and Effie were to be among them, but not out of greed. "I'm going to need you at hand, dear, dear Effie; you must stay for the whole afternoon," insisted Cornelia. "You'll give me moral support." There was nothing Cornelia Renick needed less than moral support, but Bette, her lady's maid, approved and was more explicit about why: There would be a thousand little errands to run all afternoon, she told Effie, while she herself was trapped on duty in the downstairs ladies' dressing room. In *madame*'s ear, she also made a suggestion: Perhaps Mlle. Pendergrast should be given that plum dress from three years ago? It was Bette's prerogative to dispose of her mistress's discarded wardrobe, and Cornelia would never have risked offending either woman by offering Effie hand-me-downs; but she secretly rejoiced when Bette contrived to keep all the social niceties of rank in place and still convey the dress to Effie, altered to subdue its more extravagant effects and flatter a more meager figure.

Jeanette had to settle for the dress with which she had eventually replaced the mortifying gray-and-garnet taffeta school frock, a far subtler silk in a pinkish dove-gray alluringly called *cendre de rose*. By means of lengthwise fitted seams, it lay smoothly down the front over one of the new molded corsets yet had enough fullness at the sides and back to make walking possible (the most tubular versions of the style were said to restrict the knees). A short train fanned slightly in pleats from under a tieback, but there were no ruffles, the easier to keep the dress sponged clean. Over its three-quarter-length sleeves she wore a matching jacket. The costume had been bought with the idea that it could be worn from April through October and made to last several years, as regrettably it must. It was versatile, timely, and bland; Jeanette feared it made her fade into the wallpaper. Nevertheless, before they went down to the waiting carriage, she looked anxiously over her shoulder to check that the tied-back skirt spread evenly.

"How do I look?"

"Pretty as a picture," said Effie. "Not that it will matter what you and I look like, not with Mrs. Renick in gold satin and the likes of Miss Bernhardt on the grounds."

It mattered to Jeanette. With her hands in a new pair of gray kid gloves, she touched at her party hat, a narrow-brimmed straw confection trimmed in flowers, and looked in the mirror, smoothing out the look of annoyance from her face. Carolus-Duran would be there, and other artists and writers and famous people, and Dr. Murer. She wanted to shine.

Edward arrived when he judged the party would be well under way without yet being crowded. It was his idea to pay his respects to Cornelia, look for Miss Palmer, then escape quickly if need be. The unveiling at four had no hold over him: He had already seen the painting and expected to see it again, often; he was certainly not needed to swell the throng of its first public admirers. Yet more than he was willing to admit to himself, an ambivalent curiosity inclined him to stay if possible to see Cornelia's much-vaunted Carolus-Duran, Miss Palmer's teacher, Renick's clever man of the hour.

At two o'clock, Marius Renick stationed himself in front of banked masses of peach, rose, and white azaleas at the foot of the grand staircase. People's movements stirred the gardenia-scented air; a string trio played Mozart and Haydn, the intricate, witty music he loved for much the same reason that he loved the house. After personally greeting each newcomer, he directed most of them on out into the gardens.

"Murer," said Mr. Renick, in a voice that carried, "glad you could come." He clapped Edward heartily on the shoulder while his eyes slid on to the next guests, the deputy assistant manager of a competing bank and his wife. The hand on the shoulder gave Edward a barely perceptible nudge toward the staircase as he added in a lower voice, "Go on up; Cornelia will want to see you now. She's receiving out on the balcony."

While the deputy assistant bank manager and his wife pretended to have seen nothing, Edward mounted the stairs. At the door to the grand salon, a footman guided him on through to where Hastings stood at the nearer end of the row of French windows, which led out onto the balustraded roof of the ground-floor loggia.

"Dr. Murer," Hastings announced.

On a wicker settee among more azaleas under a striped canvas canopy, Cornelia sat in the golden satin dress of the portrait with a deep red rose corsage, resplendent. "Darling Edward!" she exclaimed, holding up her gloved hand to be kissed.

"That's our exit line, Isobel," said Miss Reade, who was seated in a chair beside her, while Miss Isobel stood to one side with Effie. The sisters were dressed in the bustled silks they had probably worn to vicarage tea parties ten years before, crowned by new hats sporting the feathers Miss Isobel loved. (Hastings would have recognized the type; from Mr. Renick's having sent them up, he knew just how much respect to accord the sisters in future.)

"Oh, no, Miss Reade, please don't go yet," said Cornelia. "This is Dr. Murer, late of Cincinnati, Ohio, where I spent the happiest years of my childhood."

"We met last fall," said Miss Reade, "at Sonja Borealska's removal party."

"Of course! Wonderful! Then you will be happy to know that he has recently settled in Paris, and I am determined to keep him here for a long, long stay. You must help me do so by becoming the best of friends. Miss Reade studies with Carolus, Edward, in the same class as Miss Palmer; and you remember her sister, Miss Isobel. In a moment, I'm going to dispatch the three of you to rescue our darling Jeanette. She's down in the garden, poor thing, being chaperoned by the two dullest women in Paris."

"Why, that's the first unkind thing I've ever heard you say about anyone, Cornelia," said Edward.

"Much less about one of my own guests, you are thinking. I hope you are right. But wait until you are chloroformed by Mrs. Drummond and her daughter. You'll see."

Miss Reade suppressed a short, snorting laugh. "Legendary," she said.

"Then you know them, too!" said Cornelia.

"Only by reputation."

"They give respectability a bad name," piped up Miss Isobel. Effie, beside her, smothered a snicker as she looked down to dissociate herself from the general disparagement (Mrs. Drummond, though not active in its work, was a faithful subscriber to the McAll Mission).

"The gods of hospitality will punish me for my wicked tongue soon enough, no doubt," said Cornelia, "but not yet. Just look whom they have delivered!"

"M. Hippolyte Grandcourt," announced Hastings.

The temptation was to linger for any anecdote to come, but the social exigencies were clear. Behind Grandcourt, an exceedingly well-dressed couple approached; and the maestro, who as a favor had advised on the orchestra under the marquee, might have something for Cornelia's immediate and private ear. Rapidly surveying the grounds below in hope of spotting Jeanette Palmer, Edward offered his arm to Miss Reade and ushered Miss Isobel on ahead of them.

At the foot of the stairs, Marius Renick spoke pleasantly to the Reade sisters. (Effie's report on their brother's distillery had checked out.) As the ladies started on toward the garden, he put a restraining hand on Edward's arm. "Hang on a minute, Murer. We seem to have an invasion from Bohemia." His eye was on a young couple in most unlikely attire. "You don't happen to know this pair, do you? I'm not sure they belong."

Edward was not sure they belonged, either, but he thought it likely that Cornelia had invited them. "They're named Dolson," he said, noncommittally. "A journalist and his sister."

"Ah, yes. Cornelia did invite them, but I don't believe she has actually met them—nor does she need to. Be a good fellow, Murer; take them with you into the garden.

"Welcome," he said, smoothly, as Emily and Robbie approached. "I'm Marius Renick. I believe you know Dr. Murer? He's just on his way to look for Jeanette Palmer."

"Nothing could be more delightful than finding her," said Robbie. From years as an unwanted dependant in the houses of better-off relatives, he sensed that he and Emily were being barred from some inner circle; but for now, it was enough to have won an invitation at all. Or if not, *Noggins* could help him take revenge. Robbie ambled on out to the garden with a nonchalance pitched perfectly for the man-about-town who had nothing better to do.

Emily floated, unseeing.

Edward followed in the assurance that Miss Palmer would want to join her friends.

And so it was that when Jeanette—by now impatient to detach herself from the dreary Drummonds—happened to look back up toward the house and see Edward with the Dolsons, her heart leaped, first with a joy that embraced all three, and then with a kind of comic wail. Oh, Emily! Oh, Robbie! They had reached the shallow stairs leading from the marble terrace down to the Rose Parterre, the first of three levels of formally laid-out beds. She and the Drummonds were on the second, the Fountain Tier, where, at Mrs. Drummond's slow wheezing pace, they were making for the main refreshment marquee. A moment earlier, Jeanette had been wondering when she could decently slip away and how. Now casting convention aside, she said simply, "Oh, please excuse me, I see some friends. I must—" Without finishing the sentence, she fled.

She hurried against the general flow of hungry visitors as fast as her tight skirts would allow. The brilliance of her smile as she approached made Edward's heart lurch; he wished he knew whether the smile was meant for him or, as he feared more likely, for Dolson. She could not have said. For Jeanette, the special vividness of Dr. Murer's presence had to contend with the laughter welling up in her at sight of the Dolsons' clothes.

Whereas every other man at the party wore black, Robbie was pure Beau Brummel, a half century out of date in shades of blue and gray with a yellow waistcoat and cream-colored spats. Neither collar nor cuffs were frayed, no seam was shiny, no spot defiled his cravat. He must have found a new secondhand dealer or theatrical costumier, and he must still be in funds. Oh, oh, and Emily, Emily! Usually demure to the point of nonentity, here she was wearing an uncorseted, pea-green gown with loose folds from shoulder to hem in back, full sleeves gathered intermittently down the arms by bands, and a soft front falling from a yoke embroidered in muted greens, blues, and rose—natural dyes, Edward could have told her; Aesthetic style from London, she could have told him. After Christmas, Amy had brought back British fashion magazines, which they had all studied. One Saturday, they got the idea of each adapting a fashion plate to represent a season. Emily claimed spring and painted a brooding pre-Raphaelite woman amid masses of exquisitely delineated flowers—but who could have predicted she would go so far as this?

"My dear, we harmonize," said Robbie, holding out the blue-gray of his sleeve to the grayish pink of Jeanette's jacket. Even as he did so, his eye scanned the grounds.

I am not going to be dropped that easily! thought Jeanette, taking his arm as if it were proffered.

"The *demi-teinte generale*; we set the tone," she said, brightly. "Now, come redeem me with Mrs. Drummond. Walk briskly. We'll invite her to join us."

The mischievous way she looked up at Edward as she spoke reconciled him to anything. It also brought Robbie's attention back to her. "You sound up to no good. Just who is Mrs. Drummond, and do you think she'll come? We could always loiter among the roses."

"No, no. She's as fat as a spoiled pug. She won't come—that's the whole point!"

"Naughty, naughty," murmured Emily, dreamily.

As Jeanette, laughing, tugged at Robbie to lead him down to the Fountain Tier, Emily took Edward's arm, resignedly. Edward looked down at her. On a sunny day, it was not surprising that the pupils of her eyes were constricted, but they had been constricted indoors, too.

"How long have you been using the stuff?" he asked, gently.

"It's for my cough."

"It would be effective for that, yes; but if you wish, I can have a syrup made up that will ease a cough with less danger than laudanum."

"That's what Wee Willie Winkie says, too. He's always warning me when I need it. But would your balm ease the soul's distress?"

"No." God knew, it wouldn't.

"A garden does," said Emily, turning her head away from him. With the back of her fingers, she brushed the delicate new leaves of a shrub, pale chartreuse flushed with pink, as transparent and veined as a mayfly wing. Her fingers fluttered into the air.

From a distance, Mrs. Drummond saw Emily gesture and raised her lorgnette to scrutinize the party. At closer sight of the strange young persons' garb and the happiness in flighty Miss Palmer's face, she made up her mind: If Cornelia Renick invited such persons onto her grounds, so be it. It was now her duty as a mother to protect Zenobia from questionable influences. Without need for consultation, the Drummonds turned their backs as one and continued a stately progress toward the refreshment tent.

"B'gad, I do believe we've been cut!" cried Robbie. Chin down, lower lip set sternly, he puffed out the cheeks of his long, slender face and turned a slow quarter circle away from Jeanette. When she let go to cover giggles with both hands, he completed the turn to meet his sister's eyes. His clown's stern stare shifted to an invitation, and Emily allowed herself to be enfolded, smiling vaguely at him from far away. Edward relinquished her, doubtful of Dolson's care of her, but more than glad to bring Miss Palmer to himself. The change was as smooth as dancers changing partners.

Jeanette looked up at Edward, tentative about just how much pressure to exert with her hand when she rested it on his arm. It was suddenly very important to her to play neither the hoyden nor the flirt but instead to express just the right degree of familiarity, no more. The hand settled; her fingers registered the lean firmness that lay under his silky sleeve. She looked down shyly but stole glances to study his face. He must be about Carolus's age (by her second or third week in his atelier, she, like all his pupils, had come to think of the master as Carolus). Dr. Murer had more gray in his brown, neatly barbered beard and hair, hair that was thinning at the temples. More lines of pain were etched around his eyes, and there was something ravaged about the hollow of his concave cheek. He lacked Carolus's obvious magnetism, yet in his darkness she felt something stubborn lie hidden.

The foursome circled the central fountain and continued along the main axis away from the house to look down on the clipped hedges that occupied much of the third tier and gave the Maze Tier its name. The rectangular confines of the maze itself were flanked at either end by conical topiary from which diagonal paths rayed out in *étoiles* to beds edged in box.

"Anyone fancy frustration?" asked Robbie, the warning edge of his easily aroused boredom creeping into his voice. He stared down to where a few guests in flights of high spirits were attempting the maze.

"Not I," said Edward. He pointed with his cane farther out.

"What do you say we continue down onto the open lawn? We should get a handsome view back up at the house from there."

Upon her return from exile in England, the duchess had struggled to restore the complicated gardens after decades of destruction and neglect. Despite her best efforts, she was forced into retreat after retreat. When the Renicks took over the grounds, they honored her wishes; and by great good luck, old plans were rediscovered in a garden shed. A crew of twenty workmen pulled out tangles and brush; they dug deep and manured; they replanted scraggly bushes and clipped them into shape. They rolled lawns, relaid gravel paths, mended walls, and fixed the fountain. The result was a handsome anachronism, as rigidly perfect as it had been a hundred years earlier. But then Cornelia had asserted herself against the duchess.

At the back of the property, where fruit trees had been left untended too long, she gave orders for dead trunks to be removed, along with worthless volunteers and any tree that could not be pruned or fed back into bearing. Only some picturesquely hollowed-out hulks and decrepit snags were spared for their looks or the few disfigured fruits they put forth every year, lost flavors from another era. With gaps left mostly unfilled, the orchard became an irregular grove in a wild, grassy meadow. The children played games in it and rode a little Shetland pony there when they were small. Within the surrounding estate wall, it was carefree and romantic, much despised by the duchess and more than equally loved by the Renicks. In late April, most of the buds were still tightly closed, but a spattering of cherry blossoms opened on a few branches.

"Good lord," breathed Robbie, with a note of wonder and longing in his voice. "Tretower." He unconsciously pulled Emily closer to him; she laid her head on his shoulder. With the smell of new-mown grass rising around them, they both looked out past the bud-laden branches into somewhere far away.

"Tretower?" asked Edward.

"In Wales. A childhood home," said Robbie, without shifting his gaze from the trees. "Not ours to claim, strictly speaking, but we lived there on sufferance, for a while."

"The land claims its own," said Emily, softly.

"The laws of nature and the laws of man do not always accord," said Robbie. He turned to Edward; a glint of challenge came into his eye. "It was why I turned poacher."

And picklock? retorted Edward, silently. Very little that he knew about Dolson redounded to the man's credit—less since what he had seen of Miss Dolson this afternoon. Yet a deeper part of his mind jeered at himself: Ever stolen a starving man's filthy ration? it whispered. Who was he to pass judgment on anyone? His flash of enmity died away.

At the unspoken antagonism between the two men, Jeanette tensed.

"Emily, my dear," said Robbie, "on closer inspection, your shoes are unsuitable for leas and meadows. What say we repair to more formal ground? Don't let our retreat spoil your ramble in Arcadia," he added with a bow to Jeanette and Edward and a sweep of his arm outward.

"B'gad, I think we've been cut," said Jeanette, staring after Robbie as he maneuvered Emily back up the stairs.

"I don't mind if you don't mind. Are your shoes—?"

"Quite up to any path the gardeners have cut through the Renicks' lawn, thank you!"

An unmarried couple at a big garden party could stroll a few turns unattended, like partners during a dance. Edward and Jeanette took their time as they walked the looping path through the grass.

By the time they reached the lowest tier of the garden again, some two dozen visitors were trying to thread their way through the maze. Most trooped along, calling good-natured advice of dubious value to each other across the low hedges; but among them, a scowling

Sonja stalked just behind Count and Countess Witkiewicz, whose children's portraits she had painted. She was watched by Amy from the perimeter.

"Thank goodness, a rescue party," said Amy. "Behold, poor Sonja, the Painter Ensnared. I always knew there were drawbacks to patronage."

"You don't mean for us to lead her out, do you?" asked Jeanette.

"Not her. Me. Whisk me away; I've had enough. There's no need to linger watching while she attempts to play the good sport—at which, incidentally, she seems about to fail signally."

Rocking a little from side to side, Amy caught Sonja's attention and pointed toward the end of the parterre. Sonja mimed shooting herself in the head.

"Come along, my dears," said Amy, "there is rumored to be punch over there."

From the orchestra on the level above, the ONE-two-three, ONE-two-three pulse of a waltz floated down. A particularly lilting melody rippled out as they reached a diagonal ray. Jeanette minced a dance step. Edward caught up her hand and twirled her onto the new path. Setting her loose with only the slightest squeeze of her fingers, he clamped his cane to his chest and bowed Amy forward, too. People around them smiled; Jeanette sparkled. In the circumstances, Amy's presence restrained her from taking Edward's arm again—what a declaration that would be!—but not from feeling a little flutter of the heart. It showed in her face.

Oh, lord, thought Amy, not another one lost to Cupid's bow. Pesky winged brat.

"Look!" she said, catching up Jeanette chummily and leaning in to direct her gaze without catching the attention of others nearby. "Do you see that natty gent with the faded red hair and beard? That's Edouard Manet. He's a good friend of Carolus, so they say, a bit older.

Back when he showed a painting of a Spaniard with a guitar, Carolus is reported to have exclaimed, 'I thought Velázquez was my discovery!' and gone around to pay a congratulatory call with some other admiring lads." She looked around to include Edward. "Full marks to Mrs. Renick for knowing to invite him. Do you know whether she has bought anything from him?"

"Should she? I thought his work was much reviled."

"Well, it is very peculiar in subject and technique. Not to everyone's taste; certainly not to mine. He sends something to the Salon jury each year, and opinion is always divided about whether he means to offend them or does so inadvertently. Still, he has his supporters. *They* say he's the all-in-all."

Eventually, Sonja and the Witkiewiczes freed themselves from the maze and came looking for Amy. Somewhat intimidated by the Witkiewiczes' aristocratic worldliness, Jeanette stood as though she had a book on her head and hoped she did not look too much like a girl from Circleville, Ohio. A couple who knew the Witkiewiczes stopped to chat. The Misses Reade found the group and recommended refreshments. Everyone began moving toward the Fountain Tier. There, the party swirled the Witkiewiczes off toward the orchestra. The Reades drew in some English acquaintances; the babble in the refreshment marquee as they neared it was deafening. In spite of himself, Edward balked.

Jeanette's hand touched his sleeve. Without saying anything, she looked up toward the quieter Rose Parterre and smiled inquisitively. A momentary elation flooded him like the rush of emotion that sometimes disgraced him with tears but expanded into a wordless understanding too quickly to betray him. They veered away from their companions and moved off together. It was the most peace he had felt since a golden summer's afternoon spent with Marie. Not that long-ago thoughts of Marie more than brushed his conscious mind; he had never been more utterly aware of the present moment. No, it was instead that he recognized this tender happiness as coming

into the kingdom again, coming home to the world as it was meant
to be and always would be at its truest. Jeanette's feelings included
a sense of daring (it was *she* who had caught *his* eye), of naughtiness
at slipping away, of pleasure at being seen with an admirer, of pride
that she had guessed right about his discomfort and what to do—
and yet the more they walked, the more all of that subsided, leaving
only a settled sense of rightness.

A gong from the house sounded, a signal that the hour for the
unveiling approached.

Jeanette stiffened and turned momentarily. "We should go up,"
she said, with some regret at breaking off their conversation but no
intention of missing the main event.

"They'll give time for people to wend their way back to the
house," said Edward. "Shall we make a detour through Mrs. Renick's
secret garden?"

"Her secret garden?"

"I'll show you. From there, we can go into the house through the
library." He did not miss, nor mistake, a flash of excitement in her
eyes.

The gardener's service stairs at the end of the Rose Parterre led
up onto the terrace beside a brick wall that was largely obscured by
the overhanging branches of a beech tree. A low, arched door in the
wall led into a roofless bay enclosed on the southern side of the house.
Once upon a time, its shelter combined with an openness to long
daily hours of sunlight had made it perfect for pampering delicate
rarities and prolonging hardy blooms; but by the time the duchess
reclaimed the mansion, the copper beech had established itself and
shaded out most of the old plantings. It was a handsome tree; and
with much else to think about and pay for, instead of having it cut
down, she had installed a bench around its trunk and forgotten about
it. Cornelia admired the tree, kept the bench, and made the side
garden her retreat. In midsummer, the leaf cover was so dense that
it was possible to sit under it even during a shower. In early spring,

the light, dappled shade was almost as coral as the leaf buds were purple.

As Edward and Jeanette closed out the drone of the party, the tiny warble of a chaffinch, *tswee-tswee-tsit-tsit-tick*, sounded out distinctly from a branch overhead, but they and the bird did not have the garden to themselves. Near the library door, surrounded by four men, glimmered the thinnest woman Jeanette had ever seen. She was dressed in silvery white pongee, its nubbly paleness dim beside the lunar sheen of her skin. A dramatic, fluted collar climbed her long throat to frame a pointed chin and meet wings of crinkled, Titian-red hair. Above a fringe across her forehead sat a cunning velvet cap, like something a medieval Venetian gentleman might have worn, adorned with an ornament of pearls and emeralds. Emily in her homespun pea-green folds would look dull beside the exoticism of this woman: She might be a dragonfly, a jeweled lizard, a fairy of the most dangerous sort. An acute sensitivity to her surroundings must have alerted her to their approach; for in the instant that they became aware of her, she turned her superb falcon's profile to fix them full face with extraordinary blue-gray eyes.

"*Entrez, entrez,*" she commanded in a tone that was crystalline without being loud. Her hand wove a gesture as compelling as the look she gave them before she turned her full attention back to the men around her.

Jeanette and Edward tiptoed forward obediently and slid onto the bench under the beech tree as quietly and carefully as if they were taking seats in a theater after the curtain had gone up. It was Sarah Bernhardt, and they would never be seated closer. But they had not watched long before, to their further astonishment, they were forced to shift their attention. A woman of high coloring dressed in richest blue came briskly to the doorway and paused. Like Bernhardt, she had a nose too large for conventional prettiness; unlike Bernhardt, hers was offset, not by her eyes, but by a full-lipped, expressive mouth set in a highly contoured face. Her chin and cheeks were rounded and her figure buxom. It was Sophie Croizette. Edward thought her curvaceousness more comely than Bernhardt's sylphlike flame. It made him pleasantly aware of the plumpness beside him, aware also of how much younger Jeanette was than these two formidable actresses at the height of their powers. Either of them could play a mere girl on stage, but in person they had left all girlishness behind at least a decade ago. The one was a rare white camellia or orchid, the other an opulent hothouse rose or peony; Miss Palmer was daffodils and daisies.

"*Pas quand même, Sarah chérie, mais à outrance,*" said Mlle. Croizette, moving forward energetically. She tugged on one long glove with her other gloved hand as she spoke. "*Carolus vient d'arriver.*"

"*Avec—?*"

"*Oui,*" pronounced Croizette, with considerable asperity, though the purse of her lips and a look in her eye betrayed amusement.

Jeanette could not quite follow what was happening. Carolus-Duran had just arrived, that was clear—but with what, or with whom? After Croizette had led Bernhardt and her entourage into the library, Jeanette looked at Edward with the unspoken question dancing in her eyes: Did you see that? He, too, had perceived it as uncommon luck to witness a fragmentary comedy unfold for their eyes alone. More disturbing, pleasurably disturbing, she saw his attention now fix entirely on herself. She felt his body's warmth through his coat. Just for an instant, it was tempting to lean into his firmness. He knew and raised his arm to the back of the bench, but hesitated. She jumped to her feet.

They both knew they had to go indoors, if only to see what would happen next in the little drama just set in motion. Even so . . . Looking at him sidelong, Jeanette moved slowly, not toward the door, but away from it. Thin, scraggly grass at the edge of the beech shade ran out into a thicker stretch of lawn, which ended at the rim of a small fishpond. A cloud of tiny insects hung gold over its mirrored surface. The water gleamed. *Tswee-tswee-tsit-tsit-tick!* sang the chaffinch. "It's perfect," said Jeanette, under her breath; Edward, standing behind her, rested his hands lightly on her upper arms. But the sound of her own voice and the deliciousness of his touch were too much for Jeanette. She turned around, took his hand to pull him toward the house, and said, laughing, "Come on!"

CHAPTER THIRTY-THREE

A Garden Party (2): Who Saw What

In the front hallway, Carolus-Duran had arrived with Lucille Dobbs on his arm and a retinue of his other pupils behind him. Just as Jeanette and Edward reached the library door, Croizette, with a sweeping gesture, commandeered him. (Miss Dobbs treated her effacement as an oblique triumph and boldly surveyed the assembled guests. Her eyebrows lifted when she espied that new Miss Palmer in the sole company of an extremely well-dressed man—obviously *not* her father.)

Carolus-Duran seemed not in the least disconcerted to have his mistress, if that was what she was, replaced at his side by his sister-in-law; for the genius and good looks of one played brightly off the genius and good looks of the other. An instant after kissing her on both cheeks, he turned to divert congratulations on the portrait about to be unveiled with a gallant compliment on the sitter's beauty while Croizette, keeping firm hold of his arm, bent in the other direction to dazzle a well-wisher.

A few steps up the curved stairway, Marius Renick watched the scene in his front hallway, well content. He had Sarah Bernhardt beside him.

Gradually, the crowd parted to allow Carolus and Croizette through to join their host. They were almost at the foot of the stairs when the artist happened to see his new student with a gentleman he did not know. He was struck at once by the man's gaunt face, a type that interested him; this one had known illness, suffering. Little Mlle. Palmer he already knew to be a protégée of the Renicks. Her companion must be at least an acquaintance; and if his frock coat was anything to go by, he might be worth meeting. With a smile of entreaty and the least jerk of his head, he summoned them. Jeanette was almost disbelieving. Stardom! As she moved forward, she glanced up excitedly into Edward's face to make sure that he, too, came.

The irony of his having told Cornelia that he disliked crowds only to find himself being pulled to the center of one was not lost on Edward, nor the further irony that he was enjoying the moment. He was detached enough to know that it was neither the crowd nor the glamorous principals that pleased him, it was being with Miss Palmer and being seen to be with her. No fool like an old fool, he told himself, wryly.

At the top of the stairs, Hastings had been standing by the door to the grand salon, as immobile as a torchière. When the assembly below began shuffling into motion behind Mlle. Bernhardt, he opened it. Jeanette glimpsed a swatch of plum-colored train pull back. A moment later, Mrs. Renick emerged, walking without a cane and shining in her gold satin. It was the first that most of her guests knew that she could walk again. Her appearance was met with gasps and, after a moment's hesitation, applause. For a moment, she held on to the banister railing and smiled down on everyone else; then she turned toward the stairs to reach out to the hero of the day, Carolus-Duran. Carolus waved to the crowd, and the three lead couples proceeded into the room, where the covered portrait stood beside the piano. Mrs. Renick was conducted to the sofa in grand style and posed as she appeared in the painting.

As the line of guests began to move behind the leaders, Jeanette and Edward fell in step and were among the first to enter the almost-empty room. Jeanette looked around for Cousin Effie. She was standing in front of a panel of curtains between two sets of French windows onto the balcony, a dim silhouette obscured by shafts of afternoon sunlight flooding in from the west. From this near invisibility, she had a perfect vantage point for watching everyone and everything else the sunlight landed on, including the easel.

"Do you mind joining my cousin?" asked Jeanette.

"Nothing would please me more."

Jeanette could not have said why it suddenly seemed so important to be with Cousin Effie. Part of it was a guilty leap of affection for singular, self-effacing Effie, who had no doubt thought it a privilege to be run off her feet all afternoon on Mrs. Renick's behalf.

"Isn't it just grand?" said Effie. "The day has gone off perfectly!"

When the salon was three-quarters full, Mr. Renick signaled Hastings to bar entry to the room for the time being. From the piano, unbidden, came three loud chords, struck by Maestro Grandcourt to demand silence. Marius glanced back over his shoulder, amused. Grandcourt bowed. There were those in Paris outside financial circles who thought of Marius Renick primarily as Cornelia Renick's less interesting half. He never tried to correct the impression. On this occasion, he spoke briefly, to the point, and without a memorable word, after which Mlle. Croizette took up a corner of the velvet draped over the portrait and contrived to make pulling it away momentarily suspenseful, then a spectacle. As exclamations and spontaneous clapping greeted the painting, she and Mlle. Bernhardt departed to the adjoining picture gallery, whence they were accompanied by an adulatory footman to their carriages. The rest of the afternoon belonged to Cornelia and Carolus-Duran.

"Have you had a chance to go out to the gardens?" Jeanette asked Effie, as they along with Edward made their way slowly in the receiving line to view the picture up close and congratulate artist and sitter.

"Not yet."

"Or eaten?"

"Oh, yes! Mrs. Renick had refreshments brought upstairs."

Jeanette suddenly realized that it was she who was hungry, but she had to suppress her appetite; for when they got to the head of the line, Carolus-Duran handed her back to the honor guard of pupils whom Jacques, the footman, brought up a back way to stand behind the picture. It gave her a chance to speak to John Sargent, whom she had not seen again since they met at the Renicks' house.

"I understand you are due congratulations, too," she said. Earlier in the month, the women's atelier on the Passage Stanislaus had been as excited as the men's by the news that Mr. Sargent's portrait of the master had been accepted for the Salon. "I hear your portrait of Carolus is wonderful."

"He-he did me the honor to s-sit," said Mr. Sargent.

Jeanette, still buoyed by the flood of her afternoon's happiness, read in his alarmed eyes a shyness with girls that made her want to giggle. She stepped past him to join Miss Reade.

"Done it again, has Carolus; and I like Penders' Mrs. Renick."

Penders? A nickname? Jeanette turned her head quickly to see whether Effie had undergone other unsuspected transformations. None visible. She turned back to make light conversation about Mrs. Renick, the painting, the gardens, and the Drummonds, all the while trying to keep an eye on Cousin Effie and Dr. Murer as they were absorbed into the circulating flow of guests.

As much as Edward regretted becoming detached from Jeanette, he knew that if he stayed with Miss Pendergrast, sooner or later they would be reunited. Unfortunately for him, just as Miss Isobel was about to join them, he espied General Noyes. He came to attention. The two ladies disappeared.

"Afternoon, Murer," said the ambassador, "good to see you."

"Sir."

"Was that Circleville Palmer's girl you were with just now?"

"Yes, sir."

"Good-looking gal and good of you to look after her. Ohio must keep an eye on its hatchlings. Remind me what's she doing in Paris?"

"Studying painting, sir. With M. Duran, as a matter of fact."

"Bit of a roué from what I hear, but one of the best. Well, well, as long as Cornelia Renick has the chick under her wing, no harm likely to come."

"No, sir."

It was all nonsense—*girl, hatchling, roué, chick*—but it upended Edward's sense of well-being. As General Noyes hobbled away, Edward felt like kicking the Old Man's wooden peg out from under him with his own gimp leg. He looked with regret to where Jeanette was merrily chattering away in the young cohort to which she belonged. When, later, Carolus-Duran led his pupils along with their hosts for an enthusiastic and illuminating tour of the Renicks' collection, Edward had long since made his way downstairs. Head down, shoulders forward, he avoided being caught by anyone else he knew. His intention was to leave the house and grounds at once, but at the foot of the stairs, he paused. On the other side of the library, where the beech tree stood, the afternoon light was golden. *Everyone should have a secret garden*, Cornelia had said, and given him the freedom of hers—which would forever be his and Miss Palmer's as far as he was concerned. Perfect, she had called it. Not a hatchling, not a girl; a young woman.

As he headed for the door out to the walled bay, the last thing he expected was to be startled out of self-absorption by a sordid little crime, but a movement at the other end of the long, narrow room caught his attention. He looked just in time to see Robbie Dolson's hand come out of a display case and drop something into his pocket. Miss Dolson sprawled across a chair with her head turned away, whether asleep, in distress, or lost in a drugged haze, Edward could not tell.

"If I were you, Dolson, I would put that back."

Robbie swung around. Fear followed by a spasm of anger crossed his face, then a sort of hopelessness. In a remarkable display of either sangfroid or despair, he retrieved a small but costly porcelain-and-gold box from his pocket, examined it briefly with the air of a connoisseur deciding against a purchase, then lifted the glass cover a couple of inches and slid it back. His long fingers rested on the glass top of the case.

"What are you going to do now?"

Edward knew that at the very least he should ring for a footman. Call the police, warn the Renicks. Ever stolen a starving man's ration?

"Have you taken anything else?"

"No."

"Then I'm going to advise you to leave."

"Good man," murmured Robbie, without looking up. He smiled to himself. His hand moved to the display case catch. The snick of the lock obliterated any evidence of attempted theft.

His complacency shocked Edward. "I would also advise you, sir, to look after your sister," he said, more roughly. "Miss Dolson is not well, and too much laudanum will do her no good."

Robbie drew himself up and turned with a snarl. "I may be in no position to demand satisfaction, Dr. Murer, but I would advise *you* to mind your own business, *sir*. Come along, Emily, time to go."

Without so much as another glance at Edward, Robbie pushed a drooping Emily ahead of him out the door at the other end of the library. For a moment, Edward stood stunned by the man's effrontery. And that poor girl. Without knowing why, Edward stepped back into the hall. The front door was just closing. If Miss Dolson had worn a wrap, it had been abandoned.

"*Cet homme-la*," he said to a footman on duty in the hallway. That man—Edward was not sure what more he wanted to say.

"*Oui, monsieur.*" The footman maintained an impassive demeanor, but the look in his eye was shrewd. He spoke with finality: That man had been under surveillance all day.

Strangely enough, the episode had shaken Edward out of unhappy doubts induced by the general's careless remarks. Jeanette Palmer was young, but he could wait. He would not interfere with her education nor attempt to dissuade her from pursuing the art that clearly animated her heart and imagination. He would not press his suit too strong too soon. But neither would he besmirch himself or her by thinking ill of what he dared to hope was a growing understanding between them. The unsettling Dolsons were more troubling. As he went out into the secret garden, his lungs were grateful for the damp, spring air, cooling at the approach of dusk, and his nose for green, earthy smells free of smoke and all traces of cloying, artificial sweetness from the hall.

With his head resting against the trunk of the tree, he slipped into a reverie until a chilliness in the air made him open his eyes. Only the upper branches of the beech tree remained burnished by the sun. He had better get moving. He let himself out through the gray-painted door in the stone wall onto the terrace across the back of the house. He must find Marius Renick before he left and tell him what had happened inside (also confess that he had let the scoundrel escape); but first he leaned on the balustrade and looked out over the whole garden.

Shadows stretched across the Rose Parterre, the Fountain Tier, the Maze Level. Light trembling between silver and gold lay hazily on the meadow grass beyond; it dwindled into dimness among the branches of orchard blossom. In the general fading, water jets of the big fountain were gray; only their crests splashed white with a touch of sparkle. Emptied of people, the maze attracted him; but he felt too indolent to move, and only an idiot would enter its blind alleys at this late hour and risk the mortification of requiring release by a gardener sent out to secure the grounds.

The orchestra played its last waltz. Stragglers headed for the house. Thumps, scrapes, and desultory scraps of voices from the orchestra tent signaled that the musicians were packing away their instruments. Edward turned around to go into the house. Just in time. There, coming out, were Cornelia in her gold, Marius in black, Effie only half visible in the purple dusk, and Jeanette.

For Jeanette, sight of the solitary figure in the shadows mended an afternoon that had frayed ever since she had seen Dr. Murer leave without waiting for her. Although she had kept up light social banter with Carolus's other pupils, it had hurt when Lucille Dobbs asked, "Where's your friend?"

"He's my cousin's friend," she had answered, petulantly, and immediately wished she had said, Which one? Now that she knew he had stayed, she glowed as he came toward her.

"Edward, my dear, how perfect! You haven't left," cried Cornelia. She reached out the back of her hand. "We are on our way down to thank the orchestra and send them over to pillage the refreshment marquee. The caterers are sorting out a light supper for us and the staff. You come, too. You can't claim another engagement or you wouldn't still be here."

"I don't," said Edward, bringing the backs of her fingers to his lips. "And if I had one, I would throw it over."

"Edward! I am going to make a cavalier out of you yet!" laughed Cornelia. She clasped Marius's arm tighter and leaned a little against her husband while she spoke. It contented Mr. Renick for his wife to be surrounded by unthreatening admirers on the order of Hippolyte Grandcourt or this newest favorite, Edward Murer. They affirmed her worth and kept her entertained. As for Cornelia, she knew why he stayed. That his happiness sprang from sources other than herself in no way displeased her. A matchmaker she might not be, but she was no less excited by the scent of romance in the air than any other hostess.

The Renicks continued down to the musicians' tent, with Edward now between Miss Palmer and Miss Pendergrast; but while Cornelia thanked the musicians, he excused himself for a moment and seized his chance to speak to Marius.

"Renick, there is something I must tell you," he said, in a low voice. "In the library a while ago, that journalist, Dolson . . ." Marius Renick bent his head closer to listen. Edward had been reluctant to speak; it was more distasteful than he had foreseen. "I saw him pocket something of yours from a case. I spoke to him."

Mr. Renick pulled back and held up a hand. "Jacques told me. Thank you. Hastings and I will take careful inventory of the portables after supper. We always do. If anything is missing, the police will be informed where to look."

Edward nodded. In the face of such efficiency, his sympathy swung back a little toward the outlaw and certainly to Miss Dolson.

"You look sad," said Jeanette, taking him by surprise when he rejoined her.

"Do I? A bad habit." As he looked into her face, his own became gentle. "No, Miss Palmer, I have never been happier."

CHAPTER THIRTY-FOUR

Aftermath

That night, Jeanette went to sleep reliving the party, always with Dr. Murer beside her or coming toward her or unwilling to leave her; sometimes they did not follow Mlle. Bernhardt into the house at all. Over the next few days, fantasy overlay memory more and more, though it never altered the departure points nor belied certain moments. If pressed by conscience, Jeanette might have admitted that making herself the object of romantic attention was half the pleasure of her daydreams. Nevertheless, she also believed in the magical air that had enveloped her and Dr. Murer on their walk through the back orchard, in the secret garden, on the terrace at twilight. And she responded to him—*him*, Dr. Edward Murer, so different from anyone else she knew.

Early the next week, Edward called on Cornelia in the Poutery to offer congratulations on the success of the party.

"Darling, wasn't it splendid?" she said, as she reclined on her chaise longue. "I can rest on my laurels until we leave town in July. Pure heaven. Now, quick. Effie Pendergrast will be along any minute, and before she gets here, I want to know every detail about the thieving Mr. Dolson. Marius says you were an eyewitness."

Edward kept his eyes on his hat as he casually set it down beside his chair. "I hate to snitch, Cornelia."

"Of course you do, so hurry while we're alone, and you'll be spared dear Effie's exclamations."

Reluctantly, Edward described the scene in the library. He recounted only the actions, none of the insults.

"Where was poor Miss Dolson during all this? I can't help wondering about that girl and whether her friends should be warned."

Edward froze, wondering for an instant whether Cornelia could know about the laudanum. "Warned in what way?"

"Warned to help her or warned to stay clear, I suppose. It all depends on whether she's innocent or an accomplice."

"She was resting her forehead on the back of a chair."

"In protest or on purpose not to see?"

"Honestly, I don't know. She seemed . . . unwell."

"I'm making you uncomfortable, darling. Don't worry. I'm a banker's wife. I've had years of practicing discretion."

"You never gossip, do you, Cornelia?"

"I certainly never pass along rumors or anything harmful if I can help it, but I'll tell you a secret. If you drop incidental tidbits of information every now and again, and seem willing to listen, people will tell you the most extraordinary things. I'm a suction pump, not a fire hose. Dearest Effie, good morning! We were just wondering when you might be along. I have a thousand thank-you notes to sort and whatnot."

"I thought you might," said Effie, cheerfully. "And Dr. Murer, I'm so glad you're here. Oh, dear, I hate to ask favors, and wouldn't ordinarily, you know that; only we've come up shorthanded for Thursday . . . I should have thought of you sooner. Well, of course, you haven't been living in Paris."

Prompting brought out that the McAll Mission held a free medical clinic at one of its halls every month. It was staffed by volunteers, many of whom were dedicated and reliable, but among whom there was often a last-minute cancellation.

"I have no license to practice in Paris," said Edward, not sorry for a legitimate excuse to beg off.

"Oh, that doesn't matter. We always have a supervising physician on the spot. What we need is help treating the minor cases of ringworm and catarrh, that sort of thing. Mr. Winkham comes to help dress running sores. If I could assign you to healing salves—"

"It sounds perfectly ghastly," laughed Cornelia, "but then Effie is the saint, not I."

Edward was of much the same opinion, yet mention of Mr. Winkham put the request in a different light. Obliging Miss Pendergrast might be prudent when he hoped to draw closer to Miss Palmer, and perhaps Mr. Winkham would know something worth learning about the Dolsons. The last thing he wanted was to be further implicated in their affairs; and yet some nagging sense of responsibility, or perhaps only curiosity, drew him on. He agreed.

On Thursday at midday, Edward crossed the Canal Saint-Martin into industrial Paris in search of a mission hall in the tannery district. He was unprepared for the level of squalor or the stench. Decomposing animal waste befouled the greasy river Bièvre. In the factory blocks, stringy, half-clad tannery workers appeared to be strong, their skin pickled to a leathery brown toughness by their trade; but elsewhere, too many sullen, stunted men stood listlessly in doorways to dank basements, and too many furtive women and children looked famished for a piece of bread as gray as themselves. If Miss Pendergrast put up with this regularly, she was a tougher bird than he had realized.

The mission hall proved to be the ground floor of a narrow old building. He had been directed to look for a poster of Abraham Lincoln mounted in a window (pictures of Jesus tended to be defaced by anticlerical vandals); a line of dirty children, men with concave chests, and downtrodden women with babies on their hips identified the place just as surely as any street number or poster. At the head of the line, he tipped his top hat, saying, "*Excusez-moi, s'il vous plaît*," and shouldered his way inside without meeting anyone's eye. From his time in military hospitals, he knew better than to let irregular bids for attention start up.

Inside the door, he was greeted by an Englishwoman in a gray dress, white apron, and starched white cap. "You must be Dr. Murer," she said. "Thank you very much indeed for coming. The other medical staff are in back in the scullery." When she saw him survey the room, she added, "This place was built as a tavern; but the Lord be praised, we've turned it to better use."

The main front room was bare of decoration and dingy but scrubbed clean of surface dirt. Most of the wooden chairs used at prayer meetings were folded against the wall, with a few left ready to be occupied once the doors were open. Screens had been set up for privacy during examinations.

In the back, Effie introduced Edward to the other volunteers. The deal table around which they were gathered held medical supplies, towels, basins, and a pile of white aprons. "I'm in charge of all this," she explained, as she handed him an apron, "and you'll be working with Nurse Finch. Dr. Murer speaks French like a Parisian, Miss Finch; it should be such a help."

But not like a Belleville native, thought Edward. He hoped that between visual cues and whatever dialect an experienced volunteer had picked up, the two of them would understand enough to do some good. After doffing his hat and exchanging his coat for the apron, he washed his hands at a dry sink. Under Effie's supervision, water was constantly brought in to be heated and the slops emptied by a pair of neighborhood boys hired for the afternoon.

"Dicey water supply in the neighborhood," remarked the supervising physician, cheerfully. "We must all hope there's no infection at the pump."

From Effie's table, Edward picked up washcloths, alcohol, gauze,

and a variety of salves. Just as the teams were being dispatched to
their stations, Mr. Winkham came in, taking off his coat as he hurried to the back. At sight of Edward, he stopped. "Dr. Murer! Ah,
but, of course, you are a friend of Miss Pendergrast."

There was no time to talk. Edward hoped to catch Winkham
before it was time to leave; but for the rest of the afternoon, he and
Nurse Finch were confronted with abrasions, eczema, boils, infected
wounds, inflamed eyelids, impetigo, and a growth that was claiming
half of an old man's face. He and Winkie assisted the surgeon in
setting a drunken man's broken leg. Everything had to be dealt with
in the face of crying children and always with an awareness that the
line outside was long.

At the end of the afternoon, last cans of hot water were brought in
for a rough sort of scrub-up. Edward admired the Christian zeal of
those who would stay on to share a cold meal of bread and bologna
sausage with the locals who came for an evening prayer service, but
he would not be among them.

"What do you say, Winkham, will you do me the honor of dining with me? There's an Alsatian brasserie near Le Halles that serves
a meal hearty enough to meet my needs after all this."

"Brew on tap?"

"German."

"I'm your man."

An hour later, they were seated at a table in Les Vosges, with
mugs of beer, a basket of rye bread, and dishes of grilled bratwurst
smothered in sauerkraut, dumplings in cream gravy, and stewed
partridges. At first, conversation naturally focused on cases from the
afternoon. Winkie went on to tell Edward stories from previous
clinics, and from there they moved to general matters of public
health—the need for clean drinking water, unadulterated food, better air and less crowding. "I know when I get back home I can't

reform society by myself," said Winkie, "but I do believe a man can make a difference in his own patch."

Edward gradually drew him around to his boyhood. It seemed that the school he and Robbie Dolson had attended was neither the best nor the worst England had to offer. "Much better than a scholarship boy like me could have hoped for, but less than Dolson thought his due. He used to complain that his guardians meant to hold him back while his cousins advanced in the world, and he may have been right. Judging by his income since, though, I'd say there was always less money than he thought."

"Or that his share of an inheritance was mismanaged."

"He'd say embezzled. I wouldn't know. What I can tell you is that he took me home with him once at the holidays, and it was the high point in my boyhood in a lot of ways. Just the two of us together the livelong day." Winkie softened with a wistful nostalgia. "I'm a city boy. I'd never been bird-nesting before, nor staked out a badger's earth to watch for the badger. Well, and the house, of course: I'd never been in a house like that—portraits on the wall, mounted deer's antlers. And a library."

"Were you boys allowed to pull books off the shelves?"

"Free run, and I'd say it was that summer's reading set me on my path. Up to date on his science the uncle was, educated cove, for all he was a farmer. But the best thing, of course, was meeting Emily. Best or worst." Mr. Winkham hung his head. "Wear my heart on my sleeve, I do."

"Miss Dolson is a lovely girl," said Edward. "I saw her the other day."

"You did?" Mr. Winkham looked up avidly. "Where? I haven't seen either of them for weeks. How was she?"

"On laudanum."

Winkie bent his head and crashed his fist on the table. A few people glanced over, but Les Vosges was a noisy restaurant. He choked down his emotion.

"It doesn't have to be harmful in itself."

Winkie stared wordlessly at nothing. "No," he said finally, "it needn't be." A great sadness in his voice contradicted his words.

"It was her cough, she said. Is she consumptive?"

"Not that I know of, no," said Winkie. "Of course, I haven't examined her medically. She needs to eat better, anybody can see that, and her physical ailments aren't helped by the damp and mildew of the holes they've been living in lately. Rob's been down on his luck."

"I wonder about that. They were oddly dressed, but not what you'd call shabby. It was at a party, and according to Miss Palmer, Miss Dolson was in the latest fad from London, while I'd say your friend was in antique costume on purpose. He looked more like he was playing a part than strapped for cash."

"Oh, that's Rob for you, all right. He spent one term in a silk velvet cutaway taken from an old press at his uncle's. Look, Dr. Murer, why did you invite me here?"

"I might as well come clean: The party was at the house of some people named Renick."

"I don't move in those circles."

"Well, you'd better know that I found Mr. Dolson putting a small gold box of theirs into his pocket."

"God almighty." Mr. Winkham stared for a moment. "Are you sure? Believe me, that would be a new low. Dolly likes to play with fire and always has—flouting rules he finds irksome, dodging the landlord, that sort of thing—but not theft."

"Poaching."

"Oh, well, poor man's sport. Poaching has its own rules. Look, I'll admit Rob cadges money and he's worse than most about repaying. But outright stealing? I'd swear his sense of his own superiority wouldn't let him." In a momentary silence, Winkie read Edward's face and knew that Dr. Murer had seen what he had seen. His shoulders drooped. "Rob has fallen in with bad company lately."

"You were anxious about him the last time I saw you, before Christmas."

"Was I?" Winkie looked up, then remembered the meeting at Amy and Sonja's studio. He hunched over his mug and turned it back and forth between his hands.

"Another beer?" asked Edward.

Winkie shook his head. "Coffee. I'm on duty at the hospital tonight."

"You were pushing yourself that hard this afternoon when you had to work tonight?" asked Edward. It was his turn to sit and stare.

"All part of the training to my mind," said Winkie. "Can't sleep during an epidemic." He regarded Edward as if sizing him up. "You know there are organized gangs of thieves in Paris."

"Ever since the Middle Ages." Edward signaled to the waiter for coffee.

"Well, these days, some of them hide out in old quarries near where we were this afternoon. Rob saw them as good material. He sold a three-part article in March, 'The Underbelly of Babylon.' He used a pseudonym to protect his cover and, as a matter of fact, disguised all the details to protect the guilty."

"A prudent way to play with fire," Edward said before he could stop himself. Winkham frowned. "Sorry. Go on."

Winkie saw something sympathetic in Edward's face. He went back to rolling the empty beer mug between his hands. "What troubled me last winter was the way Rob did favors for real criminals. Delivered packages, no questions asked; carried messages in code; redeemed pawned objects. He said as long as he didn't know the details and didn't take any money, he was safe. The trouble is, Rob is smart and thinks he's smarter. He played some sort of double game and wound up having to carry a packet of stolen diamonds up to Brussels to square things. It scared me to know about it, but I thought at least he had learned his lesson."

"Maybe he learned instead how easy it could be to pick up a few francs as a runner. Are you sure he hasn't made other trips since then?"

"It wouldn't be like him. He'd rather steal for himself than be the pawn in some other man's game. He'll hate you for knowing about him, by the way, if what you're telling me is true."

"I can see that."

"If you ask me, the temptation at the Renicks' house was to see if he could get away with it, to risk ruin on the brink of advancement."

"Well, if it eases your mind, I don't think he had any other valuables stashed away on his person. He said he didn't."

"Then he didn't. But there! I've spent half my life believing Robbie Dolson, and he doesn't always tell the truth. All the same, he's the best friend I ever had. I want to believe him," said Winkie, adding with a sigh, "if only for Emily's sake."

"The best thing you could do for Miss Dolson would be to get her out from under her brother's thumb."

"Marry her, you mean? That's just what I couldn't do even if she were still in Paris. I've nothing to offer her and won't have for years; and when I do, she won't have me. She never will. I could become head of Guy's Hospital in London, and she'd still see me as Dolly's shadow if she saw me at all."

"Even if she were still in Paris—do you know she's not?"

"Know it? As one scientific man to another, no, I don't *know* anything about their whereabouts; but I can warrant you all the same that they've left for Berlin or Madrid by now. Venice, perhaps, even Algiers. Rob can't nurture the illusion he's invulnerable any more. I suppose you told the Renicks?"

"The footman already had."

"Well, then, there you are. Rob's a marked man, and he knows it. He's gone somewhere to start building new illusions and taken Emily with him."

CHAPTER THIRTY-FIVE

Impressions

Edward returned to Cornelia on Friday. "I need your help," he said.

"Anything—anything within reason, that is. I'm not nearly so foolhardy as people think."

"You once climbed a three-story crane on the wharf to hang a lantern with us boys."

"At night, too!" exclaimed Cornelia, clapping her hands as she leaned back against her cushions. "How does anyone ever survive the age of twelve? Promise me never, never to tell Marius, Jr., about his mother's exploits."

"They'll have to tie me to an anthill first, word of honor," said Edward. His grin faded. "I saw a friend of the Dolsons yesterday at Miss Pendergrast's mission. He told me that Robert Dolson has been conniving with criminals lately in pursuit of a story. It's made me come round to your opinion that Miss Palmer and her friends need to be warned, at least about what happened here—though the whole thing may be moot. Winkham is convinced that the Dolsons have left Paris for good."

"All the more reason for Miss Dolson's friends to know everything. I don't see the difficulty."

"No one loves the bearer of ill tidings, Nellie, and nobody loves the man who got a friend into trouble."

Loves, he said. So that's the rub, thought Cornelia. Oh, you silly men.

"Edward, darling, it's easy. Let me tell Effie about the incident in the library. I've been on the point of doing so all week, but I'd promised not to blab. She'll be the one to break it to the girls. All you have to do is back me up."

When Effie arrived, she gave them the perfect opening: "Oh, my, you'll never guess what that Mr. Dolson has done."

If you don't want your darling daughter to become conceited over being published or to waste her time on rubbishy cartoons, Jeanette had written her parents on Thursday night, *you will be pleased with Mr. Dolson, but I could kill him. Maybe Emily, too. She didn't come to class this week, and now I know why. Today, on the way over to Julian's from M. Duran's class, I picked up the latest issue of* Noggins, *expecting to see our piece on the organ grinder's monkey—only Robbie has made a monkey out of me.*

Timed to coincide with the buildup to the May opening of the annual state-sponsored art show, the Salon, the latest Peregrine Partout column breezily relayed artistic tittle-tattle, including a report on an open house at Carolus-Duran's studio. According to the article, the painter primped, preened, pranced, and pandered. It was more disgustingly tongue-in-cheek than anything Jeanette had feared when she begged Robbie not to write in February. Worse, from her point of view, were two cartoon figures—M. Duran with an oversized head bowing down from the top of the page like an actor on a stage and a stringy dandy in a jauntily tilted top hat gazing up from the bottom margin.

"How vile," said Amy, when Jeanette showed it to her. "The damnable thing is that if more than one hand can draw Ned Noggins, I suppose more than one can draw his chum Peregrine Partout. Did Robbie *promise* not to write about the open house?"

"In so many words."

"In so many words? Rot! I'm sorry, Jeanette, but if you haven't learned to make Robbie Dolson prick his finger and sign in blood, then you are a right ninny."

"Why bother? He'd only cross the fingers of his other hand behind his back. Oh, Amy, what if Carolus sees this and thinks I had a part in it?"

"Why would he? There's nothing to connect you to it. Hang on, whose initials are these? P.G."

"Let me see that," said Jeanette snatching the magazine back. "Why didn't I notice?"

"Pascal Gobelard. Oh, lord, Robbie."

"Bad?"

"Well, you can see he's proficient in his own low way. He's a Belgian hack who lived in London for a while and knows the Englishman's every vulgar taste. If that's the direction Robbie is taking the column, I'd consider myself well out of it."

"You don't have to pay Carolus's fees, and Peregrine wasn't your invention."

When Sonja was shown the article and cartoons late that afternoon, she had a number of scathing imprecations for Robbie in particular and men in general. Then she added, "I offer you consolation: You come with me to the *vernissage*."

Acceptance to the Salon carried with it a free pass for the entire month and the privilege of taking a guest to Varnishing Day, the eve of the official opening when exhibitors were allowed to make last-minute touch-ups to their work and varnish the surfaces for luster. It was a cross between the final dress rehearsal of a new play and a grand social reception.

"Aren't you going?" Jeanette asked Amy.

"With Louise Steadman. As usual, the jury has accepted her submission."

"A still life with kitchen pans, spoons, and a jug on white linen towels?"

"And a dead fish, rabbit, or fowl; don't forget the carrion," said Amy.

"Maybe she could paint Robbie's head on a platter for me."

"*Non,*" said Sonja, "this pleasure you reserve to yourself."

Jeanette smiled slyly at Amy. "I could put in a wedge of cheese."

"Stilton," said Amy, "something moldy. Include the maggots."

"I'd love to come with you, Sonja, if you really don't need the ticket for someone else."

"I want no one with me. That is why I ask you—you I can ignore."

Jeanette laughed; but before she left, she let out her unhappiness again. "I can't help thinking Emily knew this time. She was so withdrawn at the party."

"There is no telling what that girl has had to know and put up with over the years," said Amy. "We'll give her another week and then rout her out."

On Friday night, Effie came home with her news from the Poutery.

"He tried to steal from the Renicks with Emily right there?" exclaimed Jeanette. "He wouldn't. Not even double-crossing Robbie Dolson could do a thing like that!" Or couldn't he? Something shifty, watchful, and vulpine sometimes lurked in the back of his eyes. It had been there when he turned his back on her and Dr. Murer on the lower lawn. She had been puzzled as well as momentarily stung by that snub, but the rest of the afternoon had driven it from her mind. But here was another possibility. Had he come to the party already planning to betray his hosts?

Distress about Emily's presence at the theft did not deter Jeanette and Amy from trying to find her. If anything, it spurred them on. "Poor lamb," said Amy, "it sounds as if she was miserable."

Edward had said nothing to either Cornelia or Effie about the laudanum; it was a topic he avoided, but he did tell them that Mr. Winkham thought the Dolsons would have bolted.

"That's only a guess," said Amy, when she heard. "They may be lying low nearby. If we can only find her, maybe this time Emily can be persuaded to set up on her own."

The obvious first move was to get in touch with Winkie.

"Since I heard about . . . about what happened at the party," he said, turning his hat in his hands, "I've tried to find Rob. Just as I feared, there's no trace of him. If I learn anything, I'll let you know. You do the same for me."

Under his resignation, Jeanette saw a deeper gloom. "We're worried about Emily, too," she said, quietly.

He looked up and said cautiously, "About anything in particular?"

"No, nothing specific. I don't know, Winkie; I just think she's been carrying some great burden for a while now."

"Oh, of that, I'm sure."

"In my view," said Amy, "if she'd only break away from Robbie, half her troubles would be solved."

"No, Miss Richardson, they wouldn't," said Winkie, "and, anyway, she won't. What other reality has she ever had but Rob? You can't take away her world and expect her to thrive."

Not contented with what Winkie had to say, Jeanette and Amy asked everyone else they could think of who might know something. They left notes with stationers and porters. Effie placed an advertisement in the personals column of Galignani's English-language *Messenger*. On two successive Saturday nights, dressed in male attire, Sonja trawled the cafés where journalists, students, and satirists gathered; from time to time, she checked at the morgue. And then she declared, "Enough is enough," and dropped all thought of the Dolsons.

By the end of April, Jeanette realized with a twinge of guilt that the Dolsons had receded from her mind, too. Only on the last Monday did the strangeness of setting up at Julian's without Emily remind her of their disappearance. Meanwhile, there and in every atelier and studio in Paris, excitement had built to a near frenzy as May first approached and with it, the opening of the Salon.

On the morning of Varnishing Day, Jeanette, Sonja, Amy, and Miss Steadman took a tram to the Place de la Concorde and walked up the Champs-Élysées the rest of the way to the Palais de l'Industrie, where the exhibition was mounted. Green lawns put a pleasant distance between them and the stalled line of traffic on the macadamized middle of the avenue, but by the time they reached the exhibitors' entrance, they were part of a jostling throng. Sonja, wretched in her anxiety, grew stiffer, brusquer, and, if possible, taller. Businesslike Miss Steadman was gearing up for a long day; Amy, as usual, took charge. Once they had handed over their tickets and passed through the magic portal, she said, "I think we'd better find the *B*s first."

A dispassionately applied logic of the alphabet rather than any affinity of style, subject, or size grouped the painters into rooms by surname. The tightly packed walls of each room were a jumble; frame touched frame up to the sky of the high ceiling; but at least it was easy to know where to start looking for a particular painter. "Breton, Boulanger, Bouguereau, Borealska—not bad company, Sonja. People are sure to pause in the room."

"They will look only at Bastien-Lepage," said Sonja, in a constricted voice.

When they reached the right room, Amy followed Sonja's gaze. "Oh, brava, Sonja!" she said, heartily. "Second line, and quite a good spot!"

She took her friend's arm protectively, for Sonja stood rooted to the floor, in tears. With a mother's ability to pick out her offspring in a crowd, Sonja had sorted through a hundred canvases in an instant to land on the faces brought forth by her own brush. *"J'ne pensais jamais, j'ne savais . . ."* I never thought; I didn't know . . .

Jeanette felt a lump in her own throat. She watched as Sonja slowly crossed the room to stand in rapture under the Witkiewicz children's faces. Sonja made no pretense of wanting to join the others when, after suitable plaudits, they made a quick tour of the rest of the room. Then, when they thought Sonja had been allowed enough time in her trance, they collected her and set out to find Miss Steadman's picture.

Even a rapid passage through the building was stupefying. Thirty-six rooms, thousands of paintings and sculptures; drawings, etchings, and watercolors hung in the corridors; too much to take in, too much noise, too many people. But after the *B*s, the *D*s came quickly. Jeanette's senses were not yet deadened when, with a leap of pleasure, she recognized M. Duran's full-length *Portrait de Comtesse V——* hung centrally on the line.

"That means it's up for a medal," said Amy.

The foursome continued to route themselves as efficiently as they could toward the *S*s. Artists making last-minute changes had to be dodged. Fumes of solvents and varnish hung in the air. Jealousy, scorn, nerves. Bated breath, exhaled relief, excitement.

"My God, that's gorgeous and the man to the life!" exclaimed Amy, when they finally reached their destination.

Jeanette, too, stopped dead in her tracks to meet the piercing gaze of Carolus-Duran. He sat leaning slightly to his right, dominating the room in a painter's brown jacket and loose black cravat, with white ruffles at his collar and wrists; a triangle of dark hair and pointed beard boldly framed the face. It was John Sargent's life-sized portrait—informal and commanding, respectful where the *Noggins* cartoon was nasty. Jeanette started toward it. "Steadman first," whispered Amy.

Miss Steadman's entry hung in a corner where, despite a small size of only eighteen by twenty-four inches, its pearly tone and unity stood out against larger humdrum landscapes and a fake Dutch genre scene nearby, even against a giant gladiatorial history painting around the corner. Best of all, it was hung on the line. "My first time ever!" exclaimed Miss Steadman, breaking into a broad smile, while Amy and Jeanette cheered and Sonja slapped her on the back. "Well, what's next?"

"We'll devise a sensible plan once we've let Jeanette worship at the altar of Carolus-Duran."

"Tramp all the way back to *D*?" asked Miss Steadman.

"No, no! Come look at what she means," said Jeanette.

A mon cher maître, Carolus-Duran, Mr. Sargent had written across the top of the portrait, where he signed it.

"*Cher maître*, my grand-uncle's foot," said Amy. "He's outmastered the master."

They began to work their way back through the frantic, last-minute efforts, stopping along the way to talk to friends. Miss Steadman stayed behind with one group while Sonja headed off to the sculpture section with another, leaving Jeanette and Amy to ramble at will.

Near the door to one room, atop a high ladder, a man was literally varnishing his large landscape. At the foot of the ladder, a tarpaulin lay heaped in stiff, angular folds like the drapery in a sixteenth-century Madonna's skirt. With her eyes on the varnisher, Jeanette failed to see that behind the folds, someone sat huddled against the wall. Amy saw him.

"Charlie Post, whatever are you doing down there?" she demanded, her hands on her hips.

"Don't tell me, don't tell me, don't tell me," came Mr. Post's muffled voice, as he talked into his knees.

"Don't tell you what—to get up?"

"Where it hangs, woman, where it hangs!"

"He means where his picture hangs, don't you, Mr. Post," said Jeanette.

"You," said Post, opening one eye to peer up at her, balefully, "the discerning girl." He shut his eyes tight again and hugged his knees closer. "Go away."

"Oh, no, Post, not before you explain yourself," said Amy. "Are you telling me you have a picture in the next room—*P*, well, that makes sense—and you haven't been in yet to see it?"

"I don't dare!" shouted Charlie.

"Oh, yes, you do, and you'd better get it over with quick while you have friends with you to sing hosannahs or damn the judges as need be," said Amy. She began to haul him up by one arm. "Jeanette, grab the other arm."

"Mr. Post, please get up," said Jeanette, embarrassed, as she tugged halfheartedly. "You are making a spectacle of us."

"*Contra.* 'S you making spectacle of me."

Jeanette let go of a limp arm.

"No, no, don't leave me!" Charlie Post pulled free of Amy, too, and used his hands to push up off the floor. "Don't."

"Post, you are drunk."

"Of course, I'm drunk, you harridan. I'm terrified."

"Well, that's no good. Come on," ordered Amy.

"Spartan mother," muttered Mr. Post. "Rather see me dead on my shield than otherwise. All right, lead me." He held his arms out ahead of him and closed his eyes.

His painting was easy to find. It was huge, a long double square, five feet by ten, and monochromatic in effect, all slate blues and grays. The faint light of a pale sickle moon shone on the crests of endless, shallow waves. They gleamed. High overhead they gleamed; for as Charlie Post had feared, his painting had been hung up in the uppermost tier, skied just under the ceiling. Jeanette and Amy exchanged a worried look.

"Do you see it?"

"Of course, we see it, Post. Open your eyes."

He gave a cry of anguish. "Ruined, ruined, skied! The bastards."

"I don't know, Mr. Post," said Jeanette, with her eyes still on it. "I think the judges made a terrible mistake hanging it where it's hard to study closely; but it's very beautiful, and it's the only skied picture we've seen all day that dominates the room it's in."

Charlie Post dropped to the floor and began kissing the tips of her boots. *"Beata, beata,* your slave for life, slave for life."

"Post, stop that!" commanded Amy, in her most outraged voice.

Mr. Post took the hem of Jeanette's skirt to wipe his eyes. Hastily, she pulled it free.

*"Char-*lie," bawled Amy.

He wobbled up to one knee and looked up at her sideways, then staggered to his feet. He looked up once more at his painting, shuddered, covered his eyes with a hand, and staggered back through the crowd with the other hand outstretched. "Must get past, past, past, Post. Pass. Pass out. Piss."

Jeanette stood staring at the ground with her hands over her mouth. She held herself in, very still, to keep from shaking.

"That made me feel so ashamed, for him and for me both," she whispered. "You know something, Amy? This whole system is horrible if it can do that to a man!"

"Well, it is, in a way, and Charlie Post would hardly be the first man it has broken. On the other hand, *Post*—well, I ask you! And, remember, it is the system we have. Are you all right?"

Jeanette exhaled a long breath. "Yes, I'm all right. Sorry to have acted stupid. So we really have to compete in this?"

"We certainly do. It's the only way to be taken seriously. Don't go all wet and lady amateurish on me, Jeanette."

"As if I would!" Nevertheless, thought Jeanette, as she looked with a sudden distaste at the jumbled walls, there must be a better way.

* * *

Early the next week, on a stroll up the newer-than-new, opulent Avenue de l'Opéra after a morning in his new laboratory, Edward paused before a poster outside an apartment building: *4me Exposition de Peinture*, it proclaimed, *Du 10 Avril au 11 Mai 1879*. None of the artists listed meant anything to him, but on a whim, he went in. A lift took him to the first floor, where a franc at an apartment door gave entry into a suite of rooms that had been made over into a gallery—made over at considerable expense, with freshly painted walls and handsome fittings.

Despite the elegance, the few other visitors in the gallery ridiculed the displays. Drawings, pastels, and etchings mixed in with the oil paintings? As for the pictures, what topics—! Edward could see their point. A purplish view of snow on the rooftops out a back window in Paris was hardly the classical ideal of landscape—nor was a man in short sleeves standing on a triangle of purple shore at one end of a canvas, using a paddle to prod a canoe on green and purple water at the other. And if art was meant to elevate the mind, then it seemed an odd choice to depict a sharp-dealing broker whispering into the ear of another in front of the Bourse, or men in evening attire ogling ballet girls, or the compromising pleasures of the cafés.

And then Edward entered the largest room, the last. His mouth fell open as he slowly walked to the middle of the chamber. It was like walking bodily into summer. Even a painting of a snowy road was warmed by touches of orange-gold. His smile widened, and inwardly he laughed: silent, joyous laughter.

"Have you ever heard of a painter named Claude Monet?" he asked Cornelia the next day, when he called on her deliberately to find out.

"My dear, you've been to the Impressionists' show!" she replied. "Tell me all about it. M. Monet is a friend of Carolus's. I haven't bought anything of his yet. Not quite to my taste, and certainly not to Marius's. But look at you, Edward! You are the most undemonstrative man I know, and there's not a trace of caution in your face right now—you look downright enthusiastic!"

"I think anything from his brush would make me happy, Cornelia. I'm glad I went."

"Then go again and buy something."

Edward gave her a half smile. He would have liked to, but for a man who a year ago was cutting prints out of magazines, it was too big a leap. If he had a place of his own, maybe. But he did want to see the show again.

And he wanted to see it with Miss Palmer.

Edward invited Jeanette and Effie for the following Saturday afternoon. When they arrived, Jeanette saw a familiar name among the painters listed on the poster. "Oh! Mary Cassatt!" she said. She recognized none of the others (unless maybe M. Degas was the one whose bilious witticisms circulated). "Miss Cassatt is an American. The girls say she's very nice, very much the fine lady but not at all patronizing—she's had some of them over for chocolate. Funny that she'd show with independents this year; she's been in the Salon. What did you think of her work?"

"My opinion doesn't count. I want your honest reaction."

"No, you don't. You're setting a trap." Jeanette dimpled up at him as they went into the foyer.

Edward merely shrugged slightly with humor in his eyes.

Inside the exhibition, Jeanette was as taken aback as most visitors at the way works of different sorts were presented with equal regard. A group of etchings was one thing; together they had a sort of weight. But a single pastel sketch, quickly dashed in parallel jabs and contrasting colors—was it an insult to the public or one's fellow contributors to submit so casual a piece? Her first real shock came in the second room: a painting by M. Degas of a foreshortened aerialist seen at an angle from below, hanging by her teeth from a rope, her knees drawn up.

"I can't take my eyes off it; it makes me dizzy," said Jeanette.

"So did Mlle. La La," said Edward.

"Why, that's right!" said Effie. "At the circus. I remember! Where we sat up so high. Well, now, I wish Adeline and Harold could see this. We've got relatives coming in a couple of weeks," she explained to Edward. "Harold knows pictures, and Adeline loves a show."

Jeanette stopped in front of a little picture with a red, red background in which a woman in a delectable blue dress and white hat was eyed by three dissolute men in top hats. "The new Peregrine Partout would fit right in!" she said, vengefully. "Oh, but you know, the old Peregrine Partout, *my* Peregrine Partout could have gone to the café in that picture, too. In fact, this whole exhibition would have been perfect for him."

"Do you miss the column?" asked Edward.

"In an odd way, yes. It gave me a new angle for looking at Paris, trying to see what Peregrine might pick out. I guess I go on doing that, only I don't really enjoy thinking of him now, not in Robbie Dolson's voice anyway."

"I don't suppose any of you have heard from him or Miss Dolson."

"No, and I can't help wishing Emily would turn up in spite of everything. You must have been the last one to see her, Dr. Murer— *did* she know what Robbie was doing?"

"I don't think so, Miss Palmer. She might have been looking the other way on purpose, but—" This was Edward's chance to tell one of Miss Dolson's friends about her laudanum use. Coward, he told himself when he couldn't bring himself to do so. "She seemed to me to be . . . half asleep," he managed at last.

"Might have been squiffy," said Cousin Effie.

"Oh, Cousin Effie, Emily doesn't drink!"

"You never know who's a secret tippler, and with the troubles that girl had . . ."

As Effie spoke, they passed into a small room containing only works by Mary Cassatt, and all thought of Emily was driven from Jeanette's mind.

"Now I understand why she's willing to show with independents!" said Jeanette. "A whole room to herself!" But what did it mean for Miss Cassatt to exhibit a mere pencil sketch? Why did she use un-blended blue in the flesh across a woman's bare shoulders? And why frame canvases in vermilion or green as if the paintings extended out into the room?

A rapid stream of unspoken thoughts played across Jeanette's face as Edward watched.

"That grumpy little girl sprawled on the aqua-blue chair—well, she's vivid, but all that other aqua furniture climbing to the ceiling," she finally said aloud, "it's hideous!"

"The poor tyke was tired of sitting still," said Effie.

Jeanette was about to snap that Miss Cassatt had *posed* the child in that sprawling slump, but she was saved from a display of ill humor by Edward's pronouncing solemnly, "Aniline dye."

She looked at him inquiringly.

"Aqua upholstery," he said, "aniline dye."

"Synthetic paint," she agreed, her eyes dancing. She knew she was being teased, and relaxed. "Still, I couldn't bear to have that many blotches of that particular blue on my furniture or my walls, could you? And look at the way the sofas and chairs climb up the room as if the floor were tilted up behind. I love to draw rooms and I know they don't look like that."

"Do you think the picture was meant to pass for an illusion?"

Jeanette paused. "I guess I have to admit I don't see what Miss

Cassatt is up to, but she's a very strong painter, and she does know what she's doing."

"You care because it is your métier." As they approached the last room, Jeanette could sense Edward's apprehension. So this was the test, and there was indeed a trap. She could guess that he liked the pictures they were about to see; otherwise, he wouldn't care whether she hooted or clapped. She only hoped she did like them, for the one thing she could not lie about was—he had called it her métier. She unconsciously took his arm and squeezed it, looking up into his face. He returned the gaze with a half smile. There was no need to speak. He ushered her and Miss Pendergrast ahead of him through the door.

It was a big gallery, hung with some fifty or sixty paintings. According to the catalogue, about half were by M. Monet and half by one Camille Pissarro. They were light, bright; they seemed to float. Edward's heart rose again. Jeanette was astonished at the dominance of palettes keyed so high, at colors so pure.

"Why it was just like that, all fluttery and exciting," exclaimed Effie, heading straight for a blond canvas full of red, white, and blue. It was listed in the catalogue as *La rue Montorgueil, fête du 30 juin 1878*. "Were you still in Paris that day, Dr. Murer?"

"No."

"Well, you missed a treat. Everyone out in the streets, bands playing, confetti and flags. We all linked arms and sang the *Marseillaise* like revolutionaries. It was something."

"*Vive Lafayette.*"

Effie whinnied through her nose at his joke. Jeanette, who took less interest in politics than she supposed she should, ignored them both, keeping her focus on what had brought them here. This was the room and these were the paintings. The more she looked, the less sure she was that she knew what to make of them. She was so absorbed that she did not see someone they knew coming toward them until Effie spoke: "*Ah, bun jewer, M. Grandcoor.*"

"*Bonjour, mademoiselle, mademoiselle, monsieur.* I am glad to see you here. One must keep up with the times. Do you like what you see?"

"When I come into this room, I feel like the sun has come out," said Edward, "but I am not sure Miss Palmer approves."

"I don't quite know what to make of them. I don't see the drawing I expect, nor the modeling," said Jeanette, slowly, in a puzzled voice. "It's all so flat without tonal gradations for volume. And I wonder, isn't there just too much detail left out? When I think about how the rest of us toil away at getting details right . . ." Her voice trailed off.

"You remind me of a story Baron Haussmann once told me," Grandcourt said. "You know, *n'est-ce pas*, that the ruthless destroyer and rebuilder of Paris was a serious lover of music, eh? *Mais oui.* A graduate of the Conservatoire Nationale no less, where one of his fellow students was the great Hector Berlioz—not yet recognized as great. This was in the days when Luigi Cherubini taught composition at the conservatoire. *Eh bien.* One day, Berlioz submits to the maestro a composition. Cherubini reads the score and says, 'What is this? You have put here a two-measure rest. *Pourquoi?*' 'Why?' repeats Berlioz. 'Because by this silence I produce the effect I desire.' 'The effect you desire: a little silence. Why stop there?' cries the old man. 'Go ahead! Suppress the entirety and you produce the big effect!'"

Jeanette laughed.

"You laugh, and the baron laughed, too. He told me that story in complete agreement with Cherubini—Baron Haussmann who thought that by straightening roads and putting in bold, wide boulevards, by digging his sewers and creating parks he could build a classical city of regularity and purity. And so he did, to a degree. But by means of the big effects, the big silences, the ripping out of so much that had stood for centuries. There are those who mourn the crooked streets of old Paris, the Paris of mud in the gutter. Not I, by the way."

Nor I, thought Edward, remembering the unreconstructed tannery district.

"Nor Rosa Bonheur," said Jeanette.

"Eh?"

"From what I hear," said Jeanette, "she loves the new boulevards because she can walk in town safely and not get dirt on her shoes."

"Our great painter of cattle, she leaves her sabots on the farm, does she? You delight me. Ah, but you see, besides the baron's big effects, there is the question of all his little suppressions, too, all the little silences, the holes he left. I don't know." Grandcourt shook his head. "There is no answer, no set of rules that can replace genius, no substitute for knowing from the heart when to put something in and when to leave it out. Your academics, they know how to judge the polished surface of perfectly blended strokes; but these new men, these *Impressionistes*, perhaps they have their own sense of which notes and which silences will produce the big effect.

"*Mademoiselle*, I implore you to learn the rules; learn them and learn what it is to break them; and then look with your own eyes. Even we lesser artists, those of us who merely perform what other men compose, we, too, must make decisions. We must play from the heart."

M. Grandcourt gave Edward a shrewd look and, with a tip of his hat, moved on. A man's heart may be his own, he seemed to say, but it can be in someone else's keeping.

CHAPTER THIRTY-SIX

The Vanns

Adeline and Harold Vann arrived in Paris toward the end of May and set themselves up in a large suite in the colossal, American-style Hôtel du Louvre for a monthlong stay. Harold would attend to some legal matters for a client, but the timing of the trip was dictated by the dates of the Salon. "Harold claims he won't buy anything this year, but of course he will, so he wants to know who is making a splash," said Adeline, when Jeanette and Effie called on her on the Vanns' first afternoon. "You must show us who is up and coming before the dealers get to him."

"I'll show him Louise Steadman; she's established," said Jeanette, "and someone really new, Sonja Borealska."

"No, darling, no lady painters—except family, of course."

Jeanette was speechless.

"I'm afraid you missed the newest and most daring," said Cousin Effie. "Dr. Murer took us to *their* show. Oh, but look—here come two perfect little pictures!"

The Vanns had brought their two children to Europe for the first time, along with a nurse, who was now leading in little Laura and Joel. Laura ran straight to Cousin Effie and greeted her with a hug around the knees.

"I'm five now and can say nursery rhymes," she said. Swinging Effie's hand vigorously, she chanted at the top of her shrill voice, *"Queen, Queen Adeline / Washed her hair in turpentine,"* after which she dissolved into giggles. Effie encouraged her with a complicit grin, but Nurse had a dangerous That's-enough-Laura look on her face.

"*Harold Vann's a handsome man,*" began Adeline, in a drawl.

> *His little girl is Laura.*
> *She was rude yesterday;*
> *If she's rude today,*
> *Laur-a will be SPANKED to-mor-ra.*

The edge in her mother's voice as she bit off each of the last syllables partially subdued Laura. Looking up at Effie to make sure of her old ally, Laura settled into prim bossiness. "Show Hanky Bunny to Joel," she ordered. "I think he's old enough; he's two and a half."

"What do we say, Laura?" interjected Nurse.

"Please," said Laura, perfunctorily, her eyes fixed on Effie's pocket.

"Well, now," said Effie. She pulled out her handkerchief and seated herself on an ottoman to be closer to the children's eye level. The handkerchief was rapidly folded and tied into a passable rabbit. Joel stood at her knee, his brows fiercely contracted and his lower lip pulled up in a pout of concentration. At a flick of Effie's wrist, the handkerchief was a handkerchief again. She tied Hanky Bunny a second time; she performed another trick. Joel shook his hands up and down. After a while, he chortled, "Hanky," with such enthusiasm that Adeline began to laugh, too.

"If sweetness and light were contagious," she said to Jeanette, "we'd all float off on clouds of spun sugar. But I didn't come to Paris to worship Baby. Tell me something worldly. You are looking much improved, I must say."

Jeanette was almost thrown by this second backhanded slap but pulled herself up to look down her nose. "I saw Sophie Croizette at a party a few weeks ago," she said, archly, "and if she's anything to go by, solid colors in a combination of matte and satiny fabrics will be the fashion this summer. But there's no point in trying to emulate Sarah Bernhardt, who was in silvery white—it takes flame-colored hair to achieve the effect she makes."

Adeline pulled away to look at her. "My, my. First trick to you. Tell me more."

Jeanette plunged into an account of the garden party. She jumped from Mrs. Renick's splendor to the other ladies' dresses; she named famous guests; she described the portrait and Carolus-Duran's spectacular entrance. "We had a gracious note waiting for us from Mrs. Renick," said Adeline. "She wants to give us a dinner party."

"Say yes."

Adeline laughed. "Which is it, the food or the company?"

"Both."

"I'm to call on her as soon as possible. We'll settle on a date, after which I need a couple of weeks to acquire a new evening dress. And that reminds me—come back in the bedroom, I have some dresses to discard."

"Adeline!" said Jeanette, following her into the next room. "If you wanted to discard them, why haul them all the way across the Atlantic Ocean?"

"To wear in restaurants here and show Harold how unfashionable they are. Then when I have space for new clothes in my trunks, he can't complain so much about the money. There's a satin and tulle that, judging from what you have on right now, should be made over for you. I still like it, but it was never the right shade of blue on me."

They spent the next half hour spreading clothes on the bed and holding things up to Jeanette. The blue dress was tempting; its scooped neckline from rosettes on the shoulders would give Jeanette her first décolletage. Effie was called in to confer about altering the back. She clucked and cooed and fingered the seams.

"It would be very pretty on you, Jeanette, but—" She made rapid little sucking clicks with her tongue as she calculated mentally. "No! It's beyond my skill. What about Mrs. Renick's seamstress?"

"Perfect," said Adeline. "You must give me her name; maybe I can use her, too. Here, this is yours, and you must both come with me to Worth's."

"Cousin Effie and I can't buy dresses at Worth's!"

"No, but he has the most tantalizing system of putting together bodices, collars, skirts, and sleeves in different combinations for the staff to wear. All you have to do is study the bits while Mr. Worth bullies me into buying whatever he wants me to wear this year, then you sketch what you like when you get home. It's no good letting all that training of yours go to waste, you know."

I was indignant at the way she put the invitation, Jeanette grumbled in a letter home, *but I have to admit I was curious. Go on, said Amy: I hear it is quite the sybaritic shrine, and I'll have you know that Frederick Worth is an Englishman. So I went. A man in a frock coat opened the door on the Rue de la Paix and conducted us up a sweeping staircase. It's the fanciest place you ever saw, with deeply upholstered chairs and squashy ottomans everywhere. There's perfume in the air and potted orchids and clerks who look down their noses at you. I doubt that Cousin Effie and I would have been let into the place by ourselves, but with Adeline, we were shown right into a private consultation room. It was more like a boudoir than a fitting room except for a big table for laying out fabric.*

Although the hauteur of the staff annoyed Jeanette, she was guiltily relieved that Effie was too cowed to say or do anything humiliating. Only when decisions about fabrics were finally being made—fabrics woven to Frederick Worth's specifications and available nowhere else—did Effie forget herself so far as to finger longingly some of the lengths brought out by an assistant. When Mr. Worth curtly rejected one bolt of watery blue silk, she tried excitedly to catch Adeline's and Jeanette's attention. It was almost the very shade of Adeline's hand-me-down.

"If you've picked that out for the young lady, *mademoiselle,* you are right," said Mr. Worth, catching sight of her in a full-length mirror. His reflected eye flicked from the fabric toward Jeanette and back to Effie. "You yourself should stick to charcoal gray and black. Very nice foulard you have on, but may I——?"

He bowed and with delicate fingers tucked up the hem of Effie's basque an inch and pinched it where a dart would give it more shape. For an instant, Effie's image in the mirror had style. After he had turned back to Adeline, she pinched the hem up herself and pulled in the bodice while she studied her own reflection.

Jeanette wanted to feel that the dictatorial designer was over-rated, but she caught Worth fever enough to do as Adeline suggested and think about altering the silk dress in the now officially approved blue along lines they had seen on display. Back at the hotel, vanity impelled her to show off, moreover, by sketching neat series of dress parts, ornamentations, and the new horizontal pleats they had seen. She had an idea. "Let's make paper dolls," she said to Laura. They did—mother and daughter paper dolls, Adeline and Laura—with bits of Worth costumes to assemble. When he saw the faces, Harold asked for formal portraits of his two children in whatever medium Jeanette preferred. Flattered to be asked and flushed with the fun of playing with her little cousin, Jeanette agreed.

"Shall I go with Nurse to the Tuileries Garden for some informal studies after the children's naps tomorrow?" she suggested. "You should come, too, Adeline, and sit on a bench. I'll sketch you for a souvenir. The preliminaries can go to Aunt Maude." It would be worth missing an afternoon class for the chance to work outdoors in natural light.

Adeline's face lit up. "A picture of me in Paris! You must put in an identifiable landmark."

"The Champs-Élysées, with the Arc de Triomphe in the dis-tance?" asked Jeanette, with only a trace of sarcasm.

"Perfect. Oh, Harold, no one else we know in New York has any such thing! They'll die of envy."

* * *

The midweek party that Cornelia gave for Adeline and Harold just before the close of the Salon was a step up from her dinner for the Murers and Monroes. If the Vanns had been entertained purely as Effie's relations, the invitation would have been for tea; but ever since Marius's grandfather had engaged Harold's great-grandfather on some matter, the Renick bank and the law firm of Vann and Vann had done occasional business in New York. Cornelia's guest list, therefore, included one French and one American couple from among their legal acquaintances; a porcelain manufacturer from Limoges and his wife; and the Norwegian count with his opera-singing countess. She also invited M. Naudet, the art dealer, to hear any rumors he might bring about who was going to win medals at the Salon, and a new plum, an illegitimate half-brother of the present duc de Mabillon, who went by the name of Montrachet. M. Montrachet divided his time between the London stock exchange and Paris, where his connections within the upper regions of the demimonde were extensive. He guarded his privacy as strictly as the old duchess did hers, but he had shown an interest in the house when he met Marius one day at a club, and he proved willing to gossip with Cornelia about the rest of the family in return for invitations. Better still, with his bar sinister, she could put him in the middle of the seating chart, where his equal fluency in French and English made him perfect between Mme. Naudet and Effie, across the table from Edward Murer. For, of course, if Jeanette Palmer was coming, she must invite Edward.

On the night of the party, to the impartial eye, Jeanette in sky blue was incidental to Adeline in iridescent jade green and Cornelia in gold again, a tissue lighter than the satin she had worn for Carolus's portrait but every bit as extravagant. Yet Jeanette felt anything but incidental, and Edward's eye was not impartial. From the moment he entered the room, Miss Palmer was to him the most vivid creature there, and her throat and shoulders, seen bare for the first time, more alluring than he could ever have imagined. For an instant, it appalled him that other men should see them, too; but, of course, she was merely conforming to fashion.

Adeline instantly perceived the direction of his gaze and glanced over her shoulder in time to catch Jeanette's small, bashful smile. So this reserved man with the clipped, graying beard was the man from Cincinnati, the man who figured from time to time in both cousins' letters to her mother. Cousin Effie's eyes went to him, too. Adeline wondered whether she had set her cap for him. If so, too bad for poor old Effie! But, no, whatever water had flowed under that bridge was far out to sea. Cornelia introduced him to the Vanns as one of her oldest friends.

When the last guest had had been introduced, M. Naudet, without seeming predatory, made a point of conversing with Harold. Beautiful Adeline attracted admirers, as did the even more beautiful Norwegian countess. As the guests assorted themselves, Edward and Jeanette found they could talk for some time simply by standing still.

Neither wanted to talk to anyone else; neither paid much attention to what was actually said, except once. Jeanette told Edward that Carolus-Duran's pupils were planning to attend closing day at the Salon en masse so that they could cheer together if he won a big medal. "He's a man who craves adulation," agreed Edward.

Jeanette frowned. "Is that such a bad thing?"

"It can be sad if it means a man doubts his own worth, and worse if it leads him to compromise principles to win easy praise." Worse and worse: Edward could have kicked himself. "But then again," he intoned, solemnly, "Velázquez, Velázquez, Velázquez."

Jeanette laughed.

At dinner, Cornelia had provided for their happiness by seating them together. When the compulsory change in partners rippled around the table, Edward heard all about Limoges from the porcelain manufacturer's wife, while Jeanette, with considerably more interest, listened to tales from M. Naudet about the art trade from a dealer's point of view. She knew all the while that Edward was aware of her beside him and only keeping up a front with his other partner.

Back in the salon after dinner, Adeline made herself agreeable to Edward. Watching his detached ease with her, Jeanette suddenly realized that men responded to Adeline in much the same way that women did. Adeline was pleasant and attentive, always sure of her own welcome, often good for a pointed remark; yet underneath her polished surfaces, something dissatisfied made it unwise to expect too much from her. Not a woman to take lovers, thought Jeanette, and was shocked by her own premises.

"Are you coming to the Salon on Saturday to hear the medals announced?" asked Adeline.

"I'll rely on Miss Palmer to assess the judges' choices," said Edward.

"Oh, that's no good. We're going with her. You come, too," said Adeline. She ignored Jeanette's efforts to interrupt. "She took Harold and me through the exhibition, and I promise you, she's a marvelous guide."

"Yes, I know . . ." He caught Jeanette's eye.

"I told you, Adeline," said Jeanette, "Carolus's students will be meeting up when we get there. Of course, I do want you to come, too, Dr. Murer, if you—"

"Well, that's settled then," said Adeline. "We'll all start out together, and if Jeanette runs into her artistic friends, so much the better for the rest of us—they'll be part of the show."

Jeanette bit her lip. She looked at Edward and saw a slight lift of his eyebrow. So he was asking her for guidance! Jeanette softened into resignation; her eyes laughed. She loved the covert intimacy of their silent conversation.

"It will be my honor to join you, Mrs. Vann," said Edward.

Later, as the party broke up and Edward was taking his leave of Cornelia, Adeline whispered to Jeanette, "You'd better marry that man. It's clear he's in love with you, and back in the States, the pickings may not be so good for a girl who . . . well, anyway, marry him."

A girl who what?—got expelled from Vassar, was rumored to have had a baby in Europe, studied art? Jeanette swallowed her indignation. "Aren't you being a little premature?"

"It's never too early to know what you mean to do, goosey. A man won't catch you if you don't chase him."

"What if I've decided on blessed singleness?"

"Then look at Cousin Effie and decide again."

Marry him. Over the next few days, Jeanette's mind kept running back to those two words. *Marry him.* It was too soon to think about marriage, much, much too soon. At the end of her longest daydreams sometimes, yes, he asked her, sometimes yes, she accepted; but she always stopped short of the wedding, and well short of the wedding night. Adeline's cynicism threatened to spoil everything. Jeanette could scornfully reject the suggestion that she marry to redeem her social position. Far better to make her own way in the world, like Amy and Sonja and Miss Steadman—*with* Amy and Sonja and Miss Steadman. But what if she really was in love with Edward? The feeling of rightness that engulfed her whenever they were together was undeniable. Nevertheless, she was unwilling to put down her paintbrush, to renounce lessons, expeditions, and time spent with fellow artists. Charlie Post had cursed Mr. Moyer for marrying Miss Whitmore. Little Joel and Laura notwithstanding, Jeanette felt no desire for babies. And yet, and yet, and yet. If she and Edward were as much in love as she was being forced to consider they—might be? were? Well, then what?

*   *   *

A few days later at the Vanns' hotel, it was plain to Edward that something was off-key. Jeanette was absent in manner. He assumed she wished herself already with her friends and tried not to take it personally nor push himself on her. In any case, Harold latched onto him until the party reached the Palais de l'Industrie, where noise put an end to all conversation. It was at this point that Jeanette came out of her shell and took the lead, making a determined path through the press of bodies toward the place where Carolus's pupils had agreed to meet. They were intercepted by Miss Reade, who shouted out excuses to the Vanns, thrust Miss Isobel toward Effie, and carried Jeanette off into the maelstrom.

Edward hung on gamely until at last the medals were awarded— best to avoid offending Miss Palmer's family if possible, and Cornelia would welcome every scrap or detail he could carry back. He was rewarded with a fine tale to tell her. The announcement that John Singer Sargent had received an honorary mention for his portrait of Carolus-Duran brought cheers and foot stamping from his fellow pupils. And when it was announced that Carolus had been awarded the Medal of Honor for his portrait of Countess Vandal, loyal pandemonium broke out.

Miss Reade again kept her head better than most and steered Jeanette back to where they could beg her party to see Miss Isobel safely home while the two of them rejoined an impromptu parade that was snaking its way through the building. Jeanette flew from embracing Effie to Adeline to Edward. Springing up on her toes, she threw her arms around his neck and just for a moment pressed her cheek to his. Ever so slightly, he pressed back, and for the first time, she felt the coarse whiskers of his beard, the thin flesh over hard bone. As she dropped back, her eyes shone up into his. Next moment, Miss Reade pulled her back to their boisterous classmates.

Carolus's cohort cheered themselves hoarse. Chanting and singing, they marched arm in arm out onto the Champs-Élysées and
through the streets of Paris. For Jeanette, no prize day at school, no
win at a horse race, no political victory by one of Papa's friends had
ever been half so exciting. (Just wait until I write home, she exulted.
Wait till Mama hears this!) As they proclaimed their allegiance, they
dazzled themselves with the knowledge that they were exactly where
they needed to be, studying under the best master in Paris, while
they wrestled with their gifts and hopes and doubts. And through
it all, Jeanette felt the touch of Edward's cheek against hers and made
no attempt to sort anything out.

Edward was in something of the same exalted state. People around
him bumped, shoved, and talked all at once; he hardly knew it.
Above the tumult, Adeline asked, loudly, "Well, what now?"

"We make for the exit along with everyone else," said Miss Isobel,
"and then, Mr. and Mrs. Vann, off you go, *tzzz-tzzz*, in a beeline to
Ledoyen's restaurant—it's where the winners and fashionable set will
be, and you will enjoy telling your New York acquaintances about
it when you go home. Meanwhile, Dr. Murer, Sister has landed you
with Miss Pendergrast and me, but we are quite capable of seeing
ourselves home, quite, quite capable. We do it all the time. Unless
you care to join us for ice cream?"

Although, for Edward, only home and a rest for his weary leg
should have appealed, the momentary euphoria of Jeanette's embrace
left him expansive. He could call on Cornelia with a bottle of champagne; he could stroll out to see what Paris had to offer; in the circumstances, he would eat ice cream.

"Do you mind taking the omnibus?" asked Effie, when they
reached the Place de la Concorde. "Isobel and I always do. We sit on
top and see everything."

Why not? thought Edward. The streetcar was how he got around Cincinnati.

Their destination was Le Petit Honoré, Robbie Dolson's patisserie off the Boulevard des Italiens. Effie had retained a covert liking for it; and without telling Jeanette, she had introduced Miss Isobel to it. The two of them thought of it as their little secret.

It was a secret they shared with a growing clientele. If *Noggins* influenced public opinion less than Robbie Dolson had claimed, the excellence of Le Petit Honoré's pastries and its location had ensured its prosperity. Two lacy wrought-iron tables placed by the owner on the sidewalk were continually occupied, but there were a few more in a tiny, walled garden out back that not everyone knew about. Effie and Miss Isobel did, and it was only a short wait until they were seated in the dappled sun and shade of a chestnut tree that was piled with pyramids of fragrant blossom.

"Do you have plans for the summer, Miss Reade?" Edward asked, after they had placed their order.

"I'm so glad you asked that! We do, and you give me the opening to ask a favor of Miss Pendergrast. Now, Penders, you must listen carefully. With classes at Carolus's atelier done for the summer, Sister could leave at any time, but we shall stay in town through June. Paris is at its loveliest in June—so lovely that Sister can't see why Carolus leaves for the country. I've told her it's because the countryside is *also* at its prettiest beginning now. So sweet, all the green fields and flowers, but we saw much the same thing in Ireland year after year. We shall wait until *July* to go down to Pont Aven. And this year we plan to stay there until October. Three whole months and the apartment empty. So here is my proposal. Do you think it possible, just possible, that you and dear Miss Palmer could mind it for us? Free of rent, of course, with use of the studio."

"Oh, my, Isobel. Oh, my." Effie puffed and blew. "I'd say yes in a minute—an airy apartment in summer? *Ouff!* Only you see, Jeanette and I were planning to be in Pont Aven ourselves in August, that is, assuming we don't have to go back to the States, which I don't think we will. Even so, you might want someone else . . ."

"You'll be in Pont Aven? Oh, Penders, what *fun* we shall have! It makes no difference about the apartment, none whatsoever. The concierge can earn her keep for *one* month by looking after things. And surely you are not thinking of going home this autumn. That would be so foolish: Sister says Miss Palmer is blossoming under Carolus's tutelage. We'll hear no more about it. Dr. Murer—do *you* have plans for the summer?"

"I'm embarked on some chemical experiments, Miss Reade. I'll see where they lead me."

CHAPTER THIRTY-SEVEN

Summer 1879

Carolus's students were jubilant for days. To celebrate his victory, the ladies' class took him to lunch on Monday in a private room at Père Cagniard's. And then it was over. Carolus left for the country. On Tuesday, Jeanette carried her watercolor box and a few sheets of ready-primed paper.

"Now" said Adeline, "with all that hullabaloo behind you, you can settle down to ten days of serious work."

Jeanette swallowed the obvious retort. "I can give you mornings this week," she said, "and there is plenty of light in the evenings, but next week the class is going to the Cluny. I can't miss that."

"You mean, you won't."

"In my shoes, you wouldn't either, Adeline. Papa has let me sign up at Julian's through June, but I don't know how much time I've got after that."

"Don't be silly; he hasn't ordered you to buy a ticket, so you know you have at least July, and Cousin Effie wants to go to your Pont Aven again, so that means August. I'll write Uncle Joseph, how's that? After he hears about your dashing Carolus-Duran's medal, if you can't persuade him to let you stay as long as you like, then feminine wiles are at an end. And you need to wield them while you-know-who is in Paris, remember. I'll tell your parents about him, too, if you want."

"Adeline, don't you dare!"

"Then paint me some splendid portraits to praise, and I'll write about those instead."

Despite her irritation with Adeline, Jeanette painted the next three mornings in the nursery and devoted evenings to two horizontal watercolors of Adeline with the children in the Tuileries Garden. For herself, she would later try oil versions of the Tuileries pictures on wooden cigar-box tops given her by Harold (he produced several once he learned she could use them). On Saturday, she sacrificed most of a beautiful day to finish up the formal portraits at the Vanns' hotel. On Sunday, she triumphantly took completed park scenes to morning service at the American Episcopal Church favored by the Vanns. She and Effie ate a midday dinner with Adeline and Harold in the hotel dining room. The landscapes were delivered; the children were visited; by midafternoon, she and Effie were out the door and onto the Rue de Rivoli.

Across the street, tree leaves fluttered in the breeze. Jeanette turned her face up to the sun and closed her eyes. She felt free. The commission was done. The Vanns would soon be gone. She wanted to stretch and yawn and luxuriate with as fine an unconcern as Boots.

That being impossible in public, she linked arms lazily with Cousin Effie. "I can't do a single thing on this heavenly day. Let's walk through the Tuileries and dawdle all the way to the Luxembourg Garden, and then find chairs and just idle."

Edward was waiting for them in one of the scores of chairs by the fountain behind the Luxembourg Palace—neither by arrangement nor exactly by accident. He knew they often came here; and on a morning when he, too, felt that time spent inside four walls was time wasted, he had tucked a novel into his coat pocket and taken himself over to the Left Bank. He poked in the bins of secondhand book and print dealers along the Seine. In one, he found a single illustration from a sixteenth-century herbal, a hand-tinted woodcut of an iris—root, rhizome, leaves, and blossom. Orris root, a medicinal, the family trade. It was so handsome that he bought it. He felt a little reckless but also very lucky; for from time spent with his stockbroker friend's collection and in the library of the Jardin des Plantes, he was sure it was worth what he paid for it. From there, he went on to the park café for an omelette, and afterward found one of the few unoccupied chairs where he could sit and read, see the bright flowers of the beds around the basin, watch children sailing boats in the fountain, and keep an eye out intermittently on passersby. He was deeply engrossed in his novel when a shadow fell across the page and Jeanette's voice said, "May we interrupt you?"

He scrambled to his feet, retrieving his brown-paper parcel before it could fall to the ground. He tipped his hat—a new bowler to go with a summer-weight morning jacket. It was the first time Jeanette had ever seen him in anything less formal than a silk top hat and frock coat.

"I would ask you to sit down," he said, "but there don't seem to be enough free chairs. May I join you on your walk instead?"

"Now you two will just have to excuse me," said Effie. "We've walked all the way from the Hôtel du Louvre, Dr. Murer, and if you will take Jeanette for another turn or two around the fountain, I'll sit here a while and rest my feet. You can leave your book and parcel with me."

Jeanette squirmed at Effie's all-too-obvious tactics (what had Adeline been saying behind her back?), but Dr. Murer either didn't notice or didn't mind. They moved off in a formal promenade around the wide graveled path of the basin. Perhaps she gave his arm the lightest of surreptitious squeezes; he openly reached over to give her hand the quickest of pats. She told him how glad she was to have completed the Vanns' pictures. He told her that his parcel contained a woodcut which she and Miss Pendergrast must see. She told him that class would be held on the grounds of the Musée de Cluny all week. He asked whether he could come over to watch. She told him, yes.

On Monday morning as Jeanette walked to the Cluny, through all her enjoyment of freedom from the Vanns and the prospect of sketching outdoors ran excitement over her assignation with Dr. Murer. Assignation, tryst: shades of Abigail McLeod! She knew she was exaggerating. All the same, she would not care to have Amy know in advance that a man, that *he*, might be coming to see her later in the week when the grounds were open to the public.

Over the weekend, a few of the more single-minded students had visited the museum and could go straight to where they wanted to work; but for twenty minutes or so, Jeanette explored the gardens, the Roman ruins, and the medieval courtyard. The first thing to strike her forcibly was a clump of fragrant irises, which glowed in hazy morning sunlight as purple as the example in Dr. Murer's woodcut. She sat down in front of it. When Amy stopped by to see what she had chosen to do, she pointed to the flowers. "Emily should be here."

"*Sunlight on Single Iris: Perfection*," said Amy.

"Be fair," said Jeanette, "she would do the whole clump." Emily might, in fact, do much more: She could make a viewer wonder what lay around the corner of the broken wall behind the flowers, what strange realm lay hidden among the leaf swords. Jeanette sighed. "Wherever the Dolsons have gone, I hope there are flowers."

After Amy moved on, Jeanette looked harder. Something besides the irises and the woodcut had pulled her back to this spot. What? The response of the heart was paramount in recognizing a motif, but to make the most of this opportunity, she needed to think analytically. Up close, the urge to work with purple, lavender, grays, and greens was strong. On the sketch of a few minutes, she wrote out color notations for working up the irises as a watercolor that night, but she was here to draw. She moved to a place well beyond the spot she thought of as Emily's. The iris clump would be only a secondary, small focal point for a study of sunlight and shadow on a wall in the middle ground with a high arch farther back. Yet Emily's absent figure also became a kind of negative weight, for a diagonal in the composition implied a figure who wasn't there.

Tuesday, it rained. Indoors, always half hoping that Dr. Murer would come, Jeanette made a number of rapid sketches of objects that might be useful someday for historical illustrations. On Wednesday, with everything damp in the morning from yesterday's rain but rapidly drying, the class set up outdoors again; and in the afternoon, Edward came. He found Jeanette opposite stone steps that led up under a covered passageway into a sunny courtyard. In her drawing, a brightly lit, thick-trunked vine gave botanical life to an otherwise stony architectural study. He stood looking over her shoulder; she showed him her work from the previous two days and pointed out the irises.

"They're just like the one in your woodcut," she said, smiling up at him. As usual, only his eyes smiled back, but she could see that he was pleased.

He looked down at her sketch and pointed. "What would you place here if you were going to finish this?"

"Do you think it needs something?"

"What? No! no, not if . . . Actually, Miss Palmer, yes, I do."

"You are talking to me honestly. Thank you."

"Honestly, but ignorantly."

"Your eye is good. It's Emily Dolson who is missing. I could so easily imagine her there. The question is whether it's better with or without her. Sometimes I think an absence can be as potent as a presence."

So it could. Marie's ghost brushed the edge of Edward's awareness, then melted away; she was no longer a strong ghost and had never been a malicious one.

"Tell me, Miss Palmer, it's none of my business, but do you know yet whether you will leave Paris for good this fall? Miss Pendergrast said that you might go back to America."

"No!" said Jeanette, breaking into a broad smile. "We've just had good news. You know the Reade sisters have offered us their apartment this summer. It helped decide my father to let me stay on."

I take it that you are highly regarded by your fellow artists if Miss Reade is willing to turn her studio over to you, Judge Palmer had written. *Also, Adeline dropped us a line to say you were making good use of your time under your celebrated M. Duran. His Medal of Honor made the newspaper here and your mother has boasted ever since. I think we can take it as proven that another school year in Paris is desirable. You may count on quarterly allowance payments to take you through May of next year.*

"I've signed up for afternoons only at Julian's in July. I can't wait—a studio all to myself! What about you, Dr. Murer—are you staying in Paris?"

He smiled at her. "For now, anyway, I'm thinking of it as home."

July sent the Renicks to a rented house in Trouville as well as the Reade sisters to Brittany. Effie would miss her mornings in the Poutery, but removal to the Rue d'Assas brought new housekeeping duties and preoccupations. *Boots resisted the move,* Jeanette wrote home after their first week. *He must know every rooftop between here and the Rue Jacob. Cousin Effie was frantic the first night he didn't come in, but finally she checked with Mme. LeConte and found out he'd gone home to the* pension. *When it happened again, Cousin E said if he was a roaming tomcat, good luck to him. She can see him when she stops by to chat with Mme. LeConte, whom she regards as a great source of tips for the Lady Artist series. Her next article, by the way, is on neighborhood bootmakers, shoe repair shops, and leatherworkers.*

As for me, I've begun a formal portrait of Cousin E, and I'm doing watercolor still lifes with shells from Miss Isobel's collection and flowers from wonderful stalls on the way home. She went on to describe the artistic exercises she had set herself. What she did not put in the letter was how she felt herself to be more and more Parisian as she walked to and from Julian's each afternoon with an apartment, not a *pension,* to come back to, how she had begun to envisage living in the city permanently. Nor did she tell her parents how, on the way home from Julian's, she always peeled off from any companion to route herself through the Luxembourg Garden. After research at the Jardin des Plantes, Edward often waited at the gate by the palace to escort her through the park.

In June, when Cornelia heard about Julian's class at the Cluny, she had given instructions that Jeanette should be allowed into the garden any time she wanted to work *en plein air.* In July, when it was daylight by six, Jeanette took to rambling to see early-morning Paris before she started her own day's work. One morning, she walked out the Rue de Sevres, around through the quiet neighborhood behind the Invalides, where there were small houses with gardens, and back to the grander Rue de Varenne. A gardener at work out front at the Renicks' house led her around to a side gate into the main garden.

At the edge of the terrace, she looked out toward the back-corner orchard. Tretower, Robbie Dolson had called it. He might be a knave—thievery put him beyond the pale—but there had been deep recognition in his voice when he first saw those trees, a longing for an unrecoverable Eden. Was it possible, she wondered, to paint a landscape that would render a real place accurately and at the same time train the viewer's mind on what could be seen through it? It was one thing to imply an absent figure by including symbolic objects or leaving an empty spot in the composition; it would be another altogether to embody transcendence. Perhaps the Renicks' School of Rembrandt painting of the moon and campfire on the Flight into Egypt achieved it. But what about with no figures? It was what Charlie Post was trying to do. As a run-up to the Gernagans' orchard in August, maybe she would seek out some particularly gnarly old apple tree.

But, no. As she started down from the Rose Parterre, she espied the duchess sitting quietly with her hands in her lap in a recess on her side of the Fountain Tier, seeming to contemplate a conical, clipped boxwood. It was as though she knew the garden would never be the Renicks', not that it would ever be hers again either, but only she and perhaps the head gardener knew how to look into its heart. Jeanette retreated up the steps so as not to interrupt her meditations, but later in the morning, she returned to sketch that corner from various vantage points and sit in the duchess's seat. A final composite drawing, worked up in her studio, showed the alcove, the empty bench, and the topiary. *Portrait of a Duchess*, she called it. And she drew one other major picture from the Renicks' grounds: in the secret garden, of the beech tree—*Portrait of an Afternoon*.

CHAPTER THIRTY-EIGHT

Pont Aven Again

When it was time to leave for Pont Aven in August, Edward took Jeanette and Effie to the Montparnasse train station, where they met Amy and Louise Steadman, who had been enlisted to replace Emily at the Gernagans' farm.

While the others took their seats, Jeanette lingered on the platform with Edward. Station noises hardly made ideal conditions for conversation, but what she said about stopping at Vitré didn't matter anyway. I'm going to miss you, she thought, almost as if it were a revelation. Their train's whistle blew loud and shrill. "I guess it's really time," she said, but still did not move. The train gave a little preliminary lurch.

Edward hastily took her elbow to assist her up. "Jeanette!" He spoke in an urgent voice so low that no one inside the compartment could hear him. She half turned to look back. He could not declare himself there, not on an open platform, not in so many words—or perhaps only in the one: *Jeanette.*

Smoothly, slowly, the train began to move in earnest. "Till the end of the month?" she said, hastily. He nodded as he closed the door behind her, acquiescing—to what, he was not entirely sure; he hoped to everything.

For the first hour, Jeanette was so dazed that she could only pretend to follow what the others were saying and doing. Time and again throughout the day, she slipped into staring out the window, basking in those last few minutes on the platform, yet feeling a little afraid. Not yet, not yet, not yet, clacked a part of her mind, as insistently as the rails under the train.

On the following evening, just as the year before, it was well after dark when the diligence from Quimperlé rattled down Toullifo Hill into Pont Aven. When it came to a stop outside the Hôtel des Voyageurs, Mlle. Julia stood in the doorway to invite travelers inside to supper. On the way into the common room, Amy stopped beside a table where a pair of chess players was being watched by a third.

"Rag-Tag, Bobtail! Well, we are home, aren't we," she said. "Where's Post?"

"Ah, Miss Richardson, good evening. Long, sad story," said Ragland, shuffling to his feet.

"Not that long if you leave out the details unfit for ladies' ears," said his opponent.

"He'd been drinking, you see," said Nagg, from the sideline.

"We know that part," said Amy.

"You only think you do," said Ragland, who resumed his seat at the chess board. "I trust you never saw him in extremity."

"Lying in his own mess, choking on vomit," muttered Cousin Effie.

"Good lord, you did see him!" exclaimed Ragland, trying to get a better view of Miss Pendergrast in the semidarkness.

"Miss Pendergrast is a stalwart at charitable institutions for the deserving poor, who tend to be surrounded by their undeserving relations," explained Amy. "She has seen everything. I take it that Post sank to some new level of degradation, thereby enabling himself to rise to new heights of folly?"

"He took up a saber we had lying around the place one night," said Ragland.

"Only a prop, you understand," said Nagg, "from the Omnium Gatherum."

"He slashed his Salon painting to ribbons."

Jeanette imagined the sickle moon and oncoming waves fluttering on canvas tatters. She felt sick.

"He turned up later in Concarneau, with only a knife. Got in a fight with some Russian sailors. If only he'd stayed close to home, it might have been local fishermen and then everything would have turned out differently. Everybody around here knew him."

"They'd have soaked his head in a bucket," said the other chess player.

"But these *frics*—they beat him unconscious. Broke three ribs, his nose, and his cheek. Knocked out some teeth. The worst of it was they took out an eye."

Jeanette gasped.

"We have something for you, Miss Palmer," said Ragland. "Post said he thought you might come through Pont Aven again some day."

"Where is he now?" demanded Amy.

"Ah, this really is the worst part," said Ragland. "The gendarmes took him to a surgery. When the shreds of his shirt were peeled back, they found a piece of paper pinned inside: *In case of my demise, notify Elmo T. Post at such and such an address in Rochester, New York. Recompense guaranteed.* Or words to that effect. The authorities didn't wait for him to peg out or wake up—they just sent off a telegram. Elmo T. wired back he was on his way."

"Was it his father?" asked Jeanette.

Ragland shook his head. "Mincing bookkeeper of a brother in a pince-nez. I never saw a man with such prissy little hands. He really deserved squashing."

"A human beetle," agreed Nagg, "insectival."

"So he's gone for good," said Jeanette. "Poor Mr. Post."

"You will come by, won't you, Miss Palmer?"

She was not sure she wanted to. "Of course," she said.

* * *

On the first full day of work, Jeanette headed up into the Gernagans' orchard for her rendezvous with the Belle d'Eté. She knew at once she would keep her vow to paint its lichen-splotched trunk and bent limbs. From a higher ledge, she looked out. Oh, how she wished Edward could see this! Before her lay her major composition for the month. The orchard dropped to the farmhouse and gardens on the left—small-scale, hard-won, and human. Beyond and all around them spread untamed land, sea, and sky. Pewter, olive, amber, and silver. To bring the farm into focus, touches of yellow ochre and vermilion, while high above shone the luminous, cloud-veiled orb of the sun.

But first the Belle d'Eté. With a sense of ritual dedication, she set up a secondhand portable easel and stool beside the tree, placing them where she could peer through a gap among branches to its knobby trunk and major limbs. She worked steadily, the forefront of her mind at one with her hand, the back of her mind elsewhere (*till the end of the month; Jeanette*). Two hours, two and a half; her hand cramped. A tree demanded no break, but she did. Arching her back, she spread her arms wide and wriggled her fingers.

To stretch her legs, she wandered back up onto the ledge. She still saw her big project. Reason and experience—not to mention the difficulties of perspective—warned that accomplishment would fall short of ambition, but she didn't care. To draw and to paint was the inevitable, the natural extension of seeing; and all around her was country that endured. She would paint it so that Edward could see it, and it would be hers for life.

Jeanette held to her program for three days, until a steady rain kept them all inside. On Sunday, they decided that the sight of the devout attending church in Breton attire, followed by a hot lunch at the

Voyageurs amid company, was worth a soaking. Not surprisingly, half the painters in Pont Aven had decided the same thing, at least about the midday meal. Jeanette listened happily to arguments about the renderings of shadows with color and the old-fashioned use of bitumen until the lunch party began to break up. She slid down their bench to sit next to Ragland. "You said you had something for me from Mr. Post."

"So we do," said Ragland.

As before, in the fishy, smoky, turpentine-laden atmosphere of the converted warehouse, Ragland's cot and corner were shipshape, Nagg's side a mess. The Omnium Gatherum was more cluttered than ever by fishing gear, costumes, and the fateful saber. Yet the place was utterly different without Charlie Post's giant picture. "Here," said Ragland. From its place against the wall, he picked up a small, rectangular parcel wrapped in brown paper, longer than it was wide.

"It isn't . . ." Jeanette could feel a wooden support through the paper and had a premonition.

"Open it," he said.

On top of a canvas lay a note scratched out in a small, eccentric hand: *Beata, You saw the gleam. I no longer can. C.P.*

Amy had been watching over Jeanette's shoulder. "Oh, gawd, Post!" she exclaimed, almost angrily. "Why did you do this to yourself!"

The painting was Charlie Post's first *esquisse* of a long, low wave tumbling toward the viewer at dusk with the gleam of a sickle moon vibrant and distant on the horizon. "He should have kept this," said Jeanette, with a catch in her throat.

"Lucky it survived at all," said Ragland. "When the rage was on him that night, he kicked and slashed, left and right."

"Does anything else survive?"

"Odds and ends," said Nagg.

"Mabel Reade has offered to buy one," said Ragland. "We

thought if we could sell some of the others, just among friends, we might be able to raise a few francs to send him."

"Beer money," said Nagg.

"Oh, no, no, no, not that," said Effie, shaking her head emphatically. "No, no. He must be kept from drink at all cost."

"Elmo T. no doubt shares your opinion, ma'am," said Ragland. "He'll hold the purse strings tight. Call it pin money—but any way you look at it, a man must have a few bits in his pocket if he wants to call his soul his own."

"I ought to pay—" began Jeanette, ignoring Effie's disapproval.

"No," said Ragland, gently. "This was a gift. You are his muse."

"But I can't be! I've hardy ever seen him. I do love this picture, but—"

"You told him so last year."

"Did him a world of good," said Nagg. "Bucked him up."

"For a while," said Ragland.

"I'll hang it in my studio, always," said Jeanette, studying the picture held down at arm's length. "It's very beautiful." She looked up at everyone, fiercely. "And he did see something."

"For a while," repeated Ragland. "More than most of us."

"Post followed the gleam," said Miss Reade, when they stopped in to show the sisters the picture. "Carolus sees it, too."

Derision sprang into Miss Steadman's face. Amy said quickly, "It was very kind of you to offer to buy one of Post's daubs."

"Sister and I have been thinking," chimed in Miss Isobel, just as quickly, with a nervous glance at Miss Reade. "We believe a little charity sale with contributions from the rest of the colony might be in order at the end of August."

Miss Reade quit scowling at Miss Steadman and said, "Post's picture might bring him more if we auctioned it."

"Or perhaps a sort of artistic bring-and-buy," continued Miss

Isobel. "Everybody contributing a drawing or watercolor; everybody going home with someone else's work as a souvenir—wouldn't it be delightful?"

All doubts about the wisdom of sending beer money to Charlie Post vanished from Cousin Effie's mind. "A show," she said, "and stalls! A rummage sale, not just artwork—props, old clothes, bric-a-brac. And picnics in baskets."

"Penders, you've hit it! A charity fête for the end of the month!" exclaimed Miss Isobel. "We could have recitations and music and lovely crêpe paper streamers."

"Sack races," muttered Jeanette, "skits."

"Hush, they'll hear you and do them, too," Amy muttered back.

"Only three weeks left," said Miss Isobel, rubbing her hands. "Oh, Penders, what a lot of work you and I have to do! The *artists* mustn't be interrupted, but *we* shall make a great success."

Jeanette and Amy and Miss Steadman left them already deep in plans.

Back at the farm, Jeanette hung the little unframed canvas in a place of honor over the mantel. "There. Diana's sickle moon. A symbol of pure inspiration."

"Jeanette is given to enthusiasms," explained Amy. "We all had to paint cheeses last fall, when she was in her round, blond phase; now she's on to weirdly cropped compositions of scenes out windows. And when it comes to men, well! I'm afraid that first it was Robbie Dolson."

"A pity about your Peregrine Partout," said Miss Steadman, settling back comfortably. "It was quite good."

"And then Charlie Post, of all sorry choices."

"He chose me. I did not choose him."

"You spoke kindly to him, which was enough to sway a man of Post's weak character." Then remembering how distressed Jeanette had been by the scene at the Salon, Amy softened. "You know, I think you really did touch him."

Jeanette shook her head. "I'm a figment of his imagination."

"Beata is," said Amy. "Muses generally are." For a moment Jeanette thought she had dropped her banter, but then Amy resumed. "From Post, it was a decided step up to join the acolytes of Carolus-Duran, but your soft heart is now safe even from him."

Jeanette gave Amy a warning look.

"You protest? But why? Is it not love, true love, this time?"

Before Jeanette could answer, Miss Steadman chuckled. "You can't stand on a platform mooning—if that's the word I want in this context—and expect no one to notice."

"Oh, shut up, both of you."

"Well," said Amy, turning icy, "it's not as if you weren't going to have to make up your mind one of these days about where *you* see the gleam—in Dr. Edward Murer or in your work."

"I've never heard that artists can't fall in love," said Jeanette, who had been wrestling with the question but was not ready to admit it. "If anything, aren't we accused of being too free?"

"Certainly, the men are, to the ruin of many a model," said Amy. "But we're not talking about amorous adventure, are we? With Robbie Dolson, it couldn't have been anything else, and I'll willingly drop Post and Carolus-Duran. But when it comes to a serious affair of the heart, let me tell you it does involve choice. Look at the wives of artists! The very men who should know better quickly demote their ladies to helpmeet and secondary status. You don't see Pauline Carolus-Duran or Marie Bracquemond's work any more, do you, and they were both quite good."

"M. Bouguereau is encouraging Jane Gardner."

"Yes, but he won't marry her. Says he won't put an end to her career. And if the husband is *not* an artist, well, it's that much worse. Berthe Morisot had to absent herself from that Impressionist show you went to: had a baby, couldn't paint for a year. I don't know of a single woman artist who has gotten away with putting her work ahead of her husband's interests, and most of them simply disappear. Your Miss Cassatt knows enough to stay free, and for that matter, so does Lucille Dobbs."

"Sometimes, the best thing that can happen is to be jilted," said Miss Steadman. "I was engaged once to a most respectable young man, a desirable catch."

"You've never told me that!" said Amy.

"It was a long time ago. On the eve of our wedding, he came weeping to me with the old story: He had Found Another. My parents were all for forcing the poor lump to carry through on the engagement—*fulfill his contract* was the way they put it. He probably would have, too—I can't see so conventional a man's simply leaving a girl at the altar."

"People would talk," said Jeanette.

"Exactly. To make a long story short, I gave him his release. I think I was secretly relieved even at the time. Certainly, a few years later when I spotted him looking decidedly second-rate on Oxford Street, I realized what a close call I'd had."

"Whatever else he may be, Dr. Murer is not second-rate," said Jeanette.

"No, he didn't look it. But if he's not, Miss Palmer, he deserves more than second best from any woman who lays claim to him."

"But so does one's work," insisted Amy.

"Oh, I agree," said Miss Steadman. "You owe it to yourself to respond to the call you hear loudest."

Before bed, Jeanette stood at the window, brushing hanks of her hair their nightly hundred strokes. "Cousin Effie, tell me about Polycarpus."

Silence. "What do you mean?"

"What was it about him you first noticed? What was he like?"

"Well, he . . ." Effie hesitated.

"How did you meet?"

"He came for his schooling at Papa's little school."

"So you grew up together?"

"You might say. Well, no, we didn't. He was from a farm family and a couple of years older than me. When he got big enough to do real work, his father said a farmer didn't need schooling and made him quit. Polycarpus was smart, though; and sometimes if he got his chores done early enough, he would walk over to read with Papa in the evening. He planned on reading law someday."

"And did he?"

"Yes indeed and paid for it himself. You see, he inherited a farm from an uncle on his mother's side when he was eighteen. It was a sorry place, and his pa wanted him to sell it right away to put whatever he could get for it into the home farm. But Polycarpus said it was *his* and he'd get it in good working order and sell it for enough to apprentice himself to a lawyer. That made old Mr. Bock so mad he called Polycarpus a bug-eyed, ear-flapping mooncalf, born a fool and likely to die one." Effie shook her head.

"But did Polycarpus make a go of the farm?"

"Oh, yes. He started by selling off some acreage for capital, and in a couple of years, he turned that place right around. I don't know that he could ever have made a good living off it, not enough for the two of us; but he sold it for what he needed to pay his apprentice fees to Mr. Douglas in Utica with some money left over to invest. We thought we had a bright future."

"And then the war came?"

"And then the war came."

Jeanette laid her hairbrush on the windowsill and came over to sit beside Effie on the bed. Having been only a small child during the fighting—a child whose adjutant-major father had come safely home—Jeanette had always regarded the Civil War with the uncomplicated patriotic piety of everyone else in Circleville, and secret boredom. Now it began to feel personal. The war had hurt Cousin Effie irremediably. Edward Murer had been wounded, too; she knew that, though he never talked about it when they were together. It occurred to her that he knew a lot more about her than she did about him. *Jeanette*, he had said on the platform. *Till the end of the month*, she had answered.

"When did you know you were in love?" she asked, softly. "How?"

Effie knew what lay behind the question; nevertheless she seized the chance to speak aloud memories that had never interested anyone else before. "It was late one winter's afternoon when I was about fifteen. Polycarpus came over to read Emerson with Papa. I happened to be near the front door."

"Just happened to be?" Jeanette gave Effie a playful poke with her elbow.

"I don't remember now. Well, maybe I do." Effie glanced down bashfully and then looked at Jeanette sidelong. "Sometimes, you know, you have to put yourself in the way of chance. Anyway, Polycarpus came in all muffled up against the cold, but the way his eyes lit up when he saw me—well, I worshipped him from that moment on."

"It gives you the shivers for somebody to look, really look and see you, doesn't it."

"Just hollows you out—no, it's like you're smooth and whole and glowing from the inside. And when you're together and both feeling that way, you forget all the rest of the world. That evening, Polycarpus asked Papa to let me join them reading and it changed how Papa thought of me, too. He had called me his little housekeeper ever since Mother died when I was eight, but now he saw that I was growing up and let me take over teaching the little bitties their letters. When I turned eighteen, Polycarpus asked him for my hand. Papa said I was still too young, but that didn't stop an understanding between Polycarpus and me. We knew we'd have to wait years and years while he was clerking in any case. I felt so alive; I took it for granted then that the world was a happy place to live in."

"He made you happy, and your being together made all this possible for me," said Jeanette. "I'm here because of him."

"Yes, you are. When Polycarpus went into the army, he left his affairs in good order and good hands. Mr. Douglas in Utica took care of everything when he was killed. And then Papa died suddenly, too."

"Oh, Cousin Effie."

"It was a hard time. If I'd been older or stronger, I might have tried to keep up the school, but I couldn't have taught the older boys. Besides, I was grieving too sore. So I went to the Hendricks. Cousin Matthew used to give me a monthly allowance and call me an independent woman, but we all knew I was really living on his charity."

"Aunt Maude made you feel that way, you mean! You earned your keep ten times over in that household, Cousin Effie."

"Oh, well."

"You did!"

"I did my best. But what I wanted to say was that at the back of my mind, I always knew Polycarpus meant for me to live out my dreams even if he wasn't there to share them. And when the day came that you wanted to act on yours, I knew my day had come at last. I don't think Polycarpus ever gave one thought to Paris, France, while he was alive, but his smile was broad in heaven the day we decided to come."

"Oh, Cousin Effie, you think about him a lot, don't you?"

"No. It's been a long time since I thought about him all day, every day. Years. Life goes on, and there's plenty to occupy a person's mind."

"But it made a difference that he loved you!"

"All the difference in the world. Deep down inside I've always known I was worth something because Polycarpus Bock loved me.

We are made to love and be loved, Jeanette, lots of different ways; but when two of you are in love, well, then there's a wholeness." Effie looked out beyond anything in the room. "Now we see in a glass darkly, but then face to face. We can't look on the Lord in this world; we aren't strong enough to meet His gaze. But He sees us and loves us, and if we are lucky enough to meet His reflection in the flesh, then we know each other as truly as Adam and Eve did, that's my belief. When I die, Polycarpus will be there waiting for me, and we'll go before the Lord together."

Jeanette sat very still.

Effie came back to earth. "You're going to have to decide about Edward Murer, Jeanette."

Clasping the back of her head, Jeanette bent over her knees. "Amy says I have to decide about my career."

"It comes to the same thing."

"But why?" cried out Jeanette. "Why can't I keep on with my lessons and spend time with him, too?"

"You can for a while, but not many men want platonic friendships forever, not with the woman they love. And a man of Dr. Murer's standing won't like his wife's name in public either, which it would have to be if you were an artist amounting to anything. And furthermore—no, hear me out, Jeanette—children come along."

"So can nursemaids."

Effie sighed. "I suppose—though I think one day you'll be surprised to find out how tenaciously children take hold. And besides children, there are also the social obligations—the calls, the dinners, the committees."

"Not for Edward. He's not like that. And certainly not if we stayed in Paris."

"Paris, too. If Mrs. Renick didn't see to that, General Noyes would. But the main thing is, a wife can't give her whole mind to her work the way you girls do. Her husband has to come first."

"Oh, why is everybody putting the cart before the horse? It's not as if he's asked me to marry him!"

"Do you want him to?"

Jeanette felt an impulse to shout, No! and put an end to the conversation. For a moment, she said nothing. Effie waited.

"I don't know, Cousin Effie. When I'm with him, I feel happy and excited and proud. I'll put off anything then, *anything*, to be with him a little longer. You've seen that. All the same, when I'm up in the orchard, or back in Miss Reade's studio, when the painting or the drawing is going well—that's the best feeling in the whole world. I forget everything else, it's so right. And I never question whether it's what I'm supposed to be doing. It never, ever feels wrong to be trying, even when the work goes badly."

"Jeanette, let me ask you one thing, and I promise not to scold or to tell anybody else: Has Edward Murer ever kissed you?"

"No! Of course, not!"

"Then I'd say, you don't yet know what's the best feeling in the world."

※

CHAPTER THIRTY-NINE

A Walk in the Tuileries Garden

Although Cornelia advised against it, Edward stayed in town through August. With the theaters closed and the fashionable set gone, seats were readily available at any restaurant or café. For recreation, he had the parks, his club, and museums. And any time he could face it, there was M. Artaud's steamy fencing hall, which stayed open for the young office workers who sweltered through the month to keep the slow business of commerce and government running while their superiors went on vacation.

He needed few outside stimuli. Germany had loosened up his brain and recalled him to the pleasure of exacting experimentation. From glazes, he considered moving to the problems of unstable colors in printers' inks but turned instead to a lifelong concern of his own, the chemistry of herbal medicines. Botanical drugs had always been his primary stock-in-trade, yet plants of the same species varied widely in potency, depending on where they were grown and when they were harvested. If he could analyze compounds known to be effective and establish standards for their strength and purity, he could bring consistent quality to the production of pharmaceuticals.

He could perform his experiments anywhere supplies and equipment were obtainable—in Cincinnati, most obviously. What made Paris special was the Jardin des Plantes with its superb library and records. The plants that interested him were grown there by experienced gardeners and curators who kept careful records and were generally willing to respond to inquiries. In June, he had begun attending one of its series of weekly lectures, which followed the natural calendar, not the social, and lasted until September. From a set of specialized questions, his interests opened out into the whole realm of botany, the bibliophile's pleasure in old herbals, and Charles Darwin's more radical reading of the book of nature.

He went for a long weekend in Normandy and took Marius, Jr., on a fossil-hunting expedition to Etretat. Back in Paris, during the week when Marianne, his cook, and Gaston, her husband, were gone on vacation, he led a simple bachelor's life, eating all his meals out. He spent a good deal of time reading on a bench in the Parc Monceau. He walked regularly. And one afternoon on a walk in the

Tuileries Garden near the end of the month, he saw Carolus-Duran coming toward him.

Now, there's a man unaccustomed to being alone, he thought. Duran might like to walk a dog by himself in the country or kick up leaves in a sun-dappled lane; but from the way he kept watch out of the corner of his eye, Edward guessed that he considered going unnoticed in the city a waste of valuable time. Not wishing to presume or perhaps not wishing to lose the unobserved observer's sly sense of superiority, Edward would have passed without speaking had M. Duran not met his eye with a momentary glance, a look almost of recognition. Edward tipped his hat.

At the signal that he was known, Carolus-Duran let his shoulders fall back, his chest expand; the sun shone on him more brilliantly. All amiability, he paused to exchange commonplaces. After reminding him that they had met at the Renicks' garden party, Edward congratulated him on his medal at the Salon. Carolus-Duran expanded further.

"Come, *monsieur*," he said, turning Edward around. "If you have the time to see one of the strangest sights in Paris, the light is perfect."

He led the way toward the jagged western façade of the Tuileries Palace, talking all the time. Edward knew from his many walks in the garden that, from a distance, the palace shone at sunset with an illusory gilded splendor; in a soft morning mist, it appeared to float dreamily; in cold, gloomy weather, the burned-out, looming hulk made a man shudder. Today, as they approached it under the mid-afternoon sky, it was frankly a wrecked building.

"This was called the Salle des Marechaux," said Duran, planting himself and Edward at one of the tall ground-floor windows. "Look straight across."

Inside, the floor was heaped with old plaster dust and stone rubble. Overhead, a few studs projected from crumbled walls at each level, and rows of broken columns mapped out destruction. Yet in a glowing patch of blue sky through the rectangle of the window opposite, a tiny Victory drove her team of four horses atop the Arc de Triomphe du Carrousel.

"The Commune created an ironic frame for that vestige of lost Bourbon glory, *n'est-ce pas?*" said Duran. "It was Ernest Meissonier who perceived the strange emblem and painted it from this vantage point. He was a colonel, you know, Meissonier, during the 1870 war. He was crushed by the defeat, but as befits a high-ranking officer and a supreme warrior of the brush, he found a way to make permanent art of tragedy and hope. The art of myself and my enlisted friends was far more ephemeral."

"You were in the war?"

"*Oui, oui!* I served in the National Guard, in Paris, for the duration of the siege."

"So you saw the palace burn."

"*Non, monsieur.* That came later. For three days in May, the fire raged. The smoke was visible for miles, they say—but not all the way to Belgium. No, I did not see it. When the National Assembly betrayed Paris and surrendered to the Prussians, I had had enough. On the very day of the ceasefire, I obtained my passport. I took my family to Brussels. The tenth of March." Duran pursed his lips, and his eyes narrowed to a burning glare. It was clear that much more could be said, but a wave of his hand dismissed old bitterness. Laughter returned to his face. "What a company we were, the Seventh! Every man an artist—painters, sculptors, engravers, a few musicians. Guard units were enlisted by neighborhood, you see, and who else but artists live in the *quartier* Nôtre-Dame-des-Champs?"

The Neuner's thousand Germans from Over-the-Rhine could hardly compare, thought Edward.

"One of my best friends, a sculptor named Falguière—we had gone to Italy together one carefree winter in our youth—"

"The best place in the world to pass a winter."

"The Mediterranean—how I love it! You, too, I perceive. The warmth, the color, the soft fragrances, the beautiful women—but not, *hélas*, during the winter of '70–'71. That winter, Falguière and I, we were together again day after day, in the frozen mud of Bastion 84 on the ramparts, facing out to the Prussian encampments. It was grim, gray, cold as death—the tedium, the boredom, the endless waiting—it is the worst of war."

At the all-too-familiar note of a veteran's war nostalgia, Edward sensed a comic anecdote coming and moved to quash it. "Not quite."

"Ah," said Carolus-Duran, giving Edward a shrewd look. "No, that is true. The worst is the fear when it comes, or the horror of finding a friend's corpse on the battlefield. For me it was a painter named Regnault—such a talent. You, also?"

"I lost count." Of the comrades he had lost, of the men he had killed.

"*Mon dieu*," said Duran, soberly. "Your American Civil War. I had forgotten. How long did you serve?"

"All four years."

"*Merde*. You must have seen death to sicken the soul. You were wounded?"

Edward tapped his leg with his cane.

"It was my hand," said Duran.

Edward gave a start. "That would have cost the world much more than my leg!"

Duran shrugged. "It healed. But four years, you say." He shook his head.

"Not all of it was spent fighting. I was captured. I sat out the last year in a camp for prisoners of war."

"*Mon dieu*, we read of the cruelty. Then you, too, know what it is to go hungry. Once when I was young and ill, I almost died for lack of food. Only the generosity of a friend who discovered me famished in my bed saved my life. I cannot imagine your misery."

"You were about to tell me about your friend, the sculptor?"

Duran struck a defiant pose with his arms crossed over his chest. "*La Résistance*," he intoned, and then went on: "One day in early December, snow fell and quickly piled deep. Someone threw a snowball; his infuriated victim threw one back. Soon, snowballs were flying everywhere until someone cried out, *Attention!* He proposed that we build snow sculptures instead. From that moment, some of us were demoted from combatants to auxiliaries. We rolled and carried blocks of snow while the professionals took command. Several statues were completed, but the triumph belonged to my good Falguière. A colossal nude astride a cannon, with her arms crossed and indomitability carved into her face. Right by the guardhouse we built her. Ah, she became celebrated. Nearby companies came to salute her; civilians made expeditions out to see her. She put heart into everyone. But then, *hélas*, she succumbed to the laws of nature—she melted. Not so our resolve, but in the end we, too, lost."

"It is difficult to see so now," said Edward, turning his back on the ruins to swing his cane around the garden, the Place de la Concorde, the restored Rue de Rivoli. In the distance, the first Napoleon's Arc de Triomphe presided unequivocally over prosperity.

Duran squinted into the sun at the golden-stoned symbol of France's glory. "You would never know that the Prussians paraded in the Champs-Élysées to spite the people of Paris," he said.

"We read that afterward, people burned bonfires to purify the street."

"True. And then they burned Paris. Well, it has been rebuilt, and all reparations paid. Nevertheless, what a waste!"

"In America, my side won—for all the good it did. Since then, the politicians have betrayed our cause and returned power to the losers."

"Glory and folly, it is the story of man."

Profound and banal, it is the way of the French, thought Edward. But in spite of himself he liked Carolus-Duran. "I wish I could have seen your *Résistance*," he said.

"Gone without a trace—but not quite. Félix Bracquemond was one of us. He made an engraving of her."

"Bracquemond? He exhibited work at a show I saw in May."

"The so-called Impressionists? Bravo, *monsieur*. Not many Americans have heard of them, much less gone to see them. You must tell me what you thought."

"I admired Bracquemond's work. In America, I regularly saw more prints than paintings and felt I could comprehend him." A shy eagerness came into Edward's voice. "Mme. Renick told me that you also know Claude Monet."

"A genius."

Edward was favorably impressed by the way Duran spoke without hesitation or jealousy. All the same, tact dictated that he not overpraise one painter to another's face. "His treatment of light . . ." he began, and left the thought open-ended.

"He makes you see it as it appears in nature. It was as if the room were filled with sunshine, *n'est-ce pas?*"

"Exactly!"

"Monet is interested in physical sensation, in the impression that light makes on the eye at a particular moment as it hovers in the air and bounces off objects. We all learn from him. But most of the time when we look around us, *monsieur*, we focus on this or on that, not on everything equally."

"On a glimpse of Victory in a distant sky."

"You flatter me—but it is true, is it not? If I bring greater finish to Mme. Renick's face than to her sofa, her husband will pay a handsome fee for the portrait. Am I venal? *Non, monsieur.* For I also give M. Renick a study of the lady's character, of her generosity, of her little vanities, of what she reveals about herself over time and in her tastes. Monet is a visionary who believes that one day the world will acknowledge his genius, and so it will. But during the siege, when I saw my wife, my mother, my sister, my daughter—my little daughter, *monsieur*—go hungry, I vowed they would never go hungry again.

I, too, enjoy experimenting with new techniques, but I am no prophet; I do not feel compelled to follow methods to their logical conclusion when they can be adapted to paint beautiful pictures that living, breathing people wish to buy. *Carpe diem.* When one has endured the night, *monsieur*, it is neither foolish nor wicked to embrace the day."

CHAPTER FORTY

End of August 1879

Of the hundred or so artists in and around Pont Aven, most contributed something to Cousin Effie and Miss Isobel's rummage sale and many to the art sale as well. By the end of the month, the ladies had sold all their tickets in a raffle. On the day of the fête, they sold all their boxed teas. Everyone claimed that Town Hall, where the works for sale were on display, was as packed as any Salon; and late into the evening, everyone sat outside to listen to an impromptu concert by volunteer performers on the green between the Hôtel Voyageurs and the Pension Gloanec. Business at the two hotel bars was brisk, with a portion of the night's take going to the cause. Altogether, a sizable purse was collected for Charlie Post.

In the excitement of the big day, Jeanette forgot everything else, including the need ever to leave Pont Aven, but Tuesday brought the beginning of the end. Saying she wanted to talk to Rodolphe Julian, Amy left on Wednesday. For the next two days, Jeanette paused before every sight from the breakfast crockery to the sails of fishing boats in the harbor, aware that by the following summer, her parents expected her to be in Ohio. When her mind ran too far forward, she wrenched it back to the smell of crushed apples and grass in the orchard, the buzz of wasps feeding on the sticky brown fruit near her feet, the squealing clamor of seabirds in the distance. Yet as much as she tried to hold on to everything, she also felt a nervous impatience to be done with what was finished, to go back to the pressures of Paris, to models and classes and competition, to another month in Miss Reade's studio, to Edward.

On the train, Effie began working on a "Letter from an Artist's Colony" to send to the New York *Weekly Panorama*. Jeanette alternately read and dozed while her mind rushed forward over and over again to the Montparnasse train station, where always Edward awaited her on the platform. As the hours passed, the stories she told herself became more elaborate. They began with his ardently seeking her through a crowd. Usually, she flew into his arms. After a first scene of reunion, the daydreams took various directions. Some ended melodramatically in his rescuing her from a runaway hansom, others in her looking into his eyes and answering a silent question, "Yes." In still others, she renounced love and marriage to devote herself to Art. She half expected him really to be there, even though she and Effie had deliberately refrained from sending him the particulars of their return for fear it would seem too much like asking for a ride home. She knew it was foolish to make his being there a test of his devotion, but she did.

As a matter of fact, Edward had gone so far as to check on possible trains coming in from the west on Friday, Saturday, and Sunday, but he gave up trying to guess which one the ladies would take. To haunt the station for days on the chance of being there at the right time was for young fools, he told himself, not old ones. Instead, he left a note for them with their concierge and ordered fresh flowers— red roses and fragrant white lilies—to be delivered to the Reades' apartment on all three mornings.

When Jeanette and Effie arrived back at the Reades' apartment on Saturday afternoon, therefore, feeling bedraggled and, in Jeanette's case, disappointed, they were met in the hall by a huge bouquet and a note from Edward asking to be informed of their safe arrival. While Jeanette stood transfixed by the flowers and by the words in Edward's hand, Effie picked up a second note, this one from Amy. It was dated that morning: *Damn and blast, must see you. Let me know when I can come around.*

"I sit up all night in a second-class carriage," said Amy, that evening, having been invited to supper, "and arrive back in Paris and what do you suppose I find at home? A skeletal figure in an apron, that's what, a woman with masses of dark hair piled on top of her head: La Grecque."

"No!" said Jeanette.

"My reaction exactly. I marched straight into the studio and said, 'Sonja, is that Andrea Antonielli in our kitchen, and if so, what the hell is she doing there?'

"'*Ah, chérie, bienvenue,*' says Sonja, cool as you please. '*Oui, c'est Andrea. Sa petite fille aussi.*'

"Sonja, it seems, went looking for a model early one morning down at the foot of Rue Nôtre-Dame-des-Champs and found the beastly child Angelica gyrating through lewd poses picked up from some chanteuse. Andrea has been mostly out of work for months and spending any money she could earn or beg in the worst sort of places. According to Angelica, they've been feeding off rinds filched from the garbage."

"Oh, dear," said Effie, "something must be done."

"I did suggest delivering them to one of your mission halls, Miss P, and Sonja said—she actually said—'a good Catholic deliver Andrea to Protestants?' Ha. I asked her when was the last time either of them had dared set foot in a confession booth. No, but the point is, what she *had* done was put the pair of them in my bed. 'And what do you propose to do now?' I asked. Her answer was to put them up in the storeroom. When I said she couldn't possibly mean to house them indefinitely, she said it wasn't charity—she had hired Andrea: 'She is model; I need model.' Those were her very words. To top it all off, she's paying the poor woman only a franc an hour with five sous an hour extra to cook and clean. You'd think they were serfs."

"Does she really mean to go on with it now that you're back?" asked Jeanette.

"It seems so. There's no chance it will work, of course. Oh, but there are so many things wrong! Even simple, stupid things like head lice."

"Head lice! Then their heads need shaving!" interjected Effie.

"Well, precisely. I marched them around to a barber myself, yesterday. It's a sign of how beaten down Antonielli is that she submitted. She was tragic about it, of course. She claimed her locks were her living, which is rubbish—she could earn her living with her head in a bag if she regained that stupendous control of hers. Sold the swatch of hair for a pretty penny, too—which I have insisted must go toward new clothes and tuition for Angelica as soon as she can be sent out to school. If I am to be saddled with that child, she will at least learn to read and write. Meanwhile, the tot's wearing a scarf and scrambling all over the impasse, wheedling and showing off and making herself a right nuisance."

"How is Sonja taking it all?" asked Jeanette.

"Oddly enough, I think she welcomes a little discipline in the house. For one thing, I pointed out that if La Grecque is there to model, she must be given a raise and pose. And I must say she's interesting now, all skin and bones with that bald head. I want her to pose reclining—nude first and then in a shift. Sonja agrees she could make use of some oil studies herself. One thing I wanted to ask was, could you come in with us? Rare chance for you—"

Jeanette nodded excitedly.

"—and frankly, I think another person in the room will make it all more businesslike. I want to stymie any attempt by Antonielli to play Sonja and me off against each other."

Effie sat shaking her head.

"Well, why not?" demanded Jeanette.

"It's, it's just so cold-blooded and so indecent."

"You are cannier than the world at large," said Amy. "Few people know how much ice water runs through artists' veins. But as for indecency, surely in this case it's just a matter of a professional model doing her job."

"It's taking advantage of the *signora*'s plight. She's afraid of being thrown out."

"As well she should be," said Amy, her face darkening. "But I don't see making her work as wicked. Far better that she pose for us than be forced to sleep with men, which is what too many down-and-out models wind up doing. Given the shape she's in, one shudders to think what sort of man she might attract. I'll tell you what. Come over for tea tomorrow, you two. I promise, Miss P, you'll feel better about the whole thing."

"Can we make it some other time or another day?" asked Jeanette.

"Dr. Murer is coming to tea," explained Effie.

"Oh, I see-e-eee."

"He sent the flowers," said Jeanette, lamely.

"Yes, I had guessed whence Flora's bounty. Very well, then, we'll talk about it Monday morning on the way to Julian's to register. By the way, here's my other news: I'm giving up my job as *massière*."

"Amy!" exclaimed Jeanette. "You're going to devote the fall to a Salon piece?"

"I am. I had thought I'd work at home, but now I've decided to enroll in the afternoon class—with Antonielli around, and that brat, farewell to uninterrupted peace and quiet.

"Anyway, I'll give this much to Julian: He's being handsome about everything. He's offered me space in the atelier for independent work and criticism to help prepare a submission, and he's going to find me work doing designs for menus and such."

"Success for the students is success for the school."

"That's what Sonja says. She thinks I should spit in his eye and make the break total, but I'm inclined to take every bit of help he offers." Amy turned to Effie. "Miss P, we'll get you by the studio one day this week; you'll see it's all right about the posing."

Edward had enjoyed indulging in the flowers. For the assistant at the florist's shop, his triple order had marked a welcome resumption of business after the summer doldrums, and she led him through a careful selection of individual stems for the first bouquet. When he received Jeanette and Effie's responses late Saturday afternoon—a watercolor of a rose and a lily, and a note filled with underlinings and exclamation points—he kept the little painting beside him all evening until finally, at bedtime, it went into a drawer beside his bed. The next morning, he walked the six or eight blocks from his apartment to the Protestant American Chapel on the Rue de Berri and watched at a little distance.

Jeanette saw only him, no one else. Wordlessly, she walked right past the congregants dawdling on the sidewalk, without ever taking her eyes from his. To compensate for her rudeness, Effie made a point of greeting the acquaintances whom they had not seen for a month. When she finally joined Jeanette and Edward, she asked, "Will you sit with us, Dr. Murer?"

He would and did—not that either he or Jeanette paid any attention to the service (each was acutely aware of the other's hand when they shared a hymnbook). What the hour gave them most was an opportunity to adjust to sitting next to each other. Afterward, Edward invited the ladies to lunch at an open-air café.

They ate, then strolled to the Place de la Concorde. Across the bridge, when Edward began steering them upriver toward the Latin Quarter, Effie said, "Jeanette, I think you should tell Dr. Murer all about Pont Aven, but if you two will excuse me, I'm going to take an omnibus home. I shall expect you around four thirty or five."

Jeanette was so happy for the chance to be alone with Edward that Effie's blatancy embarrassed her only for the instant it took to exchange a glance with him. Edward himself fully understood the implications. He took Effie's hand. "Thank you, Miss Pendergrast." He would have called a cab, but Effie insisted that after a month in the country, she would enjoy a ride atop the Boulevard Saint-Germain bus. It seemed to be true; they let her hurry away. "Do you want to tell me about Pont Aven?" asked Edward.

Jeanette brought her free hand up to shade her eyes a moment. About discussions with Amy, discussions with Effie? No. About Charlie Post or the orchard? Yes, no, maybe. "It was much like last year, which was what we wanted," she said. "I painted a picture of the farm that I want you to see." They had come to a parapet in the wall at street level. Below, near the water's edge, on this side before the docks jutted out, a child with his nurse threw large chunks of bread to a frenzy of speckled ducks in the water. Jeanette pretended to watch a moment, then turned to Edward. "How about this? I'll tell you about Brittany when I show you my sketches and pictures later on. For now, you tell me what *you* did all month." Caution should have stopped her right there, but Cupid or a spirit of mischief or an unconsidered, reckless vanity led her to add, "What did you think about?" She did not say, *while I was gone*; she did not ask bluntly, *did you think of me?* But with her mouth left provocatively half open, she might as well have.

"I thought about you, Jeanette. Often."

It was as delicious to hear as she had hoped until the twinkle in his eye as he added the word *often* brought her to her senses. "You're right," she said, laughing, "conceited me. But I thought about you, too—Edward." After a pause, she added softly, "I want to see you without your hat." Her hand reached slowly up as though to brush the brim lightly with the back of her fingers.

"If I take off my hat . . ." Edward did not finish the thought— that he might be tempted to gather her into his arms right there and then. All teasing vanished from his expression, baring a glimpse of the ardor he had so far held in check. A suggestion of impropriety hung in the air. She pulled her hand back.

"Have I offended you?" he asked.

"Frightened me a little."

"Jeanette—"

"We'd better walk on." She took his arm again. "Life is so complicated, and I want this afternoon to go on being simple and perfect."

"But you do care. You could learn to care."

"Can you doubt it?"

"Oh, I can doubt any thing of joy." There was bitterness in his voice. In a wordless attempt to understand, Jeanette held his arm tighter and looked up at him earnestly. He pulled his arm free to wrap it around her shoulder and tug her toward him, just for an instant, before offering her a very proper bourgeois elbow again. "I am also accomplished at self-pity," he said, with a wry half smile.

"I realized something in Pont Aven," she said. "I realized that you know far more about me than I do about you. Let's go across the next bridge and find a seat in the Tuileries Garden. I don't even know much about what happened to you during the war. Cousin Effie was telling me about her fiancé—"

"Miss Pendergrast was engaged?" Mirth danced at the corners of Edward's mouth and in his eyes.

"Don't laugh! Polycarpus—" At the sound of the name, Jeanette had to stifle a giggle. She also had to contend with the image of a gawky boy with bulging eyes and big ears, but loyalty to sex and kin made her resume in a scolding tone. "Yes, she was, and he was killed in the war."

Edward subsided. "Poor devil," he said, and fixed his eyes on the hulk of the Tuileries Palace across the river. "A lot of men died in that war, Jeanette. If you made it back home, half the boys you grew up with were dead and the rest were crippled or gone buggers. Some of us both." Hastily, he pulled himself back. "Not everyone. Can you guess with whom I discussed this most recently?"

"Mrs. Renick."

"A good guess, but wrong, they're still in Normandy. No—your M. Carolus-Duran."

"Carolus! When?" She stopped dead.

"Maybe ten days ago." They walked on. "He was in town on an errand, and I happened across him in the garden over there. We fell into conversation about our two wars."

"And he told you about finding Henri Regnault's body," Jeanette put in quickly.

"How did you know? Tells it often, does he?" said Edward, answering his own question with a chuckle. "He also told me about building snowmen during the war."

"That's one he hasn't told in class!"

By the time they had crossed the Pont Solferino and found a bench on the south side of the Tuileries Garden, Edward was telling her about the homemade swords with which he and Theodore had skirmished, and from there he branched out into other stories about his childhood in Cincinnati and Kiel. There were things in his later life he did not want her to know, but he willingly talked about his father and mother, about the drugstore and Theodore's larger business, about his childhood in Cincinnati and Kiel. "Theodore grew rich off the war." Edward paused and gazed out at a silvery fountain, green lawns, and people on wide gravel paths, at handsome buildings on the Rue de Rivoli facing them over the treetops. He lightly kicked the tip of his cane with the toe of his shoe.

"And you were maimed."

He ceased tapping and tensed. "Is that how you think of me?"

"No, of course not. I'm sorry! I was being melodramatic. It just seems so unfair for one brother to profit in a big way while the other suffers."

"It was better than fighting on opposite sides. I never resented Theodore's luck or acumen," said Edward, settling back at an angle to turn toward her. "One thing war does for any sane man is strip away illusions about reason or justice. And sometimes"—his eyes lingered questioningly over her face—"we may be given much more than we deserve."

Carolus spoke of an envelope of vibrating light surrounding a face, the lack of hard, fixed outlines in nature, the need for the brush to blend form into atmosphere. Surely such light can envelop, can join two people, thought Jeanette, or rather she thought nothing so coherent.

"Tell me the worst."

"No." Maybe he had raved to Sophie about the worst long ago; he couldn't remember; he thought not. No woman could understand the worst, nor any man who had not endured it. Nor would he let that old darkness overwhelm this day. "Jeanette, don't let's talk about war at all."

Too much had flashed across his face for her to persist. As much as she wanted to understand him, she decided it was safer to rise to the surface. She propped her head on one hand at an angle. "Then tell me about your month."

The afternoon wore on. They strolled again. Without paying much attention to hours or minutes, they wound up at the Rue d'Assas at five o'clock, by which time the third bouquet of flowers had been delivered. If Effie had not been present, there was no telling what Jeanette might have done. As it was, she turned from the flowers to Edward so meltingly that she need do nothing. For tea, Effie had laid out little ham sandwiches, pastries, and cakes, and she now brewed an excellent pot of tea (Matthew Hendrick had taught her how to select the best). Edward, as always, was in danger of forgetting to eat, and for once, Jeanette was so rapt that she had little appetite. Inside the apartment, shadows deepened. Eastward through windows kept open to let in the welcome evening breeze, the dome of the Pantheon reflected the sunset while everything else faded. Dusk flattened the skyline. When even the Pantheon faded, they realized how dark the room had become; but by now, each time the conversation neared a close, one or another of them would be reminded of something and it would pick up again. Effie went into the kitchen to fetch the cold chicken and also brought a bottle of wine left by the Reade sisters as a gift in July. Jeanette lit a candle. They ate informally, as though at an indoor picnic, and still they talked on. The clock on the mantel chimed nine. Now it seemed the party must break up, but not until it struck ten did they admit that the next day was Monday. Jeanette had to suppress a yawn. Leaning her head against the back of the sofa, she said resignedly, "I've promised to go with Amy to Julian's first thing tomorrow morning to sign up for September."

Edward rose. "Then it's high time for me to leave. You will be drawing while Miss Richardson paints?"

"Ummnh," said Jeanette, making a lazy affirmative sound while she smiled sleepily at him through another half-suppressed yawn. Her mother and Aunt Maude would have reproved such familiarity; it made Edward affectionate. She rose and followed him into the hall with Effie.

"M. Bouguereau again?"

"No, we're transferring into Lefebvre's studio, the full nude."

Effie squawked in protest. Edward stiffened. Jeanette knew she had just spoiled her perfect day and wished she could take the words back, but fatigue and conviction made her obstinate. Ostensibly directing herself toward Effie, she said, "Well, it's the class all the best students take." She ignored the one question she knew burned hottest for Edward and Effie both: Were there ever male models? The answer was yes.

CHAPTER FORTY-ONE

Nudes

If Jeanette had been subject to insomnia, she would have had a bad night. Edward had withdrawn into an airless silence. In the briefest, most conventional terms, he had bade them good night. As soon as he was gone, the cousins had a full-blown row about morals, decency, a man's feelings, the nature of woman, and the primacy of the figure in art. It settled nothing. The next morning, reluctant to open her eyes, Jeanette dozed her way into Edward's arms in the darkened hallway until in the dream Dr. Murer shook her off. She snapped fully awake. Finding little comfort in further thoughts of him, she went to breakfast armed against Effie.

"By light of day—" began Effie.

"By the light of day," interrupted Jeanette, "I am going to make the best use of Miss Reade's studio for a month by working here mornings until Carolus comes back, and get the most for Papa's money by signing up for the hardest, most advanced class Rodolphe Julian has to offer in the afternoon. And there's nothing prurient about what we'll be doing!" At the word *prurient*, Effie ducked her head. "Oh, for heaven's sake, Cousin Effie. Write Miss Reade and Miss Isobel. They'll tell you I'm doing the right thing."

On a fast-clipped walk to the river, she continued to quarrel mentally with Effie and now with Edward, too (and with her mother, Hannah Lyman, and every small-minded restriction she had left behind in Ohio). When she met Amy at the corner of the impasse off the Rue Madame, she had hardly said *bonjour* before she started pouring out complaints. In a bitterly comic imitation, she exaggerated how much Edward had flinched.

"Don't tell me he laid down the law and forbade you to take the class!"

"He didn't stay long enough to try. No, all the vocal objection came from Cousin Effie."

"Very silly of the old girl; she ought to know better by now. But no matter; she'll come around. Not much she can do about it, is there?"

"She could throw me out, refuse to live with me—so much for respectability."

"Then you could move into our chaotic establishment. We seem to be encouraging riffraff at the moment, Sonja and I. Can you imagine what home life is like when the resident ghoul recoils at the mere sight of one? I might as well be Genghis Khan lobbing skulls as I come—except that little Demonica, as I think we must rename the hell-kitten, is fast losing all fear, indulged as she is by Auntie Sonja."

"Indulged by *Sonja?*"

"Well, tolerated. And then there's the sudden intransigence of La Grecque herself. She's having second thoughts about posing for us naked in front of the *bambina*. She claims it's not the task itself—jolly right, too; there's no knowing what she has compelled Sweet Innocence to behold or do. No, it's her ribs showing and her lack of color; she isn't pretty enough. *Thees ees not how a daughter should see a mother, Mees Richardson*—as if the child hadn't had to clean her up and feed her as recently as a month ago."

"Maybe vanity is a sign of returning health."

"I daresay, but highly inconvenient. We *are* paying her to model, and I do so want to study that haunting ghastliness before it's gone."

"Why not shut Angelica in the back room for a couple of hours?"

"If you knew how piercingly that child can shriek, you wouldn't ask."

"Here's an idea! Invite Cousin Effie to teach Demonica to read at the kitchen table. Appeal to her reforming spirit. Uplift. If she agrees, she won't be so down at the mouth about my coming, too."

"I do believe you're onto something!" said Amy. Then her voice changed: "It isn't really Miss Pendergrast who's worrying you, is it?"

When he left on Sunday night, Edward was no happier about what had just happened than Jeanette. It made him feel old-fashioned and starchy, but he could not hide from himself that he was repelled by the idea of her sitting in a room with wholly unclad models—not merely sitting, but focusing on them, thinking about them, drawing them. Of course, he knew that in the past she had regularly drawn women's breasts, men's thighs—not that she had ever shown him examples (he was touched by her delicacy when he thought of it)—and he supposed that from time to time women who dressed and undressed in the same household must see each other naked. Certainly, occasions arose when even a sheltered young lady might encounter the bare arms or chest of a laboring man. But not genitalia. He didn't think he worshipped the kind of pure-mindedness that required a girl to be kept in utter ignorance until her wedding night; but to his perplexed shame, he realized that a presumed innocence ran through Jeanette's sunny appeal to him, a promise of the world made new.

Out on the quiet Rue d'Assas, he continued northwest from one tranquil pool of yellow lamplight to the next. On such a soft, late-summer's night, despite all the walking they had done earlier, he wanted to end the day at the slow pace of foot travel, at least here on the Left Bank where, above the soft nimbus of gaslight, stars could still be seen. Paris was a city easy to perambulate at night— which streetwalkers knew, of course, and the bored women who sat in pairs in cafés, signaling availability. Usually, he was able to brush past the one and ignore the other without much disturbance to himself or them, but tonight on the Boulevard Saint-Germain, back among restaurants and theaters and restless pleasure-seekers, he could not avoid seeing how Paris painted herself after dark. At a café table on the sidewalk, beside a coarse companion who lewdly bit her thumb, sat a pretty girl, barely twenty, with eyes hooded in glum disillusionment, her skirt pulled up to show her petticoat and a bit of leg. She glanced at him. He returned her gaze a little too long. She gave him the requisite half smile and hungry, come-hither look. In a moment it would turn to flattery, though he knew she hungered for money, not for him. It didn't matter. He felt an ache in his loins and nodded.

Jeanette was not quite so prepared for the full nude as she had claimed. On the first afternoon of the new class, she wanted to look away from pubic hair and the round, inward-turning curves of the model's groin. Somehow it was easier at the Rue Madame.

Once Cousin Effie had been won over by the prospect of rescuing Angelica from illiteracy, she had, in turn, overcome La Grecque's bristly opposition to interference by telling Angelica a Belleville joke in an atrocious accent. When Angelica cawed with laughter, her mother had given way with a convalescent's sudden drop into apathy.

Regular meals and reduced access to alcohol had halted Andrea Antonielli's weight loss, and as Amy had warned, her ashen skin was already less cadaverous. She posed listlessly, but day by day, her eyes regained some of their haughty, dark gleam. Jeanette saw that she could be partner to a great picture—of Medusa perhaps, or Electra. Yet at home, it was not La Grecque's face that haunted her.

On the first Wednesday of classes, hoping against hope that she had misread Edward's reaction, Jeanette made an excuse to Amy and detoured through the Luxembourg Garden on the way home from Julian's. He was not there. On Thursday morning, while she worked at home on a canvas from Pont Aven, his three bouquets reproached her with what ought to be. That afternoon, she again routed herself through the Luxembourg Gate; again he was not there. On Friday, rather than risk disappointment, she went home another way.

Week followed week. By day, she nourished a stubborn, hurt pride rather than succumb to longing and tears (at night she often curled into a miserable knot in bed). To make use of images she had gathered at the Cluny, she began preliminary sketches for a literary painting. Her subject would be the Lady of Shalott, weaving at her loom as Sir Lancelot rode by. She encased Lancelot in rigid armor. Outside the tower window, he rode away between fields of grain sloping up to a miniature sky.

Edward knew that no man in France would condemn his lapse with a prostitute; but although the night's pleasure had been intensely real at the time, the transaction for money was sordid. He felt defiled by his own actions. He must stay away from Miss Palmer, whom he had betrayed, until—until what? Until his overly scrupulous conscience subsided, Hippolyte Grandcourt would have told him, and the sooner the better. In the meantime, he left Jeanette to pick up the threads of her busy life unmolested, thankful that he had routines of his own to follow, thankful also that the botany lectures at the Jardin des Plantes were finished so that he had no call to go anywhere near the Boulevard Saint-Germain. On the first Sunday in September, he considered attending the American chapel but was irked by the hypocrisy of his motive. The Madeleine did not beckon. He began to feel blocked, useless.

One day toward the end of the second week, he went to the Luxembourg Gate, just in case. Perhaps if he and Jeanette could resume their casual summer habit, everything would come right naturally; she need never know about his vice. But she did not appear. The longer he did not see her, the more he wanted to and the less able he was to approach her. Other desires stirred: He wanted that girl again; he wanted to kill pain; he wanted to stop the shadows lengthening; he wanted laudanum.

When the Renicks returned in the middle of the month, he called on Cornelia late one afternoon when she would be attended by a stream of other visitors.

"Darling Edward! Effie Pendergrast was here this morning; she'll be sorry to have missed you—unless you have been seeing her regularly elsewhere?" Cornelia raised an inquisitive eyebrow.

"Not lately. I have dodged recruitment into the McAll Mission this fall."

Cornelia, wise to his deflections, let it go; but when he took his leave after the socially prescribed quarter of an hour, she whispered, "Has there been a quarrel?"

He hesitated. "No."

"Come some morning to the Poutery, soon. I see we must talk. I mean it! *Chère Thérèse, bonjour!*"

Edward escaped that afternoon without having to commit himself. Thereafter, he remained simultaneously restless and paralyzed. He finally allowed himself some laudanum, though only in the evening, only a small dose to help him sleep. Mornings, he knew enough to get up and drink coffee, but he began asking Marianne for toast instead of the brioche he had enjoyed all summer, for one soft-boiled egg instead of two. She frowned and served his toast with saucers of her mother's plum or apricot confiture; he ate a little to please her. He continued to carry out experiments already under way as meticulously as ever, but ideas jotted down in his notebook during the summer were left unexplored; he added no new ones. He called on Cornelia. He fenced. He walked. In the evenings, he fidgeted through wordless games of chess with the collector of prints. As long as there was sun as often as rain, as long as the increasingly intense late-afternoon light extended into early evening, he could honestly tell himself that if he must stare down the black dog, he would rather do it in Paris than anywhere else on earth. And he wanted to do it with a clear mind, at least during the day.

Effie decided to look for an apartment with a studio that would lure Jeanette away from the afternoon class at Julian's, and the coarsening effect of nudes, by tempting her to continue working half a day on her own once Carolus's class resumed. She found one at a price she was willing to pay. Three flights up on the southern back of a building on the Rue du Fleurus, it would be hot in summer and the light, though abundant, would change throughout the day. It was dirty, and even after a good scrubbing, the gray walls would still be dingy. Its one bedroom was in the attic above; it had no sitting room, no kitchen, no bathroom, only a shared toilet down the hall. But there was a sink and running water; the stove, which was meant primarily for heat, had a griddle on which they could cook at a pinch. And the studio was large: thirty feet long by fourteen wide with a ceiling high enough to accommodate a giant canvas, large enough to accommodate a sofa and some chairs at one end and still leave plenty of room for Jeanette to work. Moreover, if they ate a simple breakfast at home, picked up lunch at a charcuterie, and dined in the evening at a nearby Duval restaurant, they could save the expense of a full-time maid of all work and spend less than they would at a *pension*.

Jeanette saw it and agreed that it would do, though she wished it lifted her low spirits more. "Just think how a clean coat of paint on the walls will help!" said Effie. "Yellow, like Mr. Whistler's room at the fair. I'll put my screen over there and find some peacock feathers."

Jeanette was about to object that cool gray was considered necessary in a studio to ensure true color on the canvas but was stopped by the thought that this would be Effie's first apartment, too. "As neutral as possible," she said, "not bright."

Edward heard about the move from Cornelia and ordered a bouquet of yellow roses and golden autumn lilies to be sent to the Rue du Fleurus on the Friday they would move in. The black dog turned in a circle and settled down.

The flowers came while Effie was out shopping for secondhand furniture. Jeanette did not even notice that they had been sent anonymously. Oh, Edward! What did he mean by it? Where had he been? She scrabbled through unpacked boxes, hunting for stationery and a pen. *Dearest*, she wrote (who cared what anyone thought), then hesitated: *Dr. Murer?* No!

> *Dearest Edward,*
>
> *The flowers are beautiful. Won't you come see them in place? Please. I thought perhaps you would let me paint your portrait now that I have a studio.*
>
> *Yours as ever,*
>   *Jeanette Palmer*

She mailed it at once, before Cousin Effie came home. She would have had it hand delivered if she had known where he was likely to be during the day.

Yours as ever, he read, that evening. *Please.* His hand shook. He told himself to summon resolve and eschew his evening dose of laudanum but took it anyway. He spent most of the evening in reverie, pondering the note: the intimacy of its salutation, the ambiguity of its valediction. No watercolor this time, but her words, her hand, her invitation. In a general sort of way, he knew he should send a reply, but one of the effects that made opium so desirable was detachment from the urgency of things. If he felt he ought to do something, it was as good as done. He took a bedtime dose and drifted off to sleep.

Next morning, he awoke to a crushing sense of failure. The onset of a headache pressed. While the base of his skull pounded, his mind groped toward the bedside table where the laudanum bottle and dropper sat. *I thought perhaps you would let me paint your portrait.* He hated the brute fact of a headache and even more his body's clamor for an opiate anodyne. Cousin Anna had given him some willow bark. He struggled to his dresser to retrieve it and rang for Gaston. Panting from nausea, he handed over the packet and gave orders for breakfast in bed with an infusion of willow bark alongside a plain roll and the best coffee Marianne could brew. By midday, he had eaten, dozed, staved off the worst, and risen. He felt rotten. A thank-you note from Miss Pendergrast had arrived in the morning post with a specific invitation to call that afternoon for tea. He pulled himself together.

He showed up at the Rue du Fleurus late in the afternoon. Although he had stopped at his barber to have his hair and beard trimmed, he felt seedy and knew he looked haggard. The crows' feet at the corners of his eyes traced deep; the circles under them were dark. Jeanette, who had hurried to answer the door, was shocked. "You've been unwell!"

"Not exactly."

"A good thing you hadn't been, Dr. Murer," chirped Effie, nervously, "or Jeanette would have sat you down for a study. She's been drawing a convalescent all month."

"Then perhaps mine is a visage to interest you," said Edward, keeping his gaze on Jeanette. He wondered what Cornelia had been saying about him. "I could sit for a portrait."

"That's not why—! Come in," said Jeanette, with her throat constricted. "You must see your flowers."

They had placed the bouquet on a small table given temporary prominence in the middle of the room with Jeanette's portable easel beside it, holding a watercolor picture of the flowers. Edward hardly took in anything about the place—not the yellow walls, not Effie's peacock feathers nor her silken screen. He was aware only that Jeanette had bitten back hurt feelings. He put his hand under her elbow.

"Carolus will be back next week. The class begins on Monday," she said, in an effort to sound unconcerned. "I shall have to put still lifes aside. He stresses portraiture."

Edward glumly remembered Carolus-Duran's ebullience and felt seedier than ever. He withdrew his hand.

The visit was awkward but not quite a disaster. Effie tried too hard and made a nuisance of herself, but she had the wit to let Jeanette show Edward to the door.

"Will you really sit for me?" Jeanette asked, her eyes pleading. "Come on Monday. Come around two while the light is good."

She wanted his face; she longed for his presence in the room. He saw it, and although he did not quite trust it, he came.

CHAPTER FORTY-TWO

Portrait of a Man

After their first sitting, he came four times a week punctually at two. The punctuality mattered to him more than to her; it was a means of holding on. Effie chaperoned from the far end of the long studio, where she made a show of writing or sewing with her back to them. Her tact and the size of the room gave them a kind of privacy, enough to have allowed a lovely veiled dalliance if Edward could have roused himself. His shame over the prostitute had ebbed with time, aided by his doses of laudanum. Now he tried to break away from the drug again but knew better than to stop all at once. With ever lower doses, there was nothing to blind him to his chance of happiness slipping away, to the old darkness closing in. The black dog growled.

Jeanette struggled with the portrait. Always, a wistful part of her mind wondered what had gone wrong between her and Edward; sometimes a more compassionate part of her was abashed to see how cruelly something gnawed at him. Her artist's mind, meanwhile, was absorbed in the search for how to portray the layers of mystery in his face. She wanted to tell truths with her brush, but how could she when she didn't understand what she saw? And with Effie in the room, it was impossible to ask the questions that mattered: Where have you been? Do you still love me? What's wrong?

It chastened Jeanette to have so little power over Edward. She quit risking rejection and stuck doggedly to the task, but the picture threatened never to be finished, never to be good. Yet he kept coming back, one week, two weeks, three weeks, four. As she worked and failed, worked and failed, she came to understand his persistence as an abiding loyalty, perhaps even a bid for some kind of solace. She left off trying to explain him to the world and aimed only to capture forever some image of him for herself. On the last Monday in October, near the end of an afternoon's work, she looked down to pick up a dab of raw umber on her smallest brush. When her eyes returned to the canvas, she caught her breath.

"It's finished." Even so tiny a dab would be one too many. Her tone was so hushed that Effie did not hear her.

Edward did. He sat up straighter. "May I see?" He came around and, from behind her, studied the intelligent, pensive face on the canvas, the lowered shoulders, which hinted at weariness but not defeat. Far from stripping him bare, she had guarded his privacy; the man in the portrait harbored a banked force.

"I am honored," he murmured. Unaware that he did so, he laid his hand on her shoulder. "You have painted me finer than I am."

"I paint what I see—and what I sense." Jeanette shifted her

weight so that the back of her head rested against him. "It took long enough, I'm afraid." Nervous modesty could not hide an equally nervous, but growing, conviction that the results were good.

Roused by the stir at the other end of the room, Effie watched them for a moment. "Is it done?" she asked.

Edward dropped his hand.

"Come look," said Jeanette.

"Why, you've made it a sad picture. It's sadder than your studies of Signora Antonielli! Well, I shouldn't say that, of course. It's very handsome, but you should smile more next time, Dr. Murer."

"I'll try to remember that," said Edward, with just a trace of his old humor.

Jeanette squeezed her eyes shut in embarrassment. "Here, give me a minute to clean up, and let's take a walk," she said.

When she and Edward were on the street (Effie had the good sense not to join them), Jeanette said, "It wasn't meant to be sad."

"No."

Nevertheless, Effie had spoken truth: It was a sad picture, a sad face, profoundly sad. Jeanette knew it, and still an inward part of her rejoiced at the painting's completion. Wishing that bugs were not crawling under his skin, Edward offered her his arm. She took it and walked at first with the lazy contented woolliness that comes after great exertion. Once or twice, she spoke on the few blocks leading up to the Luxembourg Garden. He made no reply.

When they were safely inside the gates of the park, she let her hand slip down to his and pulled him over to the side of the wide main path. The leather of their gloves blunted touch. She squeezed hard and looked at him intently, not to observe but to try to reach him. "Edward, what's wrong?"

He held on to her hand; but after meeting her gaze, he looked away and stared over her head, through an avenue of yellowing trees to a patch of green lawn. She felt his arm jerk. "I'm soul-sick," he said. "Sick in body, sick in mind."

"What does that *mean?*" she asked, with an unaccountable vehemence.

That I need brown powder, he thought, irritably, and let go of her hand. He felt it touch his arm and looked back at her face. He steered them into motion again, trying to pull his thoughts together.

He was disappearing into himself. "Cousin Effie thinks you disapprove of my studying nudes," she said. There, she had laid out the conflict she feared most.

He looked blank. "That has nothing to do with—" Or maybe it had, indirectly, a long time ago. "Jeanette, forgive me if I'm old-fashioned about such things. Your art is your art, and, of course, you must train for it."

Her heart swelled as it always did when he said such things, until she realized he was dismissing the matter as trivial. "Then what?" she demanded.

He did not answer. On a side path, he took them to a secluded bench, where he sat, bent forward, head down, rolling his thumbs in front of him. He watched an ant drag a fragment of leaf, skittering through an obstacle course of gravel. "Jeanette, what I ought to tell you is that I'm an opium-eater."

She froze. As surely as the real man dispelled her wispy daydreams with his solidity whenever she was in his company, this revelation—unlooked-for, wholly new—banished all her conjectures. She sat motionless until, daringly, she reached over to trace a gloved forefinger in the hollow of the cheek she had studied for weeks; his jaw was clenched. He tuned his face three-quarters to look up at her. The finger paused, just above his beard. He squeezed his eyes shut against tears and drew the hand around to his lips, kissing her fingertips fervently; the pressure made her tremulous inside. The scrape of a boot on the path reminded her belatedly that they were in public. Hastily she pulled her hand away. The chuckle with which he relinquished it was bitter. "I'm sorry," he said.

"No. I've wanted you to kiss me," she said, forthrightly.

"Edward—oh, why, Edward, why opium? Is this what you wouldn't tell me about the war?"

"There are a thousand things I will never tell you about the war or about myself, Miss Palmer. Can't you see I only soil you? You should leave. I don't do you or myself or anyone else alive any good."

"Stop it!" she cried. "I won't leave until I know what's been happening."

"All right, then, yes. Union doctors gave me laudanum; they gave it to everyone. It's a wonderful drug. It stops pain and coughs and—" He waved a hand and left unsaid, *the runs*. "It kills memory; it makes you feel grand, up in the clouds." His yearning was frighteningly evident until he added, "But its wonders come with a price. It ruins digestion, it makes you itch. Your body itches, your mind itches; you need more and more of it just to feel normal. I've gone off it before. If I could again . . ."

She waited.

"Jeanette, I've killed men, and I've withheld death when they begged me for its kindness. I don't deserve to live; I don't even deserve to die."

Dear lord, she thought, what on earth am I supposed to do now? On this very day, with the portrait done, the more she learned, the less she understood, and the less anything else in the world mattered.

Shaking, he scrabbled in a pocket, found a handkerchief, and raised it to his face. Eyes shut tight, he panted, face to face with the worst of his revenants—the Reb whose entrails had coiled out into the mud, a bloody, trampled mess no longer human but able still to whimper in a thin wail, *Kill me, some'ody; kill me, some'ody.* Over and over again, *kill me, some'ody. Mercy.* His cloudy eye had looked into Edward's with a stare of puzzlement at his plight and the pain he was in too much shock to feel; but Edward had saved his last bullet in case he needed it for something other than mercy. He had run and kept on running. Fifteen years later, on a park bench in Paris, he managed one more time, just barely, to push his pursuer back down. Eyes open again, gaping, he pulled the handkerchief down over his mouth.

"Edward."

He became aware of Jeanette beside him, badly frightened.

"Are you all right?"

"I told you, leave."

"No!" She knew little else; but her heart told her that if she left now, she would never see him again.

He wiped his mouth, stuffed his handkerchief away, and closed his eyes. He slumped back while his hand covered hers on the bench between them. He was hardly aware he held it, though she was, acutely. Speech was too hard; all his effort must go into enduring from one moment to the next.

Her mind raced. If she needed help, whose? She was fairly certain he would not consent to go back to the studio, not with Cousin Effie there. The Renicks? Winkie! For a wild moment, the thought of Mr. Winkham flashed as a godsend, but, of course, she had no way to reach him.

"I've broken down before." Edward spoke more calmly and looked over at her. His rattled nerves cried out for laudanum, but he could still master himself enough to delay a dose and try to think. Jeanette lacked Sophie's calm motherly authority, Sophie's assurance; but her young skin, the roundness of her limbs, her vitality, all proclaimed life to be good. False claims in Edward's opinion, yet still, in some attenuated way, he was glad of the illusion, grateful to have her beside him. "If I make less of a spectacle of myself, will you sit with me here a while?"

"Till the end of time if need be."

A sweetness altered his face ever so slightly. As his agitation subsided, Jeanette's immediate fears were allayed, though she remained unable to do more than simply let what happened happen. Only when he realized with a start that he held her hand and tried to withdraw it did she act. She held on.

"You are not yourself," she said, lacing her fingers through his.

"God, how I wish that were true."

By the time he walked her back to the studio, he would to the casual eye have looked no worse than many a morose, dyspeptic *homme d'affaires*. To Jeanette, he seemed to have lost a layer of protection, to have worsened into the next stage of an illness.

"Will you take a cab and go straight home?" she pleaded. (Oh, he would, he certainly would, straight to the brown glass bottle on his bedside table.) "And come back tomorrow. Promise."

"I will go home," he promised, and nothing more.

⁂

CHAPTER FORTY-THREE

Need

Back at his apartment, Edward took half an ounce of laudanum, not a high dose for a heavy user, but as much as he ever took at one time. Even with its aid, he could not wholly escape horror. He took another dose before going to bed. When he awoke nauseated on Tuesday morning, he took still more, the first time he had started a day with opium since he had left Cincinnati. He carried the tincture with him to the laboratory. All day long, a drug-induced indifference contended with his underlying despair. He skipped lunch. He was costive. He shrank from any thought of going to the Rue du Fleurus. In the evening, he sat with a letter from Jeanette unopened.

After posting the letter Tuesday morning, Jeanette had gone to class. All through October, working among Carolus's chosen few had countered her worries about the portrait, about herself, about Edward. But it was no refuge that day. In the afternoon, she fretted, worrying aloud about whether Dr. Murer had made it home safely, whether he was ill, what would happen if he took too much laudanum. For once, Effie's virginal encounters with the darker sides of life offered no perspective or comfort. "Oh, my. Poor man," she kept saying. "This does change things."

"It changes nothing!" insisted Jeanette. She kept her most nagging fear to herself: that he would simply desert her, that he already had.

On Wednesday, she sent another note and wondered what else she could do to reach him. *Men have died from time to time and worms have eaten them, but not for love,* Amy was fond of quoting to the lovelorn. *Nor will you, my girl,* she generally added. *Get to work.* What would Amy know? Jeanette went on to Carolus's class with a tightened stomach; she only half attended to balancing masses and shadows, to getting the tones right. Her mind wandered. Once she found herself on the verge of tears. If a milksop like Abigail McLeod could elope, she angrily told herself, the least she could do was track down Edward, compel him to speak to her, feel his touch again. Her mind flew back again and again to overblown imaginary scenes. Impulsively, after class, she walked to the Parc Monceau. The building with his address checked her by its suave anonymity. She could hardly loiter on the doorstep. When she realized a man had noticed her on her second pass along the block, she left.

On Friday, when Edward awoke yet again to physical nausea and moral disgust, he lay with his eyes closed. He had failed to obey Jeanette's summons; he had been unable to read her letter; he could not even remember on which day he had gone to pieces. His stupidity all fall haunted him. He had just enough grit left to bare his teeth at the snarling black dog. A nerve specialist was what he needed.

He had met a man named Latour at the Renicks' house in June
and gone to hear him lecture. One lecture only, after which Edward
shunned further talk of madmen and illness. Now he would ask for
an appointment as a patient. He would seek out Jeanette. He lay in
his darkness, not doubting his path but lacking the will to rouse
himself until, finally, a spasm of nausea drove him to sit up for at
least a low dose of laudanum. Once up, he rang for strong coffee and
a roll. He forced himself to eat breakfast and, somewhat to his own
surprise, actually wrote Dr. Latour. His second thoughts after dis-
patching the request didn't matter; it was on its way. At midday,
Jeanette found him waiting for her on the Passage Stanislas.

He had never looked more forbidding, more hollow-eyed, more
withdrawn. Her joy at sight of him was tinged by fright. As she came
toward him, her face moved him as little else could in his present
despondency.

"Is there somewhere we could go for lunch?" he asked.

"Père Cagniard's," said Miss Reade, stopping beside them. Edward mechanically lifted his hat. "If you join a throng, it's the same
as a chaperon, Palmer. Follow me." She gave them a knowing look.
"Take your time."

Jeanette colored a little. "It's the neighborhood café. All of Carolus's students go there, even the girls at lunch sometimes. Will
that do?"

"I'd be pleased to see you in your world."

It was the kind of thing Edward said, but he sounded so abstracted that Jeanette doubted that he meant it this time. "We won't
really be able to talk."

"I don't have a lot to say."

Actually, you've got a lot to explain, she thought, suddenly rebel-
lious to the point of anger now that she had him back.

The restaurant was noisy; artists' gear propped against chair legs
could trip the unwary. By the time they entered, Miss Reade had
allowed her table to fill. With a restaurateur's quick appraisal of what

a new customer required, M. Cagniard found them a small table for two in the back room. He recommended the *plat du jour*, promised to bring some good wine, and left them to themselves.

"Am I allowed to ask where have you been?" asked Jeanette.

"Doping."

She shrank down and bit the inside of her lower lip. "Edward . . ."

Père Cagniard reappeared with two glasses and a bottle, which he uncorked. Edward took the ritual sip and approved. "Unless you would rather have lemonade?" he asked, belatedly, after the *patron* had left.

"In this crowd?" Jeanette tried to joke.

"Very well, then—*santé.*"

"*Santé.*" Their glasses *tinked*, and Jeanette added, hesitantly, "To the recovery of your very good health, Edward."

"I'm going to try, Jeanette."

On his way over, Edward had wondered what he hoped to accomplish by seeking her out. Now, for a moment, he felt that contentment might simply be a matter of beholding her face across from him. If she had been in a lovestruck trance, it might have been, for a while. But as hard as she tried to meet his gaze steadily, she was filled with uncertainties and questions. His chin sank. With delicate fingertips pushing its base, he turned his wineglass on the tablecloth. There was still precision in his movements.

Jeanette waited. Around them, conversation hummed in the jovial, chivying tones of clever young people taking a break from work. Nobody noticed the silence at Jeanette and Edward's obscure table, not even the waitress who slapped down a basket of bread in passing. Jeanette tore off a piece.

"Bread?" she asked, nudging the basket toward Edward. He glanced up as if startled, then shook his head. She took a bite; she was hungry. "Is there something . . . ?" She did not know how to finish her question: on your mind? that I can do?

"I had been planning to ask you to marry me."

She stopped chewing. "And now you are not."

"How can I?"

Tears of chagrin filled Jeanette's eyes. "And how can I ask, why not?" she choked out. "It wouldn't be ladylike!" She grasped the edge of the table to push her chair back and flee.

"Jeanette!" Leaning forward, he clutched at her hand before she could rise. "Don't go yet. Please, not yet."

"Why should I stay?" she demanded in a shaken voice.

For answer, Edward could only gaze at her. "I can't think of a single reason." His bleakness had told Cornelia Renick much, but not all. It told Jeanette nothing that she could have put into words, but enough. Little by little, her spine relaxed, her shoulders dropped.

"I'm no bargain," said Edward, "but thank you."

"Leaving me out of it, Edward, what is it you need?"

"If we leave you out of it, there's nothing left."

The tears in the corner of her eyes flooded again. "Then what can I do?"

His hands went back to the wineglass. He hung his head. "I hated breaking down in front of you the other day."

"It was hard on both of us. But, Edward, it was worse for me when you just disappeared again, so much worse."

"Was it?"

"Of course, it was! I didn't know what had happened. I imagined, oh, *dire* things and—" Her voice became small. "I thought maybe you just didn't want to see or hear from me."

"Always I want to see you, Jeanette, always—except that sometimes now I can't desire a thing, not a single damn thing. And when my mind is clear at all, it's full of shame."

"I worried that you had taken too much laudanum, Edward. Doctors prescribe opium for pain and nerves, I know that; but I also know that too much can kill you."

"And you would mind that?"

"Oh, how can you ask?"

* * *

Unsure until he got there whether he would keep his appointment with the nerve specialist, Edward went. At the end of the initial consultation, Dr. Latour told him to come back and prescribed a regimen of laudanum sufficient to maintain his equilibrium while they probed further. A few sessions later, he offered the opinion that Edward was neither degenerate nor insane but cautioned that a return to full health would take time. He warned against solitude and recommended a gradual reduction of the drug on a fixed schedule. Edward dutifully cut his dosage by small increments and tried to believe that past failures to follow exactly this course at his own initiative implied nothing about the chance of success under supervision.

After the first, lost week of neglect, he did not disappear again. With Dr. Latour's approval, he adjusted the timing of his daily intake of laudanum to be at his most calm and alert in the late afternoon, which was the best time for him to fence or to pay the social calls that were intended to keep him from brooding too much. Effie knew always to be at home by four thirty, when he was likely to stop in. She had wrestled with her conscience, wondering whether she should discourage the attachment; but Christian compassion, her romantic heart, and a disinclination to take strong actions in almost any circumstance held her in check. If any of Jeanette's friends were visiting, Edward was soon gone; but when the two ladies were alone, he might join them at the Duval restaurant for supper. Compared to Cincinnati eateries, it was gourmet dining, he said. Sometimes he remembered to ask them to go with him to a better restaurant, which took up more time. Seeing Jeanette was the filament holding him together, he believed—until it no longer sufficed.

In the wet gloom of November evenings, he shivered. More than once as he sneaked an extra dose, he caught himself thinking that if only he could reach Sophie's kindly hands—! If only—then what?

Half-felt longing was not even an emotion, much less a prescription for what might help, yet the shadow of memory held a clue. He knew that the one thing he could still be said wholeheartedly to enjoy was a steaming shower and a massage from Ahmed after one of the rounds he doggedly pursued at M. Artaud's *salle d'armes*.

Toward the end of the month, he raised the question of a rest cure. Dr. Latour agreed it might be helpful and recommended a private hospital outside Paris. No, said Edward; he needed the sun. Dr. Latour tapped his pen thoughtfully. In that case, he had a suggestion: a colleague, who like himself had studied medicine at Montpellier, Dr. Leon Aubanel. Aubanel was deeply interested in the workings of the mind and took a few residential patients into his care at a small sanatorium beside a thermal spring in the town of L'Estaque, west of Marseilles. Latour would make inquiries about an opening.

Edward, too, made inquiries. Little by little, Cornelia had surmised a great deal about his condition without ever pressing; now he asked her whether she had ever chanced to hear of Dr. Aubanel when she was in Provence. She had not but set Marius to checking. In a few days a report came back: somewhat idiosyncratic, but respected, no quack. If his health required such a place, Cornelia advised him to go.

Toward the end of the month, Effie brought word from the McAll Mission that Mr. Winkham, whose studies ended in December, had been offered a post at the Royal London Hospital, starting in January. "Oh, no," said Jeanette. "I mean, it's good for him, but . . ." She seldom saw him but thought of him as a friend. His departure would leave a hole in her Paris. She and Effie invited him for tea on the last day of November, a Sunday, and asked Amy, Sonja, and the Reade sisters to join them to make it more festive, along with Edward and a few other men to keep Winkie from feeling engulfed by women. Rather to Jeanette's surprise, Edward accepted.

He went early to settle into obscurity before the room filled.

When Winkie came over to his corner to shake hands, Edward could practically see his train of thought as he connected constricted pupils to their discussion of Miss Dolson. With a slight jerk of his head, Edward blinked confirmation.

Before he had need to say any more, Jeanette and Amy joined them, laughing.

"Winkie," said Jeanette, "Amy has had an idea. When I told her I didn't have so much as a sketch of you to remember you by—"

"I proposed Round Robin. Now, don't look skeptical, lad," said Amy. "All you have to do is pose at your ease." She turned to the rest of the room. "Pencils out, everyone! Round Robin."

The game involved sitting in a circle, passing sketchbooks around in one direction and changing seats in the other. Played at a fast pace, it elicited much noise, scrambling, and rapid drawing.

"You can sit it out with Cousin Effie," said Jeanette, in a low voice to Edward, "but please stay."

He nodded. To the extent that he could feel anything these days, he was touched by her solicitude.

Later, while most of the players compared their pictures, Winkie pulled Edward aside. "I don't know why I'm telling you this, Dr. Murer—he'd hate me for it—but I've heard at last from Robbie Dolson. Well, I do know why: I want you to know he's going straight, at least I think so. He wrote that he knew I'd be returning to England this winter and wanted to get back in touch while he knew where to find me. It was a good letter."

"I'm glad to hear it," said Edward, who did not, in fact, care one way or another. His head hurt. "And Miss Dolson?"

"Ah. He didn't say much. Said where they're living there's a garden and she spends her time painting in it when she can."

Not all of Edward's perceptiveness had been swallowed by his illness. "Worried?"

"I wish I knew more. I'm thinking of going down to visit them just to, well . . ."

"Down?" A feeble hope stirred in Edward's mind. "Forgive me, may I ask—somewhere south of here?"

"Italy. Look, I shouldn't have spoken; I'll say no more."

"It's not the Dolsons I'm thinking of, Winkham. I don't have to tell you what kind of shape I'm in. I've put myself under Maurice Latour's care."

"Couldn't do better," said Winkie, who clearly wondered where this was going.

"So I thought, but it's not enough. He's referred me to a colleague in Provence, a man who offers a private rest cure at a thermal spring. If you're traveling south, I beg you to route yourself through Marseilles and let me go that far with you." Edward closed his eyes tight and rubbed the brow between them. "I need someone to see that I get there. If you came as far as L'Estaque, it would give you a chance to look over a private French sanatorium."

"Busman's holiday."

Edward felt himself being scrutinized by a physician's eye.

"Let me think about it," said Winkie, soberly.

"It's probably asking too much."

"I didn't say that. When would you want to go?"

"Whenever you say. Immediately, tomorrow. I can wait a week or two; but if I don't go soon, I never will."

"Go where?" asked Jeanette, approaching them. "You look conspiratorial." At their seriousness, her face went from facetious to apprehensive.

"Jeanette," said Edward, who had just enough consciousness of circumstances to protect Winkie from having to say anything about the Dolsons, "I have asked Dr. Winkham to accompany me on a journey to Provence."

"When the Renicks go for Christmas?" She knew the guess was wrong even before she finished. If he were going with the Renicks, he wouldn't take Winkie.

"Sooner. Right away."

"Oh!" Jeanette fixed her eye on Edward's. Her face said wordlessly, You hadn't told me.

"Ah, if you'll excuse me, Miss Palmer," said Winkie, backing away from palpable trouble, "I think I'd better be off. Many thanks for the afternoon. I'll just speak to Miss Pendergrast."

"Let me get back to you," he muttered to Edward.

Mutely, Edward handed him his card. As Winkie stepped away, Edward said, "Jeanette, I would have told you first—"

"Funny, I thought of Winkie myself, that day in the park."

Edward's color, which was already bad, could not drain more, but he looked more pinched than ever.

"Oh, don't let's quarrel. Excuse me, I must play hostess; the others are leaving, too."

Jeanette turned on her heel, pulled her face into an artificial smile, and went to the door, where Amy and Sonja were wrapping themselves in shawls, and Winkie in his overcoat was bidding Effie good-bye.

"Don't be hard on him," said Winkie, in a low voice, taking Jeanette's hands between his. "It was something I said that brought it up. I think I've found Robbie and Emily."

"Robbie and Emily—?"

"I'll tell you more later. Meanwhile, Dr. Murer is suffering misery neither you nor I can imagine. Go to him." He patted Jeanette's hand. "And go easy on yourself, doctor's orders. Them as loves hurts. Don't I know."

Crushed, detached by the drug from both anger and regret, wanting only to leave, yet too undone to move, Edward stared at the floor. He knew he had bungled again. He was cut by Jeanette's words. He hardly knew what to make of it when, as soon as the others were gone, she came over to where he stood, threw her arms around his neck, and, sobbing, laid her face against his shoulder. Whatever she meant, he responded by folding his arms around her and holding her close with his cheek resting on the top of her head. The two of

them swayed, body to body. It was not the embrace either one of
them had dreamed of—too disappointed, too apologetic. Effie scurried to the other end of the room and pretended not to see. At the
sound of her movement, Jeanette pulled back, placed her hands flat
on Edward's chest, and said through her tears, "Winkie says you
must go, and he'll come with you."

CHAPTER FORTY-FOUR

A Journey South

For a journey that was scheduled to require all day and most of
the night, Edward engaged a first-class sleeping compartment;
in the belief that all railway food was execrable, Marianne packed
lavish hampers for him to carry with him. Winkie, who had never
traveled in such physical comfort, did his best to be pleasant with a
moody companion. Nevertheless, to Edward, the trip was an ordeal.
In his state of health, the best he could do to repay Winkham's
generosity was to ask mechanical questions about his hospital experiences and listen to what he had to say about the current state of
French medicine. To survive the endless jiggling, noise, and over-
heated air of the compartment, Edward sank into torpor. Laudanum
helped; Winkie controlled the dosage. As was to be expected in
winter, there were long delays along the way. They were scheduled
to reach Marseilles around five thirty, before sunup; but when a
porter roused them next morning, light was already in the sky. He
assured them they had time for a shave and breakfast.

As they finally pulled into Marseilles from the north, they passed a great deal of new construction sprawling up the hillsides above the port basin. Despite pastel plaster and terra-cotta roof tiles, it seemed as raw as Cincinnati to Edward. In the huge, midtown Gare Saint-Charles, the usual station noises thundered in his brain. Local trains for L'Estaque left from a different station, which required a cab ride. In the end, although they had only fifteen miles to go, it was after eleven o'clock when Edward and Winkie, along with a very few other passengers, descended onto the little L'Estaque station platform. The driver sent by Dr. Aubanel identified them at once: two tired, pale foreigners in northern clothes. As they followed him out into bright midday sun, Edward squinted. He wanted to feel gladdened by red geraniums and overgrown nasturtiums still in bloom, by conical cedars and a spreading Aleppo pine between him and a cluster of houses opposite; but the ugly modern realities of a railway viaduct and telegraph poles spoiled the effect.

"Ah, look this way," said Winkie.

He turned Edward to where roofs, stone outcroppings, and tree-tops dropped to the harbor. Beyond, the blue Gulf of Marseilles stretched to the wedge of Chateau d'If in the distance. It was picturesque and preferable to cold, never-ending drizzle but still not Edward's idea of paradise. A few nearby factory smokestacks rose as high as the village's yellow church tower, and above, all around, the rocky limestone hills looked savage, the scrub brush dry. He wondered whether he had exchanged a brooding, glum nightmare for a glaring, harsh one. In the open carriage that took them out to Dr. Aubanel's *maison santé*, he closed his eyes against the sun he had ridden more than five hundred miles to find.

A quarter hour later, the carriage turned up an avenue of pine trees that climbed through an olive grove. At its end, two ancient, massive olive trees stood sentinel near a seventeenth-century house on the shallow steps of which two calamondin orange trees grew in large baskets and bore fruits in various stages of ripening. A few creamy out-of-season blossoms perfumed the air.

They were greeted on the doorstep by the housekeeper, who expressed sympathy over the lateness of the train. She conducted them to Edward's bedroom, where wine and biscuits had been set out beside a small, fragrant fire of cedar logs. A lavatory was down the hall. The midday meal would be served at one thirty, she told them, but first Dr. Aubanel wished to see them in his office. "Please bring the patient down when you are refreshed," she said to Winkie, while Edward sat hunched on the edge of his bed. Winkie did as he was told.

Dr. Aubanel's office, on the ground floor at the back of the house, was a scholar's study, its floor-to-ceiling shelves filled with books, antique scientific instruments, and piles of journals. From behind his desk, the doctor came around to greet them as a courteous host. At first glance, he appeared almost diffident, but his handshake was firm and his eye sharp. He was glad, he said, that they had arrived in time to visit the spring before lunch.

Outside, he led them up the hill to a newly built pavilion that resembled a Greco-Roman temple of marble columns under a domed roof. "When I discovered the spring," he said, "it was surrounded by the broken remains of an ancient mosaic pool, which I have had restored. From shards of piping, it appears that hot water was also carried down to a private villa in the Roman era."

"Was it a Roman spa?" asked Winkie.

"*Non, monsieur*, the spring is too small. As you will see, only enough water circulates through the pool to serve one or two patients at a time. It is unnecessary to drink the sulfuric water, by the way. It may be that a mineral virtue absorbed through the skin augments the spring's healing effect, but the primary benefit derives from immersion in its warmth surrounded by nature. I believe that the body forever remembers the all-embracing Eden of the womb."

Winkie raised skeptical eyebrows.

"*Non, Dr. Winkham, je ne suis pas fou*," chuckled Aubanel. "The mind is a great mystery, but so is the body. If we reawaken a primal sense of bodily ease, then the mind is free to form new habits. The spring is not magic, it but aids other therapies. In your case, M. Murer, it will help alleviate your cravings as your body adjusts to decreases in opium."

Edward felt glum.

At the porch of the bathhouse, a clean-shaven man in his twenties emerged, rubbing his damp hair with a towel. Dr. Aubanel introduced him as M. Valabrègue. He smiled pleasantly, shook hands without a word, and took Edward's arm. Edward tensed. Valabrègue glanced at Dr. Aubanel, who nodded. Edward was turned around gently but firmly for the second time that day; and for the second time, he beheld the Mediterranean, now wide across the horizon.

"By Jove, that's fine!" said Winkie.

Below them spread the rest of the estate. Dr. Aubanel explained that much of it was a working farm. Rabbits and chickens were raised for meat and eggs. A small herd of goats supplied milk for cheesemaking. Manure from the animals enriched a large vegetable garden. "We must find what you like to do, *monsieur.* Absorption in manual labor turns the mind from cankered thoughts. Exhaustion destroys health, but a pleasant fatigue brings rest."

"I tried fencing."

"*Ah, monsieur,* fencing requires focus and aggression. What you sought from opium was calm and release. For these, pure air, nourishing food, steady work, and healthy exercise will be more effective."

"*Mens sana in corpore sano?*" asked Edward.

"You are in the Romans' Provincia, *monsieur,*" said Dr. Aubanel. "We are all classicists here."

"That first afternoon, he had us both bathe in the spring just for pleasure. He knew, of course, that I was vetting the place," said

Winkie, a week later, when he reported on the visit to Jeanette. He brought with him a note from Edward.

"And is it good, Winkie?"

"If I hadn't thought so, Dr. Murer would have left with me, I promise you that. One part of the regimen is going to be hard on you, though, Miss Palmer. He is allowed no visitors for a month and no mail."

"What!"

"I'm afraid this note is the last you'll have from him until sometime into the new year."

"Can't I even write him back?"

"Not yet. The idea is to insulate the patient from all outside cares while he breaks away from old patterns and reshapes his life."

"Oh, but it's wrong, wrong!"

"It's only for a month. Thereafter, he'll begin fitting back gradually into the larger world as a new man."

"But what if I want the old one back?"

"You want him the way I saw him last May, Miss Palmer, not as he is now."

Jeanette nodded, stroking the note. "And Emily," she sighed, "how did you find her?"

"Not as well I could wish, nor so bad as I had feared. I was lucky enough to spend an afternoon with her." Winkie's luck had come at the small cost of having to make his own way to the *palazzo* where the Dolsons were staying (Robbie had failed to meet his packet boat from Marseilles and was absent from the mansion when a gondola set him down at the entrance). Despite an address on the Grand Canal, the palace had weeds growing in cracks outside, and damp stained its interior walls. It was owned by an Italian countess who had gathered around herself a following of artists, would-be revolutionaries, and parasites, none of whom paid the slightest attention to Winkie when a servant led him through halls of faded grandeur into a warren of ever smaller back rooms. The Dolsons' lodgings were on the top floor, two bare rooms and a sagging balcony. Robbie later said that it all made good copy.

After depositing his carpetbag, Winkie went in search of Emily. He found her seated at her easel in an obscure corner of an overgrown garden behind the palace. She extended a hand, which he took gratefully between both of his.

"I'd never have guessed there was this much open land in the whole of the city," he said, "nor this much greenery."

"In winter, too. You ought to have seen it in summer," she replied, in mild reproach at his not having been there.

"Ah," he said. "I wish I could have."

She withdrew her hand.

"I see you are painting." He also saw that she was still drugged, but not to the point of being dazed. "Are you able to work here?"

"I can work anywhere."

Gradually, she warmed to his familiar presence with the detached, sad sweetness he had known half a lifetime. She treated his coming to visit Robbie as the most natural thing in the world. When Robbie finally appeared, he, too, acted as if it were only right and proper for Wee Willie Winkie to bob in his wake one more time, although now he was warier, watching perhaps for a sign of just how much his old friend knew. For his part, Mr. Winkham—or Dr. Winkham, as he now had the right to be called—bridled more often at gibes and snubs than before but continued to swallow his pride out of habit. And he was careful to say nothing about having accompanied Dr. Murer south, nor to give any other hint that he knew why the Dolsons had fled Paris.

Back in Jeanette's studio, he said, "Before I left, Emily asked me to bring you this."

It was a densely worked watercolor, a pensive self-portrait curled around two sides of the picture to frame a garden in which grotesque faces peered out from the foliage. At the bottom was painted the motto, *Come buy, come buy is still their cry.*

"Oh, Emily, what fruits have you eaten?"

Chin down, Winkie turned his hat in his hand as he often did while making up his mind. He looked up at her with grief and compassion. "The same as your good man."

Jeanette clutched his arm. "I knew she took chloral sometimes. Laudanum, too?" She tried to sort through flashes of memory.

"Off and on. Not much in Paris, I think. So Dr. Murer never told you?"

"Did he know?"

"He saw it at that fatal garden party. Now, don't go blaming him for not telling you, Miss Palmer. I'd say he held his tongue in kindness to me and Emily. We're all owed our privacy."

"Oh, Winkie, it's been a longer road for you than for me."

"And I'm sorry you have to walk it now. Strange though, I'm not sorry to have a companion for a mile or two. Hurts being all alone."

Weeping, Jeanette put her arms around him to hold and comfort him while he held and comforted her.

"Remember," he said, before he left, "The road's longest and worst for them."

After Winkie left, Jeanette opened Edward's note. *Beloved*, it began. His lodestar, he called her. He asked for nothing. He promised nothing. *When next we are together—Jeanette, my hopes extend no further than that we may be so. Until then believe me, I am your unworthy, your ever devoted, Edward.*

When she had finished crying, Jeanette moped. She pined for days. She sent a letter down to him to be held until he could receive it and enclosed a watercolor of his most recent bouquet. Over and over, she sang to herself a song popular among the girls at Vassar her freshman year: *We sat by the river, you and I / In the sweet summer time long ago.* Her mind wore smooth certain memories from the perfect afternoon they had spent together by the Seine, early in September.

> *We threw two leaflets you and I,*
> *To the river as it wandered on,*
> *And one was rent and left to die,*
> *And the other floated forward alone.*

She walked along the quays, absorbed in thought when the weather was dismal enough to fit her mood; sometimes when pale winter sunlight shone, she crossed over to the Tuileries Garden. If their bench was empty, as it often was in winter, she sat a while. She went more often to the Luxembourg Garden. She sorted and resorted her preparatory sketches for Edward's portrait. She wished she had painted Edward looking directly at her, but it was truer the way it was. She had painted him with his mind beyond her ken.

CHAPTER FORTY-FIVE

Christmas 1879

Through all her December unhappiness, Jeanette worked as much as the shortening days allowed. She was nagged by a fear that it was monstrously cold of her to forget Edward for hours at a time, as increasingly she could; perhaps she didn't really love him, or not enough. At the same time, too much of what came from her hand was dogged and uninspired; she frittered away effort on trivial distractions and marginal scrawls—it was bad enough to take those walks, worse to end a day's work with chaff. To stave off dread that she was not really an artist, she never missed class. She laid out still lifes in her own studio and dedicated two hours a day faithfully to Carolus's outside assignments. At night, she modeled in clay. She obtained the necessary permissions to work in oils at the Louvre, where she began by copying a Dutch interior of receding doorways: one unpeopled room opening into the next. In spite of the prohibition, she wrote Edward a short, decorated Christmas letter and enclosed it with a note requesting Dr. Aubanel to give it to him: *He needs to know he is remembered.*

As the month drew to its end, Jeanette and Effie prepared for their second Christmas in Paris. It helped to have a child to focus on; for Angelica, who had long since lost her innocence, still had a five-year-old's capacity for wonder. On December twenty-third, in hopes of dispelling her own loneliness, Jeanette tagged along when Effie took Angelica to a marionette show in the park. On the way home, they bought an orange from a vendor who pricked out A*N*G*E*L*I*C*A on the rind in blue ink. When he held it out to her, the little girl hesitated in disbelief, then clutched it gleefully to her chest. She shook her head emphatically, *non*, when Effie offered to carry the fruit in a string bag. "Very well, then, carry it in yours," said Effie, magically pulling a miniature blue *filet* out of Angelica's pocket. Hanky Bunny was never a bigger success.

When they dropped Angelica off at the Rue Madame, Amy reported that Sonja and La Grecque were planning to take the child to Christmas Eve midnight mass.

"I told them it was a ridiculous plan. It's bad enough that the little blighter will be up for the *réveillon*; she at least ought to have a nap beforehand."

"Are you going to services?" asked Jeanette.

"Probably not."

"Oh, but you must!" said Effie. "Your father would expect you to."

"My reverend father expects me to trek across the river Seine, be it ever so frosty or dismal a night, to observe the Nativity of our Lord in the chapel of the British Embassy. We all delude ourselves."

Effie tsked. "We'll come with you. I'm sure Isobel and Miss Reade will join us."

Accordingly, on Christmas Eve, when Jeanette and Effie stopped by the Rue Madame to leave a glassy amber sheet of caramelized sugar for Angelica to shatter at the *réveillon*, they picked up Amy and went on to the Rue d'Assas. After the Anglican service, all five women returned from the embassy chapel to Amy and Sonja's studio, where other artists from the building had already swelled the company to more than twenty people and loaded the table with oysters, cooked eel, wine, and sweets. Angelica, looking pretty in a new pinafore, was shy of Mabel Reade but otherwise dodged her way among the grown-ups, shrieking with laughter and stealing food, completely at her ease. By now, she knew—and was certainly known by—everyone in the building. When the candy sheet was brought out, her destructive greed made quick work of breaking it into pieces to suck.

In contrast to her daughter, La Grecque hung watchfully on the edges, setting out dishes and speaking to no one. To all appearances, she ate nothing, although, touchingly, she had added to the table an Italian nut-and-citrus-filled *panpepato*, made on her orders by Agostino of Les Deux Hélènes. In the midst of all the eating, drinking, and merriment, Angelica fell fast asleep on the floor. After almost stumbling over her, Jeanette scooped her up and carried her to the kitchen. There she found La Grecque and Sonja quarreling in Italian. Andrea's stance expressed scornful defiance with all her dramatic skill.

"*Excusez-moi!*" said Jeanette.

The antagonists swung around to face her.

"*Qu'est-ce que voulez-vous?*" growled Sonja. What do you want?

"Angelica—"

La Grecque shoved past Sonja to receive the child but not before she closed her fist with a finger raised at Sonja's face and spat. Sonja grabbed for her wrist.

"Leave her alone, Sonja! It's Christmas!" squealed Jeanette, unconsciously squeezing Angelica tighter.

The child lifted her head and asked, in sleepy French, "*Qu'est-ce qui se passe?*" What's happening?

Andrea wailed. "*Mia piccola figlia francese.*" Angelica reached over to be taken, and Jeanette thankfully shifted the child's weight into her mother's arms. La Grecque stalked toward the back room, thrusting out a hip at Sonja as she passed.

"Sonja and Andrea are having some kind of fight," Jeanette told Amy, back in the studio.

"They would be. The question is always whether to interfere. How soon does it look like murder being done?"

"Any minute now."

Amy sighed. "I'd better go see about it. Perhaps you would start the departures?"

Jeanette rounded up Effie and the Reades to leave, calling out *Bon soir* and *Joyeux Noël* loudly to other guests as a hint. On the way home, Jeanette gave an account of the murky scene in the kitchen.

Effie shook her head. "And on Christmas morning."

"That's what I said."

For the rest of the way, Jeanette mused on Amy, generous and unhappy. On Sonja—gifted, arrogant, sometimes brutal. On La Grecque's corrosive, wrecked beauty. On Emily, fugitive and fey. On Edward; oh, most of all on Edward. You wanted to help, to be friends, to love; but so often, there was nothing you could do but ache.

On Christmas Day, Jeanette and Effie went to the morning service at their own American Protestant Chapel and afterward to the Reade sisters' apartment for dinner and an afternoon musicale. In the evening, they assisted at a McAll Mission supper. Sonja was due to spend the day at an aristocratic Polish house, Amy with Louise Steadman and English friends. At some point, Andrea Antonielli left, taking Angelica with her. They disappeared so completely that not even La Belle Hélène could track them down.

What seemed strangest to Jeanette was Sonja's indifference.

"I always said it would end in tears," said Amy. "I didn't expect them to be mine, particularly not over the loss of the demon child."

In L'Estaque, Christmas was quiet. Two residents wound up their treatment and left; day patients were few in the dead of winter. By then, any fear Edward had of being trapped among lunatics or neurasthenics was gone. Of those who stayed over the holiday, M. Valabrègue was the strangest; yet except for his retreat into silence, there was nothing overtly odd in his conduct or manner. His eyes took on a spaniel-like devotion when anyone was kind to him, but he never made a nuisance of himself. An opera singer lately paralyzed by stage fright chose to remain in hospital to avoid public appearances. The alcoholic younger son of a noble house continued to resist his proud family, who disdained to admit that he needed treatment. They all received a few remembrances and visits. When Jeanette's letter came from Paris, Dr. Aubanel, who knew who she was, hesitated. Holidays were times of tension; the effect of a hurtful letter would be magnified. He took the gamble and gave it to Edward, along with the earlier one he was still holding. A few days later, Jeanette received one line: *Bless you, my darling. Edward.*

CHAPTER FORTY-SIX

Turning Corners

January 1880. Early in the new year, Jeanette's quarterly allowance came with a letter from Judge Palmer reminding her that one last bank draft in April must cover her return passage in June. It brought her up hard against being wrenched half a world away from classes, galleries, and Carolus's teaching, from a city where art was taken seriously, worst of all from Edward.

"Well, we've always known we were going back, but, oh my," said Cousin Effie.

"If only I had a way to support myself," said Jeanette at the Rue Madame, where Amy was hard at work on her Salon painting. "The trouble is, all I can think of is piecework, which takes up time and is hard to get."

"Pays pittance, too, don't I know," said Amy. "Humiliating and tiresome, but your best bet is to think of a way to persuade the family to give you more time."

"Any ideas?"

"You could submit something to the Salon. An international success would surely impress them at home."

"Amy, this will be *your* first submission. I'm not ready!"

"No, you're not. Then again, the jury has been greatly enlarged this year; it may be more receptive to new artists. Put forward the best thing you've ever done, and who knows, you might even make a sale or win a commission."

"The best thing I've done is not for sale."

Amy glanced around. "No, it wouldn't be." After a pause, she said, "What about your *Lady of Shalott?* Nice literary scene, and you used the Cluny well. Very convincing loom and decor."

"It was no better than any other half-baked costume piece. I never finished it."

"Well, there's still time for that, as I am living proof. So would Sonja be if she were here."

"Where *is* Sonja?"

"Out examining scrap lumber. She says she is going to build her own frame for *Poland Resurgent.*"

Caught off guard, Jeanette laughed hard for the first time since Christmas. "Julian always says a woman must make a splash!"

"Not what he had in mind, carpentry, but speaks with the voice of experience, that man," said Amy. "Splash or no splash, why shouldn't you submit? If you're otherwise headed back to America, there's no harm in rejection except to your pride." She sighed. "If the Salon doesn't accept this *Breton Harvest*, I may just trundle back home myself."

"You, leave Paris, Amy?"

"Most of us do in the end."

"Not you! You know everybody here; you're so much a part of—"

"—the toilers and moilers, the hangers-on and drones? Sorry, Palmer, no; I won't play the perpetual aspirant. If I have to settle for painting potboilers to sell in London, I'll do it closer to home. It's no fun, I can tell you, being snubbed by the big boys at Julian's and now pitied by younger women all full of dewy-eyed optimism."

"No one pities you, Amy."

"Obviously, not you—you're too full of weepy-eyed despair over a man." Amy's voice lost its edge of light irony: "I'll be thirty this year."

"I've never heard you so despondent."

"Ah, well, doubts do begin to creep in, don't they? I have a friend in Glasgow who claims it's congenial. There are shows for female artists."

"But we want to be rated as artists, not lady artists."

"You may. Sonja does. At this point, I just want to work and be paid for it. I might take on illustration assignments; I might open a school. Anyway, Glasgow would put me closer to my father, poor old dear."

"What if the jury accepts your picture?"

"Oh, in that case, dear old, capable Papa is on his own. First I shall scramble out onto the cupola of the Pantheon and shout the good news to a waiting world. Next I'll swan my way to La Poupée, for a wallow in sisterly dissipation. And finally, I'll settle all the scratched feelings with Sonja somehow and renew the lease."

The more Jeanette thought about the Salon, the more compelling the idea became. The next week, when she heard that Carolus would be coming to another studio in her building to counsel an advanced pupil on his submissions, she seized a chance to ask whether he could possibly stop at hers also. She explained her dilemma and promised she would not take up too much of his time. He was more than willing, he said, beaming at his own beneficence.

On the following Saturday, he swept into her studio in a splendid Inverness cloak. He was animated; he was charming; his eye roved up and down her person for an instant, and for an instant lingered. Jeanette reacted with the coquettish devotion that everyone in the class knew he required, too flushed with excitement to be annoyed. He bowed to Effie with an airy salute, neither implying nor ruling out his remembering who she was. Almost at once his eye shifted to the canvas placed on the easel. *"Après vous, mademoiselle,"* he said, gesturing.

Jeanette had chosen to show him first her most successful painting of an invalid, worked up from studies of La Grecque. Her picture was admirably composed, he told her, the tones properly subdued, the touch of the sheets against the woman's flesh delicate. His friend Monet, he said sadly, just last year had painted his wife in the moment after death, a chilling subject, a disturbing picture, potent. He congratulated her, but no. This rendition was too morbid for a young lady's introduction to the public. Jeanette's heart sank. Without his support as a juror, it would inevitably be rejected. Before she could gather herself, to ask him to look at her *Lady of Shalott*, he had walked over to the wall where Edward's portrait hung. This, he said, was painted with real insight.

"I thought that you would say it was overworked!"

"So it is; but in a portrait of such feeling, flaws can be forgiven. I believe that I recognize the man. I never forget faces. *Ah, mais oui*, he was also at the garden party to celebrate the unveiling of my portrait of Mme. Renick. He was—with you." Jeanette wondered whether he was going to recommend submitting it, and if so, whether Edward would wish it, whether she would. Carolus spared her the decision. "If you master the technique to express such intuition, one day you may conquer New York. And now, permit me to excuse myself."

Beside the doorway, he paused to look at two small oil interiors that Effie had hung there: One depicted the Renicks' hall and stairway, the other the salon with his portrait of Cornelia above the piano. He glanced back, his eyes twinkling. "These also show feeling. *Ah, oui*, I saw the costume piece about which you intended to ask me. You have a taste for interiors, *mademoiselle*, but that one will not do. Submit this." The knob of his cane pointed to the hallway.

Elated and astonished at his approval, Jeanette asked, "Not its companion, too?"

"Even I do not compliment myself with so little subtlety in public, *ma fille*; but I think I can carry the day for this one. I should be pleased to have its painter listed as my student. And there is a career to be made, you know, in painting the houses of the rich."

"Oh, lud," said Amy when Jeanette told her. "Add gentry in eighteenth-century costume and you can sell 'em to decorators for a few francs per yard. Well, congratulations, Palmer. We'll take our submissions over together when the time comes."

A few days after Carolus's visit, Jeanette finally received a letter from Edward, no more than a few paragraphs, but a real letter. Every day, he looked at the watercolor she had sent down before Christmas, he wrote. Would she send him a self-portrait? *Not a photograph; something from your hand—it will have more life.* He begged her to respond. *Tell me about your days.* He did not tell her much about his own, how hard they had become as he was weaned from the drug; but the unevenness of his script betrayed a troubled mind. Jeanette rifled through studies of herself made when she was working on *The Lady of Shalott*. When she found one that would do, she touched it up with pen and wash, made herself pretty (surely he would want it that way), and posted it the next morning with a promise of letters to come. That evening, she wrote him about Carolus's visit and her plans to submit a painting of the Renicks' hallway to the Salon. The next day, she wrote about Sonja's attempts to build a frame *(Amy was clever and bought a fine one cheap at auction last fall, then bought a canvas to fit it).* She received no replies. As the days went by, she was less and less sure how to reach him. What she needed to say, and Edward needed to hear, was that she loved him no matter what. *I miss you*, she wrote, *I miss you.*

In mid February, Cornelia obtained permission from Dr. Aubanel to visit Edward at the sanatorium. Edward had made no attempt to reach the Renicks, reluctant to come face to face with anyone he knew; but Dr. Aubanel told him that sooner or later he must begin reentering society.

When the Renicks arrived on a Sunday afternoon, Cornelia set about to charm Dr. Aubanel in the sitting room until Edward joined them. When he came, her eyes greeted him with the candor of the Nellie he had known in childhood, making him glad she had come; but Cornelia's heart ached. For a man who had spent time outdoors every day, Edward was wan; he had gained no weight; he was, in fact, in the throes of his first weeks with no opium at all.

While Marius spoke with Dr. Aubanel, Cornelia asked, "Do you hear from Jeanette Palmer?"

"More often than she hears from me, I'm afraid."

"That may do for the time being."

"I have no right—"

"As the mother of a daughter, I must agree, darling; but as a friend to you both, I say bosh."

The day was sunny; a light wind blew as it often did so near the sea, a buffeting breeze, not the hard, bitter mistral. Before he left them, Dr. Aubanel suggested to Edward that he conduct his friends up to see the thermal spring. Edward and Cornelia arranged themselves to put their respective canes on the outside. Marius trailed behind, assessing the grounds by criteria of his own. From behind a grille between columns, the water of the pool steamed gently in the cool air. "No drowning allowed in off hours," explained Edward.

Cornelia squeezed his arm slightly and, without knowing it, echoed Jeanette. "Is it a good place, Edward?"

In answer, Edward turned her around to see the late-afternoon sun burnishing the landscape below them. The Mediterranean glowed. "If I've got any chance, it's here."

On the drive home, Cornelia said, "Marius, I need a new project, and I think that Edward Murer may be it."

"Murer is Dr. Aubanel's project, my dear; the garden is yours. But we'll visit again."

Cornelia never contradicted Marius; it was easier simply to do what she wanted.

* * *

Dr. Aubanel always greeted his patients by asking them what they were feeling, not how. Stripped of the meaningless conventions of polite conversation, the patients almost always answered truthfully. Edward, who thought of himself as an introspective man, discovered that he had more moods, body parts, and senses than he had ever realized.

During the period when his laudanum dosage was being systematically reduced, his physical condition required careful monitoring. Dr. Aubanel had him come to the office for the half hour before his scheduled immersion in the spring and again as the last patient of the day. Additionally, during the worst of it, before he set off for his office in town each morning, he had Edward step into the examining room for a quick check of his eyes, throat, pulse, and breathing. At the time, Edward accepted the order with passive indifference; midway through the ordeal, he resented it; finally, as he put it to Cornelia, it seemed good for both him and the doctor to have physical evidence that he was still alive.

Edward's knowledge of botanicals pointed to the herb garden as a place where he should work. Physically, there had not been much to do in December except fork in rotted manure, which he did, then dug more into the artichoke bed. He had never gardened as an adult except to help Sophie with an occasional chore during the year he had spent with her and Theodore after the war. Now he forked and turned soil repeatedly to make it friable and fill time, pressing his forehead to his hands on top of the pitchfork when his nerves were too jittery. In January, when apricot and peach trees were being pruned, he bundled up the trimmings and cleared them out of the orchard; in February, it was the grapevines terraced up near the limestone escarpment at the back of the property and the climbing roses near the house. By the middle of February, work was seriously under way on an addition to the herb garden; he helped construct a

stone wall as well as draw up a plant list. He was not such a fool as
to think a peasant's backbreaking drudgery enlarged either mind or
soul; he never vowed to take to the simple life as some patients did,
in a flush of grateful enthusiasm; but gradually he came to value
time devoted to manual labor. Tasks gave him measures for passing
the hours and quarter hours until his next dose or, after the laudanum was withdrawn, his next bath in the thermal spring.

The spring, a few degrees warmer than body temperature, welled
up through vents in the bottom of the pool. Currents constantly
curled around the body as bathers sat on a ledge immersed to the
neck or trod water in the middle. "While you are in the spring,"
ordered Dr. Aubanel, "you will not crave the drug." Either he had
hypnotic powers or a virtue in the water made it true.

Almost inadvertently it seemed, Edward's muscles would respond
to the warmth and relax; sometimes, he grew sleepy. As he came to
expect a level of ease, there were days when he intentionally rested
on his elbows and let the purling water lift his legs and trunk so
that he floated. Eventually he began to explore motion: the effect of
scissor kicking, of twisting, of lowering himself and shooting upward.

It was left to each man to encounter the spring's genius in his
own way. By February, it sometimes whispered seductively to Edward
when he was too much at ease to feel ashamed. It was after one such
occasion that he discussed the matter of the girl on the Boulevard
Saint-Germain with Dr. Aubanel. Aubanel agreed that prostitution
was a social ill but told him to consider desire a sign of health.
Helped by Aubanel's assurances that there was sound reason not to
burden Jeanette with a confession, Edward finally forgave himself.

When their time was up, bathers could dry off and dress at once
or rinse away all traces of sulfur in a shower of cold well water from
a cistern behind the pavilion. Edward recoiled at the thought. He
would rather smell like a hard-boiled egg all day than punish himself just when he felt best. The opera singer countered that the cold
water was invigorating. Ah, but for that, sea bathing was preferable,

said M. Pierre Turenne de Villeroy, the young nobleman who drank
too much.

Turenne was a difficult man; no one quite liked or trusted him.
Although his manners were perfect and his overt mockery always
aimed only at himself or fate, he was bitter, ironic, and far too observant. What he left unsaid could amount to a sneer. One unusually
warm morning in January, when Edward's victory over opium had
been most precarious, Turenne had found him chopping at weeds
between rows in the vegetable garden. He watched silently until
Edward looked up, ready to snarl. Turenne shrugged apologetically
and pulled out a cigarette case. "You do not smoke, I believe, *monsieur.*"

"No."

"A pity." Turenne leaned over to light up against the wind. "You
and I, we have need of a petty vice to fill a major void," he said,
directing puffs upward out of the side of his mouth. He watched as
Edward went back to chopping. "Come, I have something to show
you. You are making a bad job here anyway."

"I'll go back over it."

"So you will, another day, and another and another. Here, catch."
Turenne tossed Edward's coat from where he had left it folded across
a fence post. "I am going to show you a way down to the sea."

Edward had dropped his hoe to catch the coat. "I'll need my
walking stick."

"No, no. If you return to the house, you will not come out again.
We shall pick up something to use along the way."

Turenne cut west across the hospital grounds along one of the
narrow tracks made by the farm's animals. It plunged down into a
rocky ravine. From above, the path seemed to disappear; but after
a scramble down the bank, they landed where it continued under a
canopy of juniper, wild plum, and other brush. Turenne handed

Edward a likely stick, then led on, sometimes in the open, sometimes covertly, down a mile and a half to a deserted shingle beach.

Turenne trudged out to the water's edge and stood staring out to the horizon. "The sea," he mused, in a strangely proprietary tone, "liberty." He began pulling off his clothes, casting them aside carelessly.

Edward watched, unmoved. The day was warm for the time of year, and they were hot from walking, but he had no more inclination for that kind of chill than he had for a shower after a soak. Turenne waded purposefully into the water until it was almost up to his waist and then struck out. Suddenly, it came to Edward that he meant to keep swimming, swim to freedom, swim until it was too late to come back. "Turenne!" he shouted, and wrestled out of his own clothes. He knew how to swim but had not done so for years—paddling in the thermal pool or with the Renicks one day in August didn't count. Nor had he ever pulled a man to safety. Without knowing what he hoped to accomplish, he ran splashing into the water. He hardly noticed the shock of the cold until his lungs hurt and he was gasping. Almost at once, Turenne turned around and swam back easily.

They floundered out. Edward was furious, too angry to speak. Turenne, with the grace of young manhood and custom, walked up onto the beach ahead of him in perfect self-command. He was already drying himself off with his shirt when Edward snatched up his own.

"This is what you and I need, *monsieur*: exertion and distraction. We must measure ourselves against something hard and win in order to keep fighting."

"I thought you might drown."

"Did you? In that case, my thanks, *monsieur*." Turenne bowed. "How fortunate for you that the mistake took you into the water, which otherwise you would have refused."

Edward was not appeased. Leaving his guide to sit on the sun-

warmed pebbles and smoke another cigarette, he stalked back up
the hill alone. Nevertheless, a week later, when Turenne invited him
to slip away again, Edward went, and went again the next time he
was asked. He began to understand the need to stretch and strike
out for freedom. Ridiculous as it was in winter, he went in the water
each time—to prove to Turenne that he could take the self-punishing
challenge and because it felt good to survive. "No one who has not
gone through it can ever really understand," said Turenne, one day.

"*La mélancolie*," muttered Edward.

"Ah, that," said Turenne, "no, that is Valabrègue. I am just a sot."

"Then perhaps we should bring Valabrègue. He would have to
hear me out."

Turenne shot him an amused glance, but he also invited the
ever-mute Valabrègue the next time they set out.

No one in the hospital had ever heard M. Valabrègue speak unless it was Dr. Aubanel. To the world, he presented his gentle smile
and compliant manner; but when caught off guard, his eyes betrayed
desolation. That day, if a spring to his step meant anything, he was
genuinely grateful to be included in the walk to the beach; and he
proved equal to a brief swim.

When they came out of the water, they horsed around. Turenne
snapped his shirt at the others. Edward laughed—laughed and
laughed. His sides shook; he gulped and, with the next choking
gulp, realized he was crying. Covering his face with his hands, he
crouched down, sobbing uncontrollably—for Mutter and Papa and
Marie gone, for the men he had killed and the men he hadn't, for
too many years of his life wasted, for the recent, botched months,
for loneliness. Turenne and Valabrègue let him go until the paroxysm
slowed. A hand touched his shoulder. Reluctantly, he looked up into
Valabrègue's soft, sad eyes.

Edward sighed heavily. "I beg your pardon, both of you."

Turenne sat a little way off, smoking a cigarette and staring out
to sea. "Think nothing of it. As I have said, no one who has never

undergone the agony can understand—but then, we have, each in his own hell."

Edward pushed himself up. At the water's edge, he knelt down and splashed his face. It made him shiver. He was too exhausted for tears now; he wanted sleep. Laudanum, his system begged. He clenched his teeth against the craving and stood up. "I'm all right now."

By the time they got back to the house, lunch was on the table. Thinking there was nothing he wanted less than food or company, Edward headed for the stairs to lie down in his room. Turenne detained him. "Speaking from experience, I would say it is best to follow the rules and eat." Turenne's habitual dispassion, as if he didn't really care, was more effective than Cousin Anna's admonishments or even Sophie's gentler efforts to persuade. Valabrègue stood by and nodded. Edward, not wishing to appear more childish than he had already, gave in.

Dr. Aubanel received the truants without comment; yet he must have seen at once that something had happened to Edward; for after the meal, he ordered him into the office for an early consultation. By then, food had stabilized Edward's blood sugar and steadied his nerves. He himself recognized that he was in a crisis and that while his defenses were down was the time to lay some of it before the physician he was paying to cure him; but, God, he was tired.

"Tell me where you were," said Aubanel.

He listened carefully, asking only enough short questions to keep Edward talking for a while. "I know that path," he said, finally.

"Turenne will be sorry to hear it."

"No need to tell him," said Dr. Aubanel, with a faint smile. "I believe, *monsieur*, that it would do you good to go with him again soon."

My dearest Jeanette, wrote Edward, a few days later, *I turned a corner, whether deeper into darkness or up toward the light I could not tell at first, not until the sun shone golden.*

CHAPTER FORTY-SEVEN

Early Spring 1880

In addition to the picture of the stairway and the salon, Jeanette had painted a third view in the Renicks' house and given it to them as a thank-you. She wrote Mrs. Renick to let her know that she would be submitting *Un Vestibule dans le Quartier Saint-Germain* to the Salon and asked where *The Treasure Room* had been so beautifully framed. *Dear, darling Jeanette, How thrilling,* Cornelia wrote back, *for you and for us. Hurrah! If your piece is accepted, it will be a coup to show off its companion in May!* In her letter, Jeanette also asked about Edward, and Cornelia decided it was time to intervene. Besides sending Jeanette the address of her framer, she wrote Effie: *Marius has business in Nice and Rome this year, and so we are staying on longer than usual. At last, I can see a Provençal spring! Why don't you and Jeanette come down for a couple of weeks?*

Jeanette's heart leaped at the chance to see Edward, and for that matter to leave Paris at the dirty end of winter, but she was unsure whether she should miss any of the few classes left to her. Carolus told her to go: Ah! the Mediterranean! Take her paintbox and bring him back the sun. "If you do, I shall give you a private critique," he promised.

In the second week in March, Jeanette and Effie took a train straight through to Marseilles, second class, sitting up all night to save money. When they arrived at the Renicks' house midmorning, frowzy and short of sleep, Cornelia sent them upstairs, each to her own bedroom, a luxury Jeanette had enjoyed only at Aunt Maude's since she left Circleville. Her room in the northeast corner of the house had windows on two sides; it was full of light. To eyes accustomed to Parisian gray, it floated. Outside were trees, slashes of lawn seen through foliage in a next-door neighbor's garden, and beyond them cliffs of rock. It seemed wrong to pull the shutters against such beauty; but she wanted to change out of her thick woolen travel costume, wash up, and, perhaps, as Mrs. Renick suggested, lie down before lunch, when Edward was expected. She was sure she was too excited to sleep, but the bed had springs and a good mattress. When she awoke, for a moment she had no idea where she was. Sluggishly, she tried to orient herself in the dim room—and then sat bolt upright. A china clock on a side table read three o'clock. She had missed Edward's arrival. She had missed lunch, too, but that didn't matter. She fumbled at her back to retie her corset. Her hair! She must let it out, brush it, and pin it back up. When she hurried downstairs, Hastings showed her out into a garden. The bay in a great oval of gold-flecked turquoise tilted up toward the far horizon; the overarching sky was darkest blue at the zenith; a wedge of chartreuse lawn receded to the brink of a cliff. Only two figures were visible—Effie sitting happily in the sun and Mrs. Renick shaded by a big muslin umbrella near a palm tree. No Edward. Anxiously searching for him, Jeanette slowed her pace.

"So there you are! Come sit down beside me," said Mrs. Renick. "Did you get some sleep? You look rested, a very good thing."

Jeanette conveyed Carolus's best wishes and resigned herself to conversing with her hostess, all the while wondering where Edward could be. Surely, he had not come and gone. Had he not come at all?

Effie couldn't bear to tease. "Dr. Murer set out on a walk a while ago, Jeanette; he'll be back. Isn't this just the most magnificent view! Revivifying, I call it."

Jeanette's heart gave a hard thump against her breast bone. She could not help herself. "Please, how is he, Mrs. Renick? Is he better?"

"Yes, he is, my dear, and he'll be better yet when he sees you.

Run along and fetch him. He went down that path over there. It leads to only one place, our own small *calanque*. You can't miss running into each other."

Jeanette fled across the lawn to a break in a low retaining wall, where steps led to a path that zigzagged down steeply between rocks, junipers, cypress, and blooming laurustinas, which shielded it from sight but framed views of the dazzling, blue-green sea. Near the bottom, a huge boulder forced a bend. As she came around it, she saw Edward, standing on another boulder below her, with his back to her, naked. Covering her mouth to stifle a shriek, she jumped back so as not to be seen and then peeked around again more carefully. Sinewy, with small shapely buttocks, he was raising his arms and in the next moment lifted off into the air in a dive. Involuntarily, her hand traced the curve described by his body. She had learned to look at the nude and seminude male body posed in unnatural contortions and statuary stillness but never in the beautiful fluidity of motion. She felt a brief anguish as he disappeared until she heard the clean splash of a knifelike entry. She stayed where she was until he rose out of the water, hoisted himself onto the rock by the strength of his arms, and stood up, water streaming down off the hair of his head, the hair of his beard, and the hair surrounding his all-too-visible penis and scrotum. She pulled back in acute embarrassment and delight, smiling to herself. Holding her breath, she leaned her back against her boulder, eyes closed to recall the image. When she opened them, she started up the path, wondering what she should do, praying that he hadn't seen her. "*Un moment, s'il vous plaît!*" came his alarmed voice. She tiptoed away.

Edward had seen a slight movement, a bird, he hoped. He called out just in case, struck by the comedy of the unseemly situation as well as by distress. He dropped low and scuttled to his clothes. Quickly, he dried himself off with his shirt as he always did at L'Estaque and pulled on his trousers, still crouching as much as he could. Whatever could have possessed him to succumb to his whim and swim here when he saw the deep, inviting water of the hidden inlet? Showing off secretly to himself, he supposed, silly, puerile; and yet he was not sorry. The beauty and the privacy of the place were irresistible, his mastery of cold water a source of pride. *"Bonjour?"* he called out when he was dressed. No answer. Just as well. He whistled in assumed insouciance as he started back up the path.

At a wide turn, well below the garden, a bench had been set. Jeanette heard him from where she sat on it, looking at the ground, listening for his footsteps. As he came into sight, her head lifted and she rose slowly. He stopped. She held out both her hands to him, a welcome without reserve. When he started forward again, she walked slowly until he opened his arms, then ran. He caught her close and squeezed, harder and harder. Feeling her yield to the joy of their embrace, Edward abandoned himself to it, too. He could hardly believe his good fortune and, after many caresses, murmured as much into her ear. She rubbed her cheek against his shoulder. Gently with his hands, he pushed her back so that his eyes could meet hers.

"Jeanette," he said. A quietness in his voice made her suddenly afraid. "That day in the café, I said I had been going to ask you to marry me."

Not again, she thought.

He saw her fears and took confidence from them. "Now I can. I had meant to wait." He kissed her forehead lightly, each of her eyelids, her nose. Before he reached her mouth again, he said, "I had meant to say, Miss Palmer, will you do me the very great honor of becoming my wife?"

Edward had rehearsed this proposal for other circumstances, had expected the usual resistance, had planned to be gentlemanly and bid her to think it over before she gave him an answer. Instead he begged, "Oh, Jeanette, my darling, will you? Please say yes. Please."

Through her laughing tears, she choked out, "How could I possibly say anything else?"

The kiss that followed revealed to her hitherto unsuspected pleasures; it told him that a trusting woman's warmth could feel like deliverance. It left them both in the glowing, self-absorbed bliss that makes lovers such social bores. (By the time they got back up the hill, they thought their emotions were well concealed until Effie asked, "My goodness, are you engaged?")

"How long have you been waiting?" he asked her.

"All my life."

Another kiss. "Waiting here, I mean. Were you waiting for me?"

Jeanette murmured a wordless assent, then added, "Mrs. Renick said you had gone down this path. I—it's very steep."

"You are hiding something."

She reddened; and then with her reckless bent to blurt things out, she pulled loose and looked up at him. "I saw you swimming, Edward. I saw you come out of the water. I . . ."

Her voice trailed off as her courage failed, but he hardly noticed in his glee. "You saw this wreck of dry bones exposed and still greeted me the way you did?"

"Yes!" she said, almost defiantly. "And I will, again and again."

No fool like an old fool, Edward thought, but a newfound, cocky pride strutted out to boot aside his skepticism. He believed her when she said she would marry him. He clasped his arms more tightly around her. "It's not every decent gal who can say that and know what she's talking about!"

"A great advantage to marrying a well-trained artist."

He smiled indulgently as he continued to hold her. She did not really know, not really; but if she could take him as she had seen him just now, he had no fears about their future.

"Are we going to tell everyone right away?" she asked, as he set her ahead of him to start the rest of the way up the hill on the narrow path.

"Do you want to?"

"Part of me wants to shout it out, and part of me wants to get used to being this happy. If I touch the bubble, it might pop."

He kissed the nape of her neck. "I think your family should be told first." He turned her around, sobered by a thought. "Jeanette, do they know about me at all?"

"Of course! You've been in my letters ever since I met you, many, *many* times. They know I painted your portrait this fall."

"About the laudanum as well, that I'm here and why?"

"No, I kept that to myself, Edward."

"Will you always be ashamed?"

"I'm not ashamed! Never, never think I was ashamed. I was afraid for you, my dearest." She stroked his face, down along his beard, and touched her fingers to his lips to stop his speaking. "I missed you so, that's all. I had to tell Cousin Effie, but it didn't seem anybody else's business."

He pulled her toward him. "I wish my failings didn't have to be a secret, but what man would give his daughter to me if he knew, and how could I live without you now?"

"I'm old enough to marry you with or without Papa's consent— but it doesn't matter because they are all going to adore you." *You'd better marry that man*, mocked Adeline's voice in the back of her mind.

"How old are you, Jeanette?"

"Twenty-one."

So young, he thought, almost abashed as he held her tight. She felt qualms beginning to alloy their happiness.

"Kiss me," she begged. And with that kiss, they sealed their present hazard and their life together, whatever it might be.

Edward returned to the hospital on Monday morning. Dr. Aubanel had scheduled a meeting for the afternoon, knowing that, over the Friday to Monday, his patient would be with the woman he loved for the first time in months, a situation fraught with danger. He saw at once that he need not have been concerned. "It went well?" He could not help smiling benevolently.

"Better than I had any right to hope."

"One may not always have reason to hope, *monsieur*, but one always has the right."

A few days later, the ladies drove around to L'Estaque. After they were shown the new herb beds and the vegetable garden as well as the thermal spring, Effie and Cornelia sat in the garden while Jeanette and Edward took a walk among the olive groves. They found a place to sit on the rocks above the grapevines where they could look out over the Mediterranean.

"No wonder Carolus loves it," said Jeanette, gazing at the bay. "I've begun some landscapes in watercolor at the Renicks' house. I don't know whether it is being happy or being in the presence of something so wondrous, but I feel like I'm discovering what color is for. Will we come here often, do you think?"

"To the bughouse?"

"No, silly! To the South of France."

"Italy," said Edward, with longing, as he turned his eyes southeastward. "I've seen it in winter. I want to see it in spring—Rome and the Tuscan hills."

Jeanette leaned her head against his shoulder. "Sonja always teased us about going to Brittany instead—gray beach by a gray sea under a gray sky. Maybe she was right."

"Not if you loved Pont Aven the way you said you did." He put his arm around her waist and pulled her closer.

"Places matter."

"They do."

They talked for a while about what they could see from where they sat, about Paris, about needing to spend time in a place to know it well, about starting new. After a while, Edward pulled his arm back and bent over his knees with his hands pressed together. He looked at the ground. "Jeanette, what would you think of going back to Ohio?"

"Well, there is the wedding!" she exclaimed, starting to laugh until she registered his tone.

"I mean for good."

Surely not, she thought. No! He raised his head to look out at the water again. The lines etched around his eyes told complicated stories. He was wearing his rough-woven Provençal work jacket. So close to him, Jeanette could catch the scents of earth and rosemary and sweat that clung to it. Not even while she was painting his portrait, had she been more aware of the hairs in his beard, the straightness of his nose, the warmth and solidity of Edward. But again his mind was somewhere beyond her ken, and this time she must find him. "I guess I've just assumed we'd go on living in Paris, that you wanted to," she said, quietly. "You're saying instead that you *want* to go back, aren't you?"

Troubled but not in doubt, he met her eye. "I'm afraid I am. I thought I could make Europe home, but it's not. I've learned some things about myself these last months, Jeanette. I need you more than any other single thing, my darling, always; but I need my family, too. I depend on Theodore and Sophie more than I like to admit; I like having them around, and the boys. And I need productive work."

She found she could not give in, not all at once. "You have your laboratory in Paris."

"It can't provide the stimulation of other men, nor the impetus of real problems that need solving," he said, shaking his head. "And you shouldn't be saddled with me all by yourself. This could happen again. No one is ever really cured."

I don't care! she started to protest. She didn't care—or rather she believed that she wanted to be with him no matter what happened. She would have to take the bad with the good.

He prevented her speaking by putting his arm around her again.

"I've been thinking I could take Theodore up on a proposal to build a research laboratory at Murer Brothers. I know you love France— but could you make a life for yourself, for us, in Cincinnati?"

Cincinnati. Pig-slaughtering Porkopolis, the newspapers called it. Industrial, ugly—yet a big city, energetic; not Circleville. With Edward earnestly reaching out to her after so long an absence, for a moment all clichés seemed true. I'd go with you anywhere, she was about to vow; but before she could speak, he added, "You'd be nearer your folks, too."

She frowned and shifted in her seat. "Not your best argument. Sometimes I think the only way to get along with my mother is to keep four thousand miles between us."

"Am I walking into a lions' den?"

"No, no. Papa has moods, but he's wonderful. And Mama is intelligent and admirable and as upright as they come—witty sometimes, too, I have to admit that. But we don't see eye to eye. She thinks I'm frivolous." Almost laughing, Edward tightened his arm again around her and tugged. She bumped back, a familiarity that almost changed the direction of the conversation.

"It's not that I want to go on quarreling with Mama all my life nor avoid the family," Jeanette went on. "For that matter, going back to Ohio has been staring me in the face all along." She looked out to sea again, just as he had. "It's that I have to paint, Edward—not little vignettes in letters or decorating china. Real work, with other people who care, and real subjects that I care about. You said you needed it—well, I do, too." She turned to him. "Art is my way of making sense of the world; it's easier in France."

"A lot of things are. It's why I thought I wanted to stay—and we could come back for months at a time, often if you liked. But if you are provided with a studio, can you work in Cincinnati, that's the question. You'll miss this community, but there are artists in Cincinnati, too."

There were. None she knew, and the McMicken was hardly the same as Carolus's atelier or Julian's. And yet, had she said yes to Edward only in order to stay in Paris? No, not for a minute. She paused and took in a deep breath. "I guess we'll find out."

※

CHAPTER FORTY-EIGHT

Epithalamium

Jeanette and Effie returned to the Rue du Fleurus on a Saturday in the uncertain mood of travelers who have left one place behind but find the light different at home. While they were gone, the air had changed in Paris; life had moved on. After they unpacked, they took a turn around the Luxembourg Garden. It was more precious to Jeanette than ever. Even the terrible afternoon of Edward's breakdown there held deep significance. They bought a few things on the way back. When they set down a bulgy *filet*, the crocheted strings fell limp. I should draw those, thought Jeanette. Shops, streets, the dome of the Pantheon, French *filets*—she was seeing them as foreign again in the melancholy acceptance that she must leave.

She put off calling at the Rue Madame until the next afternoon, afraid of what her face might reveal. She need not have worried. It was the last Sunday before the deadline, and Amy and Sonja were painting too feverishly to notice anything. She soon left and, on the way out, decided to avoid an infection of nerves by submitting her picture to the Salon as soon as possible.

The next afternoon, she changed into her best blue in honor of the occasion and set out with Cousin Effie to deliver *Un Vestibule dans le Quartier Saint-Germain* to the Palais de l'Industrie. Even if it were accepted, a painting nine by twelve inches had little chance of being noticed no matter where it was hung; but it had the great advantage of portability. When the omnibus stopped to pick them up, two men already occupied the upper deck, steadying the ends of a picture too large to fit inside. Spotting the shape of Jeanette's parcel, one of them called out something rude about *les femmes dilettantes*. Toilers and moilers, she responded silently. "We don't have to ride on top," said Effie. Inside, two more men, middle-aged and dejectedly bitter, sat opposite each other with portrait-sized paintings propped against their knees. They shifted only slightly for Effie; Jeanette had to lift her package high to pass and then clutch it under her arm while she stood in the aisle holding on to a strap. Little did they know that it was Mrs. Edward Murer, the famous painter, whom they inconvenienced, she thought, with a mental toss of the head.

Near the Palais de l'Industrie, other artists were arriving from various directions to join a short queue outside the building. Jeanette walked quickly to take a place well ahead of the men on the omnibus. Every few minutes, the line would shuffle forward a foot or so. From time to time, someone coming out would stop to speak to friends, and Jeanette would try to eavesdrop discreetly. Cousin Effie openly bent around to look at what was arriving behind them. It took about ten minutes to reach the door, and then they saw that the line snaked at the same slow crawl across a long hall. "This is bad enough," said Jeanette. "Think how horrible it's going to be on the last day!"

Inside, dust rose in the cold building and the walls resounded to clanks and thumps echoing from out of sight. At last, the queue reached a table of functionaries, who handed out the inevitable bureaucratic forms. They docketed each work of art, handed back a numbered receipt, and passed the artists' dearest hopes over to workmen in smocks, who, in turn, carried them off to endless stacks and rows of frames. "My, my, just like so many pallets of turnips or yard goods!" said Cousin Effie.

Jeanette had the sickening feeling that she was consigning her pretty bauble to oblivion. "Come on! Let's get out of here!" Outside, her spirits rebounded. She threw her arms up and pirouetted on the sidewalk. Effie pulled her down and hustled her off. "Now what would Dr. Murer think if he saw you acting like that?"

"He'd think that I'm young and pretty Jeanette Palmer, his irrepressible bride-to-be!" laughed Jeanette, but she settled into a walk with her elbow linked with Effie's. "If I'm accepted, I'll bring you to Varnishing Day."

"Oh, no, you'll bring him."

"He'd hate it; you'd love it—and you've earned it, Cousin Effie."

"Well," said Effie, ducking her head, pleased. "We won't count our chickens before they hatch."

Late in the afternoon, Jeanette went around to check again on Amy's and Sonja's progress. Seeing a general disarray of crockery as well as a litter of paint tubes and brushes, she gathered up some of the mess. When she came back from the kitchen, she invited them for dinner that night at La Poupée en Bas. "My treat."

"I thought you'd be broke after a Provençal gallivant," said Amy.

"What better way to squander the last of this quarter's allowance than to celebrate a submission to the Salon?"

"We haven't yet—" Amy's hand dropped. She looked around. "You don't mean you've carried yours over already? I thought you were coming with us."

"My picture was finished and framed before we left. I didn't want to run any risks."

"How detestably pragmatic you Americans are!"

"I'll bet Louise Steadman turned hers in on the first day."

"*Non, non,*" said Sonja. "Steadman avoids inconvenience of first day as well as insane crush of last."

"Louise is a veteran and has a right to be blasé," said Amy, going back to her painting. "If anyone wants to know, the Variation on a Theme she's working on now is conch shell, nacreous side out; tulip; fish on a plate; and for no reason that I can fathom, a sleek ferret. She's in a Dutch phase."

"At La Poupée, she also has Parma violets and golden monkeys. We go next week, *chérie*."

"Come tonight. Why is it so hot in here?"

"We've stoked the stove to speed the paint drying, idiot."

"Oh, for heaven's sake, then, let it dry! I'll come by for you at a quarter to six."

Jeanette hoped that the visit to La Poupée en Bas would not be her last, but she knew that it might. In a few days, when Edward was back in Paris, they would resume their Duval suppers or otherwise dine together often. And in years to come? La Poupée would not open its doors to a married woman.

"Penny for your thoughts," said Amy.

"Are you still thinking of going to Glasgow?" asked Jeanette, gazing around at the splintery whitewashed walls, the checkered tablecloths, the side table of food.

"*Non*, she is not."

"Possibly," said Amy, with a glance at Sonja. "Why?"

"Just that if you do, you must promise to start a supper club like this."

"Oatmeal and offal every night, *ouff*," snorted Sonja.

"Ignore her," said Amy. "You do the same, if you have to go back. New York City, will it be?"

"Cincinnati," said Effie. Under the table, Jeanette kicked her. Effie assumed a look of arch reticence.

"It's the nearest city to Circleville," said Jeanette.

No one was fooled. "And home of one Dr. Edward Murer, if I'm not mistaken," said Amy.

Sonja grabbed Jeanette's left hand. "You wear ring?"

"Not yet. There's no announcement . . ."

"Mrs. Renick has recommended a jeweler," said Effie, with a grin.

"So now there is announcement," said Sonja, clinking her wine glass with a knife. *"Tout le monde! Il faut chanter 'Aupres de mon blond homme'!"*

Her call was met with cheers, groans, and clapping. The ladies had a risqué version of the old drinking song specially adapted for the loss of one of their number to matrimony, and Jeanette, like everyone else for whom it was sung, enjoyed her humiliation immensely.

Later that night she wept.

Edward and Jeanette had agreed that he would delay writing to Judge and Mrs. Palmer to ask for her hand until he was back in Paris with a reassuring address. From Provence, he wrote Theodore for a reckoning of his personal finances, saying that with the success of Dr. Aubanel's cure, he must make some decisions about his future. Explanatory memoranda and accounts drawn up by the family lawyers and bankers promptly arrived. Edward had lived contentedly on the salary he paid himself during the drugstore years, and far more comfortably of late on the quarterly dividends he had received from a portion of his shares in Murer Brothers; but he knew that he would need to increase his income considerably if he were to support a wife and perhaps (he hardly dared hope) a family. Happily, with the income from his latest patent he was, if not nearly so rich as Theodore, more than able to do what he wanted.

He sent a second letter to Theodore announcing the engagement, laid out his intention for a settlement on his future wife to give her a measure of financial independence, and suggested that he should become actively engaged in research at the company. Sophie was as amazed as Theodore. Carl reacted with a whoop: "Why, the old goat!"

"*Nein*, Carl, watch your mouth!" exclaimed Theodore, while his brain worked furiously. When he tentatively concluded that what Edward laid out contained nothing untoward, his affection for his brother took over. He and Sophie exchanged looks. It was hard to believe that a confirmed old bachelor like Edward could really find happiness in a young bride; but as Sophie wisely pointed out, bachelorhood had been at best a limbo for him.

At Edward's request, Sophie wrote Sarah Palmer to say that she and her husband would call on the Palmers in Circleville the following Saturday on behalf of the groom. By the time they went, Theodore had arranged for his lawyer to be in touch with a partner in Judge Palmer's law practice about the settlement. If any of them thought of themselves as making the best of a doubtful situation, the opinion was decorously hidden.

Jeanette had to wait for notice of a different sort: official word from the Salon jury. The day that letters would go out was well known, and on that morning nervous tension at Carolus's atelier destroyed nearly everyone's concentration. Only Mabel Reade, who had not submitted, seemed impervious. She wished Jeanette good luck on the way out to where Edward waited to escort her home. Jeanette was glad of his company; she was light-headed, apprehensive, sure it would be a rejection, not sure she wanted him to see it. For the first time in months, he drew on his professional experience to remain attentive but unobtrusive. The fateful envelope was on the table nearest the door. Jeanette picked it up and looked from Edward to Effie. The oppression in her chest made breathing impossible; her hand fumbled, but as soon as she shook out the folds of the letter, she shrieked in a most unladylike way, waved it in the air, and flung her arms around Edward's neck. After he had swirled her off her feet, she flew to Effie for a prolonged hug. The two women were both in tears when Jeanette pulled back. "This is yours, too, Cousin Effie."

"No, it's all yours, but it's the crowning day in my life."

The next thing was to walk over to the Rue Madame. There the news was mixed. Amy was elated by an acceptance, but Sonja was in a foul mood. A portrait she submitted had been accepted; *Poland Resurgent* had been rejected. The jury were fools, she railed.

"Three hundred and sixty-four days of the year, I would agree with you," said Amy, "but not today. Congratulations, Palmer."

For Jeanette and Edward, the rest of April passed in a blur with substantial orchestration by Cornelia, who would have liked to plan the whole wedding. Beginning in Marseilles, she had conferred with Jeanette and Effie endlessly over trousseau and fully intended to send Jeanette back to Ohio as beautifully attired as a good estimate of Judge Palmer's means allowed. The jeweler whom she recommended laid before Edward a selection of gems and settings for an engagement ring. The small-time druggist in him swallowed hard at the prices, and even the patent holder eliminated the costliest stones; but the younger Murer brother of Cincinnati, remembering what Theodore had bought Sophie two years earlier, approved a fair array. When he took Jeanette in to choose, she pleased him by selecting a simple setting with short prongs and a medium-sized diamond with fire at its heart.

Once the Palmers had been heard from and the finished ring was ready for Jeanette's finger, Cornelia gave a soirée at which the engagement could be announced. Since the whole point of the communal ritual was to celebrate respectability, the stodgiest leading lights of the American colony had to be invited; but Hippolyte Grandcourt and Carolus-Duran agreed to look in; and the presence of Amy, Sonja, the Reade sisters, and Edward's friend, the collector of prints, reminded everyone that Cornelia Renick knew the most unlikely people. Carolus had the kindness to present the happy couple with a quick sketch of themselves at the party. He then kissed Jeanette on both cheeks, shook hands with Edward, and vanished, leaving everyone as dazzled as he could have hoped.

Next came Varnishing Day. Amy took Effie so that Edward could be Jeanette's guest. He hated it as much as they both knew he would, but he said it was too important an event in her life for him to be anywhere else. As had been predicted, the year 1880 saw a record number of acceptances, so many that sculptures had to be placed in the outdoor porticos. Even with hastily built additional galleries, paintings were hung, not only above the line, but down to the floor and out in the corridors with the drawings. The alphabet was abandoned as an organizing principle. A rough cut segregated foreigners from French artists, but within each category things had to be fitted in wherever possible. In the din and confusion, it was hard to find anything, hard to be heard, hard for a group to hold together. After some preliminary searching, Amy shouted to Jeanette and Sonja, "Let's come back together another day, when we've each found her own!"

They parted, Jeanette on Edward's arm and Effie tagging along, the least perturbed of anyone. Edward had been studying the catalogue as a way to block out the turmoil and found Jeanette's name. "There," he pointed. She took the booklet in both hands, unable to think clearly enough to make sense of it in relation to the floor plan. Edward could. When they came into the right room, it took more searching in a welter of small canvases fitted like mosaics, but there it was: *Un Vestibule dans le Quartier Saint-Germain*, high in the double row above the line—not the best site, but less degrading than below the knees. Jeanette went very still, too choked by emotion to know what she felt at first; she understood Sonja's pride the year before. She clutched Edward's arm.

"It's the beginning," he said, "and a fine one."

Effie wanted to go back into the French section to see what Carolus-Duran was showing that year, but Jeanette overruled her, mindful of the limits to Edward's tolerance. "Hang on to your guest card, Cousin Effie. We'll come back this afternoon if you like. Right now, let's go celebrate somewhere."

"All right," said Effie, "You should become reacquainted with a landmark while there's still time."

They went to Le Petit Honoré.

The wedding was announced for mid July in Circleville. Edward's lease was up on the first of May, after which he moved back into a residential hotel for a few weeks, this one on the Rue Jacob, because Jeanette loved the street and wanted him to experience something like her first year and because he wanted to be on the Left Bank, closer to her and the Renicks. There could be no thought of leaving Paris before the end of the Salon when she could reclaim *Un Vestibule*. Meanwhile, before the established artists left in June and Carolus's atelier closed, she had her private meeting with Carolus in his studio to show him her watercolors of Provence. He assessed them and her other work candidly and with insight. Until then, she had not realized how much his seemingly off-the-cuff suggestions and occasional sharp rebukes over the past year had reflected a comprehension of her individual strengths and weaknesses. She went away inspired and momentarily in despair at having to leave—but it was time to start making real plans: to give notice, to book passage. And if leaving was hard for her, how much worse for Cousin Effie! It was telling that Effie seemed to procrastinate as much as she did herself.

"What a thought," said Jeanette to Edward one afternoon near the beginning of June, "going back to the Hendricks!"

"Had you thought of asking her to live with us?"

"Do you mean that, Edward?"

"Well, my darling, I know that every shred of happiness I'll ever have depends on your being with me, but I'm not convinced that either one of us has any idea how to run a house."

"And you'd really contemplate having Cousin Effie around all the time?"

"We get along, you know. Could you be happy with her?"

"By now, of course, I could!"

They put it to Effie. "Oh, my!" she dithered, "what can I say? Why, it's just what I should have expected from you two, only I didn't see it coming. Nothing was further from my mind—Oh my. Well, thank you, but, no. No, I'm afraid I can't accept."

"If you're afraid of what Aunt Maude will say—"

"No, no; I'm sure by now Maude has sorted out everything to her liking, and the last thing she needs is me in the way again. No, you see, I can't come with you because I'm not going back at all."

They stared.

"I'm staying in Paris," she explained, as if the fact needed to be established, which in a way, it did. "Now if you're wondering how I can live alone on what dear Polycarpus left me, you don't need to worry—not that I couldn't, but I'm not going to. I'm going to move in with Isobel and Miss Reade."

She went on to describe a scheme for running a sort of *pension* or club for lady art students, with bedrooms, a big studio, a kitchen, a lounge. If they could attract someone like Miss Richardson, perhaps the girls could hire models for a few sessions a week. "Then on Mr. Renick's advice, I took updated versions of some of my articles on living arrangements to William Galignani and he bought them for the Paris *Messenger*. If the response is good, I can redo the rest and he can run them and we might put out the collection in cheap book form, so then we could advertise the *pension*. Or even if that doesn't work out, oh, well, you know, word of mouth."

"Well, that *is* news," said Jeanette, when they had exhausted Effie's plans for the moment. "I guess I'll have to find someone else to travel with."

"Why not your husband?" asked Edward.

Jeanette was about to say that she might be a Bohemian, but not that much of one, thank you, when she realized what he had said. Husband, not fiancé.

"You mean—?"

"I mean, if you don't mind missing a walk down the aisle in Circleville, we can get married over here."

"We'll elope!" cried Jeanette, falling back in laughter.

"Not what I had in mind. We'll get old Noyes to tie the knot for us, and then we'll take a wedding trip in Europe."

"Oh, Edward, to the Italy you love, where I've never been!"

"Italy," he affirmed, smiling into her eyes. "Soon, before it gets too hot. Then we'll go up to Freiburg for me to show you off to the family and maybe all the way to Kiel and Copenhagen. We can go home by way of London."

General Noyes had the authority to marry them as Americans on the embassy grounds. Mr. Renick stood in for Judge Palmer to give the bride away. A weeping Effie was, of course, maid of honor, and Amy a second bridesmaid to prove that she and Sonja were happy about the marriage. Young Paul came from Freiburg to act as best man. Cornelia gave a reception, just friends this time, in the secret garden.

And then Mr. and Mrs. Edward Murer left, the two of them, to go where they knew no one but each other, and no one else knew them (though for the first night, this paradise was only the Hôtel Meurice). Edward, who had been shut down so long; Edward, who feared his age as a barrier; Edward, whose only experience was to his mind squalid, found in Jeanette a partner spontaneous and natural. And Jeanette, whose education had come primarily from watching stallions take mares and whispered exchanges in the dormitory after the lights were out (and from Cornelia, who had embarrassed her by sitting in for her mother with a wholly inadequate little lecture)— Jeanette found that bodies had more than contour, surface, and underlying structure; they had deeper mysteries to explore: shadows, depths, highlights, tenderness.

Edward said, later, "Tell me truly, why did you marry me, Jeanette?"

"Do you have to ask?" she said, complacently, snuggling the curve of her body around the solidity of his hip, with an arm across his chest.

"I don't believe you knew about this," he said, kissing the top of her head.

"No."

"Then why?" It was a dangerous question, and he knew it, stupid. And yet he asked it.

"Truly?" she asked, shifting up onto her elbow to look at him aslant. In repose against the pillow in darkness, the shape of his face was different again from any view she had ever had of it. "You know how I painted a picture of my studio to remember it by, with your portrait on my easel as the focal point?" He reached up to touch her hair lightly. "Well, I need more than your portrait. Whenever I see you, Edward, no matter where or when, I see you more clearly and feel you more substantially than anything else around me. And when you were gone, when I didn't know if you were coming back, everything, even the things I loved, were emptier. Without you, my world is bereft."

"Oh, my darling Jeanette," he said, pulling her back down onto his chest. "What you say is true for me, too, about you."

"I know," she said, settling happily, "which answers your question."

Readers Guide

Where the Light Falls

DISCUSSION QUESTIONS

1. Discuss the role that women play in society during the late nineteenth century. What are the major differences between American and European views of women in the working world? What do colleges in the 1870s prepare girls for? What opportunities await young women after graduation?

2. Which characters have the most to lose or to gain as a result of their reputations? What influence can a rumor, regardless of its legitimacy, have on the life of a person living in the United States and France in the late nineteenth century? What actions can be taken to stifle such gossip? Is it easier for men or women to escape the shadow of scandal?

3. Discuss the impact that war and death have on several of the characters in this book. How does nineteenth-century society view veterans and widowers? Do their shared experiences unite or divide them? What can we ascertain about Edward's character from his feelings for his long-lost love, Marie? What do we learn about Carolus-Duran from his tale about Falguière the sculptor? What does the story of Polycarpus tell us about Cousin Effie? Are there other stories of fallen or deceased friends and lovers that reveal insights into each person's character?

4. Family plays a crucial role in this story. How would you describe the environment within the homes of the Dolsons, the Hendricks, the Murers, and the Palmers? Do these families support one another?

Why or why not? What are the benefits of lineage in the 1870s and is it necessary to succeed in this society?

5. Edward Murer, Emily Dolson, and Charlie Post all struggle with their own addictions throughout this story. How do these dependence issues change the course of their lives? How do their friends and family eliminate or enable these habits? What societal pressures can be attributed to each character's substance struggles? Are there any other characters who exhibit signs of abuse?

6. Professor van Ingen, William-Adolphe Bouguereau, and Carolus-Duran are among the many teachers that Jeanette studies with during her artistic journey. However, she meets several other mentors who help her develop both professionally and personally. Who do you feel she learns most from and why? What important lessons does this individual teach her and how does it impact her life?

7. Carolus-Duran advises his students to "study where the light falls and where the shadows lie." Discuss how this quote can be interpreted beyond the walls of the studio and in each character's personal life. Which acquaintances and/or experiences would be considered light and which would be categorized as shadows? Do you feel each person correctly distinguishes between the two by the end of the novel and, if so, how?

8. After Edward sells his drugstore, we learn that "something would have to replace" his activities there, "or his demons would rip at him again." What fills this void in his life? Is this a conscious decision or is he guided toward it? Who helps him solve this dilemma? If the visual arts are Jeanette's true passion, what is Edward's?

9. Jeanette, Effie, and several other women enter into conversations about love versus work. They advise Jeanette that she will need to

make up her mind about where she will "see the gleam"—in Dr. Murer or in her work. Do you believe that it is possible for artists to fall in love? What, if anything, does Jeanette eventually sacrifice for love? Which other women in this story must sacrifice a passion or profession for love? Is this an antiquated idea left in the nineteenth century or does it still occur today?

10. Compare and contrast the dating rituals of nineteenth- and twenty-first-century life. Which method of courtship do you believe best leads to love, friendship, or both? What behaviors from 1870s romance have withstood the test of time? Which turn-of-the-century formalities would you like to see revived? How do the opinions of peers affect relationships in both periods? What role does family play in a couple's development and how has it changed over the years?

11. Why do you believe Edward engaged in relations with the prostitute on Boulevard Saint-Germain? During one of his consultations, Dr. Aubanel absolves Edward for the act of desire, but insists that he keep this error of judgment from Jeanette. Do you agree with this piece of advice? What other parts of his life do you feel should remain a secret? Does Jeanette keep any secrets from Edward? What other characters are masked by secrecy?

12. How do the couples in this story measure up to one another? What does each partner contribute to his or her respective pairing? Which of these couples are unbalanced in terms of power and respect? Which couple do you feel is married for convenience and which is married for love? How does marriage help or hurt individuals during the nineteenth century?

13. How do Robbie Dolson and *Noggins* change Jeanette's view of commercial art? What do Jeanette's peers think of her work appearing

in publications? What do these published works do to Jeanette's reputation as an artist? Have Robbie Dolson's actions improved or impaired Jeanette's future career? Explain.

14. While Jeanette and Edward find each other in Paris, Cousin Effie finds herself. What events help her develop personally? Which characters is she most inspired by? What is Effie's dream and how does she achieve it? Do you think she will ever return to the United States and, if so, what can a future in America offer her? What does her Parisian outlook look like?

15. Sonja describes the nineteenth century as "so nervous, so full of change and quickness." What social, technological, and artistic changes are happening throughout this story? How do these additions of modernity alter the lives of each character? What are the most influential changes? Which of the characters display signs of apprehension toward them and why? Which characters embrace these revolutionary ideas and inventions? What are their motives?